TROPHY BUTTERFLY©

BOOK Ten

of the

SECRET BUTTERFLY SERIES™

A NOVEL BY

Rosemary Lightfoot Ness-Bitner

To order, wherever books are sold:

ISBN 978-1-961850-20-0 for eBook

ISBN 978-1-961850-21-7 for Paperback

A caution and disclaimer

All characters, events, and conversations in this book are fictional, the product of the author's imagination, or used fictitiously. Any resemblance to actual characters, living or dead, events past or present, localities, or conversations, is entirely coincidental.

If you are offended or stressed by characters' offensive behaviors and expressions of strong opinions about   controversial subjects, you are advised and cautioned to not purchase this book or listen to this audio book. If you are a child under the age of eighteen, do not purchase this book or listen to this audio book as it contains erotic adult content. Sexual activity may cause diseases.

THIS BOOK CONTAINS SADISM, MURDER, AND EXPLICIT EROTIC ROMANCE CONTENT. IT IS INTENDED FOR MATURE READERS AND AUDIENCES OVER THE AGE OF EIGHTEEN ONLY. IT MAY BE OFFENSIVE OR STRESSFUL TO SOME READERS. OPINIONS, VIEWS, AND ADVICE GIVEN IN THIS BOOK BY ITS CHARACTERS TO OTHER CHARACTERS, AND BEHAVIORS EXHIBITED AND ADVOCATED BY ITS CHARACTERS DO NOT REFLECT THE OPINIONS, VIEWS, OR ADVICE, OR ADVOCATION OF BEHAVIORS OF, OR BY, THE AUTHOR OR PUBLISHER, OR OF, OR BY, ANY ORGANIZATION OR ENTITY TO WHICH THE AUTHOR OR PUBLISHER ARE AFFILIATED. NEITHER THE AUTHOR, THE PUBLISHER, NOR ANY OTHER PERSONS ASSOCIATED WITH THIS BOOK SHALL BE HELD RESPONSIBLE FOR ANY CONSEQUENCES ARISING FROM THE OPINIONS, VIEWS, ADVICES, BEHAVIORS, OR INTERPRETATIONS EXPRESSED BY THE CHARACTERS IN THIS BOOK; OR, IN ANY OTHER WAY, EXPRESSED IN THIS BOOK, OR BY ITS COVER.

This book is dedicated to love's triumph.

The print version layout of TROPHY BUTTERFLY was done by Andrea Reider of Reider Books. The cover design was created by Cheeky Covers; and the audio book narration was done by Minna Morinette.

Dear readers and listeners, our tenth segment explores Marty's thoughts and a flashback to her spirit soul's pagan years. Revisit history. Marty's soul, in the personage of Baalezebelle, seduces Moses and has his wife and children thrown to the Nile crocodiles. And, she's just getting started! Bob belatedly realizes he's caught up in a scheme of spirit souls that has gotten him in way over his head. He confides his agreement with David to Barbara. Will this reveal help Barbara understand David's sociopathy? Is she dealing with a monster psychopath? What horrors has David created and to what lengths will he go?

Barbara is working on two levels. Behaviors of characters Bob, Marty, David, and Susan need to fit with the evidence she's gathered during her after hours sleuthing. She's been very busy. Will she discover the keys that hold the Firm's criminal enterprise together? Will she witness the unthinkable? We are unmasking sociopathy on an enterprise scale, dear readers. Oh, the horrors! But, be not afraid. Together we can do this! Have courage.

And feel the excitement of life and budding romance when our new character, Jen, breaks out of her cocoon and meets Thor. When Jen reveals her true character, how will Thor respond? Will he run away or will hot sparks fly? Come flutter along with me, Minna Morinette, as I narrate TROPHY BUTTERFLY, the tenth book of THE SECRET BUTTERFLY (tm) SERIES.

TROPHY BUTTERFLY

**SECRET BUTTERFLY SERIES ™ CHARACTERS
(MAJOR CHARACTERS ARE BOLDFACED)**

Readers reference guide to where a character is introduced.

(CHARACTER, DESCRIPTION OF CHARACTER, AND
CHAPTER WHERE CHARACTER IS MENTIONED)

**JEN, DAUGHTER, AND INCESTUOUS LOVER OF
DOMINICK; MULTI BILLIONAIRRE HEIRESS, PORN
STAR, SADIST, CAT LOVER, CREATIVE FOUNDER OF
THE INFERNOSS DECADO CLUBS; THOR'S LOVER, CH8**

**ROGER, ROSS, ALEX, NELSON, JEN'S LOVERS, AND
PORN PARTNERS, CH8**

**BIFSTER ONE, JEN'S ONE-EYED COMPANION CAT,
TROPHY HUNTER, CH10**

**LOLITA BUNNY JOYFUL, JEN'S FAVORITE YOUNG PORN
STAR, CH10**

**THOR, ARTIST, DISTRUSTS CATS, OBSESSED OVER JEN
AND SAILBOATS, CH13**

Hello readers and listeners. This is Minna Morinette, bringing you the fascinating behavioral story of TROPHY BUTTERFLY. We spirit butterflies are going to flutter into a very secretive place where we will discover an unexpected facet of Marty's mind. We already know her mind divides between its rational, reasoning zone and its emotive, impulsive limbic zone; and we know the boundaries which separate these zones are forever, fluidly changing. But does knowing that sufficiently explain Marty's behaviors? Perhaps not!

We'll explore where her desire to separate a pregnant fiancée from her beau originated. We'll examine whether the limbic zone itself is compartmentalized between impulsive and calculating regions. Obviously, Marty's physical libido became aroused. He was a stunningly handsome prize. But what piqued her intent to steal him away? Jealousy of the other woman? Empathy for her lover's plight? Or, perhaps something darker, more sinister, directed her actions? What really activated her seduction impulse? And why did she persist until she finally had him? When she sees a man with another woman, why does she feel compelled to set him free? If she didn't really want him, why was his freedom so important?

What inspired Marty to involve herself with Dom's daughter, Jen? And what made Jen desire to become Marty's protégé? How did these three form a new family unit with diametrically opposite morality standards from Jen's mother's standards? What, Marty explains, are the positive psychological benefits of committed incestuous relationships? We'll explore the devious workings of Jen's twisted and remarkably clever mind; how she scoured nations' laws before deciding where to site her Infernal Decado Clubs; how she gained control of her father's vast business empire; and how she persuades Marty to perform live shows in her clubs. And we'll discover how devious Jen, her aspiring protégé, Lolita Bunny Joyful, and her devoted kitty, Bifster One, each captured their trophies.

CHAPTER ONE

Love your enemies. Bless those who curse you. Do good to those who hate you and pray for those who persecute you. (Matthew 5:44)

STRONGER COFFEE

"Then U, the Universal Spirit of all Living Things, left me. A serene peace swept over me and I was not afraid of the words I heard or what I must do."

Barbara related her visit from the Spirit over coffees with Bob. It was a cold winter Sunday. It had snowed hard the day before. Plains' cattle were stressed and desperately pawing through the snow for grass. People in Plaintown were cross country skiing in streets that were impassable by cars. Barbara's intuition told her there were big changes afoot at the Firm. She'd had nightmares and the spirits were visiting her dreams. She'd called Bob. She needed to talk and warn him of his impending danger.

"I know I must do as I was told," said Barbara. *"I need to accept U's commands and I must do what is most unnatural for me. I must take Marty into my heart. I must embrace her; even honor her. I must love this woman who stole your love away from me and who crushed my tender heart; and I must love her with my whole heart. I must obey. Understanding another's behavior is such a difficult leap to make. But then I asked myself; if I had known love as a little girl, and then been pushed away as Marty was, what then, would I be?*

Marty, but for the love of my parents, could be me. I needed to make an even higher leap. I needed to accept that Marty stole your love from me, Bob. But then I asked myself: would I not have done the same if I were cast in her life's role?

"But what is U expecting of me, Bob? How am I supposed to love her? Am I expected to brush her hair, massage her neck and shoulders, kiss her mouth, and perhaps suckle her nipples; maybe stimulate her vaginal crown with my encouraging fingers, while she's copulating with the man who is the love of my life? What humiliations, what mental tortures am I expected to endure? Why does the Great Spirit torture me this way? I understand I am woman and I must endure pain; but why this kind of pain? Perhaps U expects me to manicure Marty's nails while she's usurping the sperm seeds from my love; channeling his semen flows into her womb; those precious seeds that I desperately need for my own womb, to create my own children?

"Am I expected to kiss the back of her neck, wrap my arms around her waist, and hug her while she enjoys her orgasms, Bob? Am I to whisper in her ear how glorious she is while she achieves her ecstasy state? Am I to hug her like a gleeful sister, perhaps bring champaign to her and toast her exhilarating rides upon my true love's Bird of Paradise? Why did Great Spirit U single me out to have my heart torn apart in this way? How can torturing me to enhance her pleasures be pleasing to Great Spirit U? Am I a reincarnated version of the prophet Job? Is that what this is all about; for Great Spirit U to see how much revulsion and suffering I can stomach and still accept and love the Great Spirit U? I know you can not help me with this, Big Horse. Just listen, please.

"And as I struggled with my thoughts, I clung to my faith that U must have reasons to try my patience and my love this way. Surely it could not be that I was by destiny paired to forever be the innocent downtrodden handmaiden to my heartthrob's whore? Was I to

watch her fashion him into her love slave? Must I command my heart to love her perversions; those wanton acts of hers; her uninhibited orgies that horrify my eyes?

"Is U's purpose to make my love even stronger, so my Big Horse might finally separate love from lust and somehow love me more? I can only hope. But I do not and can not know U's reason. I must believe that the reason is not for me to approve or even understand; but only to accept. So, finally, I did accept. I vowed to love Marty unconditionally and with my whole heart, and to forget my own feelings. And that's when I had my first epiphany, Bob.

"I realized that U is ushering us into a new societal era where society is reverting to the days of pagan prostitution worship; openly accepting and encouraging whoring and prostitution. Marty is U's messenger. She is U's modern-day prophet. Perhaps change presents itself as catastrophic to many; an upheaval to be feared, just as established orders of old often feared the words of their prophets in their times. Perhaps instead, Marty's words and deeds must be accepted as the Spirit's will. Perhaps it is our natural progression as humans," said Barbara.

"Marty is a living statement about who we humans are, now; and whom we will next become. She's declared that she's unafraid to be who she is. She's an amazing happening. She explodes her immorality upon peoples' inhibitions and destroys their reluctance. She says we shouldn't be afraid to sin, sexually. She proclaims that adultery is beneficial and soul cleansing. There's a refreshing unashamed, proud innocence about her approach to sexual freedom and about the ways she communicates that in her films. Her fans see that. They get it. They identify with it and with her. Their minds expand and their imaginations explode when they realize how wildly sensual a woman in love can be; and what wondrous things a woman can do with her body while making love. They see what feeling and giving pleasures can be like. And they love it. They flock to her. Wherever

there's a Marty sighting, people surround her. They want to be close to her. She represents a 'Yes you can if you want to. Just put your heart and soul into it,' attitude. And they can't get enough of her. She's become a national craze. I understand it, Bob. When I watched her films, I was drawn to her, too.

"Her message is: 'It's okay to break with the past and to let your feelings and desires go. It's okay to run with your feelings.' Marty's way of seeing the world is fast becoming our new social norm, Bob. America's decline as an empire parallels the debauchery of the Romans near the end of their empire. As national and individual opportunities decline and die; more people are seeking psychological escape in Marty's films. They want to deny society's damage to their self-esteem. Her films assure her viewers that she loves them completely; madly; wildly, even if only in their imaginations. She elicits their compelling need to feel loved and be loving toward others. Marty fills their needs, Bob.

"Intimate Film Artistry seems to make a collapsing social order more acceptable. It's one of our 'New normal' euphemisms. It's a more polite term for pornography. And it helps numb us to the relentless decline in our moral standards. On screen immorality helps us fantasize and forget the crime, poverty and stresses that surround us. Watching beautiful women making love has become our national placebo. It's the preferred mental escape which makes the assault on our social order more palatable, as our moral decline accelerates.

"Intimate artistry stars are displacing traditional movie stars. Yes, they are. It's analogous to the way talking motion pictures displaced silent films in years gone bye. Actors and actresses who refused to make talkie movies were left behind while the industry moved forward. The public demanded movies where people talked. And the public got what it demanded. A breakout romantic intimate art movie with explicit sex is coming. People are demanding to see more erotic intimacy. I think we are just starting to scratch the

surface of something very deep. The demand for explicit erotica is a tidal wave. It's about to sweep over the film industry and change it forever.

"Actors and actresses who can't or won't perform scenes with explicit erotic intimacy will be left behind. The film industry will move forward, once again. And actresses who choose to perform intimate sex scenes will have to perform them well. They'll need to deliver empathy, or they will be replaced. Full length films with explicit intimate artistry scenes will become the rage. Erotic sex on screen will no longer be seen as offensive. Rather, eroticism will be promoted and seen as something wondrous and beautiful to behold. And these films and their sell through merchandise will make serious money.

"Criteria for judging a film's artistic merit will include critiques of how spellbinding the explicit erotic scenes are; how believably they are performed; how well the woman's facial expressions communicated her joys of orgasm. These movies will be a sensation and a box office bonanza for those who produce them. Their popularity will spread like wildfire. Marty already has a head start as a leading actress in this burgeoning new field, Bob. With Dominick's production company she has already made over a dozen films with explicit content. Demand for Marty to perform as the leading actress in this new film genre is exploding. She brings to the box office millions of existing fans who will pay premium prices to see her perform ever more explicit intimacy. They can't get enough of her."

"It's hard for me to imagine a world like that, Barb." Bob's sensibilities were stunned.

"Well, it shouldn't be. It's happening right before your eyes. Look at the data! Look how many people are watching intimate erotica. The growth of porn seems unstoppable. I think the public has discovered something profound. Erotica is sweeping the world like religion did two thousand years ago; but porn is moving much faster. In a

society where the monetary structure and the politics are impossibly, hopelessly corrupt, the intimate artistry trade is seen as up front and honest. It provides sex for money.

"Compare that to actresses that offer sex for a role in a film or TV show; or how about people who pay bribes to get their kids into college, depriving a smarter kid from a poor family? How about political corruption; and election vote rigging? Who do these people think they are, knowing their power was obtained illegitimately? How do they face themselves in the mirror? How long will the people put up with it? And, what will they do to assuage their bitterness in the meantime? Don't get me started on how much underhanded stuff goes on in politics, Bob. I'm certain I'm right.

"You'll soon see the day when top intimacy film stars make more money than top NFL players or marquee box office stars of conventional films. It will happen. The demand and the money are there. The public craves it, just like the public craves drugs. Like drugs, it takes peoples' minds off the corruption they live under. Prostitution and pornography will be legalized, too, just like all drugs will be legalized. Get ready for huge changes in perceptions of what is moral and what is immoral, Bob; and Marty will be at the forefront of these changes. Her immorality will be the new morality, embraced and loved by millions.

"In Rome's declining era, prostitutes were not hidden away. Not at all! They were celebrated! Cheered! Whoring was out in the open. Prostitution was glorified and respected; even honored. Prostitutes were the undisputed stars of the Roman social order. They ranked higher than stage actors and actresses. The best prostitutes were highly sought after. They were extremely well compensated and received like royalty. They were welcomed into the homes of the highest members of society. Being seen in the company of a top prostitute was an honor; actually, a status symbol.

"We have entered a similar period. As society declines, moral taboos will retreat. Prostitutes and intimacy film stars will be

honored and exalted by the masses. There will be televised ceremonies that honor their best films; best scenes; best intimacy actress stars; and best supporting casts, just like the Oscars do now for regular movies. But I expect the public's interest in the annual intimate artistry film awards will dwarf their interest in the Oscars.

"It wouldn't surprise me to see the day when the winner of the top intimacy actress award accepts her award and then performs a cameo orgy scene; on stage; broadcast live, before an adoring intimate film craving audience. The TV ratings for that awards ceremony would shatter all ratings records and the network that carries it live will make a fortune. Ad buys will cost more than Super Bowl time. More beautiful faces, better acting skills and films with broader, more imaginative themes and realistic content will be demanded by a thirsting, intimate art craving public. Every year, the annual intimate artistry film awards will be viewed by hundreds of millions worldwide.

"After foreseeing where we're headed, I had my second epiphany, Bob.

"It came to me as if the universal spirit took control of my mind. The spirit told me that Marty's soul was an eternal soul, living as different beings across the millenniums. It said Marty's words and deeds are the words and deeds from the soul of the prophet Baaleezebelle, or Jezebel, a voice that coexists with the voices of the prophets Moses, Christ, and Mohammed. Marty's role in U's plan for the world is to condition society for the rebirth of Baal worship, just as Jezebel did in the era of the Sumerians and before. Marty is leading her followers to return to a kind of modern-day fertility worship. The difference is that the Baal prostitutes ensured crop and human fertility, Marty ensures freedom of sexuality for pleasure's sake. She's a harbinger of times to come."

"You're saying that people will stop going to their churches and synagogues and temples? You think they'll go to temples of Baal instead?" Bob was trying to keep up with Barbara's thinking.

He had a hard time grasping that pagan worship rites for fertility would reemerge as similar rites for pleasure alone. Humanity's progressive movement towards immorality as its core belief seemed incomprehensible to him.

"*Yes. I believe that's exactly what will happen,*" answered Barbara with confidence. "*At least, that will become true for a large portion of the population. It's not a far leap to see what's taking place, Bob. Many people already have stopped practicing their monotheistic religions. Many have dropped out. Face it; with their sex scandals and their buggering of little boys, the Church has lost a lot of credibility. Many see their religion as a money-grubbing machine for the benefit of pampered men in fancy robes that spew incomprehensible mumbo jumbo. Once credibility is lost, it's hard to get it back.*

"And many people already watch intimate art films. The marketplace is thirsty for Marty's message. Think about it. If ten percent of the population of the United States followed some resurrected version of Baal, they would become a powerful political voice. They'd get recognition. Laws would change to accommodate them. Politicians read polls. Many politicians will seek Marty's endorsement. She will be sought out as the goddess that leads our way forward. Her 'Bottom up' approach is winning religious market share from Moses's 'Top down' approach.

"*Marty is already in huge demand. She's a lock to be a box office sensation. It's a no brainer. Romantic intimacy movie art will be accepted for mainstream big screen theater distribution. Pagan temples with open whoring will achieve tax exempt status and municipal laws will be revised to enable them to offer worship services, including open fornication, in direct competition with traditional churches, temples and mosques. Social norms will be revamped. Male controlled religions and churches will see their controls and market share eroded by pagan worship. Monogamy's grip on public mores will be pried loose. Paganism will challenge concepts of morality, family, and reproduction in the marketplace.*

"Marty's views about abortion will become universally adopted, by the mere fact that no one has standing to voice credible opposition to her. By default, her views must be the best and the only logically considered views; thus, her views are the right views for her own life. If a child might distress Marty's emotional equilibrium and potentially cause her depression, because her infant child might distract her from her blossoming career in performing intimate pornographic film art; then Marty should receive criticism from no one about her choice. She created her baby's life; so, it is her absolute right to destroy her creation work, if it later displeases her. Artists destroy canvasses that displease, in much the same way.

"Like the artist who finishes a work; finds it unsatisfactory, then destroys it; Marty, too, will be free to destroy her work, even after she births it. Her psychological well being is known only to her. If creating romantic, intimate, pornographic film art is her career passion; and if that pursuit pleases her psyche; then no one has the right to keep her from embracing her passion. If, after seeing her new born baby, she realizes it will detract from the time she can devote to creating pornography; or detract from her passionate devotion to her creative on-stage, explicit intimacy art performances; thus, risking depression for her; then she will be allowed to have a post-birth abortion. Some progressive states already have codified this view."

"But, what about the baby's life? What you are saying is it will be acceptable to commit infanticide murders. What about the father's say in all of this?" Bob was deeply troubled by what Barbara was telling him.

"Bob, the baby can't vote. It's helpless. It lives at the behest of the mother. It doesn't have money to pay a lawyer to argue against its post-birth murder. No one will advocate for its life. It can't even speak, let alone testify, so why bother trying to decide if it prefers

to live or to die in order to advance the career of its mother? The father could be a mystery person; a mere conjecture. Marty fucks lots of men. It's hard to say who did the deed without running tests. Besides, if Marty decides to make another baby someday, there will be plenty of men who will gladly do her servicing. Babies and fathers should have no say in these decisions. They are women's decisions. Period.

"Marty is a dedicated career woman, Bob. It would be tragic to deny Marty her post-birth abortion, or infanticide, rights. It would be wrong headed to force her to nurture a baby against her will. The child should have nothing to say about her decision. Even after two years from the womb the child is still totally dependent upon her nurturing. If a baby can't afford a lawyer to protest the mother's decision, then society must hold to the position that, since the baby has no access to the courts, only the mother's rights can be heard. After all, litigation favors those who have money. Marty's wishes must be determinate; otherwise, society must provide the unborn and the child an attorney to make an argument for its life. But society does no such thing. That would be too expensive for the taxpayers to bear. Taxpayers are already unfairly overburdened by paying for illegal immigrants."

"This line of thinking seems terribly immoral, Barb."

"That depends upon society's standards, Bob; and those standards are in flux. We are becoming no different than some tribal cultures where it was accepted practice to throw babies and children into a fiery volcano or to the Nile crocodiles, to please the gods. We are hypocrites if we pretend that we're somehow morally superior.

"We're sacrificing our same helpless innocents to please our modern-day goddesses: our glorious, adorable porn stars; our aspiring prostitutes and intimate art film stars; and women who simply decide they can't be burdened with motherhood. Abortion is our accepted normal social practice in our new era of The Modern

Morality Standard. We embrace whoring, pornography, and fornication. We love all of it. We no longer see it as sin or evil. We see it as our right to have sex without the consequences of parentage; and we see it as our right, especially a woman's right, to correct a mistake when we make one.

"Babies are seen as mistakes, not as blessings, by many in our culture. That's just how it is. We're desperate to perpetuate that abortion choice and we crush anything that tries to oppose it. It represents our power over procreation, and we worship that power. Worship of Baal is not far behind. Paganism will retake its historic market share of religious followers.

"In the pre-Judaic period, Baal was the dominant religious market share, reaching one hundred percent of the population in many tribes. Those who objected to the orders of Baal's priests were given a death sentence. People who opposed child sacrifice and ritual whoring were murdered and sacrificed to entertain the temple prostitutes. We seem to be drifting in that direction once again; babies and children first.

"I know of no requirement to register a fetus with government. There are no laws funding lawyers assigned to represent these unborn humans. Au contraire. Their limbs can be ripped off, their guts sucked out, their spines snipped and their skulls crushed at clinics that are already recognized as tax exempt charities. Our barbaric carnage of unborn and recently born infants continues. Oh, some politicians feign moral outrage about it. They get campaign contributions from righteous people who rail indignant; but those people are in the minority. No legislation gets passed.

"No politician fights seriously for an unborn human. They know that will cost them their reelection, because the abortion rights advocates have a united voice. So, nobody fights for the babies. The politicians care more about their reelection than these unborn humans. Why shouldn't they? There's no vote bank that gets a proxy

to vote the interests of unborn fetuses. If there was, that would be sixty million votes against abortion. But, there's no such thing. We are a society of hedonistic barbarians; collectively, we silently shout: 'Glory to our porn stars! Death to our babies!'

"Barb, do you really believe Marty feels this calloused about children? It's chilling to think a woman could have a mind that works like that."

"I'm only telling you what I've seen of her behavior, Big Horse. She's in the peak earning years of a very demanding profession. She is the creation of her own childhood and our narcissistic culture. She's driven to be a success in the only culture she knows. Marty intends to make hundreds more hours of spectacular, intimate, pornographic art films and spread her vision of uninhibited love to all mankind.

"A baby would deny the world untold volumes of the most spectacular, breathtaking fucking and orgy scenes by the world's most famous porn star, performing at the pinnacle of her beauty and career. That would be a tragic, unacceptable loss to our 'enlightened' culture. Marty must be given every media encouragement, every financial incentive, and unfettered freedom to perform her spectacular debauchery; not feeling inhibited by the distractions of a baby. She wants to hear the adulating Oohs and Ahh's of her adoring fans as cum oozes from her wanton vagina. She has no interest in hearing the wails of a helpless infant.

"Her fans demand to see her performing with hundreds of new fresh penises. They want to compare her techniques with her past performances. They can't get enough of her scintillating whoring. She's the queen of all whoredom, Bob. People obsess over every film she makes; over every scene she performs. They'd be outraged if she stopped performing. The demands of societal lust must be newly stimulated to maximize the market. And that demand frenzy must then be satisfied. She's the perfect intimate art film star to expand her industry's reach.

"Her fine work will become the cornerstone of sex education classes taught to school children from kindergarten through the twelfth grade. Her works will be treasured and shared by all, as classic films. They will be archived for the ages. I now see the wisdom of U's pronouncements, and I will humbly obey. I must and I will love Marty as a fellow sister in life. I will not judge her choices. I will embrace her soul; and I will love her for her inspired contributions to film art, and her informed, legal personal choice.

"I am ashamed that I ever presumed to judge her. I had no right to think badly of her life choice. I can't imagine what it must have been like for her as a young girl. Imagine, she was fatherless and abandoned by her mother. Her years at the WEX School for girls must have been like a prison sentence for her. And, from what I heard from Susan, her mother, the girls at the school turned against her, too.

"She only had one friend; a girl named Maria. Her mother, the WEX school, and those girls shaped Marty's life, Bob. Her psychology seethes with rage at how the world treated her when she was a child. She went from being a happy little girl with a family and a father in the home to being, in effect, an orphan with peer rejection. It's no wonder she resents everyone who has a normal family life.

"I'm not surprised Marty has become a relentless foe of family life and marriage. In her mind, other women with happy marriages are those same girls from WEX that rejected her. Marty is driven to give them payback. She wants them to suffer the same emptiness and pain that she lived as a child. When Marty sees a happily married woman, she instinctively hates her. She treats that happily married woman as her mortal enemy and engages in pitched battle to rip that woman's husband away from her. Her goal is to destroy the other woman's marriage.

"She's as relentless in her determination to rip apart a marriage as an octopus seeking to tear away the shell from a clam. The

octopus eats the clam for its reward. Marty consumes the affections of the wife's husband. Similarly, like the octopus moves on to its next clam, leaving an empty shell behind, Marty moves on to the next marriage, leaving behind the broken home, the divorce, the alcoholism, and depression; and yes, even the suicide in some cases. And, like the octopus, Marty never looks back or gives a thought to the destruction she leaves behind. She has no remorse; only her lust for more wanton destruction.

"When Marty performs in one of her world-famous orgy scenes, she must know that, on any given day, throughout the world, between one thousand and ten thousand men will view that film. Some of them may be having relationship problems with their wives or girlfriends. When a man sees Marty's film, he may, understandably, become consumed with lust. Perhaps he'll respond to a chat room advertisement, or an advertisement for a pretty woman's face that happens to be located close to him; and who offers to fuck him.

"Surely Marty knows that advertisements fuel the porn sites that showcase her orgy scenes. So, Marty knows that with every thrust of a penis into her vagina, every shot of cum into her mouth or vagina; somewhere out there, there is a man who will have her on his mind when he makes his first fateful call. He'll go forward with his fantasy and have transference sex with a local prostitute, but Marty will be the woman he imagines he's with in the aroused limbic regions of his mind. After he's had his first experience, he may decide to visit prostitutes often. Marty understands all of this, Bob. That's why she charges premium prices for her films and why advertisers pay premiums of ten times normal rates to preview or trail her films. She is to money gold to intimacy art film advertisers. She is similar to hot sports figures who are sought after for their product endorsements.

"Marty understands all of this. Behind her beautiful alluring smile and dreamy eyes lives a pure business genius. She knows she's the agent of change that affects millions of lives. She knows she's that

catalytic psychological driver that destroys thousands of marriages every single month! And, she's more than fine with that. She's proud of it! Marriages and happy family lives are like the Devil to Marty. She fights the concept of happy family life with every fiber of her being.

"Her nymphomania is her greatest ally in this fight. Fucking, felatio, orgies, cunnilingus and psychological seduction techniques are Marty's weapons of choice. She turns the light of happy wholesome family life into brooding darkness. Good became evil in Marty's childhood's. She lived in an upside-down psychological world. Marty invades the familial bond and breaks it. She overwhelms the wife; in much the same way her own childhood was invaded and overwhelmed. Susan's conduct invaded Marty's psyche and crushed it when Marty was a child.

"Susan created a monster. That monster grew into womanhood. That monster carries the memory of the empty shell of her childhood within her. It's the psychic fuel for her seething rage against goodness. The monster that lives within Marty seeks to make every other woman in the world feel her childhood misfortune. You see, Bob, most people find a way to cope. They get over their bad experiences and move on; but that's not Marty. Marty cannot cope and come to terms with her childhood. She will never move on. Her nymphomania recycles all her childhood's emotional pains into heavenly erotic pleasures. And she can never get enough of either.

"A sexually healthy, normally adjusted woman with healthy family values and average looks has zero chance competing with Marty. Marty knows that. And she uses all her seductive tools to her maximum advantage. She doesn't care how the wife feels when the woman discovers her life has been destroyed. Marty is a lot like an octopus that way, ripping marriages apart like so many clam shells, devouring the husband's affections, feasting on his love like the octopus eating the clam; and moving on. If Marty knew she could not

*be caught, she would have no qualms about murdering her lovers'
wives. That's how much she hates happily married women. Marriage
and church failed Marty as a child. So, she gave up on her Christian
faith and decided to chart her own path.*

*"How many others have church and marriage failed? When I
read stories of priests buggering children and the church hushing
it up, I wonder what is right and what is wrong. Maybe there is
no right and no wrong. Maybe there's only the choices one decides
to make. Maybe Marty's way is the right way for many millions of
people, maybe even most people. Who can say?*

*"When I asked myself that question, I had my third epiphany. It
suddenly dawned on me that U interjects all sorts of chaos into our
lives. Things we call good or evil are simply change from one way
of perceiving things to another way. And, why would U do this, I
asked myself? The answer came to me as soon as I asked it. U does
these things that cause change; that get some of us all bothered; and
some of us totally upset; because U likes to amuse U. U introduces
these changes through events or people because U likes to amuse U
by watching how people react to the changes. It's that simple. Think
about it. U can't go to movies or watch football games, so what can U
do for amusement? U causes change. That's what U does. And, perhaps U wants Marty and others like her to be U's agents of change.
Perhaps, without the Marty's of this world, the human race would
become xenophobic, inbred; and everyone would end up being a
mentally retarded simpleton. Who knows? Only U knows.*

*"But U loves Marty and all her kind. U loves all the world's
nymphs and whores because they are U's change agents; and for the
human species to thrive it needs change. Pots must be stirred! Look
at Marty as one of U's stir sticks. It's all good. Life goes on. The soup
gets some spices that give it a better taste.*

*"Humans adjust to their stirring and end up being better for it.
'So, you lost your husband to some whore,' reasons U. 'No big deal.*

The sun rose the next day, didn't it? Get over it and move along. Try something different; but continue to love your kids. Don't want to lose him? Then try injecting some variety in your lives. Yes, you know what to do. And it's okay. You don't need to feel guilty. U will always love you.' I think that must be how the Spirit views Marty's behavior. To U, it's all just one big: 'so what!'

"And how dare anyone say Marty's behavior destroys, therefore her behavior is bad, when the very foundation of the church was built upon destruction of the established order and the annihilation of entire civilizations? Did the Aztecs have a choice about their fate? Those peoples were destroyers of many peoples, but they, too, were destroyed in the name of religion. Just because the destroyers were convinced what they were doing was being done in the name of God didn't make their deeds any less evil than the deeds of those they obliterated, did it?

"Before the church demands that Marty atone and change her ways, it must pretend to not see its own reflection in her behaviors. Is destruction of the destroyer destructive, or is it creative? Perhaps creation and destruction are merely one and the same thing in some grand cycle of life? I mean, if a child is aborted so Marty can perform and her sensational performance leads to more sex and more babies being born, then how can any of this be judged and who has the right to judge any of it? How can the cycles of life be judged? What court puts life's cycles on trial?

"Marty is one of U's change agents, Bob. Creation necessitates destruction; and new life flows from creation. Life rewards the wicked, the ruthless, the clever and the strong. The meek do not inherit the Earth. That's hogwash. The last do not come in first. That's more hogwash. The last come in last. Does the cricket getting eaten by a praying mantis somehow become the big winner? Do we admonish the mantis for its nature, for what it must do to live? Do we glorify the cricket for being eaten? How about the baby turtles

eaten by birds before they get to the ocean, or baby Puffin chicks that are ripped apart and eaten by Gulls before they can fly from their nests? How about animals that eat or kill their own or abandon them to die; like spiders, felines, canines, several primates, ungulates, reptiles, and birds of all sorts? No, we just shrug all that off. We go on about our own lives, because we know that is what happens to the weak. That is natural selection at work. Are we any better; or do we just think we're better?"

"Then, tell me, Barb, how am I supposed to think of Marty? What is she?"

"Big Horse, she is woman. But she is more than woman. Marty represents what Eve knew when she gave Adam the apple and opened his eyes. Marty represents the same thing Eve represented."

"What are you getting at, Barb?"

"Oh, you men are so stupid, Big Horse. Eve showed Adam life. She opened his eyes to freedom. She showed him the source of life, the source of creation. She showed Adam her vagina!"

"So, Marty represents vagina? I don't get it. Every woman has a vagina. And, didn't Eve's vagina have a fig leaf over it?"

"Oh, you big stupid horse! Marty's butterfly vagina represents mankind's greatest leap."

"I thought that had something to do with man stepping on the moon?"

"No, no, no, Big Horse. Marty's vagina is not covered by a fig leaf. It represents woman's freedom revealed. It represents the power of a woman to make love and create life, if she chooses. Her power is highlighted by a butterfly. The butterfly represents the ultimate freedoms of choices that a modern woman has with her vagina. That's the feeling of freedom. It's opposite from the feeling of shame which once caused women to conceal their pussies, the way poor Eve did. Marty flaunts and glorifies her vagina. She is proud of her seductive, womanly powers. Eve felt shame about the powers of her vagina.

"Marty knows no shame about the life changing powers of her vagina. That difference in Marty's perception compared with Eve's perception represents mankind's greatest leap forward. Walking on the moon is trivial compared to that. Marty's butterfly tattooed vagina symbolizes humanity's enormous progress toward complete freedom. It represents woman's equality with man. It symbolizes that all barriers between a woman's power and a man's power are gone. When a man flutters with a woman who wears Marty's EYES BEHIND THE BUTTEFLY BRAND™, that man and that woman are implicitly acknowledging that their powers are equal.

"You see, Horse, Marty has birth control. She can also choose abortion. Eve was constrained. She didn't have birth control or abortion services available. Eve needed to be careful about having her pleasures. The consequence of Eve's liaison was the risk of child birth. Marty bears no risks of consequences for her pleasures. She, through her butterfly tattoo, lets the world know that she has complete freedom to make love with as many lovers as she chooses. She has that power of choice, Horse. Her eyes and her vagina create a unique brand, Horse. They represent the freedom that mankind's soul discovers when fluttering with her vagina. It's the freedom that equality brings. Marty's eyes and her butterfly vagina combined to become her brand. Her brand uniquely represents humanity's source of freedom. When someone identifies with Marty's eyes and her butterfly vagina, they discover the soul of freedom. They enter the 'EYES BEHIND THE BUTTERFLY™.'

"Freedom? Freedom from what?"

"From everything that holds men and women back from their desires for freedom, Bob. Her brand represents the soul's freedom from stresses; freedom from entanglements; freedom from responsibilities; and, for many of those who follow her, also freedom from God and religion; freedom from all of religions' commandments, mitzvahs, rituals of dos and don'ts. Marty's unique brand is the next

step forward in mankind's evolution. It is the brand of hedonism and liberty.

"Marty's ruthless assault on marriages was driven home to me after I watched one of her films. Like the Church assaulted Native Americans, Marty attacks marital tradition with her clear intent to destroy it. She was absolutely, brazenly wanton in that film. She wore a gold necklace with about fifty rings on it. Near the end of the film the camera frames her face and she seductively purrs:

'Are you feeling trapped in a relationship that doesn't satisfy you? Are you ready to discover something better? Sure, you are. I'll help you. Just click on the little red box at the bottom of your screen. That will bring you to my premium membership sign up page.'

"The camera then focuses a close-up of Marty's vagina. She's holding it open, inviting the viewer to enter her glistening pink inner lips.

'Go ahead, click the box. Come visit me, I'm waiting for you.'

"I wanted to find out what the premium membership entailed, so I clicked. The filming continued after the click. By joining her premium membership, I was paying a hundred dollars a month to see all her films from beginning to end, not just her movie trailers. In the premium part of the film, Marty brought her head forward and pulled her ring neckless over her head. The camera then returned its focus to her vagina.

"She spread her legs widely, revealing a pool of white semen cum. Then she rubbed her neckless rings up and down, through the semen pool that resided in her open vagina. It didn't gross me out to watch this. It really didn't; not the way she did it. It was loving, sensual and breathtaking. Each ring represented a man's choice to ditch his wife and worship Marty. She bathed the rings in her cum pool, as if each man who once wore one of those rings was special to her. And they were. They permitted her to drown their marriages in her sins. She loves drowning marriages. That's special to her. It's a mental thing.

"Then she placed some cum in her mouth and rolled it on her tongue, swallowed it, licked her fingers, and beamed her most coquettish angelic smile. Her invitation implies her viewer should ditch his woman and join her, too. She personifies seduction, Bob. But I guess you discovered that on your own.

"Marty sees herself as the goddess of the frustrated. And she sees her vagina as their sanctuary, an escape for those trapped in relationships they can't stand any longer. She whisper-purrs to her new premium member in her seductive come-hither voice:

'Hello, premium member, I'm so glad you came. Do you like my vagina? It's nice and soft and soooo smooth. I can't wait to make love with you. I want to take your penis inside my vagina. I want to feel you inside me. Mmmmm. I'll help you forget your relationship trap. See the red box at the bottom of your screen? Go ahead. Click on it. That will take you to my premium member's appointment page.'

"The camera man explained that Marty's premium appointments cost five thousand Dollars per hour. For that you get to meet her, at a time and place she designates; and she sucks and fucks her paying member for a full hour. Once the appointment is made and the site takes five thousand Dollars from the member's credit card, her vagina reappears on the full screen. She lovingly rubs the rings through her cum pool again. That boosts the viewer's desire to join her ring group.

'We'll make love when we meet at your appointment.' she says. Then her face forms a seductive kiss. She kisses the air, slow blinks her eyes and smiles at the camera. The film is over.

"At the appointment, while Marty makes love with her new guest, she asks him about his difficult married life and whether he's considered leaving his wife and having sensational love making sessions with her instead. If the man says yes, she makes her offer. If he'll pay her an additional fifteen thousand and give his wedding ring to her today, he'll receive five additional private love making *sessions, that's a forty percent discount; he'll also receive a package of photographs of Marty in stand alone seductive poses, close up photos of her vagina; and many poses of Marty making love with twenty of her favorite male performers, as well as photos of her performing during her orgy scenes; he'll also receive her special orgy participation invitation offers. As part of todays' once in a lifetime, bonus offer he'll be notified whenever she's filming within two hundred miles of his zip code. Then he'll get free admission to the set where he can watch her make her next film; and possibly participate as one of her performers. Once the man signs the agreement, Marty knows she's free to crush his marriage.*

'Let's have fun with your ring,' she says, taking it from his finger. She spreads her legs and rubs the ring all over her vagina. In the background, music from the Credo begins playing, fully engaging the man's emotions. The Credo repeats over and over during their love making session. The man's feelings of passion are elevated to the heavens. He believes he's having an out of body spiritual experience as he falls deeply in love with Marty.

"I remember Chief telling me about the Scalp Pole Dance. It's an ancient Lakota tribal custom. It was performed by the wives of the tribe's warriors. They dressed very sexily in their loose loin cloths dangling from their hips. They wore face paints to invite men to see their beauty. They had decorative poles in their hands and upon these poles dangled the scalps of enemy Pawnee warriors. These women danced around the poles in a seductive manner, mocking the scalps with their undulating hips to belittle the fallen and to pay ceremonial tribute to their victorious warriors with their bodies. It was their communal way of honoring their brave men who had inflicted death upon the hated Pawnee.

"Marty doesn't know about Lakota customs. What she did with that man's wedding ring was Marty acting out what she felt naturally; and yet, the symbolism of what she did struck me. Her message *was every bit as savage as the message of those Lakota squaws. Marty was honoring her sexuality. She was paying tribute to her vagina for inflicting death upon another woman's marriage. Her act stunned my sensibilities. I knew I was witnessing something debauched, perverse, and wanton. Her action unlocked her viewers' primitive psyches. She took them beyond mere pornography. She delivered them to the whole different dimension of demented pagan blood-lust craving. It's that peculiar space that exists between the sanctification of death's destruction and the simultaneous celebration of life.*

"What is happening to my mind," I asked myself. "I'm witnessing the most heinous, barbaric lewdness, yet I feel my heart racing at the splendor of Marty's vileness. I wondered, did the Lakota warriors kill Pawnee for hunting territory to feed their families; or did they kill the Pawnee to slake the blood-lust of their women? Were they able to block out the horrors of the deaths they were inflicting because their minds' limbic zones were commanding their deeds out of a desire for the passions of their women? Were they able to think in terms of the warmth of a woman's body holding them close, kissing them, and making love with them, while they murdered the Pawnee?

"And that thought trail brought me back to the present. Was Marty's seduced male able to block out the horrific devastation which he had to know she had already caused so many marriages, while he cavorted with her? Did he blind himself to that reality of Marty's true nature? Did he believe his own marriage would be spared somehow? No, I thought, that could not be true. He had to know there would be consequences. He had to know his marriage would die as surely as the Lakota warrior knew his Pawnee enemy would die when he shot the Pawnee through with his arrows. But Marty's lover didn't care, just like the Lakota warrior didn't care. Marty's lover was embracing Marty. He had flipped his limbic switch to the 'on' position. He could not be bothered by thoughts other than cavorting with Marty. His mind was gone.

"All that mattered was the lust reward, the slaking of the passion thirst of the limbic zone. Marty's seduced man could not resist her creamy skin, her soft lips and tongue kisses, her expertly feathered touches on his penis and balls. He could not pry himself away from the soft velvety sensations of her vagina or her moans of pleasure and her exhortations while he made love with her. His limbic zone would never allow him to give up that nirvana. He valued his nirvana more than everything he possessed and every other relationship he held dear.

"Marty's vagina persuades her seduced to do her bidding. Her tactics are wildly successful. They work as surely as the charms of the Lakota scalp pole dancers while winning their men's hearts, and encouraging them to kill. I saw no shame in Marty's performance. She performed her honor ceremony openly, proudly; much like the Lakota squaws performed their scalp pole dances. Both performances were uninhibited and sensual. The Lakota women performed before their tribe. Marty performed for her fan base.

"I found myself wondering if Marty thought the same sorts of thoughts my people thought while they danced. Did she, like the Lakota women, feel wonderful and blessed? Did she, like the Lakota women, believe she was doing a good thing, that she, too, was moving civilization forward? Did she intuitively understand that debauched lust was a tool of the spirits to affect change, and that the spirits believed it was perfectly acceptable and necessary behavior? From somewhere deep within her soul, I believe Marty understood the rightness of what she was doing. I believe that just like my ancestral women felt blessed to have wonderful warrior men provide for them and protect them, Marty also felt blessed to have her nymphomania provide for her. I wondered how deeply Marty felt her feelings while she rubbed the vanquished man's ring inside her vagina? Was her spectacular behavior something she had learned and practiced or was it instinctual? Then I heard her speak again:

'My vagina feels wonderful when I rub her with your ring. She's feeling very excited and stimulated. Let's show the world you refuse to allow your manliness be controlled by your marriage, shall we? Let's put that silly wedding ring to good use, shall we? Would you please rub my vagina with your ring and use it to stimulate me more?'

"The man obeys Marty. Unquestioningly, as if in a trance like state, he does as Marty implores him to do. He loses his free will. He removes the ring and uses it to probe the interior of Marty's vagina, searching for her clitoris. He is now eager to give her the pleasure she craves. His task becomes all consuming. He is smitten. He is given over to love this whore; immerse himself in her lust, even though he understands that she will use him and discard him, like she has all the other ring bearers before him. The genius of Marty's use of the limbic effect is that her lover doesn't care that his life will be destroyed. All he knows and cares about is that he loves Marty. He worships Marty. The Credo amplifies her hypnotic effect on him. He cannot resist her suggestions. Truth be told, millions of her fans watching this film would gladly take his place. She's that alluring and compelling. She coos her pleasures to her seduced:

'Did you like touching my vagina with your wedding ring? You're having fun, aren't you? Sure, you are. I'm having fun too. I love having fun, don't you?'

"She's a brilliant marketer. She asks her lover if he's receiving satisfaction after her initial sale. If he answers 'yes,' she then asks:

'Would you like to kiss my vagina?'

"If he again answers 'yes,' she invites him to perform cunnilingus. After cunnilingus she whispers seductively:

'I loved how I felt when you did that. I came so beautifully. My vagina loves you. May I keep your ring on my neckless? I'll wear it to remind myself that you care about me. While I'm filming, I'll rub it inside my vagina. It will reassure me that your love is with

me, inside me. I feel something wonderful is happening between us. Don't you feel that way, too?'

"If he answers 'yes,' this third time, she says: 'I'm ready for you now. I want you to make love with me. I want to feel you inside me and I want you to come inside me.'

"The Credo's volume increases in intensity. The man feels like he's in heaven while he's making love with Marty. She cradles him, kisses him passionately, and tells him how wonderful she feels with his penis inside her during their entire love making session. The man has never heard this sort of erotic talk from his wife. And he's never been with any woman who enjoys sex this much. He is smitten. His mind will never stray far from his thoughts of Marty.

"He'll spend endless hours remembering how she tastes; how her creamy white skin feels to his touches; how he felt while she was touching his face and body; rubbing her hands over his back while he had sex with her; how his penis felt when her silky-smooth vagina performed its unforgettable Kegel squeezes; and how blissful it was to French kiss her. For the first time in many years the man feels his soul has been renewed. He has fallen in love with Marty.

"After she makes love with her newest ultra-member, she extolls his love making like the sex-craven nympho she is. She expresses her wild enthusiasm for their love making while running her hands crazily through her hair:

'Oh baby, darling, I LOVED MAKING LOVE WITH YOU! I LOVED EVERY SECOND OF IT! I didn't want us to stop. You're SO beautiful when you make love with me, and your penis felt SO WONDERFUL inside me, I CAN'T WAIT to make love with you again. I'm getting wet and creamy inside just thinking about it. You excited me SO much. I want to be your special whore. I'll love being your whore. I want to be your love slave and I want to make love with you whenever you want to have me. And I want us to be in love. Whenever your wife gets difficult, don't pay any attention to* *her! Not one bit. YOU have ME now. Don't argue with her, just get away from her. Call my appointment service. They'll get you into a hotel and I' LL COME TO YOU. I WANT to BE with you. We'll be together again, and we'll make LOVE again and again and again! I CAN'T WAIT to have you again! I WANT YOU! I want you inside me. I love feeling your penis inside me. You're so wonderful!'*

"Then she whispers seductively into his ear while kissing him in his ear, 'Call me, please. Oh please, just call me.'

"She adds his ring to her neckless, alongside her other exclusive ultra members' rings; and she promises to wear the neckless when she makes her next intimacy art film. She'll make the film and send him a free download of it, in honor of his love for her.

"As Marty smiles her loving smiles to her latest conquest, in the back of her mind she knows another woman has just entered a living hell. She knows that, day by day, the woman will lose control of her husband. He won't take out the trash, or wash the car, mow the lawn, walk the dog, go to the store, or spend time with her. He'll go to a bar and drink, while he stares into empty space. He'll spend hours watching films of Marty on her intimacy web site. Then he'll sit staring into space, reliving those moments while he was fucking Marty. When his wife talks to him, he'll sass her; argue with her; or completely ignore her. He wants her to fight with him. He may even abuse her physically. He'll intentionally provoke her, something he's never done before. He looks for any excuse to get away from her and run to Marty.

"He knows he shouldn't call the whore; and he understands that continuing to see Marty will destroy his marriage, but he can't stop thinking about her. He needs her touches and kisses. And he craves sex with her. He can't help himself. He begins to believe that he's special to Marty; different somehow from all her other lovers. He wonders if Marty possibly really does love him. He hopes she does. He even silently prays that Marty loves him, that it's all real love. But

of course, Marty only wants his money. The man understands this reality. He knows he's playing a dangerous game, but he suspends that reality and enters a delusional place."

"Why does that happen inside a man's mind?" Bob yearned to understand this process in the hopes that he might better understand his own feelings about Marty.

"Because, Bob, when it comes to navigating the meandering pathways and hidden byways to understanding a woman's true thoughts, you men are imbeciles. Women understand extremely well how men's minds work. From childhood onward they grasp how to wrap Daddy around their pinky finger and have him do their bidding. By the time a woman reaches adulthood she has mastered most of the techniques she needs to play upon a man's emotions like a bow plays a fiddle. Marty, advantaged with her experiences with many men, has fine tuned her seduction instruments. She is the first violin of whoredom's seductive orchestra, its virtuoso of glorious, spectacular, sweetly resonating sex.

"Her sounds and movements lead her man's mind into another world. There he suspends reality. She helps him lose himself in fantasy. His normal, rational mind has lapses in judgment. It slips into a suspension-like state of dementia. He becomes incapable of rational thought. His mind visualizes an Elysium field of eternal bliss spread open before him. It takes the form of Marty's inviting body, her gorgeous innocent face, those ruby lips that invite kissing, and those disarming eyes that captivate his soul. And, her butterfly tattoo, opened now, compels his mind to dream its way onto her irresistible field, flutter in surreal ecstasy while he makes love with her.

"His mind capitulates to his dream fantasy. He has less ability to resist her charms than a child can resist candy. His mind becomes the enfeebled wanderer in his Marty fantasy opera. It drinks in her overtures; laps up the rhapsodies of her arias, unites with her passions forever in a climactic chorus of triumphant love; achieved

against all odds or reason. He hopes against hope that Marty just might love him. His rational mind knows that's a one in a million long shot, but his delusional mind is eager to risk everything to take that chance."

"You really think men are that crazy?" Bob was skeptical.

"Some are. Look at your own behavior," Barbara's ever present quick wit replied. *"Our example man has lost his mind. His capacity for rational thought has fluttered away. It's mated with Marty's butterfly. His little head now does all his thinking for him. All he thinks about is Marty; her face, body, smiles, laughter, kisses; and his tongue's and his little head's immersions in her delicious, fascinating, irresistible vagina. Her butterfly legs wrap around him and pull his soul into hers. His mind, before this moment, had teetered on a cliff edge. It then had some small ability to pull back from Marty's temptations. But resist her debaucheries now? No longer!*

"Once mated with the butterfly his mind now tumbles from its precarious cliff perch and falls headlong, willfully, and joyfully into the endless abyss that is Marty. His entire mind's devotion ardor now pledges its love and loyalty to that wondrous heaven that it can not live without. Obsession consumes his mind. It's every waking and dreaming thought is now of Marty's delicious wonderful sexuality and all other thoughts are locked out of his mind's private secret paradise.

"When her mouth opens and her tongue teasingly plays with his, he conveniently forgets he's seen her same tongue tease hundreds of penises' heads to ejaculate their semen onto it. When his hand touches her vagina, she giggles: 'Oh, I think you'd like to play, wouldn't you? Okay, let's play. I love to play.' And then, when they proceed to intercourse, he conveniently forgets he's previously seen her make love with hundreds of other penises on film; and that that's what drew him to her in the first place. His mind is in its private utopia now. He suspends all disbelief that this siren of love and sex

could be anything other than his exclusive, trusted soul mate. Marty has now locked all of him, mind, body, and soul, safely away into her sacred treasure trove of captured men whose rings she flaunts in her intimate art films.

"Moved by desperation, our lover boy's wife takes him to an opera. She knows something occupies his mind and causes him to daydream. Perhaps a brilliant performance of Giuseppe Verdi's 'Rigoletto' will snap him out of his funk and return him to her? At least, she can hope. Alas, sitting there beside her in their balcony seats, her husband's head falls back to rest upon his seat back. His eyes flutter half-closed as if they are about to drift away into sleep. He is tired. He told her he had a long day and he did. He watched three of Marty's porn films. As the opera proceeds from act two to act three, her husband's mind begins to drift.

"When the music score's intrigue hints of impending tragedy, his closed eyelids imagine a figure rising from the orchestra pit. It is small at first, but it continues rising and growing larger. It is a woman's figure. She wears only a black silk bra and black lace panties. She is stunning, beautiful. He wets his lips with desire for her. She is Marty. Larger and larger her imaginary figure grows, until it fills his imagination's entire vision field. She moves closer to him, her body shimmering before the background lights of the stage floor below.

"Marty smiles at him, then unsnaps her bra, revealing her magnificent breasts. Her smile proclaims that she wants to play and make love. Her image floats closer to him, growing larger and larger until his entire vision field sees only the cherry red nipple bud of her right breast. It is marvelous, succulent, desirous and wondrous. She cups her hand to her tit and urges his mouth to kiss its wonder. He does. His mind is in another world now, only dimly aware of the music. Marty's imaginary figure steps back from him. Her image removes its panties, revealing her sex. She rubs her vagina seductively with her hand. His mouth waters from his opened floodgates of lust. He drools.

"The figure holds open her vagina and spreads her legs. He sees the butterfly tattoo. It haunts his mind, sweeping away all other thoughts as if they are annoying cobwebs. The image brings the tattoo closer and closer to his face. The imaginary figure places her knees upon his shoulders; now straddling his head with its butterfly tattoo. Then the figure gradually lowers the butterfly tattoo until it envelopes his head. The body of the tattoo, its vagina's insatiable love channel, finally seats itself comfortably upon his mouth. Recalled vividly from his memory now, beautiful beyond anything he could have ever hoped to behold, softly, gently, the image rests its wondrous vagina upon his mouth. His mind has delivered him to the only place it wants to be.

"Then, while Marty's sex craven vagina slowly moves in synchronicity with his mouth and tongue, she releases the beginnings of her long orgasm. He imagines hearing Marty's love moans, appreciating the pleasures he's giving her. Her moans deafen all his other senses. The moment of her pleasure is indelibly etched into his brain's most sacred retentive vault. He is a success! He is pleasing to the world's number one film star of the intimate arts. He is certain that he has provided her with her fullest measure of pleasures. He has fulfilled what must surely be his calling in life. In his own fantasizing mind, Marty's opinion of him is soaring to the heavens. Perhaps now she knows! Oh yes! Certainly, his love kitten must know how much he loves her! Surely, she knows how devoted he will always be to her further glory! His hand slides into his pants. This fantasy is so good! He must share it with his best friend.

"He dimly hears 'La Donna e Mobile,' the acknowledgement of a woman's fickleness; but his mind is now occupied by something far more important than the opera. As the opera reaches the end of act two, he imagines he is the Duke of Mantua. Marty is his secret lover, Gilda. They are in their private room; in their private world. She has lowered her vagina onto his face. She wants him to ravage her; first *by tongue; later by penis. She wishes their love kept secret from her father, Rigoletto and from Maddalena, the Duke's other love interest; and secreted from the world.*

"In his addlepated mind as Marty's lover, her vagina and the music convince him that he is about to again savor the sweet love juices of the world's number one intimacy art film star, in secrecy from his wife. While his wife listens intently to the Belle Figlia, daughter of love aria, his mind is reliving the most memorable experience of his life. He dreams. He still has Marty's taste on his tongue. He silently smacks his lips. Yes, he can still taste the love of his life.

"The darkness of the theater and the music return his mind to earlier today. He was not at work. He lied to his wife about that. He was on a film set with Marty. He had persuaded her to allow him to play a role in her latest film. Instead of paying for a performer, he assured her he would gladly pay her to play any part she wished. She agreed. He would be the compliant mouth, within the unseen head, faced up upon the bed, upon which she would repose her sex craving vagina. His tongue's role was to locate and stimulate her clitoris while, above him, she alternately performed exquisite fellatio with six hard, fabulously oversized penises.

"Her experience with cunnilingus was a great contributor to his success. Her pelvic movement was a slow rhythmic persuasive help mate to his tongue. Her knowing vagina first yawed gently forward and down, helping her clitoris receive the full upward stroke of his extended tongue; and then her vagina pivot-yawed backward and upward creating an exhilarating downward stroke of her clitoris gliding over his tongue. This gentle yawing continued, allowing him to catch his breath between his tongue strokes as Marty performed fellatio upon her partners' penises above him.

"When her orgasm flow began, her vagina pitched ever so slightly from side to side, like a ship rolling peacefully between gentle swells. He could tell by the way her pink walls contracted and

relaxed that she enjoyed her orgasms immensely. She long continued these contractions, thus assuring him that she was savoring every second of her prolonged release. He could only imagine how her mouth became even more sensual and loving to the penises which it hosted above his head, while her vagina flowed freely below.

"She was spectacular. The camera captured her ecstatic rapture state. He had dutifully performed his part. Marty had released her orgasm into his mouth while she enthusiastically, joyfully sucked penis after penis above his head. He felt profoundly honored to per-form his role in honor of her pleasure, thus affirming his commit-ment to her and proving his unrequited love to her. In his mind, the role he played was anything but sordid. It was exquisite, shameless, undying devotional love.

"He believed that by continuing to stimulate her and helping her have a long enduring orgasm, he assisted her credibility before the cameras. He was right. Marty's sensual ecstasy while in the throes of orgasm showed as joyous radiance in her facial expressions. The film was much more erotic, thanks to his contribution to its success. He faithfully, lovingly helped Marty perform her explicit artistry at her lust crazed best.

"He recalls the pride he felt. He played his small role by helping her persuade all her fans that surely, they were witnessing the undisputed number one intimate art star on earth, while in her throes of pleasure's passions; and surely, he helped her add to her great fortune. By doing his part in furthering her cause he believed it might be possible that she will find it within her heart to love him. And if she does not recip-rocate his love, that would be okay with him anyway; because he loves her. That's all that matters to him now. He knows his love is enough for the two of them. He ejaculates into his hand, inside his pants. His wife is engrossed in the opera. She doesn't notice.

"That marvelous day, he tasted the rapture flows of Marty's whore-lust and felt selfless gratitude towards her. She allowed him the

honor of pleasuring her! On stage! This simple-minded idiot thinks he's arrived at her inner circle. Then, after she had her professional performers sufficiently stimulated, he was removed to a chair and allowed to sit and watch her continue her performance. Seeing her performing live, in the flesh, was far more riveting and stimulating than the hundreds of times he'd watched her on film. Watching her vagina's thrusts while contracting upon penis after penis; then seeing those penises' ejaculations flow from her was vivid and breathtaking for him, because it was real! He relived Marty's moans and bantering during her orgy scene, in his mind.

"Here's where a strange phenomenon occurs, Bob. I cannot fully explain it; but it is a transference process during which the male's mind goes off the rails. Our opera goer recalls a film he saw. Marty was reclined, receiving oral sex; her hand on the head of her lover; her fingers kneading his hair. He remembers her look of serenity; the way her eyes rolled back to their whites; her expression of eternal happiness.

"Something happens. His mind flips to a different state. It wants to do everything it can to ensure her pleasures will last forever. It's a similar hormonal drive to the drive that makes deer, elk, and buffalo battle for mating rights; but it's different in the human male. It's something akin to what a Black Widow male spider or praying mantis male feels when he mates. He's perfectly okay with letting the female devour him afterwards. He wants to make sure her pleasure continues, even at the sacrifice of his own life. Other, higher ordered animals are not this way. The male mates and leaves the female. Also, this is true of most human males; but not all human males. Some human males; not all, are susceptible to female infatuation. When these males become smitten by a woman, they willingly destroy their own lives for her betterment. These males must have a DNA quirk that makes them like black widow spider males. Chief has thought on this. Nothing else, he opines, explains the behaviors of these males.

"Our opera goer is one of these rare males. He has found his way to Marty like the male spider finds his way to his Black Widow mate. He has found his nirvana in Marty. He wants Marty's feeling of eternal happiness to last forever; even if he must sacrifice everything to enable that. That's how I think of Marty's victims. They know she is wicked, heartless, and cruel. Those immoral traits are what they love about her; and they love her, regardless of her capacity to destroy them. That's the only way Marty's male victims make sense to me. And this is how I imagine our opera goer's mind misfunctions while seated beside his wife. His imagination remembers only what he saw Marty doing while making her film.

"Like a performing virtuoso tuning an instrument for play, Marty scrutinized each penis presented before her lips. Had her assistants done their work well? Was it ready to ejaculate? She kneaded each testicle sack with her knowing, loving touches. Yes, she ascertained. Surely this penis was eager for the joys of her mouth. And this one is primed for its entrance into her vagina.

"Our bedazzled fellow watched her beautiful mouth lavish kisses upon the penis's head. Obviously, she loved what she was doing. Her tongue and lips played expertly upon its circumcision ring and penis head. Its erection response was magnificent. The penis swelled and reached skyward, proving to her mouth that it felt honored. Her hands and mouth next massaged its balls. Her skills are unrivaled. This phase of her performance was intoxicating. The penis understood that it was impossible to resist Marty's coaxing; and it didn't want to. It loved her attentions. It shuddered and strained to be larger than itself, as if it felt privileged to have a role in the film. Millions of penises would gladly perform with her; but her hands held this penis.

"She strokes the penis with lips and tongue and hands. Her loving kisses convinced the penis that she was giving it the love she craved. It surrendered, ejaculating spurt after spurt of its creamy

white essence into Marty's lusting mouth; sending gushing volumes onto her triumphant tongue. Her performance was exquisite. Her fans were able to discern her thoughts and feelings. They were seeing the genuine Marty. She loves romancing a penis. The intensity and genuineness of love for the male stem elevates her above the other adult actresses. Her voice purred her softly spoken vignette, while continuing to receive the penises' ejaculations; a truly remarkable talent:

'Oh, yes, I'm taking in all your cum. I'm the woman you love. You know that's true. You're proving that to me. Do you know that you're giving me an orgasm right now? Yes, you are. You KNOW you are. I'm coming, right now. Can you tell? Yes, baby, you are SO wonderful. Kiss me. I love being kissed while I'm coming. It makes coming so beautiful. I feel loved, really loved when you kiss me. I love coming with one penis inside me and another penis in my mouth. You boys make me feel SO erotic! You want me to have all your cum, I know you do. And I want you to give me all of it, too. Yes, all of it.

'OH YES, that's good, baby Yes, that's exactly what I wanted. My vagina loves what you're doing. My vagina wants you to come inside her. Yes, I'm sure. I feel you coming now. You are so sweet! Your cum feels so hot and warm. You're filling my whole vagina. He, he, he! (Giggling). Oh, that's really nice. So warm! Kiss me. Kiss my mouth. I love being kissed.

'Oh, hello. You're a big hard one, aren't you? Oh, yes! I love how you feel in my hands. I can't wait to feel you inside me. Yes, perfect. You're a perfect penis. Go on. That's it. Oh, so good. You ARE a big one, aren't you? You're very strong and sooo firm inside me. Oh, I love what you're doing right now. Yes, yes, yes. Are you ready? Yes, I absolutely do want you to come inside me. You're not afraid to give me all of it, are you? I want all of it. Yes, all of it. Yes, of course I know. Don't worry, I'm on the pill. Just come. Please come. I want you to come. Are you coming? Yes, I feel you now! Oh, that's really

good baby. I feel you shooting. So hot and so much! Give me your cum. Prove you love me. I want it; you know I do. I want all of it. Yes, keep coming. Keep flowing, that's it, yes, give me all of it. Don't hold anything back Oh, kiss me. I want to be kissed. Yes, that was sweet.

'Well, hello there. You're certainly huge, aren't you? Is this true? Another big penis wants me? Is this big penis for real? May I have all of you? Okay, let's start nice and easy. That's it! Oh, that feels sooo good. Yes, all the way inside me now. Yes, of course I can. I want to. Oh, now I think YOU'RE ready, aren't you? Here, inside my mouth. Yes, I want you to come. Oh, yes, that's it, sweetheart. Oh, both of you at once! How wonderful! You boys are so wonderful to me. I love fucking like this. I never want to stop. Keep going. Yes, harder. I love getting fucked like this! My vagina feels soooo gooood! Oh, keep coming, yes, yes. Oh, Oh, Heee (giggling).

'That was fun! I love having fun while I'm making love. Whew, so deep! That one took my breath away. You're not going to share that penis with any other woman, are you? Promise you'll save yourself for me. I loved what you did to me. I want you all for myself! When you tickled me like that you made me come again. Yes, you did. Yes, you really did. Did you feel me gushing inside? Oh, you're so sweet! You remembered to kiss me. You know how much I love to be kissed! I love you. You need to visit me more often. Please come back. Your penis felt so nice. You had a lot inside you, didn't you? Do you know how much cum you gave me? You were wonderful! Are you always so full like that? I love how you tasted. You liked giving me a lot, didn't you? Ha, ha. Yes, that's it! You boys are my special protein shake!

'I love getting naughty with you. I'm serious. I love making love with you. You make me want to be a very naughty girl. Let me suck you some more. I know you have more. Yes, of course I want it. I love it. Yes. Yum. You are so yummy! I love your beautiful penis. Will you

remember how wonderful we feel, right at this moment? Will you call me? Please call me. I want to make love with you again. Don't wait long. I want us to do this again, just the two of us fucking for a whole hour, okay? Let's be you and me, straight sex, nice and slow; and in every position. We'll both come like crazy. I want your penis and I want to feel your body all over me, okay baby? You'll love it. Call me.'

"Marty's oral sex stimulator watched her orgy sequence. His mental processes slowed the action down and committed it to memory, one spellbinding still frame after another. He captured every lip caress, every tongue lick, every flick of her cum basked tongue, every eruption spurt of hot white semen onto her extended tongue, every pulsing rivulet semen flow from her vagina. He forever burnished every image of her casual, nonchalant, sin--loving debauchery into his mind. He noted Marty's untroubled relaxed manner as she sucked penis after penis, while he pleasured her clitoris. He relives each of his tongue's strokes upon her pleasure receptor while watching her face in the film. His mind sees divine serenity in Marty's face. That image suffices to cause him to offer up his own immolation to her, like the male spider. Marty's confidence, that she is the best at her vocation, shows. She never displays the slightest hint of boredom. She shares the same performance traits as champion figure skaters or prima donna opera sopranos; unruffled, securely in command of the men and penises she performs with. Our fellow knew he had witnessed a consummate professional who knew and loved her profession and adored her for the splendid whore she was.

"When she turned to face the camera and opened widely her legs, he gulped. She revealed the triumphant fruits of her glorious debauchery. Proudly, brazenly, she held her freshly fucked vagina widely open and displayed a gigantic pool of white semen still burbling its fresh thick cream from the three penises she had milked. Her butterfly wings appeared to be carrying white nectar paste

extracted from the penises. She smiled boldly, unblushingly flaunt-ing the incontrovertible proof of her fornication successes. She had sequentially copulated with three of her partners' penises. Each had ejaculated into her; each had entrusted its life elixir essence to her.

"This was the transformational moment in the film. Her vagina was no longer merely the source of pleasure for her performers. It was much more than that. For our opera goer it represented the holy chalice, the ultimate repository of the seeds of life. It held untold billions of sperms. And every one of them desired to mate its life to her egg. But Marty next used this reservoir of male sperm for a different purpose.

CHAPTER TWO

Logic will get you from A to B. Imagination will get you everywhere else. (Albert Einstein).

Butterflies do not eat steak sandwiches, potato chips or ice cream. But some butterflies will gladly swallow a penis. (Rosemary Ness-Bitner, author)

SIGNATURE ACT

"Marty performed her signature act. She did the singular thing that separates her from all other intimate art stars, and all other women. She showed the camera and the world why she alone stands proudly, unchallenged as the number one Queen of Intimate Artistry Films. She unfastened from her neck her gold neckless. Upon its gold strand were fifty wedding rings. She held the neckless and the rings above her chalice pool of white cum and smiled boldly, defiantly, into the camera. Her face exuded a wonderment of pride in what she did before and what she is about to do now.

"Marty understands the male mind and her craft. She knows that many of her male viewers already have regrets about being married. She understands they stay married because of feelings of guilt or fear:

'Could I really leave my wife? Wouldn't that be cruel? Her life might end in poverty. What would people think of me? Can I make a life of my own without her? Where will I sleep tonight if I leave her?'

"*These thoughts and countless others like them race through the troubled minds of her viewers from time to time. Marty knows this. She's listened to men talk. She's gleaned their thoughts between their spoken words. Marty understands men.*

"*And, she knows how to play them to catch more of them. She takes a page out of every fisherman's book of tricks. What better bait to catch a fish than eggs from another fish? Why not use sperm to capture more sperm producers?*

"*With her smile, her brimming cum filled chalice, and her neckless of wedding rings, Marty understands how to tease action from men's thoughts. While their minds express frustration thoughts into the abyss of worlds unknown to them, Marty baits these eros starved males. Smiling, she dips her neckless string of conquests in her chalice of cum. Her echo answer to male minds' frustrations is given. Her beautiful smile, her alluring mouth-watering vagina, her act of dipping the rings, all say to the troubled viewer:*

"'*I know what you are thinking. I understand how you feel. It's an easy choice. Look! See my smile? I will love you. See my vagina? It's for you. You can have sex with me. Yes, you can. We will make love. I WANT to do that. Don't you? We'll have a wonderful time. See those wedding rings I bathed in my pool? Men just like you chose to leave their marriage for me. Do not be afraid. Make the right choice for yourself. Choose me for yourself. There's nothing to fear about being with me. Everything will be wonderful. Others have made the right choice. They are much happier now. I want you to be happy. I want you to choose me, too.*'

"*While she dips the rings, a click icon appears on the video screen. It directs the viewer to her premium service. Thousands of men will click on the bar. The sticker shock will winnow out most of them; but ten will join. Like fish that swallow bait eggs are dreaming of food, these men dream of placing their semen inside Marty's cum pool. They will spend a fortune to experience having sex with the world's most famous porn star.*"

"So, it's kind of like an assembly line for her. Is that what you're saying, Barb?" Bob's voice betrayed his dejection. He felt small and downtrodden by these revelations about his lover.

"Yes, Big Horse. I am sorry to be the one to break this to you." Barb put her hand on Bob's arm.

"I don't know which could be worse; to learn she loved another man; or to learn this, that she makes herself available to many men. And these other men fall so easily, don't they?" Bob shook his head. His thoughts were far away.

"Yes, Bob. Men can and do lose their minds over a woman's vagina. Many succumb to Marty. Look no further than yourself. For many men the female vagina is the greatest stumbling block in their lives. They want it but they don't know how to get it. It drives them crazy enough to take unimaginable risks to get it. Marty understands male needs and psychology. Her performances hold them spellbound. Then, she dominates their minds in a different way. She openly attacks the relationship bond the male has with his partner. She offers him not only sex, but also a refuge from his troubles. She's very aggressive, Bob. She attaches a psychological bond to her followers."

"I had no idea." Bob shook his head.

"Sure, you did, Horse. You knew she was gone away from you a lot. You just tried to protect your feelings by denying reality. That's normal when you love someone." Barbara nodded into Bob's eyes. Her smile was understanding.

"That promise of more to come, later, is Marty's psychological bond. It's how she separates herself from most women who make adult films. That's how she holds her number one ranking in all the Porn World surveys. Her films are great, Bob. I'll give her that; but the reason she commands premium prices and top ranking is because she understands the male mind. I kept watching her film.

"She next, indecently, and immodestly, toyed with her cum pool before the camera. She spooned a portion of cum onto her fingers,

lifted it to her mouth, rolled it on her tongue, and burbled it before swallowing it. Her subtle silent message again answered the male mind's worries:

'Don't worry. You won't get me pregnant. I'm on the pill. I'm clean, too, completely disease free. All my partners are tested. My love making is all about pleasure and fun. I take all worries out of it. And, as you can see, I also dispose of the evidence. See me swallowing it? I'd like to swallow yours, too. Your wife will never even know you are seeing me, unless you want her to know. I've taken all the risks away. It's completely safe for you to have an affair with me. Go ahead, everything is safe. Click on the premium membership bar.'

Unbeknownst to Barbara, during the scene that Barbara was describing to Bob, from the deepest recesses of her spirit mind's memories, the voice of Miss Iniquity was whispering to Marty:

'Are you feeling what I'm feeling? Close your eyes, listen to my voice, and concentrate. Can you recall seven thousand years ago? Sure, you can. You were a priestess of Baal in many of your previous lives. Remember? Sure, you do. Remember. Think hard and remember. You are now acting out the exact same things you did back then. You are converting a man to your beliefs. Think. Can you see yourself? Can you recall that glorious morning? Close your eyes; remember. You were pampered. Every day the young altar girls massaged your body with oils; coiffed your hair; cleaned and polished your fingernails and toenails. It was the morning of special offerings. The temple matron had just freshly shaved your vagina's mons, using her sharpest obsidian blade. Then she salved and anointed your sex with her prized gardenia scented salve and lilac scented oils, in preparation for your fornication rituals. Remember?'

'Yes, Miss Iniquity. I remember now.'

'Good. Now see yourself. Your name was Sheila; Goddess from the Heavens. You were in the center of the temple. You were the most revered, most highly prized prostitute among the ten prostitutes

selected to perform the ceremonial ritual of earth's rebirth. You were lying upon the altar, awaiting your supplicant. Your tribe was at war with the ancestral forbearer tribe of Hagar; mother of Ishmael. The time was three thousand years before the birth of Abraham. Their tribe was ruled by leaders who subjugated women, and your tribe venerated women. Remember?'

Marty nodded her head. Miss Iniquity's trance was having its effect. Marty's ancestral past was coming into focus.

'Yes,' whispered Iniquity, *'I see that you can remember now. You were lying upon your pedestal bed, completing your holy preparations to fornicate. The day before, your tribe had captured a band of men and boys from the enemy tribe. You were being honored as the most exalted prostitute of your tribe. Your vagina was to receive the best offerings from amongst the tribal warriors. Fornication with you was their ultimate form of honoring you. You were about to perform pagan worship.*

'Placing his penis inside your vagina was considered a warrior's most holy act. That act was his pathway to eternity and continuation of life eternal. Your temple acolytes had brought you a bowl of food to eat and a cup of wine to drink to sanctify your fornications and increase your strength. In the bowl were boiled and sliced testicles, hearts and livers of men and boys from the enemy tribe who were conquered the day before by the warriors from your tribe. The night before this holy day the captives were brought to the temple. They stood bound before all the prostitutes so that you could examine them to be sure they were all healthy and satisfactory. Then the high priestess used an obsidian blade to remove their testicles and their hearts and livers while they were still alive, ensuring the freshness of their organs. She also collected their blood. Do you remember?'

Marty nodded to acknowledge her recall from seven thousand years before.

'Very good, Marty, it pleases me that you can recall your past lives. Now remember when you watched the high priestess chop the testicles, livers and hearts of the captives and mixed them together; and then cooked them for you and the other prostitutes. Remember how you ate your full portion from the bowl? The meat of your enemies was your staff of life. It was the hors d' oeuvres offered to sustain you. It gave you the strength of the conqueror and provided you with the sustenance you needed as you fornicated throughout the morning. Can you remember how enthused you became to fornicate?

Again, Marty nodded.

'Then,' continued Iniquity: *'Into a vessel cup of wine the high priestess mixed the blood of your captives. You supped from the holy vessel cup to stoke your passion blood lusts. The tentacles of your clitoris came alive with a burning heat and desire to continue fornicating; remember?*

Once again Marty nodded.

'Then the man whom you prostitutes called Adonis, because he was so beautiful and well endowed, offered the most magnificent bull and cows for sacrifice. The high priestess selected him to honor you. He had already cautiously, reverently, entered you. You felt sublime and honored. You were about to orgasm for your fourth time that morning when his wife shouted out to him from the congregation:

(Stop! You are offering her too much. We can not afford this great a sacrifice.)

'Then you stopped your thrusts. You felt affronted and alarmed that the woman interrupted your fornication; and you sat upright and pointed to her; and then you said to her:

(You have dishonored me, your goddess, in favor of your wealth. You have put wealth as your god before me. You must be punished, for I shall have no other gods or goddesses before me.)

'And then the high priestess pointed out your offender and ordered her to be taken away from the tribe, away from the circle

of worship. And the high priestess sentenced her to be hacked into pieces for offending you. Do you remember?'

'Yes, Miss Iniquity, I remember,' smiled Marty, pleased with her ability to recall her spirit's memory.

'Then, after your defiler was removed, you fornicated wonderfully and wildly all that morning. You had two more orgasms before the afternoon. Then you rested from your holy duties.

'Remember how you made love with no fear of becoming pregnant because you had eaten portions of woke roots, which sealed your womb from conceiving? Yes, I see by your smile that you do remember all the glory of that day. I want you to always recollect how idyllic that day was.

'Your challenger was taken away to be hacked to death while you wrapped your arms around her husband and cradled his penis within your loins. You heard her fainting pleas for forgiveness, and then her screams of horror from far away as she was being hacked to death by swords while your altar girls dutifully massaged your head and neck and shoulders and while your antagonist's husband's penis reentered you, thrusted deeply inside you and stimulated your clitoris as he made love with you so beautifully.

'Remember how ecstatic and erotic you felt in that moment of your ultimate triumph? You heard your enemy yell out her horrifying death screams as swords ran through her stomach and blood from her liver wounds gurgled up into her throat; and at that exact same moment her husband's hot semen flows coursed freely over your clitoris making your orgasm juices burst free.

'That was the moment when the little white periadies butterflies fluttered around your head and made you laugh. You knew the spirits were blessing your beautiful whoring. You experienced nirvana. You dug your nails into her husband's naked back and behind. You kissed his mouth to let him taste your deep passion lusts. You whispered you were extremely pleased with his submission to you. You

assured him that you would raise his daughter, Cecilia, the maiden who was unaware of her own wondrous beauty, as your own child; and you promised him that you would teach her the ways of temple prostitution and all its religious rites.

'You had two beautiful orgasms with him that glorious spring morning while the tribe adored your wanton promiscuity and applauded and cheered, watching you scream out with joy. While you orgasmed, your spasms were priceless. Your loins were hot and slippery because you knew you had complete power and control over your worshipper. After that day he and his daughter faithfully attended to your every need; and he came to every service to honor you.

'You are now experiencing what people today refer to as a flash-back. It is a reincarnation remembrance. You are the same beautiful goddess prostitute that lived seven thousand years ago. You entered your present life with your spirit carried through the millenniums by the butterflies. Always be proud and shameless of who you are.

'You are a modern-day living goddess. You are a butterfly in spirit because, like the butterfly, you represent freedom from oppression of every kind. And you must insist that you are to be worshipped; and that this man before you now may have no other gods before you; not his money nor his wife. Like your ancestral forbearer you must convert this man to accept your belief system, your New Morality Standard. And you must totally own his soul. We both know that this conversion is only right because the female organ is the true and time-tested morality standard. It is the source of life that human kind has always worshipped, naturally. And you bear that true source of life between your legs.

'So, go with full confidence. And encourage this hopelessly lost and conquered man to taste your sex and pine for you. Once you have competed your control of him, convert him into a slave to serve you. Then, turn his life inside out for your benefit. Pay no heed if he *whimpers to you about the baleful protest cries of his forlorn dispirited spouse. She is nothing to you.*

'Love him, like you loved and conquered the others on your ring neckless, but never completely love him; or any of them. Love yourself above all else. Remember always that you are his goddess and you will tolerate no others before you. Goodbye my goddess; carry my voice with you and always remember to love and cherish your way of life.'

The voice of Miss Iniquity then departed from Marty's mind.

Marty lastly smiled and made her signature lip kisses to the camera. Her on-set oral sex stimulator-viewer gulped. His heart leaped into his throat. He was smitten with lust for her, just as men who had lived seven thousand years before him lusted for her ancestral body and her passion filled spirit. He became spellbound. He trembled with an uncontrollable passion. His penis became so hard and erect that it hurt him to restrain it; yet he did restrain himself, because he knew if he acted upon his impulses he would be overpowered by Marty's protectors.

Lust sweats for her poured out of him from every pore of his body. His heart beat wildly and rapidly. His chest heaved with crazed desires for anything of her, a touch, a kiss, even a look of acknowledgement. The captivating effect of her glorious whoring was overwhelming him.

"Marty was beautiful," remarked Barbara. *"She was stunning, dazzling. She was glistening, naked, shameless sin; performing before him live, in the flesh. She was every taboo he was always told he should avoid; yet everything he desired in a woman. Words can not express the depths of his passions for her. Her whoring sent him into an infatuated rapture state from which he could never be recalled.*

"He was convinced she was the most glorious woman, the most alluring whore in the entire world. Aphrodite and Cleopatra were merely faded shadows in her brilliant light. Her vagina, with its

beckoning cum pool, bedazzled him. His hormones sent him into a state of delirium lust. If asked, he would gladly die for her. Love lust erased every other memory he ever held. He restrained himself from rushing onto the set, embracing her, and kissing her delicious mouth. And he watched penis after penis flowing cum onto her tongue, seeing her lips smack and savor the essences of her partners, while her cum covered tongue flickered wantonly, signaling she thirsted to suck yet another penis.

"He became so stimulated that he attained an erection hardness he had never imagined possible. He sat there, entranced, and spellbound by her wanton revelry. A transference of sorts took place. In his mind's limbic zone, he projected that those gorgeous lips and tongue which so lavishly romanced the head of each penis were, instead, his own lips and tongue.

"He began identifying her carnal pleasures as his own. His heart and soul slipped all conscious control and poured out passionate empathy for her need to embrace the pleasure fruits of sin in her most flagrantly debauched way.

"His mind floated away from all his rational thoughts and cautions. It rejoiced in her uninhibited pursuit of shameless lust. It inwardly acknowledged that by venerating her whoring it was aligning with her mind and subjugating itself to her addictive powers. Something happened within the moral essence of this man, her latest conquest. It was more profound than falling into love; far more binding than making a vow of fidelity.

"It was mesmerizing, that unique, hitherto never defined process whereby Marty's seductive genius caused the man to become beholden to only her; and whereby, through this process, he surrendered his heart, mind, and soul. She now held his thoughts, desires, passions, and dreams, indeed his very life, in bondage to her. She understood this. And she knew this attractive force was so strong that it compelled him to willingly obey her every request; serve her *every whim; and give her whatever she asked him to give her. Watching penis after penis ejaculate into her insatiable vagina drove this enraptured man into fevered lust madness. He wanted her.*

"Bob, I asked myself, who was this man? I mean who was he really? And I thought he must be typical of Marty's premium members. As he sat there watching her fornicating, seeing penis after penis ejaculating semen into her craven vagina, he must have lost his sense of time and space and self. And when the last partner's penis withdrew; when he saw her lying on her belly after her final fucking; when he witnessed yet more semen spilling from her victorious love channel; and when he watched her then twerk her hips and Kegel her vagina, inviting an imaginary fresh penis to enter her, he must have then known what his place was in time and space and soul.

"He must have known then that the game of life was rigged against him, although he willingly played the game in hopes that he could beat life's stacked odds. He had to have known when he was passed over for promotion that the boss's son would someday be his boss; or that the other guy would get tenure at his college and he would not; or that he'd never be the top salesman because the owner gave the best sales territory to her secret paramour. He had to know that his marriage was a sham and that his wife knew it was a sham, too. But they were still married and playing the game of pretending there was love there; when in truth their love had walked away years ago.

"And then I asked myself: What was in that man's mind as he watched Marty's vagina beckoning him to come and enter? What was he thinking while he watched her vagina twitching as it itched to receive still more pleasure; as it yearned to feel the strength and lust cravings of yet another penis, as it penetrated beyond her outer lips and descended into her hot slippery wetness; as it took her breath away with the sheer majesty of intimate copulation with her? And then I knew what was in his mind. It came to me, because I was able to imagine that my mind was his mind.

"In that instant he knew that he loved her, not in a platonic or romantic way, but in a lusting, life-altering way. It was adoration love; unconditional love from an eternal effervescence fountain. He was experiencing a sensuous passion sort of love; the love of the smitten; the kind of love that comes from the desperation drive to escape what is; what once maybe was, but what surely was never as good as what he imagined love would be with Marty; and what will never be again; and what he doesn't want anymore; and what he desperately wants to flee from, forever; shake free from his mind, forevermore; and forget that the biggest mistake of his life had ever happened.

"He is the man who suddenly recognizes who and what he is. He knows he is lost and now wants to lose himself completely from his lost soul and escape into his ether nirvana land. He wants to lose his damnable soul. He wants to feel it slip away; enjoy life while he can, as his immortality transcends all evil or shamelessness over what he is about to do. He wills himself to escape to the Elysium realms; not caring that he has not died yet. But he knows that, in his soul, he really has.

"He suddenly crystallizes in his mind all those things that Marvin and David said about the entire society being dishonest because of dishonest money. He now also sees society as a stinking heap of hypocritical bull shit, slipping into its doom beneath the ocean's waves. He wants no more of it. He wants out of all of it, no matter the cost in money or soul. And now he looks at Marty's throbbing, seething, pleasure craving vagina with a newfound perspective and appreciation. And yes, he seeks complete capitulation to its wonders. He adores her beautiful, insatiable whoring vagina like nothing he has ever known or felt before.

"He intuitively knows that he must make this choice for his soul to survive. He must give all of himself and his soul to the mesmerizing vagina. He must commit unconditionally to this voluptuous

shameless whore, and to this path of self destruction that lies before him, smiling to him, inviting him. Now he sees Marty's pulsing, tasty, flesh-peach as his salvation hope. It is the beckoning, beautiful portal through which knows he must pass.

"His mind sees itself and his tongue as brethren of the many millions of desperate sperms that struggled mightily to pass her fallopian channels and enter her sacred ovaries; yet he knows that mind and tongue can not travel that far into her holy reaches. But mind and tongue can pretend, can't they? He can wish he was all the way inside her sacred vestibules of procreation. He can imagine his tongue will satisfy the whore's clitoris and cause a bursting rush-flow of her orgasm fluids; and that would be a sort of conception, a life spark of lust's passions, wouldn't it? And that might greatly please her, might it not? Like a sperm launched upon its mission, he, too, must enter the glorious soul-ravaging vagina, with his mind and mouth first; and then, hopefully, after he earns her pleasures, with his penis.

"In his aroused state and from this time forth the man wants her badly enough to give her everything he has, if she will only permit him to taste her vagina or allow him to copulate with her one more time. His mind is exploding with passion lust. His desires for Marty, his love for her and his fealty to her, from this moment forward no longer knows any corporeal boundaries. He is smitten insane with devotion to her. An unquenchable passion-driven devotion fire rages within his breast. It must be fed. It consumes him. It is as deeply held and as powerful as any saint's or prophet's devotion to the Creator; even more so. She is not some inert religious idol, image, or icon. She is real. She is tangible, touchable; taste ready, alive, and so imminently fuckable.

"She is not some invisible man in the sky with a list of dos and don'ts, who decides if you are good or bad in his secret book of life. She is tangible; real; here and now; alive in her dreamy, perfect

flesh; smiling her exhortations for him to join her in sin. Her mere presence forces the choice of beliefs between the imaginary and the living; the lifeless metallic and ceramic statues; and the breathing and touchable yearning flesh. Boldly, shamelessly in his midst, in her naked wantonness, she chortles, laughs, smiles, cavorts, and banters gleefully. She moans, squeals, and enthusiastically exhorts her partners to fornicate with her more often, and harder; and keep her orgasms flowing. Her laughter erases all other thoughts this smitten man ever had. He is spellbound.

"As our opera man watches Marty fondle the testicles, stroke the penis shafts of her orgy partners, and kiss and suck their penis heads, he can only pray that this magnificent nymph will allow him to partake of her favors. His adoration knows no limits. He worships and glorifies every second of her performance. He basks in the heat radiance, the splendid shameless wonderment of her whoredom. And he knows with every fiber of his being that he can never have enough of her or do enough for her to fully express his devotion to her. Marty has become his goddess. Then the director said: 'Wrap it.'

"After Marty finished filming, she became a woman transformed. Suddenly her acting ended and she became a professional, prudent businesswoman. Her intimacy switch was turned off. Now she could as easily be the woman at the reception desk in his office: cool, cordial, and professional in a downtown Ms. sort of way. It was understandable. Sex is a business for Marty, that's all.

"She did not allow him to make love with her or even touch her sex. That was not part of their agreed arrangement. Instead, she got up off the bed and walked boldly to him and stood before him. She cupped her breasts and placed her nipples squarely before his eyes, blocking out everything else from his entire field of vision. He desperately wanted to suck her nipples; but she only allowed him to look at them. Then, she touched his penis, stroked it caringly, and

*kissed him on his forehead. She spoke to him in a confidential low-
ered voice tone:*

*'You did well, sweetheart. I was proud of you. Your tongue got
me into my favorite mood. You helped make me come. You did your
part beautifully. Until next time; okay, baby? We'll fuck then, baby.
We'll have a good time then.'*

*"Then, she placed her hands on both his shoulders and bent
down to softly kiss his lips before she left him sitting there, spellbound. She walked with regal insouciance away from his desperate
need to make love with her, carrying her naked body in majestic
fashion, as if making a bold statement that any garment, however
sheer or seductive, would only detract from her beauty as the undisputed Queen of Intimate Film Art.*

*"Before exiting the set, she stopped briefly to tenderly embrace
and hug each of her partners and kiss their lips; laughing and teasing each of them about how she appreciated their penises and their
performances; encouraging all of them to cast themselves for her
future films; congratulating them for their stamina and enthusiasm;
and lovingly touching and tugging softly on their penises, one last,
final time.*

*"She was casual and nonchalant with her cast, as if they were
neighborhood men she knew from her local pub. And, making films
with them as she did and as often as she did, it was her natural way
of bidding adieu, until they would all meet again on another set,
and fuck again. This was the matter-of-fact nature of Marty's sex
work. Then she made her way through the filming room and exited
through her private door.*

*"Our man sat there, awestruck. He stared longingly at the door
she had closed behind her. Her body was gone from the room now.
His body was still in the room where he had just witnessed and par-
ticipated in the most riveting pornographic performance of his life;
but his heart, mind and soul left the room with Marty. She took*

those parts of him with her to keep forever. She knew exactly what she was doing."

"Which was?"

"Whore tradecraft. She fully understood the effect that her live performance would have on him. That's why she had her service handlers escort him through a different door. He was not permitted to join her. In his lust crazed state of mind, he could become dangerous to her. They treated him more like her mascot dog than one of her screen partner lovers. Now he needed to be returned to his kennel."

"How do you know all this, Barb?" Bob had hopes that Barbara was only making things up.

"I found her appointment calendar one night after everyone left the office. I copied it. I backtracked the dates to when Marty was filming. I got the production schedules from her production company." Barbara didn't flinch. She was always sure of herself.

"How did you get the production schedules?"

"Bribery, Bob. You'd be surprised what people will do for money. Breaking confidences is small bribe stuff. Everybody does it. So, now that we're on the topic of your sweetheart's schedule, would you like to know what Marty did after she left the production set?"

"I guess I need to know, don't I?"

"Yes, Bob, you do. Marty's service rents rooms by the day in the same hotel where her studio makes her films. After she walked through that door she freshened up. An hour later she visited one of her premium members on a floor below. She spent an hour there. Two hours after that she was in another room on another floor with a different premium member. She spent an hour with him also; then, she went to the office for a half hour to check her messages before she went home to you."

"So, you're telling me that between that film she made and her premium member visits she fucked eight men before she came home

that night?" Bob's eyes searched Barbara's in hopes she'd show uncertainty. She didn't.

"At least eight men. Look Bob, this is a woman with a sex addiction who has figured out ways to make her addiction pay. Good for her. I did some math, Bob. She fucks an average of six men every day and it ranges as high as eighteen men in a single day. Those are days when she does multiple film shoots or multiple orgies."

"So, you're telling me I fell in love with a whore, aren't you? You're telling me Marty is a low-down whore and I'm just a fool, aren't you?"

"No, Bob, I'm not saying that. Your love for her and her love for you may be as honest and wholesome as any lovers' love anywhere. She's just an extraordinary woman, Bob. Any woman who gets ranked as one of the world's top twenty sex film stars is an extraordinary woman. She must love her work far more than many women who do sex work only because they need money to survive. Those top sex film stars do very well. They make fabulous money from their films and they also have private member services with all sorts of tips and side benefits.

"But, in Marty's case it's even much more than the money. Sex is her disease addiction. She needs it like some people need nicotine or alcohol. But that does not mean she can not be a normal well-adjusted partner in a marriage. She can love you and care about you as your wife or partner. Her condition is nothing for her to be ashamed of, Bob. Everyone has faults. Everyone deserves understanding, not ridicule.

"In her deepest heart, that's the tiny kernel of human feelings, encapsulated within her otherwise heartless dark heart, Marty truly does love you, Bob, I'm certain of that. She can be, for you, a very loving, caring person; perhaps even a devoted wife. I just want you to know what you've gotten yourself into, that's all. Marty loves to make expressive sexual love with many partners. But I believe that

she also deeply loves you in a way that is profoundly meaningful for her; and in a way that she feels on a deeper level than a sexual love. I think she sees you as her one and only true love. I've never said she doesn't love you.

"I don't know what all goes on inside that mind of hers, but to most people, she's heartless. She must be that way to be a successful porn star. She can not allow herself to fall in love on a long-term basis with every man who falls in love with her. But, she can and does fall into a kind of committed intimate love with lots of her premium members. I wouldn't categorize those loves as fidelity love. They are more of a camaraderie type of love. She encapsulates that kind of love in her seduction method. She must love her premium members as friends and enthusiastic sex partners on that camaraderie level to do the kinds of things that she does with them. She includes BDSM in the things she'll do with a premium member.

"I'm telling you this so you know what kind of life your sweetheart is into, that's all. But it doesn't end with premium members. She has a similar, but even more intense love with a few of her most favored performing partners, but those relationships are also anchored in the money she can make by performing with them. Segments of her fan base obsess over films she produces with certain specific partners; so, I'm sure you can imagine that her on screen love making with those partners is so realistic that even Marty has a hard time distinguishing between real true love with you and love with one of those partners."

"She doesn't stop, does she, Barb? I mean, it's like nonstop sex for her, isn't it?"

"No, it doesn't stop. But there's a difference in the loves she has. That's what I'm telling you. If you, for example, could not perform for her; for example, if you couldn't get it up for some reason for an extended while, I think she would still feel love for you. You are a different kind of love for her. You are in a category in her mind that only you can occupy. She will never leave you. I'm sure about that.

"But if a screen partner couldn't perform, even for one scene, I think her love for that partner would evaporate instantly. That's the difference. With you, she can disassociate you as a person from you and your penis. But with a screen partner, there's no real person in her mind. It's just a man with a penis attached. It's the partner's penis that holds her love interest. The man just happens to come along with the penis. Marty cannot allow herself to stay in love with her premium members or her film partners. Some of these naturally become her regular lovers for a while. She'll even get infatuated with them and have off screen private liaisons with some of them. But she has no fidelity to them. Even her most intense liaisons are transient matters. Once the money is gone; or the objective of destroying a wife is accomplished; or her infatuation is gone; or that partner no longer helps her film sales; those lovers are discarded. Consider the dupe she took along to watch her make that film.

"She gave him what he had bargained for, but nothing more. She was being polite and honest by the way she informed him that he was not her lover. He was just another customer. It's laughable that he holds out hope that she'll fall in love with him and run away with him. She's already worth over thirty million dollars from her films, her private service, the gifts she's received, her sales income from the Firm and her bonus money that David gives her for something nefarious which I can't yet explain. She already makes more in one week than that clueless dupe earns in a year. Sex is big business.

"The film she just made will have a million men drooling, dreaming, and masturbating over her. It will produce a hundred thousand downloads at twelve dollars each in its first month of release, and net Marty at least twenty new private service members. Her dupe is no billionaire. He's a nobody. He has no chance with her outside of his usefulness to her as a toy. What's more, there's an even greater mismatch.

"She's a consummate professional, a virtuoso at the top of her profession and she absolutely loves her work. When she's on set, her *audience is millions. She understands this. She knows the economics of reach and sell-through.*

"He, on the other hand is an at-will employee, easily expendable; and he hates his work and his life. His next hour with her will cost his account balance with her service another five thousand dollars. But he doesn't care about the money anymore. For his limbic zone's erotica lusting; for his little head's moments of joy; for the delicious savory taste of her vagina in his mouth; for the wonderment of just being present with the world's number one whore for a mere hour on her film set, that fool will do anything, pay anything, and sacrifice everything. He continues to hope that their relationship might blossom into love. Until that happens, he feels honored to be her love slave. His mind has off the deep end. He thinks he's Casanova. But, really, he's just roadkill.

"That night, after the opera, our man lay in bed with his wife. He made no move to touch her, kiss her, or show her any affection whatsoever. That would betray Marty, the woman to whom his contorted mind believes it must stay faithful. After all, once he's tasted the vagina of the world's most famous porn star, every other woman, especially his wife, becomes an inferior being. The wife is a huge let down; a sexless nothing. After a long while his wife rolls over and pretends to be asleep. Then, she hears him making mouth sounds that she can not distinguish.

"He is reliving those moments when he watched her perform on set. She paused from licking a partner's penis to speak to him:

'Does it excite you to see me sucking another man's penis?'

"Her eyes were dancing, laughing, beguiling. They told him that she loved what she was doing.

"He remembers nodding his head.

'Are you feeling jealous of the man I'm sucking?'

"She laughed at him, teasing his situation. He was forced to stay in his chair and watch her. He told himself that by watching her he

was stimulating her; helping her to perform at her most erotic sexual best."

'I feel like being a very naughty slut today. See my partner thrusting his penis into my hot pink vagina? Can you imagine how wet I am inside? I'm so wet and so hot. He's got a very big penis and he's stretching me. Oh, now his penis is reaching way up inside me. Oh, yes! I can feel him coming inside me now. His cum is so hot. Now I'm coming too. Oh, this feels so good. Don't you wish that your penis was inside me right now; fucking me right now?'

"Again, he nodded his head."

'Yum, his cum is dripping out of me now. I'd like you to prove to me how much you love me. I feel very sexy now. I'd like you to come here to my bed and lick my cream-filled vagina. I want you to prove to me that you love me, even when I'm being a totally raunchy whore. Would you like to prove to me that you really love me, no matter what I do?'

"Again, he nodded his head."

'That's good, baby. I want you to lick me now. Lick me until I have another orgasm. We'll stop filming until after you make me come again, okay baby? I want you to prove to me that you love me enough to lick me, even while cum from another man's penis is oozing from me. I need to know you'll do whatever I ask, to pleasure me. Will you do that for me?'

"Without hesitation he complied with Marty's request. He knelt before her widespread legs and held her vagina open with his hands. He performed tender loving cunnilingus while cum from her partners flowed from her vagina. After she came another time, he told her that he loved her.

"Marty pulled her body up and propped herself up by her elbows. She looked down at the head between her legs, her mouth opened. She mouthed some ooh and ahh sounds. She enjoyed what the man was doing"

'*I know you love me, baby. You love me because I'm not ashamed to be a slutty immoral whore, don't you?*'

"She smiled her coquettish smile and rolled her tongue over her lower lip.

'Yes,' he gulped."

"He strained his neck so his head could look up at her. She leaned forward and kissed his mouth. He felt her tongue probing his, teasing it. She pulled her head back and looked at him again, as if she was seeing him for the first time."

'*Your wife isn't at all like me, is she? She wouldn't fuck other men in front of you, would she?*'

"Marty shook her head in a teasing sort of way. The coquettish smile blew mouth kisses to him."

'*No, she's not like you.*'

"The man grinned, enthralled by the immorality of his questioner."

'*Would she let you lick her vagina while it's still filled with other men's cream? She wouldn't let you do that, would she?*'

"Marty's smile widened. Her tongue searched her lower lip again, this time very slowly, seductively. She was imprinting her immorality upon his limbic mind, putting images of herself inside his thoughts, knowing he'd keep them there all his life."

'*No, she'd never do that.*'

"Now the man became beholden to Marty's debauchery. He wanted what she offered. His wife and other, more modest, moralizing women wouldn't dream of doing the things that he loved watching Marty do."

'*Would you like to slide your penis inside me, baby? Would you like your penis to feel how hot and juicy wet I am inside?*'

"Her eyebrows lifted and the coquettish smile reappeared on her crimson lips."

'*Yes, you know I would.*'

"His doe eyes looked his love into her face."

'We will, baby. I promise. We will. But now I need to first finish my filming. I need to do another scene with two partners. The set is ready for me. Two men will make love with me. Their penises will take turns coming inside me. I'll fuck them until I have more orgasms for the cameras. You'll know when I'm getting my orgasms off, baby. I'll shout out that I'm coming. That way, you can feel my excitement with me. Okay, baby? You can stay and watch us. You can imagine how you'll feel when your penis is inside me. Okay, baby? I'll need some time after I do the scene. I'll come for you when I'm ready; and then we'll make love. Okay, baby?'

"She reached her hands down and held his face. Then she bent forward again and kissed his mouth again."

'I'll wait for you, whenever you're ready. I'm fine with that. I want you to know I love you.'

"He was awestruck by her wanton immorality, her shameless mockery of sincere love and its tenderness. She is not a trusting, loving kind of woman. She is the kind that seeks pleasure for its own sake and makes no pretenses about her wantonness. But that's what he wanted and needed; her casual way of abandoned morality dominated his psyche. Her love making was unvirtuous and sinfully lewd; but at the same time, it was refreshingly honest; and completely ethical, by her immoral standards; so much so that it seemed holy.

"He deified her. Her unprincipled sinfulness became his imaginary shrine to her iniquity. He adored her evil intentions. He knew full well Marty would strip him of his assets and leave his wife impoverished; and he welcomed all the sin lust Marty would employ to achieve her goal. He was her willing victim; her humanized male Black Widow. He was smitten by Marty's promiscuity, mesmerized by her immorality, and hopelessly addicted to the touches of her flesh. He had fallen in love with her. There was nothing he wouldn't do to make love with her again, and again, and again.

"After a while, his wife felt their covers move as his hands fondled his erect penis. He was reliving every delightful second of his afternoon on the film set. His mind was on Marty's glorious ravaging vagina. Yes, in his imaginary fantasy state she came to him again as she would night after night for years to follow. He believed her soft, pink velvet vagina was there; about to settle over his face and envelope his mouth once again. His tongue believed it was about to relive its finest hour. It had stroked the clitoris of the world's most spectacular sex star. It had coaxed her to orgasm into his mouth before the entire world. He fanaticized that Marty now loves his tongue, and him.

"His wife has some sense that an intractable vexation is taking place within her husband. Her marriage is in the process of imploding. She knows that's true. A tear rolls from her eye. She understands something is lost. Whoever this other woman is; whatever she represents, the wife knows instinctively that she can't compete with her licentious sexuality. She shudders, understanding there could be harsh changes coming in her life; knowing that she is powerless to prevent them from destroying her. She clenches her jaw in fear. She grinds her teeth. Then she falls into unsettled sleep.

"That man isn't mentally strong enough to walk away from Marty on his own volition, Bob. His self-esteem; the essence of who he is as a man now depends upon Marty's approval. He's like a puppet on a string, hoping Marty puppet master will signal him to lift his arms and wrap them around her in a tight embrace. He listens for her slightest word of encouragement; wishing she'll praise his sexuality; hoping that will lead to love. He is no different than a young kitten drawn obsessively to catnip. Touching Marty's vagina with his fingers and his lips; sniffing it and inhaling her pheromones; kissing it; plunging his craving tongue into it; finding her clitoris and making love with it; then imagining its succulence; beholding its carefree wantonness when he can't be with it, now consumes all his mental faculties.

"His soul is smitten and overcome by Marty's iniquity. His mind is no longer strong enough to think for itself. It only does as Marty commands it. It only seeks to please her. Whenever he can give her sufficient money and gifts to prove his worthiness, Marty rewards him with enough sex to sustain him. Marty knows she controls his mind in this cruel, heartless form of human bondage. She, like a female Black Widow, is in the process of devouring her lover's life.

"Marty must be careful about how she handles this man. She must slowly ease him out of his fantasy. Sexual favors become more measured than they were initially. She understands that separating assets from a family is a process. It requires tradecraft. And she knows her trade very well. Only her newest Premier Members get the fullest measures of her favors. Our opera goer is an old conquest. He has been a member for a while. Marty knows his finances are depleting. He's on the clock. She paces her sessions with him. Like an hourglass losing sand, his dwindling accounts command less and less of her time and interest. He gets minutes now, not weekends, not evenings, not hours. Only minutes. If he becomes a nuisance or a belligerent, Marty's service steps in to enforce his contact terms. Marty has lawyers and muscle if those forceful steps are required. Marty leaves nothing to chance. Her work is all business. After she has finished with him, when she has taken all his possessions and consumed his marriage, she expels him from her vortex of iniquitous lust. Then, and only then, his life, less wealthy than before, becomes his own again.

"Meanwhile, the slightest provocation from his wife suffices to send our man running to Marty. His wife knows by the way he looks at her that she now disgusts him. She feels unwelcome when she's in the same room with the man she has loved her entire adult life. She aches inside; but she doesn't understand what causes her crushing emotional pain.

"Marty cleverly keeps herself hidden from the wife. Meanwhile, her venom does its work. She delivers her poison vaginally to the

husband's penis, as orgasm after orgasm becomes a drip-by-drip infusion of marital death which steadily poisons the wife's marriage. Marty's voracious vagina has already devoured the husband's affections. Now, like a snake-bitten rabbit, the wife feels a strange paralysis-like effect taking hold of her marriage. She lives in a fog of uncertain madness, hopelessness, and disorientation. She enters the early stage of a process.

"At first, she has no comprehension of the overwhelming psychological powers arrayed against her. It is inconceivable to her at the early stage of things that another woman could use her sexual and psychological powers so effectively that, in less than a month's time, twenty years of marriage, their home, their children, and her husband's career, could all be uprooted and demolished. If someone had told her that this was happening to her, perhaps a lifelong friend who meets her in a coffee shop, she would not believe her.

"But she suspects something is askew; possibly terribly wrong. She knows her life is being slowly but surely devoured somehow, by some vague force; but she feels powerless to stop it. Her enemy is unseen. Her enemy is clever, elusive. She suspects there's another woman in the picture, but she can't be sure. She wonders who this enemy is. Is it vicious? Does it really intend to harm her? Doesn't it know that she is a good Christian woman with a loving home and family? Why would it wish to harm her? What could she have possibly done to bring this onto herself? But this vague enemy has experience with this sort of thing. It plans its moves carefully, keeps its locations secret, uses a service with an unlisted, untraceable phone number for communication, and uses code words to verify whom it is communicating with. It is a determined enemy. It keeps her off balance.

"The wife doesn't fully comprehend it yet, but her enemy plays for keeps. She feels uncertain whether she even has an enemy. She thinks that, perhaps, she is becoming paranoid. All she knows is that

she seems pitted against mysterious shadows and secrets, and she knows, in her gut, that somehow, she's losing this mysterious fight. She's not glamorous and seductive like Marty. She doesn't possess Marty's techniques or her stamina or her passion for sex; and her face and body can't compete with her unseen nemesis. Her sagging boobs and waistline are simply overmatched by the stunning body of the world's most famous porn star. Some wives get face and body work when confronted with a marriage threat; but that won't work when Marty is the other woman. Despite lubrications and romantic settings, noting on earth can make a vagina become twenty or thirty years younger, and more appealing, than the vagina of the world's most heralded and adored star of intimate film. Marty understands her fabulous vagina is her trump card advantage. And she plays it, always, expertly.

"The wife develops a vague, nagging sense that, somewhere out there in her husband's world, another woman is determined to eat her alive and spit out the remains of her life. She may sense that the other woman is ruthless and has no conscience. But she cannot understand what could possibly motivate such a woman. She can't imagine that another woman's loveless childhood is taking out its full vengeance on her.

"She cries at night. She fears she's losing her marriage. Her husband does nothing to comfort her. He keeps his affair a secret. His dreams and wealth have already cast her aside and married themselves to Marty. He's placed all his chips on the long shot slot bet that Marty, the lust dream of millions of ejaculating penises, will fall in love with him. His wife is on her own.

"The wife doesn't know the man she married anymore. His body lives with her, but his mind has checked out of the marriage and checked into the Lust Hotel. It has a room there. It stays in its imaginary room with its imaginary Marty, kissing her over every inch of her body; touching her; hearing her laughter; hugging her; loving

her; loving just being with her, even as she fornicates with others. He has no pride or self-respect about his love lust. He can't help himself for feeling the way he feels. His mind can't leave its room. It doesn't want to. It stays there while his physical presence pretends to live in the real world.

"He suspects his boss has picked up on his changed behavior. Going into the weekly sales meeting the boss's face always gave him a warm smile. They've been good friends for years. They socialize with their wives. But this day the smile face carried a concern frown. Likely his division's fall from first in sales to third caused the frown; but he assured his boss he'd soon be back on top. During the meeting, the boss noticed he wasn't turning his pages and following along in the sales reports like the other nine division heads were. He wasn't paying attention. He wasn't keeping up. There was silence. All eyes turned to him. The concern frown on the boss's face was now a worry frown. Our daydreamer scrambles for cover:

'Sorry boss, I must have eaten something that's gotten me off track. My tummy's been bothering me. I think I'll go to my office and sit this out. I'll read the report when I feel better. I'll catch up.' He lies. It would be the first of many.

"He goes to his office and shuts the door, puts his head back. His mind is a million miles away. It's not on sales. It's in another world entirely. It's in the world of creation space. It's inside Marty's vagina, thinking about his tongue licking her clitoris. He's in dream world, locked into the sixty-nine-sex position with Marty; his arms wrapped around her hips; his face buried in her vagina. He's licking her clitoris; she's sucking his penis. He's in neverland bliss.

"Sales are the furthest thing from his mind. He already spent fifty thousand on one hour appointment sessions. His cash balances are gone. She's told him she desperately wants to make love with him for an entire weekend. But she has a small problem. That will play hell with her appointment schedule. He'll need to pay her fifty

thousand to make up for her deferred and canceled appointments through her agency.

"He has five hundred thousand in his pension plan, a lot of that is in company stock. He figures he can swing it. He'll borrow against the plan. He'll pay it back before he needs to pay taxes and penalties on the withdrawal. He tells himself his sales will go back up. He'll demand an advance on his annual bonus. He'll buy back the stock he sold to stay in good standing with his boss. He'll just need to tell some more lies. Everything will work out!

"And he'll accomplish his new objective, which is pleasing Marty. He'll sacrifice everything for her. He'll have many more hours to lick her delicious insatiable vagina and give her so many fantastic orgasms that she'll realize he's the greatest lover she's ever known. He believes she'll fall madly in love with him. Then, they'll run away together to New Zealand. They'll live happily ever after on a ranch, raising sheep and fucking their brains out. He's delusional. He's gone insane. New Zealand is the furthest thing from Marty's mind. Our man has become a hopeless idiot. He doesn't know it yet, but the fifty thousand is only the start. Marty will want to see him for ten weekends, until his pension plan is gone, and the IRS is chasing him.

"His wife doesn't know it yet, but her husband will soon ask her for a divorce; or, if she can't find a way to bring him back to his senses, she'll divorce him to salvage what little marital assets remain. If unopposed, Marty will ravage everything they have. The wife can't bring him back. Church and therapy won't do it. He won't reveal his incurable addiction to Marty's vagina.

"He'll sit in therapy with his wife. He'll stare at the shrink, but he'll imagine he's licking Marty's insatiable, wanton vagina. He has promised the whore that he'd keep their love a secret. They sealed their promise with a kiss. He is P. T. Barnum's proverbial, borne every minute, sucker; a true idiot. His loyalty now belongs to Marty and her glorious irresistible vagina. He'd rather chance death than

betray his secret promise of confidence to the whore. Both he and his wife have been outplayed.

"Their home will be sold to pay off his debts. The ex-wife will take the kids and move in with her mother. When the mother passes away, his ex-wife will work retail jobs, scrub floors, and beg friends and relatives for month-to-month expense help. She manages to feed herself and the kids somehow. But, after essentials expenses, there's nothing left for her. Her life becomes drudgery.

"The ex-husband will continue seeing Marty until his money is gone. Then he'll call her appointment service and discover that she's unavailable unless he adds credit to his account. But of course, he can't add credit. He's broke. He now finds himself in Marty's dustbin, spent and useless. He'll never see her or her vagina again, except in her films. His mind still wants to be in the Lust Hotel, but now it dawns on his mind that it's been evicted. He's a broken man now. He's older; starting new with debts and support payments. He's lost his job over his fling. All he has are memories. The road back will be long and painful. Hell is where he lives now.

"Some men who've had his same experience will try to go back to their wives. And some wives will take them back; other wives will slam the door in their faces. Some won't ever go back to their wives. Such is the lot of these men in their version of a man's world, where idiots pretend not to be idiots by commiserating with like idiots. They complain that giving bitchy women the right to vote destroyed the entire world. These idiots turn to booze, gambling, and wasting mindless hours by watching football on TV.

"Still other men strive mightily to rebuild their credit with Marty's appointment service. This last group is hopelessly addicted to precious one-hour experiences with her vagina. For these devoted admirers, that hour is the highlight of their month. Her catnip allure never leaves them. They know she doesn't really love them; but they no longer even care. They are addicted to her, like an alcoholic

becomes addicted to alcohol. It's enough for them that they love her. They dream of making pornographic films with her. They imagine they are her film partners, instead of the well-hung stallions who perform with her. They scrape together enough money for a priceless half hour with her; then love the way she says lewd immoral things to them while they have sex with her. They don't object when she challenges them to bring her more money. They can never get enough of her. She has become their addiction. They've lost their money, their pride, and their minds.

"That film section with the wedding rings told me a great deal about Marty," continued Barbara. Barbara's logical mind didn't need every detail of Marty's seduction method to methodically explain the behavior she witnessed.

CHAPTER THREE

When you finally understand yourself and can accept who you've become, take into your heart life's lessons, and live them unafraid and unashamed. (Rosemary Lightfoot Ness-Bitner, author)

METHOD

"What did it tell you?" Bob's head was spinning.

"First, Marty is contemptuous of marriage as an institution, especially monogamous marriage. When she has a man interested in her she'll leave hints of her presence, phone calls to the home, things like that, to intentionally taunt the wife. She understands the wife will become furious with the husband; punish him by denying sex.

"Like a soldier can't fight hour after hour without food, a husband can't endure harangue after harangue without love and sex. Marty fills the sex void. The husband is trapped in a reinforcing loop of sex from Marty, anger from his wife, resentment of his wife and then, back to more sex with Marty. Marty displaces the wife, shoves her out of the sex loop. Eventually, the wife gives up and goes away. Marty drives this outcome. She simply does not believe in marriage.

"She's openly hostile to marriage. She does all she can to destroy marriage as an institution. She believes the institution of marriage is immoral. She is that institution's mortal enemy. When she gets an Ultra-Premium member into a hotel, he can quickly run up a fifty-to-hundred-thousand-dollar bill, all legitimate under her Ultra

contract. The Ultra member incurs a debt that places liens against marital assets when the marriage breaks up. Courts enforce Marty's lien ahead of any assets the wife or the husband get. Lawyers and whores get paid first in today's courts.

"Second, Marty's decision to become a whore and star in intimate sex films was a highly rewarding career choice. She was fortunate to come into the profession on her own terms from a solid platform of existing customers that she gathered through her contacts in sales and her moonlighting escapades at orgy parties.

"Most women in the sex trades are far less fortunate. Many are captured into the business as sex slaves, or they fall into the hands of a pimp because they are desperate. They become the victims of violence, disease, and sometimes death. Marty was too smart to become someone's victim. She kept her wits about her and stayed in control of her relationships. That provided her the psychological comfort that she needed to compensate for her lack of nurturing as a child. For many women, employed in the sex trades or not, work days are pure drudgery. Many women in today's stressful society have forgotten how to enjoy life or even how to smile. Not Marty. She loves every day of her life because she doesn't think of her sexual activity as work. Her life is like a waterfall, endlessly cascading from one enjoyable experience to another.

"Sucking and fucking are not work for her. They are a pleasure, and every day brings the promise of new, joyous cum filled celebrations. Her career path compliments her nymphomania in a continuous self-reinforcing loop. The intimate film artistry field is wide open for woman. There are fewer female sex stars than lawyers, doctors, and dentists; and the financial rewards for these top stars dwarf other professions' average incomes.

"There are fewer than two hundred top ranked competitors in Marty's world. An attractive woman, who sincerely loves making love with an endless stream of handsome lovers, can carve out an *exclusive clientele niche, fine tune her selections of partners and grow her following of fans to produce a huge income. And, she can expect opportunities. All expenses paid travel, escort and entertainment gigs will frequently come her way. Marty recognized the opportunity and seized it.*

"The biggest barrier to entry for most women is their own apprehensions about making passionate erotic love, in front of a camera for the first time, with a man they've never met before. It requires the woman to flip a mental switch and convince herself that she loves that man; otherwise, her performance will be void of emotion and it will likely fall flat. Her career will never get off the ground.

"For the married woman, stepping outside the boundaries of monogamy presents an added, sometimes insurmountable, challenge. Her most difficult psychological leap requires that she make love with a total stranger, knowing her husband is aware that she's doing it. After her first time, this inhibition becomes easier to overcome. For married women it's essential to have accepting, enthusiastic, supporting, and unconditionally loving husbands.

"Most women are psychologically unwilling to take that first step. That sharply narrows the field of entrants. Many women who could possibly become wealthy and famous never even consider the field. Marty was different. She became promiscuous early, while still in boarding school. Barriers of 'first fuck fear' and marriage were non- existent for Marty. She enthusiastically jumped at the chance to make intimate sex films. She entered the field with her eyes and legs wide open. And, because her work showed that she loved performing intimate scenes, she became an instant success.

"I watched one of the fellatio films she made, Horse. She was on her knees at the foot of a bed. Her naked partner laid on the bed with his legs spread. His penis was there, right in front of Marty's face. The entire film hour was about Marty performing fellatio with that penis. This was not an ordinary fellatio scene, Horse. It was about

Marty's passionate love of the male penis. She treated that penis as if she was a smitten kitten. She rubbed her face cheeks against it. She licked it with a loving, patient ardor that communicated to the viewer that she considered that penis to be her god. She placed its testicles, one by one, into her mouth and tongued them. All the while she licked its shaft and tongued its balls, she spoke softly to it. She heaped praises upon it. She promised it that she'd love it forever; that she couldn't wait to slip it inside her vagina and give it the most wonderful experience it could ever imagine. Her love came through to me as I watched the way she stroked it and kissed it and used her tongue to stimulate it, especially upon and around its head. It was an act of compassion, adoration, and respect for the life-giving cream that she ultimately coaxed from it.

"As she spoke with the penis, she pampered it with continuous loving stimulation; never hurried; never disrespectful or violent towards it in any way. There was a silent majesty about the way she treated that penis. I witnessed Marty's devotion to the pleasuring of that penis. I became fascinated by her face and her words to the penis. And I asked myself: why is she so ardent, so obsessive, so fervent? She did not need to make this film for the money she would make from it. She is already a rich woman. She does not need the notoriety. She is already notorious. I watched her and I thought about what was happening inside her mind. It is a trait that Chief has taught me.

"Then, suddenly it came to me. Marty was reaffirming herself to herself. She was proving to her soul that she was of a pure and loving disposition to that penis; that she loved it with all her heart and soul; and that she asked it to accept her love and acknowledge its acceptance of her love by ejaculating for her.

"I thought more about what I was seeing. Then I understood the film's deeper meaning for Marty. I have seen my own mother become entranced this way. I have even behaved myself this way. I was watching Marty performing a novena! Yes, a novena! Only she

wasn't making a special prayer to God for nine days to have God give her something that was vitally important to her. No, not nine days; but one hour! Yes, Marty had compressed her novena from nine days to one hour! Then I understood her mind. She is a Pagan. Her rules are different. Well, basically, she has no rules.

"But her ardor for what she believes in, the penis, and her faith in her belief are no different than a Christian's belief in God. Her belief is just as sincere. She was performing an act of unadulterated love. It had all the elements: submission; adoration; acceptance; begging to be heard and answered; all those things. She had the same sorts of overwhelming needs that I have. But Marty's are of this earth. She seeks the spirits that reside among us; not where I seek my spirits, in the heavens. She implores the penis to hear her speak of her adoration for it; not as I ask my God in the heavens to hear me. I think I got inside her mind, Bob. In truth, her beliefs are every bit as strongly held as mine.

"But she does not have one God, Bob. She has multitudes of gods. Every male penis is one of her gods! When I understood the way her mind works, I no longer saw Marty as a base whore or degenerate porn star. I saw her as a profoundly devout woman; a virtuous woman expressing her devotional love to her god, the male penis. Then, when it ejaculated, I saw the serenity of unity with her god bless her face. she was experiencing her enlightenment. Her sweet innocent smile shortly followed. In her mind she had just performed a holy, wonderful act. Her novena was answered. Her prayer for acceptance was accepted by her god. She swallowed her god's acceptance. And that strengthened her soul and her belief in the rightness of her life and her worship of Pagan beliefs. I was so taken by her sincerity and the beauty of her fellatio that I wanted to take her head in my hands and kiss her face in a thousand places."

"So, you believe her Pagan beliefs are, okay? I mean you are okay with her believing in not one God but millions of them?"

"Yes, Bob. I am not empowered to judge Marty or what Marty believes. While she was romancing that penis, I knew that causing it to ejaculate was incredibly important to her. I found myself in sympathy with her; praying that the penis would ejaculate for her; and it did! The ejaculation moment was beautiful, Bob. Her novena was answered! She received her blessing. By ejaculating, the penis affirmed that it loved Marty; that it accepted her love; that her love was worthy to receive its reciprocal love. I knew that loving penises and receiving their love in return meant everything to Marty. I understood that her feeling was not any different from the feeling I have when I receive holy communion. We both, in our own way, ingested the essence of our god. I found myself feeling so happy for her. I knew then that I accepted her as a loving, human person. I knew I was falling in love with her.

"But then Marty revealed her deeper inner essence. There was a nuanced, perceptible change in her demeanor. A certain intensity of purpose passed over her face. She placed her mouth over the penis's head. Her eyes glowed with a sort of focused mission quest. She vacuumed up all the penis's ejaculated semen with her mouth and tongue, and swallowed it. Then, she proceeded to suck intently upon the penis head, drawing up from the male scrotum and testicle sac every vestige of semen, as if she were, once again, a young girl drawing the last drops of a milk shake up from a straw and into her mouth. All the while she sucked up this semen, she patiently massaged her partner's balls and continued lovingly stroking the penis's shaft.

"As I placed my own mind into hers, I realized that I was seeing more than the follow on from a whore's whore lust. Her eyes told me that she had to do that final part of her fellatio. Her eyes were saying that she did not ever wish to stop; that she needed, for herself, to prolong this love fest with her penis friend as long as the penis could possibly sustain it. She was a woman who had become obsessed with her love for her god; the penis."

"But if she has all that money and she sees the penis as her god, why does she stay with David?" Bob couldn't see any logic in Marty's behavior.

"That is the mystery, Big Horse. I have asked myself that question a thousand times and I cannot come up with any rational answer to it. The relationship that she has with David is, I think, the key to everything. But it is disguised from everyone, even you; even from Susan, I think."

"And why, if David is so special to her, would she become obsessed with men's penises? Every man has one. There is nothing unique about them."

"It's not just a physical thing with her, Bob; although in her films she does seem to partner with men who have very impressive sizes. It's a religious thing with her. She's no different than any other person who becomes fanatic about their love of their religion. People will go off the deep end for their faith. There have been Christians who have killed to spread their faith. There have also been Jews and Muslims who have killed to spread their faiths. Marty, I'm afraid, is no different. She's deeply obsessed with her belief system. She even has a shrink who encourages her obsession. When I understood that, that's when I finally grasped the full effect of her affliction. She has an obsessive-compulsive disorder of the most shameless and base kind.

"Marty must romance penises. She must obsessively adore them, worship them, and love them. They are her life's truest loves. She was taking from that penis all the love that it could possibly give to her. She could not leave her love obsession with that penis until she knew that she had consumed all its semen. She had to know that that penis loved only her; that she had all its love; that it would have no love left to spare for any other woman. Finally, I knew within my inner self that I now fully understood her and why she is the way she is. She is a faultless victim of her childhood. She is obsessed, still, because of not receiving her mother's love. I feel deeply for her now;

and I very much love her. In fact, Bob, I adore her. I want to run to her and hold her and kiss her face and hug her and tell her that I love her and that I understand why she does what she does. And that what she does, her immorality, is all right; because in her Pagan worship reference frame, what she does is perfectly moral and good; and that is beautiful."

"But Barb, you have told me that you can't stand her."

"No, Horse. I can't stand her behavior. I despise what she does to marriages and to children of those marriages. And I can't stand it. I can't stomach the effect of it; the pain it inflicts; the return of her pain to others; the way she indirectly transfers her pain to the innocents. It's necessary for her to do it. I see that now; but it's still sinful and horribly wrong. Her conduct is purposefully sinful and evil. It is opposed to everything I believe and everything my values represent.

"But at the same time, I understand what happened to her during her childhood. She had an experience that was worse than never being loved. She was, at first, loved. She knew love from her father, but then her father died and her mother abandoned her. She had love; but then she experienced that love being taken away from her. That is an incredibly painful experience, especially for a child. Marty has spent her entire life trying to replace that lost love. She is on a futile quest. It's as futile as a man trying to find a leg that he lost in a war so he can stick it back on. It's not possible. But the man keeps hoping and believing. Marty keeps hoping and believing.

"I know that she'll never be able to replace her lost parental love; but she doesn't know that. She's on this perpetual quest to replace it. And she has settled on penises as her love substitute. I now understand her human need, Horse. It explains her specific need for your love, Horse. You are as close to her father as any man could ever be. You are kind and gentle and loving and dependable, just as he was; plus, she can access your penis, when she wants it. It's a sad kind of love in a way. As part of her obsessive-compulsive disorder, her love

for you is a sadness. But it is real love. It is also beautiful love in the way that the spirits work out our human needs.

"The spirits told me to look at her need that way, through her eyes. And the spirits told me to accept her ways because that is the way the spirits want us to think about life; to accept life as it is. I now understand why she does the prostitution and the porn. And I understand that, for Marty and others like her, prostitution and porn are good things; actually, beautiful expressive human things with redeeming qualities. The spirits have told me that I must broaden my thinking and I must understand her expressive human need and that I must love her. And now, I feel her crying out to the world for love. Her needs have touched my heart, Horse. Her needs come through in her work. I see them now. And I love her, Horse."

"You love her? After everything?"

"Oh, yes, Horse. I do love her. Very much. My spirit understands her spirit. Our spirits are like sister soul mates now. And my spirit loves her spirit. I feel that I must do everything that I can to help her in every way that I can. I also want to kiss her lips and feel her tongue with mine; and I want to kiss her nipples and her sex. Yes, Horse, it's true. I also have those erotic feelings for her."

"Barb, if you feel that way, why don't we approach her about it? Why not both of us be honest with her and tell her how you feel; and about how I feel about her and how I feel about you? Why not ask her about doing a threesome with her?"

"No, Horse, no! Absolutely not! I was just explaining my feelings. I didn't say I wanted to act on them. Don't you know the difference? Having sex with her would oppose all my values. I would be betraying my people and the trust that Chief has placed in me. I would never do that. I know that I must control my feelings. You really do not understand women, do you, Horse?"

"Well, how am I supposed to understand you? You just made my head spin. You women are complicated."

"No, we are not complicated, you Stupid Big Horse. We are not complicated. You men just do not pay attention to us when we talk. Just listen to us when we talk. There's a difference between what we feel when we talk about our feelings and what we feel when we talk about what we intend to do about our feelings. Oh, never mind, Horse. Kiss me, Horse. Just kiss me. I must be kissed now."

Bob took Barbara into his arms. He squeezed her tightly to him and kissed her. She took his hand and placed it upon her breast. Her kisses became deeper, more passionate.

"Barb, I thought you said we must wait? Why did you…….? What has changed?"

Barbara pushed Bob back. Now she was crying. *"Nothing has changed, Horse. I am sorry. I just let my feelings take power over me. I am sorry. It is also very hard for me to wait, Horse. I am woman. I need you. I need to have intimacy with you. I must have that and I know I must have that. It's very hard for me. I made a mistake, Horse. Sorry."*

"Well, couldn't we? Kind of like have a trial run? I mean, just one little sample? Who would be hurt?"

"No, Horse. We can't."

"Not even once?"

"No, Horse, not even once."

"Why not?"

"That's the discipline, Horse. I can not allow my emotions to interfere with what I must do. If I did; if I, I mean if we did it, I could lose my concentration and my objectivity. I have already strayed too far. I must stay focused; otherwise, I could cause great harm."

"Strayed from what? Focused on what? Harm to whom; to what?"

"On my path to my journey's end, Horse. I must follow it. On my task, Horse. I must stay focused on my task. I must learn more and work more to put pieces into place in my own mind of many things

that still need to come together. And I must understand all of it, Horse. I must understand what David does and has done."

"Why do you have this obsession with David?"

"Because, he likes to cause harm, Horse. I see how he treats his staff; the mortgages, the fault findings, the enslavements, the entrapments, the trickery, the firings. He enjoys causing harm to others. He's an unusual animal, even as a human animal. Animals do not seek to cause harm for amusement, except for killer whales and cats that use prey animals to train their young. But those animals have a purpose to teach their young how to survive. David harms with no purpose, except it amuses him to harm others. I and Chief believe that he is capable of great evils. And the harm I fear is to you, Horse. Chief and I think that you may be a danger to David. We must be careful, Horse. And Horse, I heard a spirit voice. It told me we may never see Marty again."

"Spirits again? The same spirits that will get upset if we make love? Really?"

"Yes, Horse. I am sorry. I hope it is not true; but it may be true. We must allow ourselves to consider that possibility. We must keep our minds open, Horse. She may be gone from us, forever. If so, it is the way of things. Some speak of it as karma. I said I made a mistake when I got you excited, Horse. I am not her, Horse. I cannot just fuck you because my crotch feels hot, even though I really want to. But my ways of love are better than her ways, Horse. You will see. You will come to understand that. I am sorry I got you excited, Horse. But please know that I love you. And I do not think that we must wait too much longer.

"Anyway, we were speaking about why Marty is so successful. Let me finish that thought. The third reason is that Marty has immense personal pride in her appearance and the quality of her work. That results in fan loyalty. She has become accomplished in her profession and has a healthy professional desire to continuously improve her

trade craft. Her body is as good as mine, although she's four years older than me. Habits that enable her to perform at a high level include nutritionist prepared meals, work-outs with light weights three days each week and aerobics on three alternate days. She exercises every muscle group in her body. She stays conditioned like a professional athlete. She drives her body to match the demands that she places on it.

"Intimacy is not just a romantic expression of love for Marty; nor is it her profession. It's her life; her entire life. She is the reincarnated Sara of our modern time. She's rebranding Paganism and marketing it and living it. She's reintroducing it as the western world's fourth religion.

"When I watched her perform, I realized I was seeing something many other women simply cannot do. Many women grimace and wince while they make love. Not Marty. She smiles joyfully. She loves love making! Most women become exhausted after they climax. Not Marty. She demands more sex. Her energy level increases. She's like an Olympic runner experiencing a runner's high; but her endorphin surges come from having sex, not from running. Most women would have the man withdraw his spent penis and then they would also withdraw from sex and relax themselves. But not Marty. She immediately replaces the spent penis with a fresh, hard one. Her orgasm flows continue uninterrupted. Her conditioning enables her to prolong her climax experiences for long extended times. She allows nothing to distract her from her orgasms. They absorb her full concentration. Speaking as a woman. it's beautiful and inspiring to watch how much she enjoys her flows. I now understand why she needs a ready supply of hard penises to slake her nymphomania and sustain her performances. That need for fresh penises explains why she stars in so many orgy films.

"Why does she drive herself? I now see the world through her eyes. Religious messaging never rests. Hollywood's violence messaging

never rests. Thus, Marty never rests. Perhaps she sees her work as the love antidote to all the pompous divisiveness and dehumanizing violence that bombards people every day of their lives. Whatever causes her driven work ethic, her messaging resonates. More and more, people accept her and her work. She's gaining market share in the public square, and she's doing it without the benefit of those early indoctrination classes that all religions depend upon. She gains her following through the persuasive appeal of her messaging. Her ribald nakedness is, after all, refreshingly honest in a dishonest world.

"Through her psychosis, libido, and liberal use of lubrications she continues copulating at an inexhaustible pace. She's like a beautiful champion racehorse that never breaks stride. During the entire length of her films, she remains fresh looking and irresistibly sexy. She never allows her male partners to shoot their semen onto her face or hair, thus maintaining the screen image of a lustrous goddess with her creamy white skin and porcelain perfect doll face. Cum shots are filmed going either into her mouth or into or over her vagina. This enhances her screen image of pristine goddess who is accepting her partners' offerings. Weekly manicures, pedicures, frequent hair coiffing and daily massages keep her looking relaxed and fresh. Her teeth are hygienist cleaned weekly. She doesn't eat candy, cookies, cake, ice cream or junk food. And she keeps herself well hydrated. Her viewers and clients always see her body at its performing best.

"Her wardrobes are unsurpassed. If she's performing for a patriotic theme, she'll wear a bikini with red white and blue bunting material; if its a seduction scene she'll look like a bejeweled Cleopatra with a serpent headdress; for an Easter theme, she'll wear a bunny bikini complete with a fluffy tail. Her ensemble of miniskirts, teddies, designer stockings, and transparent panties is endless; her props are varied and inexhaustible, from teddy bears and pillows to vibrators, whips, crops, clamps, spreaders and other assorted BDSM items.

"She's an accomplished actress. She can pretend to be any character. She can play the innocent baby sitter, anxious to be ravaged; the oversexed teenage cheerleader with hot pants and bangs and bows in her hair; an oversexed nurse with thermometer and blood pressure equipment; a sexy secretary with gorgeously coiffed hair and professional looking eyeglasses; or a prim and proper lawyer; a nun, housewife, retail clerk, job seeker, doctor, striptease dancer, sun bather or cocktail sipping party girl. Her mind can convincingly play any sort of character that her film role requires. And, she plays all her roles convincingly. I have no doubt that she'll star in a full feature length film series someday, with a real extended plot and a role that allows her sexuality to shine. She'll break all box office records. If it's offered in three-dimensional film, many viewers will see it a dozen times. She's that addictive. And she'll ring the cash registers.

"Lastly, Bob, your Marty is a brilliant marketer. She studies her markets and targets them with specific offerings. She created her wedding ring promotion just six months ago. That has already corralled her fifty Premium Member lap dogs. She has those men wrapped around her finger. They paid her twenty thousand Dollars each for their initial membership and their five premium ultra membership fuck sessions. That program is on track to earn Marty an additional two million Dollars a year, above her film royalties and Fund sales commissions. She'll likely soon reach the maximum number of ultra members that she has time to service. Then she'll raise her prices to whatever the market will bear. She's a living cash register, Bob. Her lovers are like adoring little boys, mindlessly bidding up the price of a precious baseball card.

"She's also figured out how to leverage her previous work. Marty is highly creative. She recently collaborated with her film producer to create a compilation piece. It's done in synchronicity with Tchaikovsky's 1812 Overture. It opens with Marty being mouth kissed and nipple suckled by her performing partners to the

awakening titillating music. It then proceeds to the compilation scenes of penis after penis after penis, each in its final throes of ejaculation into Marty's vagina or mouth. There are about a hundred of these snippets that capture the climactic shootings of the penises' ejaculations, all beautifully choreographed to the overture's reporting cannon fire. The effect leaves the viewer gaping spellbound as each pronounced hard note during each frame of the overture is timed perfectly. It coincides perfectly with the pulse and recoil of the penis in its frame. The penises appear to be cannons firing their discharges. Marty's vagina attenuates each penis's recoil, after accepting its semen. This goes on and on until the finale of the overture, when freedom is proclaimed and liberty erupts. The cannons report. The cymbals clash. The church bells chime loudly with their joyful telling of emancipation.

"Throughout the overture's finale the compilation focuses on Marty's own finales, when she opens wide her legs in synchronicity with the pealing church bells to reveal her signature cum pools. The film flashes from one opening reveal of her vagina and its cum pool, to another, and to yet another, in rapid succession. Ever the genius, Marty's cum pool shots were all performed with her vagina resting upon differently colored satin pillows of reds, crimsons, purples, purples laced with gold, gold, soft hues of orange, and pink.

"The compilation piece contains twenty such open cum pool scenes with Marty dipping her wedding rings into her cum pools. Looking closely at these scenes the viewer can see they are all different because of the different pillows and the growing number of wedding rings that Marty dips into her cum pools as the sequence progresses. In her clever way, Marty documents the ever-increasing male lusting's for her vagina. Between each scene she is kissed by a partner, and she is seen smiling her signature inviting lust smile and sending her mouth kisses to her viewer fans through the camera while her nipple is being sucked and her breast is being fondled by

a partner. The implication is that, as the world's consummate porn star, Marty can never get enough erotic sex.

"On the very last scene of these cum pool extravaganza reveals, Marty lifts her neckless of cum soaked wedding rings above her face and slowly lowers them into her mouth. She smiles, sucks away all the cum from the beholden rings, then swallows it. She lifts the neckless and rings, now sparkling cleaned and free from cum, above her head. She lays the neckless and rings upon her chest between her breasts. The subliminal message to her viewer is clear. She is joyously proud that she has devoured those marriages. It immensely pleases her to be immoral, sinfully wicked and obsessive over enjoying her own pleasures.

"For the children affected by her whoring, this act struck me as sadistic, but that thought doesn't stop Marty or give her pause to reflect. She has no reservations about her wantonness. She's like a Black Backed Gull leisurely resting herself over a nest of fledgling Puffin chicks. Every time she fucks her Premium Member, his account balance declines more and his children's futures are diminished. This goes on until the Member's money is gone and the children have no future.

"With similar unconcerned heartlessness, the Gull holds down a chick with its clawed foot while its beak rips off a wing or leg; or it opens the chick's stomach and casually devours its entrails. As the Gull holds its beak skyward and slides the chick's body parts down its gullet, it feels nothing. No shame, no guilt, no feeling for the chick or the nest's remaining, terrified chicks. They are like menu items to be devoured without fore or after thought. Marty has no more conscience than that Gull has.

"Bob, your Queen of Intimate Film Art has no misgivings about her methods and no patience for men who equivocate. If they want her, they must meet her demands. If a man wants to partake of her pleasures, he needs to honor her by joining his wedding ring to the others. He needs to join her premium service and forsake all others.

"*From the time her viewer fan sees one of Marty's films for the first time a process begins to take form in his mind. He first notices that her films are different from the ones he has seen of other intimate film actresses. Other women grunt and wince while having sex. Generally, they speak very little. There are the 'Oohs' and 'Ahh's' and the frequently spoken words of 'Yes,' and 'fuck me,' but little else is spoken.*

"*Marty's work, by contrast, is vastly different. She giggles and laughs openly and frequently. She freely banters and teases her partners. She lavishly praises them for how they are making her feel during her sex with them. She continuously finds opportunities to kiss them and touch them lovingly, all over their bodies. It's obvious to the viewer that Marty loves making love, and that she loves the men who are making love with her. Her wholesome dazzling beauty and constantly encouraging words and praises uniquely set her apart. Her viewer discovers he likes Marty as a person. She's fun. She's no longer just another porn star having sex on screen. She's a fellow human, with honest feelings. He wants to meet her and get to know her; because she's likeable.*

"*Once the viewer empathizes with Marty, his limbic zone elevates her to a type of prominence. What she does is no longer naughty or evil. Her sex acts become beautiful scenes. He hopes Marty will satisfy her insatiable lust. While this phenomenon is occurring an opposite effect also occurs. His past learnings about morality, goodness and family values become an annoyance. They interfere with his mental remembrances of Marty performing in her films. His mind becomes conflicted. His moral anchors hold him fast to his past life. His wife, children, parents, extended family, and church set a drag against that portion of his mind that lives in his limbic zone and wants to run free. The more he watches Marty's films, the more his limbic zone chafes at morality's resistance drag. It yearns to expand into and occupy the whole of his thoughts. He finds himself no longer content to watch Marty enjoying cunnilingus and fornication for a mere one hour a* day. Soon he is watching her films three; then five to eight hours a day. Eventually he discovers her compilation of orgasms synchronized in perfect harmony with Tchaikovsky's 1812 Overture.

"His inner mental conflict comes to a head. The learned thoughts about familial love, moral rectitude, avoidance of sin, and high morality are preventing him from fully embracing his thoughts about making love with Marty. The infatuation he has developed begins living in his dreams. He must purge his learned morality and the objections from those who detract from porn's immorality, so his mind can fully embrace Marty's debauchery, unencumbered by nay saying. He confronts his learned behaviors and his familial morality, concluding that they no longer serve him well. They are obstacles to his happiness and his imaginary love lust with Marty. He corrals the detractors, mentally binds them up. He ignores their appeals to his senses and tosses them onto an imaginary funeral pyre.

"Imagining himself locked in Marty's embrace and kissed by her wanton lips, he tosses a flaming torch into the pyre. His learned standards of moral conduct, his wife, children, parents, extended family, friends, and church all scream out to him. They beg for mercy and help:

'Save us!'

"They cry out while searing flames lick their clothes and flesh."

'AHHH, OWWW, EEEE!'

"They howl in anguished pain as their flesh burns away and their bones disintegrate into ashes. He ignores their screams and turns a deaf ear to their horrors. He can't be bothered by them. He imagines that he's French kissing Marty while everything and everyone from his moral life dies and crumbles into ashes.

"His flesh presses closely to Marty's. His hand feels her warm, welcoming mons as it presses against his hand, informing him that Marty wants to play. His fingers enter her vagina's outer and inner lips. Her kisses deepen. They reach into his soul. While her enemies *are writhing in their death throes, she touches his penis and strokes it. She moans her approval of his horrific deed. She whispers:*

'I'm very proud of you.'

"Silence. His mind can not respond. It can not acknowledge the horrific thing that he has done. Silence lingers longer. Then he knows. There is no longer a choice to be made. It's done. Marty is all he has now. His arms squeezed her closely to him; tightly now, as if to crush her soul into his. She is no longer his devil temptress; but his salvation. Without her, he has nothing. She knows this. She responds to his crushing embrace with a tongue teasing French kiss, deflecting his thoughts away from what he's done; then, assuring him that he will be spared from his own desolation deed:

'I'm here for you, baby. You're safe with me.'

"He has made his choice. He's rid himself of his moral baggage and joined Marty in unrepentant lust. She steps back and smiles at him and beams her approval of his arson murder. Then she hugs and kisses him again, as if to tell him that, as far as she is concerned, his heinous deed never took place. His family and his past were always inconsequential baggage to her. Their immolation pleased her; relieving her of a superfluous nuisance. But in any event, if he should remind himself of the deed he did and looks to her for approval; by her hugs and kisses, she tells him that she's very pleased by it. He is her hero. He has vindicated her whoring. She has scored yet another glorious triumph over provincial morality. She has gained a convert.

"His imagination races forward. From his life's disintegrated ash pile a spellbinding figment of Marty arises anew. She floats naked in mid-air, her voluptuous body arrayed on satin pillows, lying before him, inviting him to join her. Her arms are open, her legs widespread. Her smile beckons him to lie with her. He imagines himself by her side, his flesh pressed against hers. He holds her, kisses her, feels her delicious breasts; then he performs delicious cunnilingus and makes love with her.

"*His conversion is complete. His mind is committed to love Marty; love her whore lust; love her debauchery; surrender his soul and fortune to her. He will view more of her films and join her premium service. More determined about his decision than any decision he has ever made before, he patiently follows the instructions that her service gives him.*

"*Soon thereafter, he realizes his dream. He experiences delicious, unforgettable sex with the world's most glorious, unrepentant, shameless star of intimate film art. She confirms his decision was the correct decision. She adds his wedding ring to the growing trophy trove on her gold neckless. She praises him for his choice. She assures him she deeply values his decision and that she will always love him for it. Her reassurance of love, given after her membership sale, binds him to her for the lifetime of his finances.*

"*Marty's download results from her overture compilation are wildly successful. They break every record for intimate art film downloads and are expected to exceed a million copies in the first year of release. She receives several offers to endorse apparel lines of clothing, lingerie, and shoes. Film producers propose a series of full-length films about her life and meteoric rise to stardom. Sex magazines rave about the overture compilation. It is hailed as the singularly greatest, most explicit, best choreographed, mesmerizing intimate film work ever created. They opine that every aficionado of intimate film art must acquire it. They declare it is the 'must have' signature film for every erotic film library. They assert that the compilation sequence will permanently endear Marty's face and cum gushing vagina to viewers' hearts. And these aficionados of porn know what they're talking about.*

"*One writer stated that: 'the viewer's thoughts of foreplay, love, romance, and sex enmesh with visions of Marty in her fabulous compilation. She breaks all barriers and sets the all-time high bar for outstanding intimate film art.' Another writes: 'She is irresistible.*

She displaces all other stars and takes center stage. She instantly becomes every viewer's sex addiction-obsession. I promise that you will salivate witnessing the ascendancy of the world's most provocative, evocative penis magnet, ever. Her overture compilation is your unforgettable must-have film. She's spectacularly shameless and so sinfully deliciously wonderful!' Another writes: 'Unless you have the willpower of a superhuman you will not be able to resist Marty's latest film homage to the male libido. Don't be surprised if you find yourself unable to resist signing up for her premium service. Only well-heeled gentlemen need apply. This is no ordinary woman you'll be seeing. This is the sex goddess you'll never stop dreaming about. She is the undisputed Creme de la Creme of Sexuality, the adorable, penultimate Queen of all erotica.'

"Marty's work is one reason why so many new entrants to the sex film field fall flat on their faces. Most aspirants believe they can rig up a camera and film themselves having sex with a boyfriend or a few male friends. Frankly, watching them grunt and hump quickly becomes tedious and boring. No one likes to sit through ten or twenty minutes of some guy ramming a vagina in five different positions, until both partners are exhausted, before he finally gets off; and then watch them lie moaning until they recover their stamina. The viewer feels sorry for the woman taking the inconsiderate pounding from her bloke partner. But they will not buy her films.

"Marty eliminates that boredom. Unseen by the camera, she has two or three assistants giving blow jobs to her male partners. When it's a partner's turn to join Marty in an orgy scene, his penis is already extremely sensitized, and primed to ejaculate semen. When he enters her hot lubricated vagina; feels her educated vaginal muscles contract and release on his already stimulated penis; and experiences the subtle coaxing pressures of her pelvic undulations, her partner's penis simply can't hold anything back. It can barely contain itself. It comes, and comes and comes.

"Marty's camera crew expertly captures tight close ups of her pelvic gyrations. The viewer imagines all the sensations the performing penis is experiencing. He mentally participates in the erotic sensual moment of the male's ejaculation, while the performing penis is captive within Marty's love channel. He watches in wonderstruck awe while the world's most adored vagina contracts over the penis, extracts its life force and devours it. Marty becomes awesome splendored magnificence, a veritable fountain-pool of semen releases. The viewer is spellbound; mesmerized. His thoughts are riveted to the scene, never to be unfastened from his sense of admiration and love of Marty.

"Consider this, Bob, with only so many hours in a day, what are viewers going to choose to watch? Marty's films or some unknown woman's single film that shows her getting poked for a half hour by her boyfriend? By understanding all the nuances of her craft and the male eros psyche, and by doing the spending necessary to achieve perfection, Marty dominates the sex film market. I expect she'll hold her number one ranking for at least five years. Males love and adore her. They're not about to waste their time watching an unknown woman. But they'll eagerly wait to see Marty's next performance. The demand for her erotica is simply insatiable. She literally sucks all the money out of the market.

"Her web site offers a free download, screen-saver application. Each time her fans boot up, they see a photo of her in a fresh erotic pose. She also offers a sex tutorial series for the public schools' sex education programs. It starts with kindergarten and goes through grade twelve. She discuses the importance for girls to give their consent to many different boys so they can know lots of boys on a more personable, intimate level; thus, making an informed choice about which boys they want to choose for frequent sex partners. She even has one segment that encourages young girls to experiment often with their love making techniques on many different boys, if their *goal is to become a highly paid erotic film star like her. Marty studied the cigarette industry. She learned it pays huge dividends to get your customers addicted to what you're selling while they are young and impressionable.*

"Realize how genius she is, Bob. Every single day the very first thing millions of young boys and girls see when they boot up their computers is a full-size screen shot of Marty, posed seductively, provocatively displaying her butterfly vagina. Millions of the world's youths start their day, not with a prayer to God or a pledge to their nation's flag, but with a visual imprint of Marty's inviting lips and beckoning vagina, explicitly oozing white cum from her latest sexual conquest. And at night, millions of boys watch pictures of her perfect face, her body in skimpy outfits and sexy poses. They fall asleep dreaming they are holding the world's most beautiful sex goddess in their arms. That's brilliant marketing!

"At the end of her films she enthusiastically declares: 'That was WONDERFUL! I LOVED it! Let's do that again, soon!' Contrast her enthusiasm with most other intimate film actresses who ask in a deadpan voice, 'Did I do Okay?' It's those clever touches that bind the hearts of Marty's fans to her and make her work stand out, far above the others."

"But Barb, if she's doing so well, what doesn't she leave the Firm and just do porn full time?"

"I think for two reasons, Horse. David is one of them. He has some sort of hold over her that I do not yet understand. And there is a second reason. It's not the glamor of creating porn. It's a deeper reason. She is, I think, a lot like David this way. Marty also enjoys hurting people.

"She's not a dunce. On some level she surely knows that she's leaving in her wake crushed children's lives, broken hearted wives, and wrecked households; yet she turns a willfully blind eye to the suffering and havoc she instigates. Their miseries please her because

she knows she can leverage their pain to her advantage. She cleverly uses their tragedy to advance her image of this vixen goddess and to promote her brand image. She focuses her social media followers on the most recent family break up that she's caused, and cleverly gloats about her romance with the estranged husband. Her messaging is that no other woman can match her allure and sexuality.

"Here, Bob, I have a transcript of Marty's live television interview with Consuelo Lovely, the WORLD INTIMACY BEAT television show reporter from INTIMATE ARTISTRY PERFORMANCE MAGAZINE. Consuelo's TV show and magazine recently changed their name to upscale their brand image. This was her last interview before she changed the name of her column and the magazine. It's all about your sweetheart, Marty. I'll read it to you. Just listen how Marty demolishes the wife of Dominicko Castro. Dominicko is Marty's most recent tabloid lover, promoter, and convert to her cause.

CHAPTER FOUR

This world is not for aye, nor 'tis not strange that even our love should with our fortunes change. (William Shakespeare: Hamlet)

You attain an endearing symbiotic relationship with your man when he stops talking about himself because he prefers performing cunnilingus. (Rosemary Ness-Bitner, author)

METAMORPHOSIS

"That porn magazine and Marty have a symbiotic relationship, Bob. They endorse her exotica PREMIUM LINE of transparent brassieres, bikinis, and lingerie; and Marty and Dominicko extensively advertise her PREMIUM LINE in the magazine. Her product sales are sizzling hot as a result of her promotions. This interview was done as an exclusive magazine supplement for its aficionados, those devoted subscribers who pay to have print copies of INTIMATE ARTISTRY delivered to them. It targets readers who seek psychological bonding with adult film actresses by delving into the innermost workings of their thoughts. This reprint of Marty's latest televised podcast interview is just one of a series of cooperative efforts between Marty and this magazine, Bob. Notice how Marty uses every opening to take a dig at Mrs. Castro."

"Hello, you beautiful fans. I am Consuelo Lovely of WORLD INTIMACY BEAT, the live television interview channel of INTIMATE ARTISTRY PERFORMANCE MAGAZINE, and the voice of millions of people seeking *"PEACE THROUGH INTIMACY."*

And I want to give a special shout out, today, to our viewers for keeping INTIMACY BEAT ranked number one among all television talk shows. With me today is our honored guest, Marty, this year's QUEEN OF EROTIC INTIMACY. Marty was voted by our magazine readership as the world's number one adult film star by our fan's poll near unanimous agreement. As many of you know, Marty has made over four hundred exceptional intimate artistry films. She also designed and created the exquisite PREMIUM line of see-through lingerie, bikinis, and evening wear.

DOM AND CANNES

To show a man you are a decisive woman, don't suck your thumb. Suck his penis. (Rosemary Ness-Bitner, author)

"Marty, I'm not going to ask you why you are so successful. Our loyal fan base already knows how much enthusiasm you have for making spectacular adult films. I want to launch right into the latest news about you and your most recent love, Dominicko Castro. As our fans and the entire world already know, you two have been making a sensational splash in the tabloids with your white-hot love affair. Can you tell us all about it? What's the attraction between you two and how did this whirlwind romance even begin?"

"Sure, Consuelo; and thank you for having me on your program. Oh, that Dominicko, he's such a man! I'm so lucky he came into my life. Now that we're together I can't imagine what life was like before I met him. I'll never forget that first phone call I got from Dominicko. Hearing his dominating masculine voice sent tingles of anticipation through my entire body. He said he had watched my latest film, 'The Immaculate Conception Story.' He told me that film made him decide the two of us should get acquainted. He told me he loved how I smiled with my eyes and facial cheeks as well as my mouth when I made love. He raved about how much he enjoyed

seeing how pleased I was with my sexuality. Well, the next thing I knew he picked me up in his helicopter and whisked me over to Cannes in his private jet. We stayed on his huge yacht. I never imagined myself with a multi billionaire like Dominicko; but now that I know him, we've become inseparable.

"Whenever I'm with him I feel intense desire building like a pressure inside my mind. It wants to release from me and go into him, through my kisses, my nipples, by wrapping my legs around him and ultimately by having our intimate connection, inside my vagina.

"Dom understands the ways I love to be touched. He knows how to make my skin come alive with fires of desire. He lifts me up and sets me on this cloud of sublime ecstasy. He's different from other men in the way he brushes his lips against mine; and by how he sends my mind spinning when he softly nibbles his lips over my breasts and kisses me lower and lower over my tummy as his lips follow the trail to my eager vagina. I can feel his kisses becoming sweeter and sweeter; more and more tender, until his lips are finally nibbling and kissing my vagina lips. Teee-Heee, his lips love my lips. We tease each other about that. And Dom loves the electrifying feeling he gets when I dig my fingers into his back. I do that spontaneously while he's loving me with his mouth. I feel so much passion when he does that. I become like a bundle of highly charged electricity; and I release my charge into Dom when my nails dig into his back. I become like a wildcat. I REALLY love our oral sex, Consuelo; can't ever get enough. I always want more.

"Dom explained something to me that I never understood before. Many people who watch my films have an initial repulsion to seeing explicit sex. Dom said he felt like that too, at first; but the more he watched my films the more his perceptions changed. He was no longer repulsed by seeing penises ejaculating into my vagina. He no longer felt squeamish about seeing cum oozing from my vagina or by seeing penises ejaculating into my mouth.

"A completely opposite feeling started taking root within Dom's mind. He began seeing me for the loving woman I am. He began his understanding of me. He began to understand that I create porn because I totally love lovemaking; that I'm obsessed with the artistic expression of lovemaking. That' when my film art began to fascinate him. Eventually, over time, he became obsessed with me and my films, so much so that he set aside more and more time each day to view me making love. After some time of carefully watching my films, stopping the frames to study the motions of my vagina in the throes of love making, Dom had his epiphany.

"He recognized that he was observing the mysterious miracle of creation. He knew he was being divinely inspired to rethink his original prejudices about my explicit art form. He could no longer accept the dogmatic teachings of his religion. He no longer felt beholden to the whims and demands of his wife and her social calendar. He no longer felt there should be any stigma or guilt or feelings of shame over being seen with me. He felt himself coming full circle in his belief system and choosing to repose his faith and his love in me."

"And why do you think that was, Marty?"

"Because, Consuelo, he had come to understand that my morality and my pornography was all love based. He recognized that I do what I do out of love. That's when he decided he needed to venerate and adore me and my whoring, before the entire world. He needed me. He needed me to share my boundless love of intimacy with him. He wanted to join me in that love and share our love with the entire world. Dom is a very loving man. He didn't care what his newfound love might cost him. His family life and his businesses, he knew, would likely suffer terribly; but Dom didn't care.

Consuelo wanted to understand exactly what, in Dom's mind, caused him to cast aside everything he believed in and make his lifetime commitment to Marty. *"Marty,"* she asked, *"Is there any one thing in particular about you or your films that brought about*

Dom's changed perception of you and your work? I mean, this famous man made a radical change in his life choices. Essentially, he decided to give up everything for you. Can you think of anything specific? Did he comment about anything that caused him to change? Tell us, please, if you can remember anything; anything at all."

"Well, a lot happened that first time we were together. I mean, he said a lot to me. But one thing does kind of stand out in my memory. I had asked him what it was about my films that he liked the most. He told me it was my endings. Well, I thought he was putting me down; like telling me he was glad the film was over. But that wasn't it at all. He explained that my endings brought on a revelation for him. He told me that he became fascinated by the way I flexed and bounced my tush and shook my bootie and then held myself open after my partners had come inside me. He said he couldn't stop thinking about those movements I did. And he couldn't get his mind off of all the semen that oozed out of me. His mind would not rest. He had dreams about that ending sequence I perform.

"Then his thoughts jelled. He remembered something from scriptures about how a man is forbidden from spilling his seed. Suddenly he saw that dictate as religion's way of keeping control of women by making them not use contraception; and by essentially making them submit to the chance of becoming pregnant. He realized it was another male ordered religious way of controlling and dominating women. And there I was with my films, flaunting my mons pubis, and sending a completely opposite message. Dom saw my endings as confrontational messaging. He saw a woman declaring herself to be free of religious influences; declaring that she had free will; free choices. I suppose he had something there. I do intentionally spill my males' seeds after I and my partners have had our pleasures. Essentially, I mock God when I shake my bootie and spill out my creamy white semen like I do. Yet God did not and has not since punished me for doing that; not that I believe in God in the first place.

"And that got Dom thinking that perhaps the reason God didn't punish me was that there really is no such thing as God; there's no such thing as a divine being. That's when Dom decided that, all his life, he'd been worshipping the wrong thing. He came to believe that he should be worshipping the miracle of creation and the miracles of nature and intimacy and pleasures that join men and women together; not a God that places men above women. He began seeing my films as demonstrations of human love and the freedom to enjoy pleasure. That's when Dom became happy for me; overjoyed, actually. He began feeling this deep wonder and happiness for me the more he watched me having sex with my on-screen partners.

"He felt awed that hundreds of penises have ejaculated into my vagina. He adored me for my commitment to sexual freedom. It was what Dom refers to as his acceptance moment. He said that's when he began respecting what I stood for and that's when he started falling in love with me. From that moment onward, Dom decided that my vagina was what he should worship. He has since worshipped it, and me, as the source of life and humanity's pleasures; intimacy, harmony, and beauty. He believes my smiling, bootie shake routine, where I proudly display the seed I've spilled from my vagina, is the explicit essence of beautiful freedom and human love. It's those closing moments in my films where my smile essentially invites my viewers to call me and have the same wonderful experience. That's what prompted Dom to call me. He believes that everyone should interpret my display the same way he does.

"I'm so glad that Dom thinks of me that way. I was so happy to hear him confess his feelings to me. I knew I had the love of a man who saw me in the same way that I see myself. And he accepted me for being me! Such a beautiful feeling came over me. Here was this wonderful man telling me that he saw me as a woman who was committed to bringing joy to the world; unlocking freedom from peoples' souls. And he was telling me that he adored me and loved me for

doing that. My heart leaped when I heard that. I cannot express how wonderful I felt. Dom is not a possessive man. He's totally fine with sharing me with other men; that is, during those times when we're not together.

"Then, during that first time when we were together, he told me that he felt something very profound. This feeling replaced all his previous assumptions about life. The more he watched how I enjoyed making love and performing felatio, the more he became converted to the holiness of my creation art. He felt an overpowering desire to make love with me. He sought to cast out his life's demons and commune with me and all my fans who love me.

"He desperately wanted to perform cunnilingus with me. He yearned to use his tongue to experience my orgasms with me and explore my sexuality with me. He sought the sensation of being one with others who are now and who have been my lovers. But mostly he wanted to honor my sexual triumphs, my erotic accomplishments, and my film art. He said performing cunnilingus would be his humble way of paying homage to the majesty of my erotic film artistry. After that confession of his profound heartfelt love, we finally came together. It was beautiful beyond words to describe how I felt about making love with him."

"When did you first realized that Dom sincerely loved you; that this love was the real deal? I mean how did you know it wasn't just a fling for him? And when did you realize that he would leave his wife to have more time with you?"

"A woman knows when her chemistry makes a man catch fire. Up until that moment it could be just sex, you know? But then, there's that defining moment that's different from all the others. It's that moment where you know you've really connected, you know?"

"How could you know, Marty? You have so many lovers and you're doing your film work. What told you that Dom was serious, that he only wanted you? Was it something that he said?"

"He didn't have to say anything. He took me to dinner in New York that night. It happened when we got back to our hotel. It wasn't until later that he told me about the thoughts that raced through his mind while we rode that elevator. I was wearing my crimson red lipstick that night, the same shade I usually wear while I'm performing fellatio on film. Dom told me the things he had said to himself while riding with me in that elevator:

'Here I am. And right beside me stands the woman of my dreams, the woman that I've obsessed over. I've studied hundreds of her still framed porn pictures. I've memorized her beautiful, innocent face while she sucked the semen from hundreds of penises and the way she smiled while making love with hundreds of men.'

"He told me:

'I visualized the hundreds of times in your films when your lips and tongue caressed a penis after it had ejaculated. I was awed by the ways you honored those penises for giving you pleasures. I loved that your morals commanded you to seek pleasures and human intimacy. I was spellbound by how you chortled and smiled while you swallowed semen from your vagina's semen pool. Your uninhibited and open commitment to human love and pleasure made my heart race.

'You took my breath away. I was overcome by my adoration for you. I trembled inside. I was in awe of you. I wanted to take you in my arms and kiss you; and hold you and never let you go. I wanted to join my life to yours and yours to mine. I wanted you to be my trophy; wanted to hold you high; carry you majestically on my shoulders; honor you; glorify your immoral lifestyle; be seen at conventions and dinners with my arm around you; raise my glass and toast you, your beauty, and your immorality, at social functions for being the most accomplished actress in the world. And if people asked actress of what, I want to tell them: Explicit erotica! Beautifully erotic, explicit erotica!'

"*That would be so Dom. Other peoples' opinions never bother him. He was imagining that our worlds would collide, like two intersecting galaxies; and that there would be casualties; but he didn't care. I was more important than anything else in his world. He told me he wanted me and everything about me. He said he wanted to touch his tongue and lips to mine, to profess his adoration for my immoral beliefs. He wanted to surrender his beliefs to mine. He wanted to unite his life with mine. All he could think of was how much he wanted me. He told me he wanted to ravage me. When we got off the elevator, he couldn't even wait to walk those few steps to our room. His need to have me overwhelmed him.*

"*That was the moment I knew it was happening for us. He took my face into those huge hands of his. His eyes had this: 'I can't walk another step with you. Look, I need you. Now, look at me! I must have you. I need to make love with you right now. Look into my eyes! Right this minute look.' Dom's eyes had this: 'I'm hungry crazed for your body' look. He was experiencing a lust rush. I could tell. It's the way a man's eyes look into a woman's eyes when he absolutely has to have her. This is where some men can lose all control of themselves and when they will forcibly rape a woman. But that wasn't Dom. He was filled with passion; but it was controlled passion. He was never violent.*

"*That's when he kissed me. It was a sudden, spontaneous kiss. I wasn't completely sure that this would be our moment; that moment when we would have our first intimate sex. I know I was hoping it was that moment. I remember hoping he would take me, right then, right there in the hotel hallway.*

"*And then it happened. Sparks flew. I felt the electricity. My blood turned to fire! My uncertainties flew away when Dom kissed me that first time. It was the way he kissed me. It was a hard, possessive kiss. Very dominant kiss; very hard kiss. That kiss, the suddenness of it, the intensity of it, took my breath away. Totally spontaneous. Passionate.*

Made me gasp. Set off this yearning fire inside me. I instantly wanted to have sex with him. Made my heart leap. That kiss communicated that his soul was ablaze with lust for me. It declared to my soul that his passion heat was going to torch his world to a crisp, proving his love for me. That's how hot his heat felt.

"The press of his lips assured me he would go into our love with everything I imagined he would; and more. I sensed it then. It was his nonverbal commitment to me. He was making it to me. He wanted me to be his goddess; goddess of everything immoral and unholy; goddess of immoral sins and passion lusts that would set him free. His tongue was in my mouth. I welcomed it. I wanted it. I could feel his hunger for me. I wanted to be his goddess. I wanted to answer his need.

"In that moment I wanted to make love with him more than I ever wanted to make love in my entire life. My fire suddenly roared higher, like air from a blast furnace was fanning my flames. Made me crazy hot! Heat blasted into my vagina. It all happened so fast. It was so strong, so intense that I feared my panties would soak through from my wetness. My clitoris suddenly caught fire, like a hot wind from a nuclear blast had rushed over it. Its lust pangs throbbed through my tentacles into my thighs. I was so totally ignited; so eager to keep going. I tongued him back. I instinctively let him know that I was ready. I wanted him to enter me; to come inside me. I put my arms around him and held him close. Oh, Consuelo, I really wanted him. So badly. So much!

"Then suddenly, a volcano erupted like a pyroclastic blast inside my sex. The tentacles of my clitoris surged hot pulsations from my vulva into my loins. My tummy tumbled over and over. Wildly. Crazed with insatiable lust. It shot up my spine into my brain. My neck and face flushed with this sudden, raging heat. The heat stayed with me. It intensified. I couldn't control it. I could not put it back where it came from. And, I didn't want to. I desperately wanted to

make love. I wanted Dom's penis inside me. I kissed him very hard. I became like an animal. I could not think about where we were or what time it was or who might see us there in the hallway. Nothing except lust was in my mind. I only felt lust.

"I groaned and said: 'Yes. Yes!' I felt so primal, like a wild mink or something, I don't know; but I was absolutely crazy out of my mind with this overwhelming desire to have sex. All I could think of; the only thing in my mind was how badly I wanted to do it. I couldn't wait another second. I wanted Dom to take me right there in the hallway. He understood my feelings. My body. He had to know that I needed him right then. Right there in the hotel hallway.

"His hands slipped down my sides to my waist. He pulled me against him. I could feel his hard hugeness. I had this handsome, powerful hunk of a man who wanted me more than anything. I felt his need for me. I knew it was real, Consuelo. I knew it. I just knew it! Then Dom dropped his hands to my thighs and started to hike my dress up. I said: 'Yes. Yes!' again. He didn't care if anyone came into the hall. Nothing was going to stop what was happening. I knew that, too. I desperately wanted him to keep going. I wanted him to take me. I said: 'Hold me, Dom. Hold me close. And fuck me. Yes! Fuck me and fuck me and fuck me!'

"We couldn't wait to walk those few steps to our room. That would take an entire minute. And we simply could not wait that long. We had to do it now. Right now. Dom was so intent about having me that I knew he had to be in love with me. Nothing else mattered. Love happens like that. We both knew it was happening. He had lust rage. For me. For my body. For my vagina. I welcomed his rage. I wanted it. When he hiked my skirt, I felt hot fire running wild through my blood. Volcanoes popped and spewed hot lava inside me.

"I needed to make love. I had to. I wanted to fuck like a wild animal and I never wanted to stop. I couldn't get my panties off fast

enough. I wanted Dom's penis. Inside me. Now. Right now. Right here. I said: 'Yes! Yes! Now!' He lifted me onto his penis. He's incredibly strong. What a man! I put my arms around his neck and kissed him. The wildness I felt at that moment was completely natural; so beautiful. He penetrated. His penis was inside me. I was ecstatic.

"I said: 'So good! So wonderful! I love it. Fuck me. Fuck me good, Dom.' I loved how he felt inside me. It was electrifying. I can't completely describe it. I only knew that Dom needed me. I gladly surrendered myself to that need. I moved my hips to take in more of him. He needed to know how much I needed him. I wanted him to need me. I wriggled my bootie; helped him feel all of my sensations; let him know our sex would always be fabulous; let him know it would always be loving; special; wonderful! He responded. Held me tighter. Signaled that he loved me. Body language. Our bodies knew. They told each other that this was real. I loved that Dom needed me; needed his penis inside me; needed to let me know we had joined together in love. Together now. We were together. Intimate! One! We made that instantaneous decision, right then and there, to join our souls together. That's how love happens. It was love. I knew it was love.

"Consuelo, Dom thrusted so hard into me while holding me against that wall I thought that all the sex I ever had before was just practice for that moment. I knew I needed to submit to him; let him do whatever he pleased with me. This was the real thing, with a real man. My, oh my! He was like a wild animal, a bull charging wildly inside me; and nothing mattered to Dom, other than having me, loving me.

"My legs wrapped around him. I pulled his penis deeply inside me. All the way inside. I loved how I felt in that moment. His penis was heaven for me. It was so huge and so hard! I wanted to hold him there, inside me like that, all night. When he came, he looked into my face with eyes I'll never forget. There was a light from his eyes. It was love, Consuelo. It shined. His soft eyes told me that he loved me

before his mouth ever spoke a word. There were no games in his eyes; only love, honest love. I knew in that instant that Dom was mine; forever mine.

"My eyes, looking back into his, told him that I always wanted to be there for him, like I just was. My eyes flowed out my love to him. We didn't need to speak words. It was all there for the two of us, just like that. When he held me close and kissed me even longer, and tenderly, I knew right then and there that he would leave his wife for me. I was absolutely certain of it. I felt this internal surge of happiness. I knew that this was right for both of us. It was love. It happened that fast for us. It was only our second date. But that didn't matter. The feelings were all that mattered. And the feelings were real. A woman knows when her man loves her to the exclusion of everyone else.'

"Is he always so spontaneous?"

"Oh yes, especially when he gets that urge to dominate me. He sometimes loves letting me know that he's the man. Then I submit to him. He is never demeaning or anything like that. He is always beautiful. His dominance is his way of letting me know how much he needs me; how much he needs to keep me close to him. Dom needs to be a dominating lover. He knows I completely understand and accept that about him. That's why we love each other so much. I love being with a man who knows how to dominate me, without hurting me.

"He loves to push me, face down, on the huge California King bed in his yacht's stateroom. He gets on top of me and gets me all hot and wet by nibble-kissing my neck and ears. That drives me crazy. I dig my fingers into the sheets to contain the pleasures that he gives me. I wait patiently, getting wetter and wetter inside, hoping he'll soon enter me and begin ravaging my vagina. I go crazy anticipating having his huge penis inside me, absolutely out of my mind crazy. I hear myself saying to myself:

'Come, Dom, come inside me now. I want you. I can't wait
another second.'

"He always enters me so lovingly, so gently; and all the while he
always continues kissing me. I can tell by that initial entry whether a
man respects my body. Then, once Dom's inside me, we just explode
in this unbelievable torrent of wild animal lust. We can't fuck hard
enough or long enough. We release each other from the world and
fly through heaven together. It's like I'm riding a powerful stallion
horse. My horse has endless stamina. Dom satisfies me like no one
else ever has.

"Dom treats my body in ways that are hard to describe. I've
never had these same feelings with any other man. He makes me
feel like being with me is his special bliss; like I'm his escape from
his drudgery at home and at work; like he knows every moment we
can find together in our busy lives is extra special time. I knew that
on that first night. After we made love in the hall; after we were in
our room and naked, Dom washed my feet. Then he massaged and
kissed my feet. No man had ever done that before. When I asked
him why he washed and kissed my feet; was this some kind of Greek
thing?

"He told me he did it because his spirit soul told him that he
needed to commit himself to helping me on my journey. I told him
that I wanted him to come along with me on my journey. And he
answered me that his spirit told him in a dream that he could only
come part way with me; that he could not cross over into my next
life with me; that I was destined and ready to become an immortal
spirit in my next life; but that he was doomed to be a mere mortal
spirit after his present life.

"He said my spirit was about to emerge, like a new and free
butterfly. I would leave my mortal life and enter chrysalis and transform and emerge again as a spectacularly beautiful butterfly. His
spirit, on the other hand, would need to wait two more generations

of spirit life before it could enter my spirit world beyond the life it has now. In the meantime, his spirit needed to toil on Earth, between the womb and the grave. His spirit, in the person of a woman named Susan, my mother's name, would need to first confront a very evil spirit that tormented me. His spirit needed to destroy that evil person who carried the evil spirit. Only after his spirit did that could it progress to its next spirit life; and only after that next spirit life had been reborn could it be free to seek my spirit.

"And he told me that his spirit would ultimately rediscover my spirit in the body of a woman named Cecilia; and that our two spirits would know passionate love again. Our spirits would join again in the bodies of Sheila and Cecilia and we would become great lovers. He said that, for now, we needed to love and cherish each other with all the love that our spirits had blessed us to have while we were together. Then he laid down beside me, rested my head on his arm and kissed my cheek until he fell asleep. He is such a sweet man, Consuelo. He's like a giant-sized, real-life teddy bear. It's like the two of us have our love inside this magical time warp of slow-motion bliss. Every second feels like we can make it last forever. I enjoy every second of it. I simply close my eyes and float away like I'm being controlled by a greater power and I'm helpless to change anything that is happening.

"I sometimes feel like I'm this little girl, riding on a gigantic bird that flies upside down with me riding it and its penis is far up inside me. It flies me anywhere I wish to go and it makes it possible for me to do anything I want to do and have anything I want to have. This splendid, beautiful bird has its huge, loving penis all the way up inside me. It feels wonderful beyond words to describe it. A lovely nymph is flying alongside us. She is playing a harp, making the most beautiful melodious sounds which are resonating in perfect harmony with the dreamy sensations that the penis is making me feel inside my vagina. Her harp music makes my thoughts go dreamy.

My mind drifts far away from everything, except how much I love feeling this gigantic, wonderous penis inside me.

"*While this wonderful love making was happening with Dom and me, I just knew that his wife would fall away from him; from us. I decided there was no point in even bothering myself by thinking about her; so, I simply stopped thinking about her. I knew that nature would take its natural course. Every time we made love, I imagined her spirit was flying further away from us, going out of our solar system; then leaving our galaxy and drifting infinitely further away, into the vast universe beyond. Every time I held Dom in my arms, while we kissed and hugged and made our sweet love, I had that thought about his wife's spirit flying further away until I couldn't see it anymore; until I could no longer imagine that it even existed. Whenever Dom came inside me, her spirit disappeared forever. It no longer had any effect upon my feelings or on his. And that absence of her spirit made our love making that much more beautiful.*

"*Now, whenever I'm riding Dom's gigantic penis, I imagine that we are flying weightlessly through the air. Dom places his huge hands on my shoulders and pushes his penis deeper and deeper inside me. It reaches further into my vagina and expands larger and larger until my joy meter blows through the top of its scale. I scream with pleasure when Dom and I make love like that. There's an intensity about it; like it's all that matters to both of us. I know I must sound like a craven, shameless animal; but I don't care.*

"*Dom and I both know that I'm a fallen woman. He understands that I'm not the kind of woman that people would ever call a 'good girl.' He knows I'll never be a 'good girl;' not for him or for any man. And I know he understands that and loves that about me. He has told me that he doesn't want a 'good girl.' He told me that 'good girls' are a dime a dozen and that he wants to stay away from them. He tells me that he adores the whore in me. He tells me that a 'bad girl' needs love every bit as much, or more than a 'good girl' needs love. And he tells me that he is totally in love with his 'bad girl,' and that he will love me forever. That's when I urge him to push harder and harder into me, until he releases his massive cum load and collapses in exhaustion on top of me.*

"Every time we make love; I want to keep Dom inside me forever. Having Dom's penis in me is like living inside a wonderful dream that never ends. I'm sure he's had other women before me. That's why I was so surprised when he told me he loved me, and couldn't live without me, and when he sincerely swore that he needed me. When two people have a wonderful chemistry together, love just sort of happens. Teee-Heee. Love can't be faked.

"When Dom finishes inside me and I feel my vagina has been filled with his creamy hot cum, I then feel his love flowing through my entire body. He's a very caring lover. He does not try to pull away or come out of me. He loves staying inside me while he hugs and kisses me; caresses me and pets my hair and face. He continues kissing my nipples long after he finishes; and when he finally does come out, he uses his fingers to keep me stimulated because he understands my body now; and he knows I like to continue coming, long after he's done. He loves being together with me; holding me close; sharing my pleasure throes while I come.

"We have 'sweetness love.' That's when your partner wants you to have all the pleasures you can possibly have; and you feel the same way towards him. That means a lot to a woman, even to an erotic, explicit romance actress with many lovers, like myself. I love hearing a man telling me that he loves me. I never tire of hearing Dom telling me that he's in love with me. Teee-Heee.

"Marty," Consuelo inserted herself, interrupting the vignette; *"You were saying the two of you have sweetness love. Does that mean you've fallen in love with Dom?"*

"Why yes, of course I have. I love him with all my heart. I just love the stuffing's out of him. He's my great big lovable teddy bear. I totally love Dom."

CHAPTER FIVE

Licking postage stamps is a thankless one-way street. Licking penises is different. They will give you something back. (Rosemary Ness-Bitner, author)

OTHERS, ETC.

"But, Marty, in previous interviews you've given you said you were in love with a secret boyfriend named Bob; and in another interview you mentioned that some man named Carl was the love of your life. So, help me understand here, just which of these men are you in love with?"

"Why, all of them, of course. I love all of them, Consuelo. I also love a man named Darren, another named Donny; and then there's Fred, big Ed, Johnny, Marshawn, Josh and about another dozen men or so in my Premium member group; and then there's a secret obsession I have with a man named David, although David and I haven't had sex yet, but I'm working toward making that happen for us."

"But, Marty, how can you possibly be in love with all these men at the same time? I mean, don't your feelings ever tell you that you need to choose one man and forget the rest of them, except for your work on your erotica, of course?"

"Well, no. I really do love all of them. And I love each one of them with all my heart. I don't favor one over the other. But I do especially love spending my nights and my time with Bob, whenever

I can; and I do that about five nights out of seven, unless I'm away with Dom somewhere.

"The thing about Bob is that he makes me think about what's possible in my life. When I'm with him it's like I can flip a switch in my mind that makes me feel all warm, lovey-dovey domesticated; and peaceful. It's a kind of bliss. No one else makes me feel that way about what could be possible; only Bob. I mean, sometimes I find myself wondering what life would be like if I changed everything, you know? Like, maybe I could be a housewife with some kids and I could love them totally, unlike my mother who didn't really love me. I could do two little kids a lot of good. I could be the perfect mother and I would give them a lot of love.

"Bob makes me think that I could do that if I wanted. See, Bob loves me for what I could be if I wanted to be that different kind of person; and he wouldn't care that I made hundreds of erotic romance films. Bob knows I've done lots of naughty things, but he loves me and he accepts me for me; you know, like a good father accepts and loves his daughter, no matter what she's done. Bob is very giving emotionally. That's why I always feel safe with him and in our relationship. When I'm with Bob, I feel like I'm safe and at home. He puts that kind of love into our relationship and I need that kind of deep unconditional love.

"Carl loves me for the explosive sex tigress that lives inside me. It's sort of like Carl has a voyeur's love for me and all the naughty things I do with him and with others; and Carl loves my films. He can never get enough of them. It's like the more I whore, the more of a 'bad-girl' or wicked woman I am, that's what makes Carl love me; that's what brings out his love for me. And I love Carl very much. I know he needs me to be a bad girl, so that motivates me to be my naughty best. It's that driver to be lovingly naughty, to be a totally uninhibited fuck crazed whore; loving the erotic intimacy I'm having, which is why my film art is so adored.

"But Bob loves me for the gentle nurturing sweet wife and mother that I could be if I wanted to be that. So, I guess there's some duality in my personality or in the way my thinking goes, but the only man I can imagine settling down with and marrying is Bob. I totally love him. He knows I need to be away some weekends and he's okay with that. And I know Bob understands my need for Carl. He understands that I sometimes absolutely must have my special times with Carl, because that satisfies my lust so well. But, honestly, Consuelo, whenever I'm with any one of my lovers I give that lover all my undivided love. I'm completely his. I just block out all thoughts of my other lovers and I think only about the needs of the man whom I'm with at the time. I turn on my love for him and turn off everything else."

"Don't you find that difficult? I mean don't you ever feel any guilt about telling one man you love him one day and telling another man you love him the next day?"

"No. I never feel any guilt. What is there to be guilty about? I mean, none of these men own me, except maybe David sort of owns me because he has a sort of hold on me even though I haven't had sex with David; not yet. I'm working toward that, though. David is extremely complicated. I'd need to have hours with you to explain that; but I don't want to do that because it wouldn't be fair to David. He has a special need thing about women, especially me. But no, I have no guilt about being completely, totally in love with one man one day and another man the next; or even about being in love with five or six different men on the same day. Here, this may help you understand. When you change the channels on your television do you feel guilty about leaving the channel you were just watching to go watch something new?"

"No of course not."

"Well, changing my feelings between the men I love is the same as that, like changing the TV channel from one man to another.

I just love the man I'm with; and while I'm with him, I forget the other men. It's very easy for me to do that, mentally, once I start kissing and making love. My shrink assures me that having a variety of lovers is excellent for my mental health. I'm certain she's absolutely correct. I think I'd go insane if I had to confine my love making to one man. Yeah, that would make me go crazy."

CHAPTER SIX

Morality and immorality are different parts of your mind. If you aren't having fun, change to the other part of your mind. (Rosemary Ness-Bitner, author)

MARTY'S MORALITY

At that point in the interview, Consuelo, reporter from INTIMACY BEAT, had an epiphany of sorts. She realized she was observing Marty through a sort of medieval hagioscope, that notch behind the altar where lepers stood while observing the Christian service; but keeping their diseased bodies away and apart from the others by staying in their outcast, outside world. Consuelo sensed this was her great opportunity to make a splash. Here she was, face to face, with the widely acknowledged goddess of erotica romance films. Unlike many adult film stars whom she'd previously interviewed, Marty was totally open; not holding back her feelings or secrets. The interview was going extremely well. It was the chance of a lifetime to go into the mind of the number one erotica film star. Intuitively, Consuelo grasped that Marty was unique in her field; but why? There seemed to be a void in her subject's life, a willful detachment from morality. She felt emboldened to probe deeper into the thoughts of the sex goddess:

"Thanks for clearing that up, Marty," she said. *"It strikes me that your moral code allows you to freely love men who are already in*

another relationship, like Dom was. Can you tell us what enables you to do that?"

"You're asking about my moral code, Consuelo. Sure, I'll answer that for you. I think what enables me to be the uninhibited woman I am is I don't believe in most religious teachings. For example, I do not believe that Moses was given the Ten Commandments by God. What I believe is that a power crazed old man went up to a mountain top and chiseled those commandments into stone all by himself. I believe he was just like a lot of men who want to control people. And I believe that he used those tablets as his theater prop to pull off his act.

"So, great for him and his followers! Whoopee! It's a narrative that controls people and keeps them paying money to be a believer. It controls people to this day, but I don't think it's the truth. It's the same with the Immaculate Conception story. I do not believe that is the truth, either. It works splendidly for those who get off by controlling other peoples' minds and purses; but not me, because I do not believe it is the truth."

"So, by not believing, your moral code says it's okay to disobey the adultery commandment?"

"Not exactly, my moral code says that the adultery commandment never even existed in the first place. I don't believe it ever was real. I believe it was made up by a power crazed man to keep women in their places so things would run smoothly for the men. If the prohibition against adultery wasn't in the commandments, I think society would run more smoothly than it does and there'd be fewer neurotic guilt crazed people."

"Do you feel the same way about killing, stealing and lying?"

"Well, yes and no. As far as forbidden by the commandments, I don't think those commandments ever existed in the first place either; however, there are secular laws that forbid those things and I feel I must obey those laws. There's no secular law that forbids

consenting adults from having sex, but there are laws that say we may not kill, steal, or lie."

"I see. Thank you, Marty. Can you share with my readers what events most shaped your life choices?"

"Oh, sure, first there was Father's death and Mother's decision to abandon me. Those were horrific experiences. They turned me toward promiscuity and sex as replacements for parental love. Then my quest for sex developed into my nympho addiction. I suppose that's it in a nutshell."

"How about events that affected society in general, did anything in particular shape your attitude?"

"I think so. I still vividly remember the day Kennedy was assassinated. I was on a sailboat in the Chesapeake Bay. We heard about it on the radio. I was terribly frightened. I knew something was very wrong about that assassination. I remember crying and being grief stricken. I felt that somehow his death would hurt me, too. Shortly afterwards the Naval Academy started shooting off those terrible huge guns that they have. Those huge naval guns make a horrifyingly loud boom, like they could blow the entire world apart. Well, those cannons went off every fifteen minutes, or so; all day long until it got dark. I started trembling and crying because I knew the world had changed. I was terrified. My boyfriend Darren had to hold me to keep me calm.

'I was terrified because I felt that there was something very big going on that would affect my life and I didn't understand it. I'll never forget those cannon booms. I felt the concussion waves from those booms, way out on the water. It was horrible thinking about what those naval guns could do to people. It was only days or weeks later that I started making sense of it all.

'Those future Naval and Marine Corps officers were frustrated by Kennedy's death too; and with every boom of those cannons, they were getting angrier about it; and, they were determined to make *somebody pay for it. Then, later, I realized that a lot of those men were going to go to a place called Vietnam; and basically, they were going to destroy that entire country; totally shred the place to pieces; kill millions of helpless, innocent people; bring down holy hell upon them. And these were people who just wanted to live. They didn't even know there was a place called America.*

"I think that's when I had a fundamental change in the way I viewed life. Up until that day when those big guns went off, I was only concerned with how much pleasure I could get out of every situation. After the sun had set and we sailed into Weems Creek past the Naval Academy's Trident Point, I looked at the Academy's huge gray stone buildings with those green copper roofs; and do you know what I felt I was seeing for the first time, after all those other times that we had sailed past there?"

"No Marty, what?"

"Death, that's what. Horrible, fucking death for the entire world. Then, when we were tying up at the boat dock in the early twilight, I realized I needed to look at life differently. I needed to start thinking in terms of how much pleasure I could give to others. I think that change in my mindset happened that day Kennedy died; and that change in my thinking is what propelled me to becoming the world's number one erotic romance star. I made up my mind then and there to just love freely every man that wanted to make love, instead of making war. That's when I decided men didn't know what they were doing. That's when I started thinking that men should not be allowed to run the world. A lot of men get war crazed. They even mix up their emotions with religion in many cases. They are dangerous to everyone; even to their own people, when they get crazy like that. Men can become totally fucking clueless about life, Consuelo. Women should run the world."

"Oh, wow, Marty, do you still believe that?"

"Yes, absolutely I do, only more so. Men should not be allowed to produce and direct motion pictures either; not the way they make them with gangsters shooting everyone and cars being driven by crazy people; and with stuff blowing up, and all their stupid violent murder shows. It's no wonder our society is neurotic. Children see that stuff. It fucks up their brains. Movies should be about love and sex; and intimacy- promoting adult film movies absolutely should become mainstream movies. Society would become much calmer and more understanding of the needs of others. I absolutely believe that with all my heart and soul. The world would be much more peaceful and loving."

CHAPTER SEVEN

Eating oatmeal every day can become boring. Sex gets like oatmeal if you let it. Don't be bored. Change your lovers, like you change cereals. Make love in exotic new locations too, like you change restaurants. (Rosemary Ness-Bitner, author)

CONNOISSEURS

"Thanks for sharing your thoughts and feelings with our readers, Marty. I know they'll appreciate that. Now, it's occurring to me that you promised to fill us in about your experience at Cannes. Can you let my readers know what the rest of that trip was like?"

"Sure, Dom wanted us to make the rounds in Cannes together, introducing me to about a hundred of his friends as the world's most sensational adult film star and the love of his life. He wanted me by his side wearing my transparent bikinis and spiked heels. Of course, I did as he asked.

"As Dom introduced me, friend after friend paid me his compliments on my work:

'Magnifique, bravo, excellent performances, all!' exclaimed one gentleman as he bowed low to kiss my hand and my vagina through my transparent aqua bikini bottom.

'You've given my life divine inspiration, Madam,' spoke another man who kissed both my cheeks.

'I have yearned, since I saw your first film, for this opportunity to be graced by your presence, Miss Mallory,' spoke another as he fell

to one knee and kissed my hand. He also kissed my vagina and told me he adored me and my remarkable thought-provoking films:

'I have never seen such divinely inspired wonderment. You are liberating many such as myself, who thirst for your inspired commitment to freedom.'

'You are the second coming of the French Revolution!' spoke another who kissed my cheeks, embracing me and holding his kisses longer than any of the others.

'I cannot live without watching one of your films each day. You are my goddess and my idol,' spoke another who knelt to kiss my hand. He also kissed my vagina through my aqua sheen bikini bottom, telling me: 'I worship your vagina. You are my new religion. I would be honored to dedicate my life and fortune to be assured that you can continue making your life-inspiring films.'

'The warm sunshine that lifts my heart glows eternally from between your glorious legs; and the white love that streams from your beautiful sun lifts my spirits to the heavens. You refresh my faith in love more than a newly fallen snow. I worship you and I love you. You are the world's most delicious morsel. You are glory. You are amore. You own my heart,' proclaimed one French gentleman who kissed my hand and then proceeded to continue placing kisses upon my arm, raising his kisses higher and higher upon my arm until he also kissed my cheek.

'Madam,' said another man named Pierre, 'I have chateaus all over France and Switzerland. I beg you to feel free to use them as you wish. Live in them; visit; film in them and their surroundings. My many homes are yours. You and your glorious work give me divine inspiration. Never have I felt such rapture, or desired to be so close to any other woman. I am beholden to you. It would be my greatest honor to be of service to you in any way you please. I only request; no, I beg you, allow me to become one of your Premium Members. Please take my card.' Pierre then proceeded to kneel before me and kiss both of my hands and my vagina.

"One clever fellow captured that iconic photo of Pierre's lips pressed against my vagina. It was beautiful, like the loving kiss to the forehead of a newborn. I heard that photo earned him a pretty penny. It's the one that got centered on lots of tabloid cover pages, exposing Pierre, and causing all sorts of articles and op-ed pieces to be written about him and me. I was simply there with Dom, in the moment; realizing that my intimacy promoting erotic films had achieved world-wide acceptance as beautiful Nuevo art; and not understanding that photo would cause such a dam burst of pent-up feelings.

"When I looked up from Pierre's kissing my vagina, I found this gigantic man standing before me. I recognized him immediately from his appearances at porn show events and in two porn movies that he had performed in with other porn stars. Here he was, Kendrick, the Celt, towering over me. He was at least six foot, seven inches tall, very broad shoulders, and completely bald. He had an industry nickname: Torpedo. That's in reference to the head of his penis, which is at least three times larger than the head of other typical male partners' penises. I'm not exaggerating, Consuelo, Kendrick's penis has an enormous head.

"Kendrick stood there and leveled his gaze upon Dom and me, without speaking. It was obvious that the giant had something on his mind. I believe that Dom intuited that Kendrick wanted to speak to me privately. Dom stepped aside to allow Kendrick to move into my personal space."

"Miss Marty Mallory," began Kendrick, *"It is my extreme pleasure to finally meet you in person. I am an ardent admirer of your work. My name is............"*

"I know who you are," responded Marty. *"I have seen some of your work as well. And I was very much impressed. Please, call me Marty."*

"Yes, Marty," grinned Kendrick. *"Then, would you please call me Celt?"*

"All right, Celt. What can I do for you?" Marty knew her industry well. Celt owned a large film distribution and prostitution services network; but Marty had no idea how extensive it was.

"I'd like to discuss a business proposition with you; privately, if I may; and, of course, if Dom here has no objection."

Dom looked at Marty and shrugged his shoulders, indicating that the decision to meet Celt privately was hers alone. Marty's eyes lifted from Dom to Celt. *"You may; and Dom, here, seems fine with it."*

"Excellent," beamed Celt. *"Let's see. It is 1:30 now. Let's say I'll have you back here with Dom no later than 6. Is that all right with both of you?"*

"Marty, you're a big girl. You know I don't keep a harness on you. Take as much time as you need." Dom bowed his head to Marty in a magnanimous gesture that matched his words.

"Very well, then," smiled a pleased Celt to both Marty and Dom. *"Marty, let's meet on the rooftop heliport in a half hour. I and my helicopter will pick you up. We'll fly to my yacht. It's only a few miles offshore. I'm sure it will meet your approval and we'll have complete privacy to discuss my proposition."*

An hour later Marty found herself in Celt's mirrored stateroom on his three-hundred-foot yacht. He knew that Marty didn't drink. Respectfully, he offered her a club soda.

"Celt," grinned Marty, *"Surely you didn't bring me all the way out here to have sex. You know we could have done that back at the casino's hotel. Tell me. What's on your mind."*

"Do you know about my business?" Celt took a sip from his scotch and water.

"I know you distribute films and you offer escort services. But I have no idea about the size of your operation. And I have no idea how it works. But I am more than curious. How do I fit into what you do?"

"I am the largest distributor of pornographic films in Great Britain and continental Europe. That's for starters."

"I'm impressed," purred Marty. "Please go on."

"Through my holding company, I operate an extensive network of prostitution and escort services companies. Altogether, I control over ten thousand prostitutes in Great Britain and another thirty thousand prostitutes here on the continent."

"I'm impressed, Celt. I had no idea. So, what does a big operator like you need with a porn actress like me? Forty thousand whores aren't enough for you? You need one more? Enlighten me, please."

"Marty, Marty, Marty," sighed Celt. "It's not about the number of prostitutes I control. It's about the profits they make me. You need to understand that I've gotten to where I am by carefully studying my markets and what I would call, 'The Human Condition.' I constantly look for opportunities and ways to create them."

"And, somehow, you think I am an opportunity for you? What is it that you see, Celt?"

"Ah, first things first. When we are agreed, I will explain why it is in your interest to work closely with me."

"And what am I to agree to?"

"I want a five-year exclusive to distribute your porn films in China, India, Russia, Latin America, and twenty Islamic countries."

"And, why would I agree to that, Celt?"

"Because, as I've said, I know my markets. And right now, you have virtually no sales at all in any of those markets. And, by giving me a five-year exclusive, I will change that. I will make sales happen. I will more than double your overall film sales; and I will at least quadruple your merchandise sales."

"And how would you do that, Celt? And why an exclusive with me? Why not with some other porn star.?"

"Marty, Marty, Marty. You need to respect my knowledge of markets and the human condition. I have analyzed data from thousands

of porn films. Your films have a unique appeal to the human condition. More than the films of any other porn star, your films leave a man's libido in such an aroused state that he is three times more likely to click on a site link to a prostitution service than he is when watching some other woman's porn films."

"Really? Is that true? I had no idea."

"Surely, Marty, you must have some sense of how appealing you are. Your private member services are indicating your demand is going through the roof!"

"Celt. How did you find that out?" Marty gaped perplexed, and a bit peeved.

"Let's just say it is my business to understand my markets, dear Marty. My methods are confidential."

"Okay, I'm interested. I'll give you a three-year exclusive to distribute my films in those countries; and if it's working, bringing in sales, I'll renew the exclusive for five years. Agreed? But I need to understand how this is supposed to happen. You need to sketch in some details about how you'll make this happen."

"Agreed. And I want more than your handshake on this, Marty."

"Agreed."

"Okay. First, here is what I see. Your porn films are far and away more evocative and stimulating than any other porn star's films. That is a given. What I propose to do is approach the right people in each of our target market countries with a simple proposition. I will give these 'right people' a ten percent cut of all the prostitution services my organization brings to their national market, provided they use their control authority to forbid all other prostitution services from operating in their country. Now, in the Islamic nations, there are morality police. Any woman caught offering prostitution services who is not a woman in one of my organizations will be severely punished. Likely, a repeat offender will be decapitated. You need to be okay with this."

"Well, marketing is your strength, Celt. Of course, I'd be okay with it."

"Good. Well, country by country, then, I'll have every one of your films dubbed with a woman's voice in the language of that country. Your films will be available in Mandarin, Hindi, Spanish, Farsi, Arabic, and Russian. I'll begin by promoting your premium porn films. I'll offer promotional codes for customers to get your premium films for half off your offering prices."

"Wait, Celt. I never give my work away for free."

"I do not expect you to. I will personally eat the cost of the other half of all my promotions."

"That may cost you millions."

"I know. I expect that it will. But, Marty, dearest, I believe in you. I believe in the seductive powers of you and your fabulous irresistible vagina. It's my bet. I expect that, once a customer has begun viewing your porn films, he will not go back to whomever he was viewing before. I will follow up my initial promotion with a referral promotion. If a customer refers someone to your films and that referred person buys one film, then the one who referred can earn one additional free film. I expect, based upon my knowledge of markets and the human condition, that your films will rapidly penetrate these new markets and demand for you glorious whoring vagina will race through these new populations like a grass fire over tinder dry prairie."

"And, how will you make money, Celt?"

"Marty, Marty, Marty. I know the human condition, remember? I know that many legions of these new customers will click on my links to arrange a session with one of my prostitutes. I will have already recruited many thousands of women in each of these new market countries. They will be the most appealing prostitutes in each country; nothing but the finest, most seductive, and accommodating woman. As an inducement to join my prostitution network, each

woman will be given five promotional codes that allow her to access one of your porn films while she is performing sexual services for her customer. It's been my experience that women who perform while watching a porn film with their customer is three times more likely to have that customer call her for a follow up session than a woman who performs without an erotic film playing. With your films playing, Marty, I expect the demand for repeat prostitution services will exceed all previous levels of demand. I'm a believer in you, Marty. Your porn films make men want to fuck."

"And you expect that the demand for your prostitution services will more than make up for your loss leader film promotions, right?"

"I don't expect, Marty. I know. I know my markets; and……"

"And you understand the human condition." Marty finished Celt's sentence for him.

"Exactly right. Now, if I may be so bold, would you care to consummate our understanding? I know I would enjoy that very much."

"Yes, Celt. Let's consummate our understanding." Marty pressed her body to Celt's. She kissed him and placed one arm around his neck, while she began stroking his penis with her free hand.

Later, after she had rejoined Dom, he asked her: *'Well, how did it go? Did you reach an understanding?"*

"Yes. It went very well."

"And your understanding?"

"Celt will earn his way into distribution control in many new markets for my films."

"I see. And, how would you like me to relate to Celt?"

"Oh Dom. Celt is mainly a business associate. He's harmless. We merely consummated our understanding in his stateroom. I've made you proud. Yes, of course, I fucked him. I think we both expected that. I must tell you; his reputation of 'Torpedo' is well deserved. The head of his penis is at least three times larger than the penis heads of any of my porn partners. It was a 'stretch' for me to take it inside* *me and past my inner vaginal lips. But once my vagina adjusted to accommodate that huge head, our sex was marvelous. It was unlike any sex I've ever had before. He positioned that head way up inside me. It was like I had this huge ball rotating inside my vagina, as its socket.*

"So, unlike most sex where I thrust with my partner, with Celt, I sort of rotated my vagina forward and backward over his penis's head; and the I rotated my vagina sideways over the head. This gave me wildly erotic sensations. I loved fucking him, Dom; truly, I did. Well, after a time of my rotational movement over his penis's head, Celt began to thrust into me. Understand, he is a very strong man and his thrusts were extremely powerful. Well, he drove into me like he was this huge bull and I was just some rag doll that had her vagina impaled on his monster penis. He went at these thrusts until he finally released in a series of gush-pumps."

"Gush pumps?"

"Yes, gush pumps. Remember the old farmhouses? They usually had a water well somewhere near the kitchen. When the farmer or his wife wanted water, they went outside to the well and pumped the well handle for a while before anything happened. Then, suddenly, gushes of water came flowing from the pump. Well, fucking Celt made me feel like I was waiting for this deep well to be gush pumped. Celt kept stroking me, methodically, for what seemed like an eternity. I was beginning to wonder if he would ever come.

"And then, when I least expected it, he gushed these sudden spurts of semen into me. Semen just gushed out of him like water coming up from a water well. And this happened repeatedly. He gush-pumped me this way five separate times before he emptied himself. It was very sweet. He hugged me like he was a big baby who needed to cling to his mother. That's when I knew that he was beholden to my sexuality. It's a psychological thing that a woman just knows she has with a man when she has it. It seemed like time

stood still in that moment. I realized that I bore some responsibility for the way Celt felt about me.

"There was more going on than his obsession with my porn films that was driving this. I knew he needed this relationship with me. He needed the relationship with me to be able to prove himself as a successful man. That relationship would be Celt's driving force which propelled him to success with his new venture. I understood that. He was not only fucking my body. He was also fucking my mind; getting me to put my good will behind his effort to please me. It was more than the money. He needed me to approve of him as a man. I was flattered by how completely he needed me. I've never been fucked as completely as that before."

"So, where is this new relationship taking you?" Dom's grin was more of an approval of Marty's seductive prowess than any concern that she intended to stray from his orbit. He adored his whore and he especially loved hearing about her amorous exploits. He was easily a hundred times wealthier than Celt. Dom had arrived; Celt was still making his way in the world. Dom knew that Celt could never mount a serious challenge to his dominance. But if it amused Marty to gain Celt as a lover, then Dom was more than willing to accommodate her. After all, he knew her libido was insatiable. He also knew that her proclivity toward promiscuity was what he adored most about her. He cherished her as his incorrigible, innocently immoral, joyous, sweetly lovable fuck bunny. Her exploits and sexual capers and romps amused and excited him. He was happy for her ability to slake her nymphomania this way; and for the vitality and love of life that her liaisons brought out of her. And he loved her for being exactly whom she was.

"Well, Celt and I have agreed to make a porn film together. Based upon his intensive data research, Celt has determined that the features in a porn film which make a male viewer most like to

click on a link to one of his prostitution services are: first, the female porn star's inner vaginal lips; second, the female porn star's facial lips as they express her pleasure with experiencing a penis's penetration of her inner vaginal lips; third, the female porn star's facial expressions as she experiences the joys of fornication, especially her own orgasms; and finally, the ejaculation of semen from the male partner's penis into the vagina or the mouth of the female porn star.

"So, based upon Celt's research, we are going to create a unique film. It will be a silent film. It will show full screen close ups of my vagina with Celt's huge penis entering my inner vaginal lips. The cameras will pan between my vagina and my face, while I grimace as I stretch myself over his penis's head. Then it will show my vagina's gyrations on Celt's huge penis and pan back and forth between my vagina and my facial expressions of amazement and wonder over how satisfying I feel to be fucking such a marvelous penis. Then it will also show Celt's penis as it ejaculates in gush pump fashion onto my vaginal lips while semen from an inner cream pie is flowing out of me. It will present this powerful image of confluence, as if my vagina is the great, irresistible, inevitable, mixing place for male semen; like two mighty rivers are joining together and commencing their unstoppable, inevitable flow toward the ocean. The film will psychologically imprint the powerful imagery of immorality's unstoppable, growing inevitability to dominate human behavior."

"So, no script; no background plot? Just your vagina, your facial expressions, his penis contributing to a cream pie flowing out of you? That's it? That's the entire movie? How long?"

"Yes. That's the entire movie. No plot; no background; one hour of vaginal gyrations, facial expressions of wonderment and a ten-minute segment at the end of semen flowing and Celt's huge penis basking in my vaginal semen flow while it continues to pump out additional semen."

"No hugs; no kissing; no touchings; no foreplay at all?"

"No, none. Just my smiling face; my honest innocence expressing my adoration of Celt's penis while it is fucking me and while it is contributing to my semen flow. What do you think?"

"I don't know. It will be different. I can see where, once the viewer gets into it, especially your sweet innocent face accepting and adoring that huge penis inside you, the viewers just might go crazy over it. What are Celt's thoughts?"

"He believes the viewers will go crazy over it. He thinks the clicks for his prostitution services will go through the roof; break all previous records. He thinks the film will be in huge demand and people will want to have it playing on their big screens while they have sex with his prostitutes or with their steady partners or mistresses."

"He's probably right. It's pure eroticism. He knows his markets. I wish you success with it."

"He's betting heavily on it. He's making a million copies of it available for free in his new markets. And, guess what, Dom?"

"What?" Dom smiled and grunted, wondering what Celt was up to; wondering if the European had serious hopes of edging him out as Marty's most intimate lover.

"He's so certain of the film's success, he's going to get me a gift to celebrate. He's going to the Yukon to kill five mountain lions; and he's going to Botswana to kill a leopard. Then he's going to have this furrier fashion them into a lion skin coat with leopard trim, to honor me as the world's most glorious, most incorrigible, most immoral vagina. Can you believe how smitten he is?"

"Yes, I can. I understand it. You do have that effect on men." Dom smiled a reflective smile.

Three days later, a huge package arrived for Marty. It was wrapped in white gift paper and a big red ribbon was tied around it. *'What could this be?'* she wondered. *'It can't possibly be from Celt. He has not had time to kill those mountain lions and the leopard, or have their skins tanned and fashioned into a coat. So, who could be sending me a surprise gift? What have I done lately, and for whom, to earn a gift?'* Slowly, Marty untied the red ribbon. She peeled back the white wrapping paper and carefully opened the box. And there it was!

'Oh my! It's huge! It's beautiful beyond words to describe it. There can't possibly be another one like this anywhere in the world!' Marty squealed as she lifted her present out of its box. It was completely unexpected. It was a full-length Russian sable silver and black fur with puffed sleeves and a detachable chinchilla cape and hood. And there was an envelope! She trembled as she opened the envelope to read the message. It was from Dom! It read:

'To keep you warm, darling. Love, Dom'

Marty was spellbound. She cried. How could Dom ever feel that he needed to one-up another man like this. Dom was her one truest love. She pressed the coat close to her and cried tears of joy. Dom loved her! Yes, he loved her. She rushed to the internet and did a search. She found the coat! There it was, at Her Majesty's of London, the world's most exclusive furrier. Breathlessly, she read the description of her fur:

'You love her. You love her more than anything or anybody in the world. Show her that you love her. Prove to her that there is nothing that you would not do for her. Show her that there is no gift too great to give to her; to let her know how much you appreciate her; to let her know that she, alone, is the most wonderful and most deserving woman in the entire world; and that you value her love and you cherish her. Go ahead. Prove yourself. Show her you mean it by giving her this unique gift. It tells her what you feel in your heart: That she's the one; your one and only; that you adore her and you want only the very best available in the entire world for her. Just for her. Just for your one and only.'

Marty looked at the description below the picture of the fur. It read: *'Check for availability and price.'* When she checked, what she saw took her breath away. The screen showed that the price of the coat was $12 million. The availability stated: One. After the availability, there was a notation that stated: *'This item has been sold and is no longer available. We have no substitute and no replacement item of this quality available currently. We do not expect to have another item like this for another one to three years as the Silver Russian Sable is an exceptionally rare and extremely elusive animal. We assure you that we are doing and will continue to do our utmost to obtain for our valued customers the most luxurious garments available anywhere in the world. Please check with us periodically for availability.'*

Marty sat down in a table chair. She was in near shock. *'Dom heard me tell of Celt's desire to give me a fur coat. That prompted Dom to search the world to get me the most luxurious fur coat in the entire world! Oh Dom, my dearest, sweetest Dom. You do love me, don't you? You love me more than any man could ever love any woman in the entire world! I see that. I always knew you loved me; but I never, until now, appreciated how much you love me. I understand now that I am your trophy woman; your ultimate prize! Oh, my dear sweet Dom, tonight you shall know the fullest measures of my love. I want to make love with you so much. Oh, Dom, I really do!'*

"Consuelo, I loved my visit to Cannes. A world of opportunities was opened to me. I was besieged by reporters, radio and television talk show hosts and columnists. Everyone wanted to get their exclusive story about me. And I discovered that I was suddenly the subject of intense debate. Did I represent a new low in social morality; or was I the standard bearer for a new and refreshing art form genre that was enlightening the mind of mankind; leading humanity's way forward?

"Some were saying that I was the reappearance of biblical Belial, the princess of wanton depravity. Some cursed me for being iniquitous, in my godless pursuit of mammon wealth; soulless in my profligate

sinful debaucheries. But I felt something else happening within me. I was feeling a presence urging me onward, like a Great Spirit was awakening inside me, assuring me that what I was doing was right and holy. It was telling me that I was tearing down a confining established social order and replacing it with a new, liberating one.

"I was freeing the imaginations of millions from oppressive dogma and showing them that my way was the path to happiness and fulfillment. This spirit within me loved me for my work. It was telling me that my artistic film work was beautiful and that I needed to be proud of it. It told me to do more of it. That convinced me that I needed to ignore all the negative commentary and concentrate on producing more and better films than ever before. I'm working on a new film now. It will be my greatest ever.

"When I granted those interviews that followed, I had no idea how extensively I would be quoted. Soon the T Shirt shops were spinning out shirts with sayings attributable to me, like 'Sex is good,' 'Making love nourishes my mind,' 'Penises deserve to be loved,' 'I crave cunnilingus,' 'Oral sex is beautiful,' 'I love to Kegel; especially with penises,' 'Cum once, cum often,' and other quotes like those. I had no idea such an explosion of public opinion could be released by that one photo of Dom kissing my vagina; but it was.

"Those introductions in the casino went on and on throughout that afternoon with about a hundred men bowing, kneeling, kissing my hand or cheeks. Many of them also kissed my vagina, rubbed their hands over it, and raved about how much they loved, adored, and even cherished my artistic adult films. Dom knows marketing. He understood adult films had come out of the closet and were going mainstream."

"Do you believe that yourself, Marty? I mean are you sensing that adult films are about to go mainstream?"

"Oh, yes. I feel it. It is already happening. Just take the way all those established gentlemen approached me in that casino at Cannes.

Five years ago, men would not have kissed my vagina like that with all those cameras taking pictures of us. They wouldn't have risked being stigmatized by kissing an adult film star's vagina like that. But, now, attitudes and mores have changed and it is acceptable. Those men were feeling honored to kiss my sex. A porn star's vagina with semen streaming from it is no longer considered offensive in any way. It's now considered symbolic of the beautiful triumph of sexual freedom. It's now considered glorious and beautiful and the porn star's gift to humanity. I love doing those scenes in my films where semen flows from my vagina. I know I'm giving an honest salutation to the world. I'm declaring that being a porn star is nothing to feel shameful about; rather, it's beautiful and glorious to whore and help penises ejaculate their semen. It's like I am sharing a holy rite with my viewers. I love flaunting my vagina, all filled with cum cream. Dom says our times today are like the last days of the Roman Empire when prostitutes became honored guests in the homes of Rome's ruling classes. It's kind of like when gay people first came out of their closets. At first it was hard for them. Now, it's not a big deal. Someone is gay. So what? Someone loves intimate erotic film art. So what? Some people adore and idolize their porn stars. So what? It's humanity's progress. Get used to it."

CHAPTER EIGHT

When that awkward moment presents itself and your man does not know what to do, kiss him while you place your hand on his penis. (Rosemary Ness Bitner, author)

The more I see of the moneyed class, the more I understand the guillotine. (George Bernard Shaw, author)

REINCARNATED

"Well, I think you are on to something there. Our magazine readership keeps growing at an accelerating rate, which confirms what you and Dom are saying. So, assuming erotic romantic adult films are a burgeoning new career field, do you have any advice or tips you'd care to share to a girl who's over eighteen and who is seriously thinking of entering the adult film business?"

The voice of Miss Iniquity entered Marty's mind and spoke:

'This is a great opportunity to convert many young women to your New Morality Standard. Make the most of it. Think back once again to one of your earliest reincarnation remembrances. I want you to remember that time when you were Ishtara, high priestess temple prostitute in the Temple of Baal, progenitor of Ishtar, and the grandest whore of Babylon. In your congregation was a man who had married a woman from outside the tribe, from the tribe of idols, and their daughter, Cecilia. When that woman shouted out to her husband to stop fornicating with you, complaining that your cost was twice his required tithe, you pointed to her as your defiler; and

*you caused her to be hacked to death, dismembered, and disembow-
eled. Do you remember?'*

'Yes,' answered Marty's mind, *'I remember. Her morality was
suffocating her daughter. Murdering her was a good thing.'*

'Good,' continued Iniquity. *'Then remember how the father
begged you to spare the life of his half-orphaned Cecilia, daughter
of the woman whom you pointed out to be slain and dismembered.
And how did you answer him? Do you remember?'*

'Yes, I told him my price to spare his daughter's life was high.'
Answered Marty,

*'Then tell me what was your price. I must hear it again as you
said it,'* urged Iniquity. *'You pleased me so.'*

*'I told him I would spare her life only if he agreed that I would
raise her in my own image, as a temple goddess; incorrigible in her
commitment to wanton whoring; and that I would scrub her soul
free of all morality taught to her by her mother; and I would train
her to please all men in the connubial ways of a wife; but that her
ways of consorting would eclipse all forms of immoral debauchery
that he had ever dreamed of enjoying with me; and that he must
never utter a protest nor express a frown at the immoral ways of his
daughter, lest I have her put to the sword. He agreed to my terms
whereby I would liberate her from pretentious virtuousness; and,
thusly, I converted him and his daughter to the immoral ways of the
Temple."*

'Good,' approved Iniquity. *'You remembered. Then recall when
you went with the husband, now among your converted worshippers and lovers, to the dismembered woman's empty home. There
you found idols of male gods for paternity worship and many other
gods: Gods for peace; gods for prosperity; gods for health; gods for
wisdom; and many other idol gods. And then you and your lov-
er-worshipper smashed all these idols. And the husband gave you all
the woman's jewels and all her gold, and all the household foods and
herd animals to honor you for your glorious whoring.*

'Then, when Cecilia asked what had happened to the God of her fathers and all their lesser Gods, you told her that Baal, her new and more glorious God, had come and destroyed them because they were dishonest and weak gods; and that she would now live in the ways of Baal, the honest true god. And, with the blessings of her father, the husband of the woman who defiled you and whom you singled out to be murdered, you told the girl that her mother's ways were wrong; and you told her that the right ways were your ways and the ways of the Temple. You said to her that you, with her father's blessings, would teach her your ways and the ways of Baal.

'And then, that little girl hugged you tightly for she was afraid for all that had happened; and she looked up to you for your understanding and your acceptance of her. She thirsted for your guidance, teachings, and wisdom; and you clutched the fair Cecilia to your bosom and comforted her. Do you remember?'

Marty nodded.

'Good,' continued Iniquity. *'And then remember how you took Cecilia with you to live with you in the temple. Remember how you taught her to serve you and please you? You taught her to massage you with creams and salves and anoint you with the precious oils, and to properly serve you. And then, when she became old enough, you acknowledged to her how spectacularly beautiful she was and told her that your loins ached to know her as your lover; and you told her that it was time that you taught her all the ways of a temple prostitute.*

'You explained to her that the only true way of belief was through the worship of the mighty Penis of Baal; by honoring him with the glories and blessings of the feminine vagina. You taught her the intricacies of all the pagan worship rituals and prayers; and you instructed her in the pagan belief system of fertility and reincarnation of life that manifests it holiness within, and through, and in union with the female vagina. You taught her that the female vagina must always be revered and honored and loved. You explained how

worship services and whoring with the Temple prostitutes freed the congregation from their concerns over trivial matters; and how prostitution worship freed the souls of congregation males from concerns about their wellbeing. You explained that the Temple took care of all members of the tribe and shared its sacrificial bounties with them.

'*You introduced Cecilia to the beauty and pleasures of fornication and oral sex. You trained her how to appear and how to dress herself to be inviting; how to seduce the tribal males; how to enjoy the many different positions of copulation; and how to feel wonderful and exhilarated with her progress through every phase of her training. You taught her to love and cherish her life as a sacred Temple whore; and you were with her in all her teachings until she appreciated that her life as a whore was a special honor. She learned that her life was above the lives of the ordinary women who bore children and did household duties. And you convinced her that the ways and teachings that her mother taught her were wrong and punishable by death. You explained that her mother's death was good and for the betterment of the tribe.*'

Marty nodded: '*I remember.*'

'*You eventually sponsored her to the high priestess of all the Temple prostitutes. You averred that she would make a good Temple prostitute. You promised the high priestess that she would be a great credit to the Temple. Then, you were there by her side when she performed her first Temple rites of fornications and orgies; and she was admitted into the order of sacred Temple prostitutes. You were very proud of her. You and she became as one in your commitment to whoring for the Temple; and, you also became intimately fond of each other. Her beauty and promiscuity pleased your eye and made your loins throb in lust for her. Remember?*'

Again, Marty nodded: '*Yes.*'

'*When you were certain that you had captivated her mind and converted her to love your iniquitous ways, you presided over her admission to the Temple Priestess's Order of Triumph. She was with you when your tribe captured her old village of idol worshippers. You then watched her baptism into your most sacred order. You witnessed her complete renunciation of her old ways as she ran her sword through the stomachs of those men, women and children from her old tribe who refused to convert to your ways.*

'When you observed her smiles of murder lust while she committed treason against her blood relatives and their virtuous ways, you knew you had succeeded in purging morality and righteousness from her thoughts. Then, after seeing those captured men who did agree to convert and accept their lot as life-long slaves of the Temple of Baal, you watched her perform the sacred fornication rites with those new converts. You watched her as she fornicated with each of them to defile their souls' old ways; and you watched her as she took their semen seed into her body to defile their virtuous seed and to symbolize that they would never again reproduce with any of their kind; but that their seed would become absorbed into her immoral ways of sinful whoring; thereby strengthening her.

'You watched her smile as she tempted and seduced those captives who had once vowed that they would never succumb to the ways of Baal. You watched those men clamp their organs down with their hands in their futile efforts to restrain their lusts; only to fail in their attempts to resist the alluring charms of beautiful Cecilia. You judged her perfect in her touches and kisses. You watched with pride as her beckoning beguiled them. You were pleased to see their moral struggles fail, as the rich dark forces of natural lust within them welled up and overpowered their thoughts of virtuousness.

'Their limbic zones shot flames of lust heat through their loins until their members rose in defiance of their will to restrain them. Their penises commanded their minds to surrender their desires to Cecilia and to make love with her; even knowing their deeds would

foretell their deaths. She was so beautiful and tempting that they could not resist her any more than a moth can resist a flame.

'Even knowing that their certain deaths followed their act, each of these men surrendered his will to her, and copulated with her; and renounced through his deed his virtuous will; and each of them clung to her and loved her with all his fevered might in the moment before his imminent death by the sword. You watched her fornicate with the damned. She proved her kisses pierced the artificial veils of virtue and righteousness that men parade for their public fronts. She was as swift and deadly to their morality as her sword tip, when she thrust it into their bellies. You watched her smile into their eyes her smile of confidence that spoke to their minds. It told them that her carnal lusts were more powerful than their virtues or their gods. And that smile, which beamed from her face, assured you that she felt no stain upon her conscience that their whoring had damned these men, by their own gods, to live their afterlife in hell's valley of death. Her smile told you the damnation of their lives, and their murders by her sword, meant nothing to her. Pleasure was now her god.

'You noted that Cecilia's appetite for sex had matured and blossomed and that she much preferred cavorting with two men at once, while on her knees and elbows, rather than copulating with only one man. You felt joy for her as you watched her enthusiasm for orgies grow. She progressed to become a sex addicted nymphomaniac. You were immensely pleased that she now sought sex for pleasure's sake alone, and that nothing else in life held a greater priority for her.

'And your eyes filled with great pride as you watched her exquisitely perform the sacred castration ceremony. You felt heat in your loins while she sucked the penises of the Temple's male enemies to remove all their seed from their loins. Your breast swelled with adoration for her as she cupped her hand to her vagina and then transferred their semen to her mouth as she joyfully swallowed their

semen down her sin loving gullet, never to give fertility to any virtuous woman ever again.

'And you beamed with your pride in her, while she then castrated every one of those virtue loving male enemies; and ripped their virtuous testicles from their gonads; then tossed their testicles into the boiling pot, for the sacred offering meal of your order. She proved herself to you and the Temple sisters that she was now worthy of your Order. She demonstrated that her immorality was as pervasive and natural as the air she breathed. She joined you and the Women of Triumph Order at the Victory Celebration Feast of the Conquest of Virtue, where you and she and all your sister prostitutes ate the boiled testicles and hearts and livers of those men who refused to convert; and the testicles of those men who had become your eunuch slaves.

'After you sisters consumed the testicles and organs of your enemies, you lovingly bathed her in the blood of all the men, women, and child victims your tribe had conquered and killed. As you washed away all vestiges of her own virtuousness, you kissed her passionately on her mouth and you confessed to her that you loved and adored her. You told her you felt great passions for her love. You confessed that she immensely pleased you as a lover. She then thanked you for rescuing her from the prudish teachings of her mother and her mother's old tribe; and she swore her eternal hostility to the suffocating moral ways of her old tribe; and she swore eternal allegiance to your immoral ways and the new morality of the Temple of Baal.

'The price to consort with you skyrocketed. Your fortunes and the temple's fortunes multiplied. Men from distant lands came to receive your favors and surrender their wealth to consort with you. Your pedestal bed was raised high above the beds of all the other prostitutes. Your fornication bed was declared the Holy Altar of Baal; and it was there, before the assembled congregation, that you *performed your copulation ceremonies. Then, as now, you were top ranked above all other temple whores; and your pleasuring ways were glorified by song and dance and offering tributes.*

'Wives whose hearts voiced protest over the price of tithing to you were beaten and bound; their hearts stabbed silent from a dozen dagger thrusts; their bodies disgorged, hacked into pieces, and fed to dogs; and their children sold as slaves. Throngs gathered around. They kneeled before you to praise your glorious majesty, and watch in awe your wondrous fornications; and your performances always pleased your audiences.

'It was immediately after you performed your orgy ritual on the festive feast of the longest night that you had your epiphany. Remember? You were being massaged and rubbed with oils as you lay upon your altar bed. A musician was playing his lute to please your mind and assist your moods. Another artist was carving a likeness of you from white alabaster, when it struck you. The sculptor was muscular and handsome.

'Your eyes were pleased with him. Then, suddenly, a searing hot flame shot through your loins. You had to bed him, right then, at that moment. Outside of any ritual or temple rite, you fornicated with him there on the sacred altar. You couldn't help yourself or stop once you began. Later, the high priestess explained that this happens often enough. She called it the lightning awakened. She told you it comes from repeated fornications.

'That was when you discovered the disease of nymphomania controlled you. You've been afflicted with it and you've carried it within your spirit for all your reincarnated lives; for seven thousand years until the present day. Its affliction cannot be cured, only accommodated. That's why you took the handsome sculptor artist to your chamber quarters every night after that, and laid with him; even after your day of temple fornication rites. Even today, in this life, when you have Bob with you in the evenings; no matter how

much whoring you've done during the day, even after creating orgy films, you feel the need to copulate with Bob every single evening. Don't you?'

'But there was yet one more test you put to your protégé to assure your order of her total allegiance to the Temple. You told her there was one man in the congregation who had only given half his tithe to the Temple. He cried for mercy and blamed his misfortunes on the insects and the weather. He said his cattle had not produced as they had in years past and he begged forbearance. You trusted eyes to speak truth to you and listened carefully what the eyes told you.

'His eyes bragged of his confidence in his worth to you. Had he not often tithed more than required, just to have you, the most desired whore in the temple? Surely, his eyes demanded, you would give him no less than complete absolution for this one shortfall. You nodded politely to his eyes, as if perhaps you agreed with their demand for forgiveness. But you perceived a well disguised and faint uncertainty that lied behind his challenging eyes. And in that hint of fear, you glimpsed an opportunity far greater than the man's favors. Your skin felt the inkling. You knew his lusting for the taste of your juicy peach was as fateful as the lure of Venus Flytrap nectar to a fly. This was the moment to close your trap! You knew he could not possibly be of further use to you. It was time to end the ridiculous dance he tried to have with your mind. It was time to say goodbye to him; but in a special, final way.

'You took account of the man's worth to you in another way. You instructed your guards to hold him while you deliberated what should be done. You decided that a betrayer deserves betraying. Then you had his daughter brought to him. Again, you studied his eyes as you passed sentence on him. Death! His eyes glared their anger and screamed their disbelief at you, for they presumed you held his favors towards you closely in your heart. Alas, his eyes had never, before that moment, glimpsed the deepest heart of a whore.

Too late! Your trap was closed! His lesson, hard learned, would be that a true whore takes every possession a man has; even his life and the lives of his children, while never surrendering anything she can not easily surrender again and again.

'His eyes recovered their hope when you announced the honor of his execution would be given to Cecilia, his daughter. His eyes even flashed a hint of contempt for your proceedings at what he presumed must be a joke. But it was no joke. Cecilia was no longer his doting daughter. Cecilia was now fully indoctrinated into the iniquitous ways of Baal worship. At your hand she learned well the profession that you taught her. She loved to whore. Now, filled out and highly promiscuous, she relished every opportunity to advance her status within the temple. Her eyes spoke their pleasure at your sentence, for her eyes knew it was her opportunity to prove her worthiness to join the temple's most sacred Coven Order. Her face and eyes smiled their profound gratitude to you. Those eyes were eager to seize this chance to accelerate her advancement.

'Without hesitation she stood before her father. Her eyes were cold and uncaring. His were panicked at the unthinkable horror that was about to befall him. Her eyes stayed unblinking and will-ful. She ran her sword straight through her father's guts, then with both hands she lifted her blade to disembowel him. She smiled her most endearing adoring smile to you. Her eyes met yours. They shouted out their glee and pleasure while committing this special murder. She knew this assured her acceptance into the temple's highest order.

'Her father's eyes spoke of their horrified disbelief while looking far away as if to recollect distant past times to savor in his final moments. But you did not allow him the pleasure of his memories. You could not show him that mercy for his defiance of the temple. His snubbing had cheated you. He had angered you. You decided a swift and merciless end to this usurper would set the best example to

all others who would challenge the tithe demands of the temple. You nodded your signal order to Cecilia to finish it.

'Again, Cecilia eyes smiled into yours with the joy of blood lust as she took up the heavy obsidian bladed axe. Her eyes held no equivocation or hint of hesitation; only enthusiasm for her opportunity to prove her worthiness. Your protégé's eyes spoke only of love for you, for giving her this fabulous advancement opportunity. Behind her eyes were thoughts of the fine clothes; the feasts; the celebration parties; the perfumes and aphrodisiacs and hallucinogenic mushroom drugs; the constant pampering by servants, and the opulent living quarters lavished upon the temple's most valued, most revered, sacred prostitutes; and the immense riches of gold, silver, ivory, and jewels that would be showered upon her as a member of the Coven Sisterhood, the temple's most sacred order of prostitutes. She saw herself transported through the nearby villages, her honored way made holy by palm fronds and roses strewn on the road before her litter; the peasants bowing low before their divine goddess as she passed. Her eyes showed no compassion for her father, not even a fleeting thought to allow him the luxury of his memories, before death closed his eyes forever.

'The father's eyes pierced a far away nothingness in their horrified disbelief as Cecilia came around behind his head with the axe. With her full unhesitating might, she swung the axe blade down hard upon his neck and decapitated him. Then, Cecilia's eyes shouted their triumphant glee when she lifted her father's head and danced about his corpse; holding the bloodied head high above her in celebration of her deed; well performed. Before the assembled congregation throngs of yelping, adoring blood-thirsty witnesses, she jammed the errant head onto a spike post as an example to others who might think of cheating their temple tithes.

'Through tells from her blood lusting eyes, you and all others gathered to witness her murder then knew, without doubt, that

Cecilia was fully committed to the whoring ways of a temple prostitute. She had no compassion or feelings for anything or anyone other than her own pleasures. She would advance to become a full temple prostitute of the highest order, easily three full years before her peer group. Service to the temple as a temple whore would be her life's work. She proved she had extinguished the soul of her old tribal ways and was now worthy of admission to your order.

'Young Cecilia, in full view of her father's dying eyes, then smiled her eyes' most comely smile. She embraced you and kissed you fully upon your mouth. She told you she enjoyed the pleasure of murdering her father and proving to you that his life had meant nothing to her. She swore before you and the other sisters of your order that from this day forward, until her death departed her from the earth, she would only worship her sexual pleasures and the sexual pleasures of her temple sisters.

'You felt rapture flowing through your veins as she swore to you that your ways would now be her ways; and wherever you would go, she would follow you and go with you; and that whatever you would do, she would also do. You knew when she took her sacred Oath of Prostitution that her mind had now been completely washed clean of virtuousness. Your spirit and hers became lovers then. Reincarnation after reincarnation your spirit knew it would rediscover Cecilia's spirit and you two would be eternal lovers. Her vagina had become captive and committed to the ways of Baal, and it would, in turn, feel guilt-free and blessed to seduce and convert ten hundred penises to those same ways.

'You felt a great strength and sense of rightness and well being in your loins that night as the high priestess blessed your Order and declared that its purposes and all its sacred acts of murder and all its sacred fornications were good and holy and very pleasing to Baal. Cecilia had proved again what all the sisters already knew, that morality was but a bridge, easily crossed by men, when their whore

lusts invited them to cross; and teachings of virtuousness were but a slender thread, easily cut, when lusts for passion or power tugged upon it. All men raced swiftly across those bridges of their pretentious morality. All purged their moral teachings from their minds the instant their lips touched the lips of a welcoming whore's.

'And then you kissed your understudy's experience proven sex. You made passionate love with her before the other Coven Sisterhood's Sisters of Triumph. Remember how she thrusted her sex into your mouth as her youthful juices gushed and flowed? Remember how she screamed out her joys and thanked you profusely for casting out her virtue; and helping her escape morality; and helping her discover the glorious freedom of whoring? Remember you told her you loved her and now accepted her as a full sister member of your Temple's most holy order? Remember when you held her in your arms and kissed her and cleaved her blood drenched body closely to your own? Remember how you also felt divinely blessed? Remember the orgy of the sisterhood that followed her indoctrination? Remember the glories of that day and the goodness you felt? Remember the countless nights afterwards when you and your eternal partner, Cecilia, made sweet feminine love after your days of prostitution duties in the Temple?

Marty smiled and nodded: *'Yes, I remember.'*

'And do you remember those times, after her conversion, when you and she were selected to lead the temple's blood rites? Remember when you joyfully put your swords through many captives of your temple tribe; and how the love between you grew ever stronger as she performed those rites with you? The high priestess chose you to select three newly born infants for the sacrificial offering of rebirth. Into Baal's bonfire you tossed the purest, most perfect babies; assuring fertility of the tribe's lands and cattle.

'You flawlessly performed the sacrificial rites of infants. Murdering the newborns made you notorious as the most desirable, glorious,

immoral whore in all the lands of Baal. You were acclaimed Baal's most highly revered and iniquitous whore, the one most favored and most pleasing to Baal. Lust for your approval and favors could not be contained. To touch you, to kiss your lips were considered the pathways to eternal blessings and happiness. This was the time that your spirit discovered the uniqueness of prostitution in commerce. Men laid the world at your feet for a touch, a kiss, an invitation to fornicate. You offered only your shared pleasures in return; joyful fornication in exchange for payment.

Marty's mind returned to the present and to her relationship with Jennifer, Dom's daughter. She recalled the time just a few months past. They were basking in the sun. She and Dom were lying on one side of the pool and Jenifer was lying beside a boy on the other side of the pool. That's when Dom first noticed the changes that had taken place in Jennifer. Dom opened the subject with a question:

"*Marty, do you know the boy that's lying there beside Jennifer?*"

"*Yes, Dom. His name is Roger. She's been seeing him for over a month now.*"

"*Have you noticed the way he's holding her; how he has his arm around her and how he's kissing her? And, if I'm not mistaken, he also has his hand inside her bikini bottom and her hand is inside his trunks.*"

"*They are in love, Dom,*" replied Marty, matter of factly.

The young couple must have sensed that they were the subject of Dom's curiosity. They got up and left the pool; only to return about two hours later. Dom's intuition told him that he needed to learn more about the boy and his own daughter.

"*Marty, have you noticed the way Jen dresses lately? She wears very skimpy clothes. She also wears make up like a woman wears make up, with fake eyelashes, eye liners, facial blush, and lipstick. I swear, she looks like…….*"

"Like a beauty queen, perhaps? Perhaps a hooker? What?" Marty finished Dom's sentence for him. But her tone indicated to Dom that she was entirely supportive of Jen's new look. Dom noted Marty's protective attitude toward his daughter's new permissive look.

"Well, yes, frankly. And have you noticed her swim suit? She's wearing a thong bikini. Its napkin isn't wider than a postage stamp. It's barely an inch wide. It doesn't even cover her. And Roger always has his hand inside it. And her top? It's just a string with two thimbles that barely cover her nipple tips. Did you know she had that bikini?"

"Dom, I helped her pick it out. She loves it. She loves the sense of freedom it gives her."

"I see."

"Dom, it's what she wanted. I told her I thoroughly approved. I complemented how it looks on her. She looks uninhibited, free, confident, and smashing; stunningly sexy. Jen has a beautiful body, Dom. That bikini helps her show it off. It's perfect on her."

"Well, I suppose I agree. That's what progressive women are wearing these days, isn't it?"

"Progressive, liberated, confident and uninhibited sensuous women are wearing them, Dom. Yes, we are."

"Well, I certainly want Jen to feel she's part of the new women's liberation. I shouldn't say anything about it, should I"

"No, Dom, you shouldn't. Not unless you want to alienate her."

"Oh no. I certainly do not want to do that. It's just that her bikini makes her look like........."

"Like a tasty, delicious bon-bon?" Marty finished Dom's thought for him.

"Well, yes, I suppose that describes my thought. It's just that she's my daughter and that bikini, and the way she lies there with her breasts arched up and her hands behind her head and the way she's smiling while that Roger fellow has his hand down her bikini, makes her look like she could be......"

"A stunning, drop-dead gorgeous centerfold right out of a por-nography magazine, come to life right here at your pool, right before your eyes. A remarkably beautiful young femme who is just about to remove that bikini bottom and leave you gasping in awe and wonder; taking your breath and your heart away." Again, Marty finished Dom's thought.

"Well, yes, frankly. And when she lies on her stomach, I can't help but notice that her thong doesn't even begin to cover her where I would think it should cover her. And I can't help but notice that……"

"She has gorgeous long legs and very tightly-muscled buttocks." Marty was smiling at Dom. She enjoyed her taunts; noting how Dom was appreciating his daughter's sexuality.

"Yes. It's a look that, frankly, makes a man salivate. I mean, my little Jennifer looks like she could……"

"Take in a man's penis; fuck his brains out; and drive him out of his mind crazy with lust for her." Giggled Marty as her hand began stroking Dom's penis. *'Or, how about this, Dom? That she could spread wide her drop-dead gorgeous legs and invite a man to perform oral; give her such a sensational orgasm that it would join their souls together?'*

"Yes, she does take a man's mind for a spin; no doubt. But tell me, Marty, did you notice that Jen and Roger left poolside together and returned together, after being away for two hours?"

"Yes, Dom. I noticed."

"Do you have any idea where they went?"

"No Dom, I don't."

"Well, I know that this is a little delicate to ask; but do you believe they went somewhere and did it?"

"Are you asking me if I think Jen is fucking Roger?"

"Yes, I guess that's what I'm asking you."

"Dom, I'm one hundred percent certain that Jen is fucking Roger, and I'm totally certain that she is loving the experience."

"How can you be so certain?"

"Because, I'm the one who introduced them, Dom. I know Roger from one of my porn sets."

"What!" Dom sat bolt upright, spilling his drink over his chest.

"Don't get excited, Dom. Please let me explain. Let me take you back to the beginning; about three months ago, when Jen came to me and asked me for my help."

"Please do. I'd like to know what's going on. I suppose a father is the last one to know anything that's going on in his own home. Enlighten me." Dom was obviously miffed.

"You were away somewhere. I was in our bedroom when she knocked on the door. I opened it, and I noticed right away that Jen had been crying."

"She was crying?"

"Yes, Dom. And not just teary-eyed crying; sobbing cries out of desperation. So, naturally, I asked her what was wrong. I held her in my arms and I told her she could open to me."

"And, did she?"

"Yes, but not at first. I could tell she was frightened. I asked her to come to the settee with me and sit down."

"Did she?"

"Yes. Oh Dom, Jen needed me. When I sat down on the settee bench, she didn't sit next to me."

"She didn't?"

"No Dom. She crawled onto my lap, put her arms around my neck, and hugged me. She rested her head on my breast and cried like a despondent little girl. She was terribly distressed."

"Oh, my poor, sweet Jen. What was troubling her?" Dom looked perplexed.

"Dom, I wish you could have seen how tightly she clung to me. I didn't know what to make of it. I just held her and patted her back while she sobbed and cried. She was deeply troubled, and badly

needing comforting. I slowly rocked her, like a baby, and told her that everything was going to be all right; that, together, we could work out whatever it was that was troubling her. She just continued clinging to me and sobbing for the longest time. I kept whispering to her:

"Jen, it's okay. You can talk to me." Then, finally, she blurted out in a pained, wounded voice:

"It's my mom, Marty. It's Mom! She's driving me crazy! I don't know how to handle her. She puts everything on me: her divorce; her anger; her drinking; her lack of friends; everything! I don't know what to do for her. I can't take this anymore. I can't do this by myself. Sometimes I just want to dive out of a window or throw myself in front of a train. I just want to end my life so I can stop myself from thinking about Mom and her troubles. I've tried thinking about horses and birds and hiking and the ocean; stuff like that. But nothing works. She has me so mixed up and crazed. I don't know what to do!"

"Shh, shh, there, there. You are not going to dive out of any windows or throw yourself in front of any trains. You are much too wonderful and special for that. You have your whole life ahead of you; and you are going to have a wonderful, beautiful, and happy life,' I whispered to her, while I patted her on her back. 'Maybe you should start by telling me what's going on.'

"I think Mom is losing it," she said. "She's just become so impossible. She hates everything and everyone; even me, I think."

"Tell me, Jen.' I searched Jen's face, Dom. I've never seen a young woman in so much anguish and pain. I gave her a huge hug and I kissed her cheeks and forehead. 'Just talk it out, Jen. Start at the beginning. I'll help you get through this. Go on, Jen; keep talking. What is she doing, Jen?" Marty's eyes searched Jen's.

"Well, she always wants to fight about everything. If I say black, she'll say white. If I say up, she'll say down. No matter what I say or whatever I do, she disagrees with me about it. Everything is an

argument; a constant argument. I can't even talk to her and com-plete a thought. She interrupts me every time. She doesn't even want me dating any boys. She doesn't like me being out of her sight. She makes me wear these baggy dresses and jump suits instead of shorts and skirts; and these awful clumpy boots instead of sneakers or slip-pers. I can't even have a descent bathing suit. She makes me wear this totally lame thing she found from the nineteen thirties. It fits me like a potato sack. It makes me look and feel like I'm a hundred years old." Jen had begun to air her grievances, but she had just scratched the surface of her problem.

"It sounds like she's just caught up in the past, Jen. Maybe if you talked to her about how things are with your friends and how you feel out of place......; maybe if you told her that your friends all date boys and you don't want to become an outcast......"

"No, Marty. It's not as simple as that. There's so much more going on. I think Mom hates me because she knows that I like you; and because she knows that I like being here with you and Dad."

"What makes you say that? Your mother agreed in the divorce that it was best for you to know both your parents and to share your living with both your mother and your father. She should be okay with you staying here, with your dad and me, half the time."

"That's when Jen gave me the hardest, tightest hug that I've ever gotten from anyone in my life, Dom. She literally began squeezing the stuffings out of me. Then she looked into my eyes and began sobbing again."

"Marty, you don't know my mom. You have no idea what she's really like. She can tell you something to your face and then do the complete opposite behind your back. She can be really, really mean. I mean, she can get mean as hell. I mean roaring ugly mean."

"Well, mean; what do you mean by saying she's mean, Jen?"

"Oh Marty. You have no idea how much Mom hates you, do you?"

I don't know. Your father's divorce decree stated that all parties agreed to be amicable; all parties agreed that friendly relations were best for you and your well-being; so, I assumed and I'm sure your dad assumed that she would abide by that. We try to abide by that; although I admit I have said a few catty things about your mother to help promote my films. I have privately apologized to her in writing about that. But I've always tried to respect her time with you and her feelings about the divorce. I understand that the divorce has been a sensitive subject for her. But I feel that I go out of my way to respect her boundaries and her sensitivities. I've tried to be very cordial to her ever since the divorce, Jen. I think she knows that." Marty nodded her head and smiled. Her feelings and her facial composure were at her most sincere, confiding best. She cocked her head slightly and lifted her eyebrows, encouraging Jen to open up more.

"Marty," Jen shook her head slowly and dropped her jaw, disbelieving that Marty could be so naïve. *"Mom doesn't just hate you. She really, deeply hates you. She even prays that you will die. And she tries to get other people to hate you, too."*

"Really, Jen?" Marty scoffed and gave a smile of disbelief, implying that Jen surely must be exaggerating.

"I'm not making this up, Marty. Mom makes me go to church with her every Sunday. And after church we meet these people in the church basement for coffee and donuts. They are Mom's support group. Well, after coffee and donuts, me and Mom and these people; there are seven of them, five women and two men. We bow our heads in prayer."

"Well, that all sounds very sweet, Jen." Marty looked puzzled.

"It's not sweet, Marty. It's evil. They hold hands and say this awful prayer together:

"May Marty be struck dead by lightning." "Then they say: "Lord, hear our prayer."

"Gosh, that's terrible, Jen. And your mom makes you sit with her and listen to this?"

"Yes; and that's not their only prayer. They also pray:

"May Marty be killed in a car accident; and

"May Marty contract a terrible disease in her whoring vagina; and may she die a horrible, painful death from it; and

"May Dom become disgusted with Marty and her whoring, immoral ways and may he throw her out of his home and return to the sanctity of our church and his loving former wife; and

"May Marty's teeth and hair fall out; may her lips rot away; her bones turn to dust; and may syphilis rot her flesh away and may she be eaten by worms; and

"May Marty's evil be understood for the destruction that it is. May her followers turn on her and stone her to death; and may they bash in her skull; and may they all spit upon her grave; and

"May the love of our lord and savior drive out this despicable whore from our lives. And then, after each request to their God, these people all say: 'Lord, hear our prayer.'"

"So, that's it? They do this every Sunday?" Marty's eyes were wide open in disbelief.

"Yes," nodded Jen, *"and then they conclude every one of their little prayer sessions by taking out a centerfold picture of you from one of your porn magazines. They pass around a basic kitchen table knife, and they all take turns stabbing your centerfold picture. They especially concentrate their stabs on your vagina. Then we all stand up and hug each other and everyone tells Mom that things will get better for her."*

"And they make you join them in doing these prayers and these stabbings every Sunday?"

"Yes, Marty."

"Oh, you poor girl. What else does Mother do?"

"Well, she started taking me to this social worker whom she met through her friends at the church. I sit there and listen to this woman, who looks like a miserable unkept person, while she tells me that I only need one parent; that what my father is doing with you

is wrong and sinful; that a girl doesn't need a father in her life; that she only needs her mother; and that I should tell Father that I want to leave him and you and your immoral life-styles and live full-time with Mother." Jen pressed her head into Marty's breast and shook her head slowly.

"And, what do you think about that social worker's advice, Jen?"

"I don't know what to think, Marty. I'm terribly confused. I've always loved Dad. I've always loved pleasing him and making him proud of me, ever since I was a little girl. And I always loved Mom, too; although she was never as much fun as Dad. I could never talk with her like I can talk with Dad. She was always bossing me around and criticizing me and telling me that I wasn't behaving properly or that I shouldn't be playing with boys. Especially boys who were older than me.

"Lately, she's gotten impossible. She won't even let me date a boy. Imagine that? Here I am, sixteen, going on seventeen in three months, and Mom thinks it's wrong for me to kiss a boy, even though I have several girl friends who have been having sex with boys since they were thirteen or fourteen. It's just crazy, trying to reason with Mom. I feel like she wants to keep me locked up in a cage and never let me become a woman. It's like she wants me to stop growing. Sometimes I even feel guilty for eating food. Sometimes I think if I stop eating, I'll stay a child and that will make Mom happy.

"And Mom especially wants me to stop seeing you and Dad. She wants me to have nothing to do with either of you. She says you are both immoral pigs and the two of you are going to rot in hell. I can't believe that she expects me to stop seeing Father; or you. I mean, why would I give up two people whom I love dearly; and why should I give up our many houses, our ranches, our private jets, our yacht, and all our club memberships? I mean, why should I impoverish myself just because she has become bitter about her divorce? I love her. She's Mom. But honestly, I cannot stand living with her any-more." Jen squeezed Marty tightly, again.

"So, Jen, where do you want to live?" Marty looked into Jen's eyes and gave her a kiss on her cheek.

"Well, I need to tell you my feelings, Marty. I know I'm still a kid; but I can see things. I see how you are with Dad. I see how much love the two of you have for each other; how much you kiss each other; how the two of you look at each other with love in your eyes; and how often you two are always touching each other; and I've noticed how Dad often feels you and squeezes you in your woman places and how much you love it when he does that."

"How does seeing me with your dad in those ways make you feel, Jen? It's okay. You can tell me."

"Well, honestly, at first, when I saw Dad take you in his arms and hold you like he does, while he kisses you and squeezes your breasts like he does, I thought it was wrong and that the two of you were hurting Mom. But, the more I saw the two of you doing that, and the ways you will lie on top of each other and kiss each other, and when I hear the two of you in your bedroom after you think I have gone to sleep; well, then I feel good and warm inside about the two of you being together. But I also wonder about you, Marty. I wouldn't want you to ever hurt Dad. I've heard him and you talking about your other life at your investment firm and about some man named David and another man named Bob. I've even heard you explain to Dad that you love both these men, only in different ways than you love Dad.

"I've heard you explain to Dad that you would consider making love with David your ultimate triumph in business; and that you love Bob in some special, tender way; and that you love Bob so much that you may even marry this Bob some day; and that you'd even like to murder some woman named Barbara, because she also loves Bob. So, honestly, Marty, I am totally confused by your lifestyle. I don't understand how you can love Father like you do; and have designs on this David fellow and have some sort of long-term goal of having a life with Bob; and possibly have children with Bob, as long as having a family will not interfere with your porn career.

"I'm just terribly confused. And I don't understand how I fit into your life and Dad's life. There's so much going on with you; and yet your life is all so loving and beautiful. And you have all these men in your life. And they all truly love you. There's Carl and Fred and Ed and Marshawn. Honestly, Marty, there doesn't seem to be any end to the number of men in your life. Plus, you have your private member service where you have sex with men who pay you a lot of money to have sex with you.

"That's prostitution, Marty. It's prostitution, pure and simple. Everything I was ever taught about prostitution told me that it was very wrong. And yet I see that you enjoy doing it. And I can tell that Father is perfectly okay with all of it. In fact, it seems to me that he encourages it; and that he loves you even more for doing it. But I often ask myself: what is it that is unique about you that makes Father love you so much? Why you? Why not some other porn star?"

"Jen, I think your dad was hungry for a woman to love because things were not going well in his marriage. And he didn't just want any woman. He didn't want a replica of your mother. He wanted a woman who had a head for business. He wanted a woman who had no hang ups about morality; in fact, he wanted a woman who totally rejected conventional morality because he was ready to reject conventional morals himself. Your dad had gotten to the point where he decided to hell with religion; to hell with marriage; to hell with morality.

"He wanted to involve himself with the most promiscuous, immoral whore he could. He decided a good place to find such a woman to include in his life was in the world of pornography. Naturally, he viewed my films. I'm ranked first in the world on several internet porn sites. Obviously, your dad wanted the best that the world had to offer. He's a man of tremendous means. He can afford anything or anybody he wants. So, he called my service and we started dating. We talked and shared ideas about where our lives

where and where they were going. It didn't take us long to see that we were very compatible, as well as being physically attracted to each other. We joined forces in some business ventures; and we are successful together.

"And, Jen, the more we know each other; and the more we understand each other, the more we love each other. It's more than a physical thing with your dad. He's told me that he loves the essence of me; of who I am; of my immorality; of my creativity in my porn films. He's told me that he adores me and everything about me. And, Jen, I feel the same way about him."

"You love Dad, don't you, Marty?"

"Yes, Jen. I love him very much."

"Mom didn't really love Dad. I see that now. If you love someone, you wouldn't treat him the way Mom treats Dad, would you?"

"No, Jen. You wouldn't."

"You'd never hurt Dad, would you, Marty?"

"No, Jen. I will never hurt him. I really do love him. I'm blessed to have him in my life. He's a very special, extraordinary man. I love him more with each passing day."

"And, Marty, you honestly don't have any misgivings or doubts about the rightness or morality of doing your porn, do you? And Dad is totally okay with you doing that, isn't he?"

"Yes, Jen. He is totally okay with it. He encourages it and gives me creative ideas that help make my porn more spectacular than it has ever been. He's even going to produce ten full length films, each featuring me staring in several explicit erotic scenes. Your dad adores my acting in my porn films. He considers what I do a wonderful, expressive art form. He considers it my gift to the world. He's very enamored by all of it and he adores me for doing it. And he believes the world needs more of my work. He's going to be instrumental in promoting the new films. Jen, I love your dad for accepting my career and the work I do."

"Marty, I know that you are highly successful at doing porn; and that you are a notoriously famous and highly compensated prostitute and that many men absolutely adore you. I honestly don't know how you do it all? I want to trust you as a friend. I know that I want to. I really want to. I hope you'll explain your world to me, so I can understand how I should feel about it and so I can believe that everything you do is all right. Because I think it must be. It must all be filled with tremendous love, somehow; or Father wouldn't stay with you. But he does stay with you.

"And as time goes by, Father seems to grow ever closer to you. I mean I can see how he is building his entire life around you; he loves you that much. I now see that Father truly does love you and that he probably could never have a happy life without you. And I hope that you'll let me be your friend and that you'll show me how we can have a good friendship, like a big sister, little sister kind of friendship. Because, honestly, Marty. I have no friends. Honestly, I have nobody. Mother keeps me under lock and key. I can't even use my phone without her permission and without her listening to my conversations. She tells me she needs to control me this way because the world is an evil place and she needs to protect me from all the evil people, especially you."

"Oh, Jennifer, here. Let me just hug you for a while. Everything is all right. Honest, it is. I love your dad very much. It's hard to explain this; but even though I may someday have a life with Bob, I will never leave your father. He will never be without my friendship or my love. And neither will you, Jen. I do love you, Jen. I love you very much. And I very much want us to be friends. And we will be friends, okay?"

Jen nodded her head. Her doe eyes looked into Marty's eyes. *"Yes, Marty. We will be friends. Hold me and hug me close and say it to me again."*

And Marty hugged Jen tightly and assured her that they were friends. She told Jen that it was safe for Jen to confide in her and that she would do her very best to help Jen break out of her confining situation and discover freedom and happiness.

"So, please help me, my new big sister friend. Tell me what I should know about sex and love. I'm pretty much a blank slate, except Mother says it's all bad and I shouldn't think about it. I know, now that I know more about you and I can see how you are with Dad, that Mom is wrong. But I don't know what is right, either. And, Marty, I feel I must be completely honest with you. I have secretly watched some of your porn movies and my breath was taken away by how you were in those films. And, I secretly watched you and Father in the den while the two of you were watching one of your films together. I was like a fly on the wall, looking down through the louvered doors in the setting room of the master bedroom. I took everything in. It was fascinating. You, Marty, were fascinating."

"Really?" Marty's eyes opened wide. She had no idea Jen prowled around at night. She was shocked to learn that she and Dam were being observed by his daughter.

"Yes! You were lying there on the huge day bed, beside Dad; the two of you were watching you performing in your porn film. You were prancing around in that film, bouncing your titties, and rubbing them and licking your own nipples, and oiling yourself. You were putting on a display for your porn partner. And I saw how Dad hugged you and kissed you and put his hand down your panties and fingered you while, on screen, you were taking down your panties and showing both a front and rear view of your vagina while you were fingering yourself.

"You were saying to your porn partner that you were a total penis hungry whore who desperately wanted a penis to fuck you. And you went on and on about how you couldn't wait to have a big thick penis inside your vagina and how much you were going to love fucking a big penis. And then this man appeared. You took down his pants; and he had this huge, very erect, penis. You seemed surprised that his penis was so huge; and then you licked it and began sucking

it. You love to lick and suck male penises, don't you, Marty? I mean, that wasn't just an act for you, was it? You really enjoy doing that, don't you?"

"Yes, my dear friend Jen, who seems to know and see all, I do love licking and sucking penises. I feel all warm and wonderful inside while I'm doing that. A man's penis is a beautiful wonderful thing. We'll talk a lot more about the male's penis someday. I promise.

"Oh, would you? I'd love to know how I should feel about the male's penis and what I can do to make males' penises want me; like the way penises want you, Marty."

"We will, Jen. And I know just the boys that you should meet to help you with this, okay?"

"Oh yes, Marty. A thousand times yes! Thank you. And Marty, I noticed that Dad seemed to adore you and the things you were doing in that movie. He didn't appear to be the least bit jealous about the fact that you loved making your pornographic films. He seemed thrilled to see you lying there with your legs spread while one of your partners was performing oral sex on you; and while you were sucking the penises of two other porn partners. Dad kissed you fully on the mouth and told you that what you were doing was beautiful and that he loved you. Then, after a while, on screen, three men ejaculated into your vagina. You held yourself open and revealed a huge semen pool."

"You knew what you were seeing, Jen?"

"Yes. I've had tenth grade biology, and I've also looked at quite a few porn magazines and online porn web sites; so, I knew you were displaying your vagina's cum pool in the film. But, here's the part I'm not sure I know how to understand. You wore this neckless. The cameras closed in on it. I could see that it contained about fifty wedding rings. Those were wedding rings on that neckless, weren't they?"

"Yes, Jen. You are very observant."

"Well, I'm just trying to understand the messaging that was going on in that film. I think you are the only porn star who wears

a neckless of men's wedding rings. That's unique to you, isn't it? And those rings on that neckless are highly significant, aren't they?"

"Yes, Jen, I am the only porn star who wears a neckless of men's wedding rings while I'm performing in one of my porn films. Jen, to aficionados of exceptional, discriminating porn those rings are extremely significant. They are the essential message of the entire film."

"Okay, well, then I watched while you removed the neckless from your neck and you drenched those wedding rings in your vagina's semen pool. And then you lifted the neckless of rings, dripping in semen, above your head and you sucked all the semen off those rings and took the semen into your mouth. Then you sort of burbled the semen on your lips while you smiled and mouthed kisses to the camera. No other porn star does that with wedding rings and semen, Marty. Just you, right?"

"Yes, Jen. Just me. It's my unique signature. It defines my persona as an unrepentant, righteously immoral whore. It declares to my viewing fans that I'm not about to compromise who I am or apologize to anyone for the marriages that I've destroyed; and that I've loved those experiences; and that, by dipping those rings in my semen pool, I'm reminding the world that I'm proud that I did what I did; that I feel no shame in it, whatsoever; and that I'm more than willing to help more of my Premium Members leave their marriages. Let's say it's my unique advertising message. Okay, Jen?"

"Yes, absolutely, Marty. But would you please help me understand what was happening there, Marty?"

"Sure, Jen. Well, the secret to creating exceptional pornography is to use your body and your prop, in this case the wedding rings, to deliver a powerful, impressionable message to you viewing audience. Each porn star, if she wishes to be successful and in the very top ranks of porn stars, must develop her own unique message. The particular message that I was sending was that my love making and my insatiable, uninhibited vagina have successfully liberated fifty men from

the confines of oppressive marriages. And, that's an accomplishment that I am very proud of. Now, that message infuriates a lot of married women; but it resonates strongly with my viewing audience, which is largely males. Those viewing males take that message to heart. It tells them that I am the uniquely immoral porn star who would take immense pleasure in facilitating the destruction of their marriages. They see, by the fifty rings, that I'm perfectly capable of delivering on my implied promise; and that I relish the opportunity of doing it again. So, if they are willing to pay my price and engage me, I'm more than willing to be the unapologetic, shameless, cheerful, sinful destroyer of their marriage.

"And my message encourages my viewing fans to join these fifty liberated men in rejecting marriage in favor of choosing an immoral lifestyle based upon freedom, honesty in the relationship; and respect for the human need for love and pleasure, and acceptance of the need for variety in relationships."

"And marriages and morality do not stand a chance against your whoring ways, do they, Marty?"

"No, Jen, mostly, they really don't. Once I can get a man's penis into my mouth or into my vagina, it's highly unlikely that his marriage will survive. Once a man chooses me as his sex partner over his wife, it's extremely unlikely that he will ever go back to her."

"And why is that, Marty? Can you explain what takes place in a man that makes him decide to leave his wife for you?"

"Sure, Jen. It begins with the porn films. I use the rings as my prop to stimulate the male penal gland at the base of the brain's amygdala gland. The imagery I used was designed to switch on the male viewers' limbic zone in their brains. That's the portion of the brain that makes the males' penises become erect. It's the psychological driver that makes the males crave sex. When it is successfully activated, which happens when males watch my porn films, it creates an unstoppable urge within the males' minds. They become out

of their minds crazed to make love with me. That's what drives the sales of my films and the many requests for a prostitution contact with me. That's when they call my Premium Member Service.

"Jen, in that film, I was psychologically assuring my viewers that it's perfectly normal and healthy for them to leave a marriage that they find oppressive; and that they should have no inhibitions about calling me, or clicking on one of my sponsors' advertisements for prostitution services. By burbling the semen and blowing kisses to the camera, I was whipping the males' sex drive into an erotic frenzy; and intimating that I wanted them to call my service; that I wanted to help them leave their marriages; and that I very much looked forward to fucking them."

"*I see,*" Jen nodded in acceptance of all she'd heard. "*Then, tell me, honestly, Marty: was the wedding ring that Mom gave to my dad one of those rings you had on your neckless? Did you drop Dad's wedding ring into your semen pool?*"

"*Yes, Jen. You dad's ring is on my neckless.*"

"*And, does Dad know that his wedding ring is on your neckless and that you dip his wedding ring into your semen pool?*"

"*Yes, Jen. He knows.*"

"*And he's okay with you doing that?*"

"*Oh, yes Jen. He's more than perfectly okay with it. He's told me that he feels highly honored that his wedding ring gets bathed in my semen pools. He's often told me that my vagina is the perfect place for his wedding ring; and that it's the perfect repository and final resting place for his former marriage. He's very pleased to watch me doing that with his ring. He's told me several times that my semen pool is an iconic holy place; and my dipping of the rings there represents the ultimate triumph of human love over institutional oppression. He's often complemented me on that scene in my films.*

"*He's told me that it is breakthrough, breathtaking roman-tic intimate artistry, and exceptionally clever, expressive erotic communicative work. He's said that, while some people may think it is immoral and wicked, he believes it unifies his human soul with mine in mutual consent and purpose in our lives. He's told me that every time I perform that scene, he adores me even more than he adored me before. He loves the scene. He's held me and kissed me while he paused and replayed that scene at least a hundred times. He tells me that I'm very courageous and uninhibited to perform that scene and that he loves and respects me for doing it."*

"Yes, I could see that he does. It's like that scene is a declaration by Marty that she's releasing her formerly married lovers into a new, immoral life with her. Honestly, Marty, until you've just explained it from Dad's point of view, as you just have, I felt badly about that scene; because I thought that Dad's wedding ring was likely on your neckless and I knew that his marriage to my mom resulted in me being born. And I felt that, by loving you and your pornography, Dad was choosing to reject me. So, I'm glad that you explained it as a psychological breaking free of an oppressive marriage."

"Jen, you better than anyone can see what's best for your father. Tell me what you see." Marty looked deeply, searchingly, into Jen's eyes. She understood that it was critical to their relationship that Jen give her an honest answer.

"Well, Marty. I do see both sides of things. And I have come to understand that Dad's relationship with you is what's best for him. You have no idea how hard it is to live with Mom, Marty. She's always drinking vodka. She's always ready to argue with everybody at the drop of a hat. She rants and raves around the house and in grocery stores and shopping malls. It's embarrassing. And she's always cursing: God damn this and fuck that. And then, at night, she sometimes breaks out into these horrifying screams. And then she throws things. Sometimes she'll break a few plates by throwing them against the wall; or she'll smash them on the floor. And then she'll cry. I've told her that she should see a therapist to help her get on with her life; but she just tells me to fuck off."

"I'm very sorry, Jen."

"Don't be sorry, Marty. It's not your fault that Father called you after seeing one of your films. He approached you. He was attracted to you. If it wasn't you, I believe it would have been someone else. Dad was simply ready to leave Mom and move on with his life. The two of them had simply grown apart; or, rather, Dad continued growing and Mom just couldn't keep up with him; or she didn't want to. Mom wanted the world to stand still for her. But the world never stands still for anyone. It keeps on moving, like those lyrics in that song: Old Man River: 'Life just keeps rolling along.'"

"You have very mature insights for a young woman, Jen."

"Thank you, Marty. I think watching your films and sitting here, talking with you has helped me understand one important thing. Father needs you, and he loves you. He loves everything about you. He loves you with his whole heart. That's Dad. And he loves your porn films and he loves you for making them. I've always believed in Father. He's very smart. I know he must have very good reasons for loving you like he does. I'm glad now that he loves you. And I'm glad that I know you better. I feel so much better about you and Father and your love. I know the two of you have discovered something very precious. And, Marty, if you'll allow me, I'd like to be part of your love. I mean, if that's okay with you, Marty, I don't know how to say this."

"Just say it, Jen. It's okay."

"Marty, I don't care anymore that you came between Mom and Dad. I can see how good you are for Dad; how happy he is. I want you to know that I'm okay with you; and everything about you. I love you, Marty. And, I'd very much like to kiss you, if that's all right."

"Of course, it's all right, Jen. I love you too. Here." Marty clasped her hands to Jen's face, pulled Jen's face close to her own, and kissed her mouth. It was more than a motherly kind of kiss. It was an adult woman's kiss with another adult woman. It communicated to Jen that Marty was very pleased to learn of her love; and it portended that their relationship would grow and deepen.

"Marty, in that film you told your porn partners that when they sucked your nipples a certain way, that they made you come. Was that true?"

"Yes, sometimes I have an orgasm just because my nipples are so sensitized that the thrill of a partner sucking on them gets me thinking erotic thoughts. And that will make me come."

"But that wasn't the only time that you came in that film, was it? I mean, you had two penises inside your vagina at the same time. I heard you shouting out that you had so much penis inside you; that you loved having so much penis inside you; and that you wanted them to both, please, please, come inside you. You came again then, didn't you?"

"Yes."

"And then those two men came inside you at the same time, didn't they?"

"Yes, Jen. They did."

"That was a very erotic moment in the film, wasn't it?"

"Yes, Jen. I thought so, didn't you?"

"Well, yes, I did. And then you dipped the wedding rings into the semen from those two men."

"Yes, that's right."

"And then, after you licked the semen from the wedding rings and swallowed it, I saw one of the men bury his face in your vagina and give you oral sex. Do you remember that?"

"Yes, I do, Jen. Why?"

"Well, it appeared to me by the way that you moaned and thrusted your vagina into his mouth that you were having another orgasm, I think that made it your third orgasm for that film. Is that right?"

"Oh, Jen. I think I had at least three orgasms before the males ejaculated inside me in that film. While my two partners were fucking me in the different positions that we filmed, I'm sure I had at least three or four more earlier orgasms. Why?"

"I was just curious. I mean, you seemed to be enjoying them so much. I've never had one, so I was wondering what it felt like?"

"It's impossible to describe it, Jen. It's a beautiful feeling of wellness with the world and intimacy with your partner. It's like your body is telling you that everything is all right and beautiful and wonderful. I love having orgasms. I try to have at least one every day. If I don't have a partner, I'll stimulate myself, just to have one. They are so wonderful. But when I'm creating a porn scene or when I'm with a lover, like your father, I often have multiple orgasms; sometimes three or more; sometimes as many as six or seven."

"And are all your orgasms the same? I mean do they all make you feel the same way?"

"They are not exactly the same; but they are almost the same, Jen. And they are all very wonderful and beautiful."

"I would like to know how it feels to have an orgasm, Marty."

"You will, Jen. I'll help you have one. You'll see. It's beautiful. You'll love having them."

"Well, does Father also give you orgasms?"

"Oh, my goodness, yes. He certainly does. Your father is a very sexual man. He has a fabulous penis. It's very large and he gets extremely hard. And he has exceptional sensitivity to a woman's clitoris, inside the vagina, which releases the orgasm flood. He's exceptional at oral sex and his penis makes a woman go wild with desires. Your father is one of the greatest lovers I've ever known. I love making love with him."

"Well, I noticed that you paused the film while that man performed oral sex with you. And while the film was paused, Dad seemed frozen, almost trance-like; like he was in awe of you; like beholden to you and he seemed compelled to worship you. That's when he kissed you and squeezed your breasts pretty hard. Why did he do that, just then?"

"Heh," Marty laughed, *"that was your dad's amygdala gland. It caused him to respond to the stimulus he was receiving from my porn film."*

"What? I don't understand."

"Jen, in every human brain there is a tiny gland called the amygdala. It's a hereditary gland from the time we humans evolved from our reptilian ancestors. We have the gland; and reptiles have it, too. It's highly sensitized and highly evolved in humans. When reptiles are stimulated by warmth, their amygdala tells them to hunt and kill their prey; and eat. It's nature's instant gratification mechanism. And it is easily triggered. It impels reptiles to kill everything that comes within their sphere of influence. It's not a rational controlled or thought-out impulse. The reptile only perceives that it gains something by killing that which is within its ability to kill. This destructive kill impulse causes reptiles to kill their mates; even their offspring. They have no attachment to any other being whatsoever while they are stimulated by their amygdala gland.

"But the amygdala gland also stimulates the urge to procreate; to create life. The reptilian amygdala tells reptiles to mate. In this aspect, the gland acts in a similar way in humans. Most humans, not all humans, are no longer influenced by the amygdala's summons to kill; but instead, their amygdales have evolved to become hypersensitized to sexual stimuli. Some humans have extremely sensitized amygdala glands. The slightest hint of sexual possibilities triggers their urge to copulate. I am convinced that your father has a highly sensitized amygdala. He responds instantly and passionately to my slightest sexual stimulation. When your dad observed me performing in that porn film, his amygdala secreted a massive dose of its hormone. It overpowered your dad's limbic system and initiated his reptilian response. Essentially, this instantaneous lust for me took over his mind in a flash. It made his mind become spellbound with desire for me. And when any male's mind is in that state, especially

your dad's mind, it simply must worship the female vagina's creation ability. It's even something more than needing to have sex with the woman. It's that; but it's also an adoration state; like the woman becomes a holy vessel into which a man must repose all his love. The woman and making love with her becomes the man's destiny; his whole reason for living."

"The male feel compelled to worship the female vagina?"

"Yes. Worship with adoration. It's a holy experience for the male. It has that effect. The limbic mind addled male is powerless to resist it. It's what caused your dad to forget and forsake everything else that was in his mind. Thoughts of getting intimate with me swept all his other thoughts away. It made him think only of adoring me; worshiping me and my sexuality; and having sex with me. He received a command to have intimacy with me. That command came from nature. It overpowered your dad. You see, Jen, it overpowers the Church's commandments about coveting and adultery. There's no way the rational mind can stop it. Your dad wanted me. He needed me. He had to have me. He needed intimacy with me at the exclusion of everything else. You observed your dad entering his limbic state. And when he became under the spell of that limbic state, nothing was going to stop him from having me."

"And this is why some men cannot help themselves when a woman tells them to stop, isn't it?"

"I think so, Jen. But this is a tricky area. Sometimes, in some men, they just cannot stop themselves. They become beholden to the female and nature tells them they must have her. But there are other men who disdain or even hate women. They misdirect their frustrations with their lives by turning them on women. They have a 'get even' or 'conquer the bitches' mentality. Those men rape to degrade and humiliate women. And nothing humiliates a woman more than being impregnated by a man she cannot stand and carrying his fetus, which she does not want."

"But Dad wasn't raping you, was he?"

"Oh no! Not at all. I wanted his advances. I wanted him to make love with me. I encouraged him to kiss me and touch and squeeze me. I was consensual. He knew I was consensual. He knew I would welcome his advances. So, he squeezed me like that because he knew that would stimulate me. Did you notice how my nipples protruded when he did that?"

"Yes. I did."

"Well, that was my body signaling to your dad that it wanted him to suckle my nipples; stimulate me; and make love with me."

"And he did, didn't he?"

"Yes, Jen. He certainly did. Weren't you watching us? What did you see?"

"Well, I saw Dad clasp his hands around your waist. Then I saw him kissing your breasts and your nipples. Then he kissed you lower, between your breasts; and then, he kissed you lower still. He kissed your stomach for the longest time. He seemed obsessed with you."

"He is. Jen."

"Well, there's nothing wrong with that, is there?"

"No, Jen. There isn't."

"And then Dad did just like your porn partner in that film. He kissed your vagina. Dad was giving you oral sex, wasn't he?"

"Yes, Jen. He certainly was."

"And he helped you have an orgasm, right there on the day bed, didn't he?"

"Yes, Jen. It was a beautiful orgasm."

"But then, something happened that I didn't understand. Daddy lifted your vagina onto his face; but instead of facing his head, he positioned you to face his feet. Can you explain what the two of you were doing?"

"Oh, yes Jen," Marty giggled seductively, *"that's just another position for performing cunnilingus. It enables the woman to receive*

her partner's tongue fully extended; and without the partner needing to strain neck muscles. The tongue can naturally slather the clitoris over the clit's full length. It's highly erotic and very stimulating for the woman."

"But you and Daddy don't do it that way very often, do you?"

"Well, no. You see, there's a risk to your Dad when he does it that way. His nose is completely shut off from receiving any outside air. Your dad's entire face and nose are completely immersed within my tushie cheeks. Understand?"

"Yes, I think so."

"So, your dad can only hold that position for about forty-five seconds. After that, he can no longer hold his breath and he starts to suffocate. So, I must then lift off of him so he can breathe. And when I life off, I lose a little of that dreamy erotic feeling I'm having. And then when I rest my tush back over his face, we almost, essentially, need to start all over."

"And if you didn't lift off?"

"Well, that could be catastrophic. Your dad could likely suffocate and die."

"So, a woman can murder a man that way?"

"Yes, Jen. If the man can't get the woman off his face, he would most certainly suffocate and die."

"Wow, Marty! That's profound. I wonder if a man has ever loved his woman so much that he stayed with giving her pleasure like that until he died?"

"I don't know, Jen. I never thought about using my vagina and my tushie cheeks to murder a man. But I suppose it could be done if the man couldn't throw the woman off of him."

"But if the woman leaned forward and put her body weight into her arms, couldn't she hold her man's arms down and prevent him from throwing her off him while she was suffocating him with her vagina and her tushie cheeks?"

"*Yes, I suppose she could commit murder that way. But you saw your dad and me. Remember? He gave me my second orgasm very quickly. I never considered overstaying my position. I would never hurt your father. I'm surprised you have thoughts about using that oral sex position to commit murder, Jen.*"

"*Oh, it's nothing, Marty,*" Jen brushed away Marty's comment. She didn't want Marty to become alarmed about the darker thought that had entered her mind. "*It's just me being Jen; me wanting to fully understand things. I get that from my biology class, I guess. Anyway, after you had that second orgasm, Father lifted you on top of him. This time, he moved your vagina right onto his erect penis, didn't he?*"

"*Yes, Jen. He did. We often make love in that position. Your father loves it because he loves to hold me and kiss me while we are having sex.*"

"*And you had another, third, orgasm while Father's penis was inside you, didn't you?*"

"*Yes. Why Jen? Does any of this trouble you?*"

"*Oh no. None of it troubles me. I thought it was all very special and beautiful. Was one orgasm more beautiful or more special than the others?*"

"*They were all beautiful and special in their own ways, Jen. It's the positioning of our bodies that makes each intimate connection wonderful. I totally loved each orgasm. I totally love all my orgasms. I live for having them. They are all beautiful. Why?*"

"*Nothing, really. Your thoughts about life and love and your approach to life and love are so unlike Mother's thoughts and approach. You are totally opposite women. You are more like a bunny rabbit and Mom is more like a porcupine. I was just remembering how Mom always told Dad to keep away from her; and how she was always shouting at him and telling him how unhappy she was. You're just so different than Mom, Marty. I see how much you*" *love Dad; how warm and cuddly you are; and how much you love making love with him. There's such a sharp contrast between the two of you. I'm not a child anymore. I now see the difference between you and Mom and I want to be more like you. I don't want to be like Mom at all; not anymore."*

"Well, you don't have to be like her, Jen. You can be anybody you want to be. I'm highly honored that you'd like to be more like me. If that's what you want, just try to find love in your heart for people and don't be afraid of having intimacy with others. Feel sincere about connecting emotionally with people. And, above all, when you feel love for someone, tell them or show them. Be open with your feelings. And never feel afraid or inhibited about love or about making love. Love is a wonderful thing, Jen. Live your life with love; and honesty. It's not terribly complicated."

"Well, I have some things I'd like to accomplish to start out on my new path in life, okay?"

"Okay, sure. You are sounding a lot like your father; very goal oriented. Tell me."

"All right. First, I'd like to have an orgasm. I feel I must know what having an orgasm feels like. I want to know whether I like having them. I assume I will like having them."

"Trust me, Jen. You will love having them.' I'll help you have your first one to make sure you have a good first experience."

"Thank you, Marty. Then, I'd like to make love with Father. I want him to accept me as a grown woman and no longer see me as his little girl. I want to have a mature relationship with him; not like your relationship; but a relationship where he can accept me as a woman."

"All right, Jen. I can help you with that also. But there are some things you need to understand first."

"Okay, shoot." Jen nodded her head and looked into Marty's eyes with searching seriousness.

"Well, for starters, you should wait to have sex with your dad until you are seventeen. That's the age for consensual sex between adults in this state. If anyone found out that you had sex with your dad when you were sixteen, your dad could get into legal trouble. I'm sure your mother would try to get the law after him. So, let's just wait a few months, okay, Jen?"

"Sure, okay."

"Next, there are religious and moral prohibitions against a father having sex with his daughter. It's called incest. Going back to biblical times, incest was common, even normal. But it resulted in children being born with deformities. Children with disabilities were often disposed of back then. They were tossed into the communal fire and forgotten, or simply abandoned when the tribe moved on. The misogynist religious types eventually became rulers of the early biblical tribes. They decided to prohibit incest to help ensure that the tribe's offspring were healthy. Those moral and religious prohibitions carry over to today's religions and today's secular laws."

"But do you believe in them, Marty?"

"No Jen. I don't. I don't think they are based on solid reasoning. Frankly, I believe they are ridiculous. Today's women have birth control pills. I'll be getting an initial supply of them for you, soon. Remember to take your birth control pill every morning so you will not become pregnant from having sex."

"Okay. I'll remember."

"Good. So, you can see that, if you can not become pregnant, the original reason for not having sex with your father becomes a moot point. He can't get you pregnant when you are on the pill, so there's no risk of having a deformed child. Therefore, there's no logical reason why you should not be able to have consensual sex with your father."

"So, I'll be able to make love with him?"

"Yes Jen. But let me talk with him about it first. He needs to hear from a woman's perspective how important it is for you. I can help you here, okay?"

"Okay. Well, please just let me know when he's ready. You know, I mean please let me know when I can make love with him."

"I will, Jen. I'll set it all up so it will be a beautiful experience for both you and your dad. Okay?"

"Yes, okay. Thank you, Marty."

"You are welcome, sweetheart. Now, there's another thing that I think you need to do before you make love with your father."

"What's that?"

"I think you need to make love with some boys your own age."

"I'm not sure I know how to go about that."

"That's okay, Jen. I do. I know four young men from my work in pornography. They are all eighteen. That's an age that's close to your sixteen years, so I think the law lets you have consensual sex with them. They live together in the same house about four miles from here. Their names are: Roger, Ross, Alex, and Nelson. I've worked with them. They are all very considerate of a woman's feelings. They are all very handsome, loving, and gentle; and they are all wonderful lovers with very exceptional penises. We'll need to schedule a session with Roger. I think he is the most sensitive one. He'll be breaking your hymen membrane. That's kind of like a red shield that stands between you and womanhood. He'll need to push his penis through it. That destroys it. It will hurt some; but it will stop hurting after about a day or two. And then you'll be all set to have sex."

"Gee Marty. You think of everything. You're wonderful!" Jen hugged Marty and kissed her a second time.

"I'll be a good friend to you, Jen. I Promise. I'll give the boys a call and set things up so that you can meet them. If things go well, what I propose is that you make two very sweet and simple porn films with them before you approach your father, okay?"

"How will I make these porn films?"

"Leave that to me, Jen. I have a film production company. I'll finance and arrange everything. All you'll need to do is perform sex acts on screen. I'll be there to guide you through the entire film shoot. And after the filming, I'll finance the distribution. I'll trail your films along with several of mine as bonus films for my film buyers. I'll also set you up with your own phone line and secretary in my Premium Members Service; so, all you'll need to do is review the photos and the information of the men who call to date you. It will be up to you to decide whether you want to have dinner with them and whether you want to have sex with them, okay?"

"Gosh, Marty. How can I ever thank you?"

"You've already have thanked me, Jen. You told me that you'd like to be more like me than your mother. That's thanks enough for me. Okay, Jen?"

"Okay, Marty." Jen embraced Marty and kissed her again.

"Marty, there was something else I wanted to ask about that film you were watching with Dad. I saw Dad lower his face to your vagina and lick you there. You were smiling and laughing the entire time. I could tell that you were loving what Dad was doing with you. You giggled and sighed in the film and with Dad. You love having intimacy with men, don't you, Marty? And then I watched while Dad made love with you; and in so many different positions! You two were just like the many ways you made love in your porn film. I never appreciated that making love could be so enjoyable and so much fun like that. You make love-making fun, don't you, Marty?"

"Well, I hope so."

"And, what really struck me, was that Dad seemed to love you more and more; and the more naughty and more promiscuous you became in that film, the more Dad desired you. I watched Dad become crazy over you. I mean, there you were, lying with your legs open and receiving oral sex from one lover, while sucking the penises

of two other lovers. And laughing and bantering with them about how your vagina felt the whole time.

"I can see why Dad gave up Mom for you. She would never even consider making love with multiple partners like that. I think, if I were a man, I would give up my wife for you, too; even though you make your porn films and you obviously love having sex with many different men. I didn't know, before that night, that the two of you made love while watching you performing in your porn films.

"Honestly, I was happy for Dad and for you. I just can't get it out of my mind how much you loved what you were doing in that film and what you were doing with Dad. I mean, I saw how you loved licking your porn partners' penises; how you loved having their penises inside you and how you loved thrusting your vagina with their penises inside you; and how you lovingly kissed that one huge penis after it came into your mouth; and how you burbled that semen from that penis on your lips and then continued kissing it and stroking it. You really loved doing all that licking and sucking and kissing that penis, didn't you?"

"Yes, Jen. I really get into having sex like that. I love having a man's penis in my mouth and in my vagina. I think it's the most wonderful experience in the world; the most happiness that any woman can have." Marty nodded her sincere affirmation to Jen.

"And I noticed how much Dad loved you for being promiscuous and uninhibited; and for doing all those things you did with those men's penises. Dad does love you for being that way with other men's penises, doesn't he? I mean, he loves watching you making love with other men, doesn't he?' I mean, he totally approves of all of it, doesn't he?"

"Yes, Jen. He does. He's told me many times that he adores my promiscuity; that he adores how much I love fucking and sucking other men; that he's in awe of me because I am a woman who has no moral compass; that I am a fallen woman who does not care one

iota what the moralists of this world think of my behaviors or my porn films. Your dad considers me the icon of freedom and sexuality. He has told me that he believes my persona is in the Avant Guard of the new, immoral world order; and he loves me for it. He adores me for my immorality. And he often tells me so."

"Yes. I can see that now. I can see that Dad is completely right about the way things are and the ways they are going to be. He's uncanny that way. Dad is always right about the future. It's like he can see things ahead of time. And, Dad is not like other men. He acts. He does something about it; like joining many of his business ventures to you and your pornography venues. But, tell me honestly, Marty. Do you really, truly love my dad?"

"Yes, Jen. I do love him. I love him very much and our love is a very deep. It's good, honest love. There's something you should understand about love, Jen. It's not an exclusive thing. By that I mean, that if I love a man, and then another man comes into my life and I also fall into love with that second man, my love for that first man does not end or go away or die. That love continues. And I bind my love with all my lovers with intimacy. And I totally love and adore all my lovers; especially your father. He's very special to me, and he knows that. I truly love him. And I will always love him, no matter what the future holds for any of us. Understand?"

"Yes, I think I do understand now. Love is not like a piece of fruit, is it? I mean, it's not like something you eat or give away; and then you don't have it anymore, is it?"

"No, Jen, it isn't. It's something that you carry inside you. You can share it with others. And you can love many men. And you need never feel ashamed about sharing your love with many lovers. There is nothing wrong with having many lovers."

"I'm so glad to finally understand. I never understood the right way to look at love before. I guess that means that if a boy or a man loves me, he may also love other girls or women as well, doesn't it?"

"Yes, Jen. And that's the beauty of loving in the way that I see love. You never need to feel like you must be distrusting towards the men that you love. All you need to be is open and honest with them. If you have a loving relationship with a man and another man comes along that you want to make love with, be honest about it. Don't sneak around and pretend that the new lover does not exist. Tell your beau that you want to include another man in your love making. Chances are, he'll understand that and he'll accept what you want to do. If he loves you, he'll accept whatever parameters you wish for your relationship. Just love your men for who they are and their intimate friendships with you."

"Thank you, Marty. Now I can see why Dad loves you so much. I suppose when people love each other the way you love Dad and your other partners, there's nothing wrong about your loves. It's all based on acceptance and honesty; never about possessiveness. Right?"

"Yes, Jen. You understand it."

"I see that now. And there's nothing wrong with it. It's beautiful. I believe I want my life to be lived that way. I want to be like you, Marty. I've been wondering whether I could ever have sex like you do and whether I could ever love having sex as much as you love it. I mean, honestly, Marty, when I watched you in that film while you made love with Dad, I knew I was seeing something special and beautiful. So, I guess what I'm asking you, is will you please help me break free of Mother? Will you please teach me the things I need to know about sex, so I can eventually enjoy it and love it as much as you love it?"

In the months that followed their talk, Marty followed through on her promises to Jen. She introduced Jen to Roger, Ross, Alex, and Nelson. Roger and Jen were immediately attracted to each other. And, as Marty envisioned, Roger made love with Jen and broke her hymen. After that, Jen gained the experience of having multiple lovers. She frequently drove her new BMW to visit the boys. Soon she was there every day, enjoying sex with Ross, Alex, and Nelson, as well as Roger. Then, with Marty's guidance, and after Jen turned seventeen, Jen created her first porn films. Marty set up a private member account service for Jen. Soon, Jen had a following of men who desired to have private time with her. The service weeded out the unacceptable candidates and those who might pose a legal or physical problem for Jen. And, Jen began dating men; and having intimate relations with several of them, for money. She was, at the tender age of seventeen, a beautiful fresh face sensation in the world of pornography. And her stage name and films were favorably mentioned in several columns by reporters who followed the industry.

Jen had reached the age of legal consent in her home state. But the consent laws only provided for consent between adults who were not related, and close in age. If Dom were to have relations with Jen, likely he would risk imprisonment and heavy fines. It was time for Marty to deliver on her final promise to her understudy. Marty did her research and made a few phone calls. She broached the subject to Dom one evening, after the three had dinner and after Jen had left for a visit with Roger and Ross.

"*Dom,*" Marty purred, "*I need to talk with you about Jen.*"

"*Is she having a problem with school? What?*"

"*No Dom. She's getting straight A's. Nothing like that.*"

"*What then?*"

Marty related her conversations with Jen to Dom, apprising him of his ex-wife's psychological abuse: The cursing, the temper tantrums, the general bellicosity. She also related the after-church meetings, the hate prayers, and the picture stabbings to Dom.

"*Why, those things are clear violations of the divorce decree. I'll call my lawyers and put a stop to it immediately!*" Dom was infuriated.

"*Wait, Dom. Think for a moment. A legal action would just end up in family court. Fathers never get a fair shake there. Nothing*

would come of it. You'd just drive your ex's behaviors more under-
ground; and Jen would still be stuck in the same situation. Is that
what you want for your daughter?"

"No, but what can I do?"

"Plenty. But first, I need to bring you up to date with what's
going on with Jen." Marty kissed Dom and nodded authoritatively,
while sliding her hand into his pants and resting it on his penis. As
she began stroking him, she also related Jen's budding promiscuity
and her increasing fascination with pornography.

"I don't know, Marty. Is getting involved in pornography a
healthy thing for a girl as young as Jen? Don't we need to tread care-
fully here? What has she been up to?"

"Let me fill you in, Dom. Remember that boy, Roger?"

"Yes, you told me he was having sex with Jen; and you thought
it was okay."

"That's right. Well, he has three friends. These boys all live
together in a house about four miles rom here. I've used all of them
in my porn scenes. They're all very clean, safe, and considerate;
and very loving toward women. Jen wanted to explore creating
porn, so I financed two productions with Jen and the boys. She
made two very sweet, adorable films, Dom. And, Dom, she loved
the experience."

"She's all, right?"

"Yes, Dom."

"She wasn't hurt? I mean these boys? They respected her? They
still respected her afterwards?"

"Yes, Dom. She's good friends on best terms with all four of them.
They adore Jen."

"That's a relief. Tell me about the films."

"Sure. The first one shows Jen at a waterfall. She's naked, of
course. One by one, each of the boys hikes up to the waterfall and
discovers Jen. They kiss her and fondle her. Then each boy, in turn,
makes love with her. After she does all four boys, Jen goes swimming

by herself in the pool below the waterfall. The film ends with Jen smiling and waving to the cameras from her swimming pool."

"That's it? Did the boys……?"

"Ejaculate inside her?"

"Yes, did they?"

"Yes; and she took their semen from her vagina and put it into her mouth and swallowed it; and she smiled to the cameras afterwards; after each ejaculation sequence."

"Oh Jesus, mother of God! What did Jen say about it afterwards? How did she feel about it?"

"Oh, Dom, if only you could have seen her. She shrieked and laughed; and she hugged and kissed all four of those boys. She told me that she positively, totally loved it. She loved fucking each of them and all of them. And she loved swallowing their semen."

"Jen loved it, huh?"

"Dom, love doesn't even begin to describe how Jen felt about it. She was delirious with joy; enraptured. She was very thankful to me for setting up the film. She hugged me and kissed me and thanked me at least ten times. And she told me she wanted to make more films like that, with the same four boys."

"She did, huh? I mean, you're not just putting me on, are you? My little Jen really loved making a porn film?"

"Totally loved it, Dom. She was out of her mind with happiness. It was like a huge weight had been lifted off her shoulders. I could see a new sense of confidence come over her face. And I could see how she hugged those boys and kissed them that she had taken full possession of their love and their feelings. They love Jen, Dom. I mean, these boys all love her. They think of her as their private goddess."

"Whew! I don't know what to think! Well, what about the second movie? You said there were two of them."

"Yes. Well, in the second movie, Jen is wearing a bikini, sitting on a blanket in a meadow. She has binoculars and she is watching songbirds in the trees. After a time, Roger comes along and sits

beside her. He looks through her binoculars at a bird. They talk a while; then they kiss. Then Roger undoes her bikini top and kisses her nipples. Next, Roger takes off her bikini bottom and performs oral sex on Jen. There's a sweet sequence where the viewer can see that Roger is giving Jen an orgasm; and she's loving it. Then, Jen assumes the missionary position and Roger makes love with her. He comes inside her and the cameras show his semen flowing out of her. Then, Roger puts his clothes back on and gets up and leaves. Jen puts her bikini back on and resumes looking at this bird through her binoculars. The end of the film shows a close-up of the bird fluttering its wings and sitting on a nest in a treetop. The imagery suggests to the viewers that two young people innocently met and innocently did what two young people naturally do. It's a very sweet film."

"And you two are marketing these films?"

"Yes, Dom. I've set her up with my distribution company. Her films are free bonus add-ons to ten of my most popular porn films. Jen wanted to get recognized for her work. I've helped facilitate that. I also set her up with my Premium Member Service so she can develop a private clientele."

"My daughter as a porn star whore. You're going at warp speed with this, aren't you?"

"Dom, I'm just listening to Jen. She confides in me. That's very sweet and precious. She's been so oppressed by that mother she has. She's desperate to become independent. She wants to stay with us all the time. She wants to become closer to us. She loves us, Dom. And she trusts us. She's becoming a confident woman, Dom. And it's beautiful to see her blossoming the way she is."

"But what about her schooling?"

"Dom, Jen is brilliant. She gets straight A's. She'll be matriculating into college next fall. She's adamant about completing college. She wants to become a doctor. And she wants to do much of this on her own. She has an independent streak, like her father."

"*Marty, I'm worth over twenty billion. She doesn't need to do this. She knows I'll pay her costs of everything. Have you told her that?*"

"*Yes, but she wants to pay as much of her own way as she can. And she wants to do it by performing porn. She's very determined, Dom.*"

"*But, she's seventeen. She's barely flying under some legal radars doing porn at that age.*"

"*Relax, Dom. I've checked with counsel. As long as the boys are no older than eighteen; and she's representing to the production company that she is seventeen, in this state, everything is legal.*"

"*But don't you think she's a little young to be creating porn?*"

"*Oh Dom, no. I often wish I had started at her age instead of waiting until I was twenty. I mean the level of confidence she already has, compared to a twenty-year-old just starting out, is so noticeably higher. Jen is completely confident with males' penises. She's very much in control of herself and her scenes. And you can see her enthusiasm glowing in her face. She's unafraid. She's delighting in doing the explicit sex scenes. She's a joy to watch; and, she's a joy for the boys to work with. I often wish I had started as young as Jen. I could easily have a hundred more films to my credit; and they'd be some of my best work, because I was so enthusiastic and juicy then.*"

"*Marty, you're still the most enthusiastic and juicy woman on the planet. Don't diminish yourself.*"

Marty took Dom's penis out of his pants and began licking and sucking it.

"*You sure do appreciate a compliment, Marty. Oh, yes! That feels wonderful. And I assume you are teaching Jen how to romance a penis. You are, aren't you?*"

Marty slipped out of her panties and straddled Dom, inserting his penis into her vagina.

"*You wouldn't want your daughter to receive instructions from any woman other than the world's most notorious porn star, would you Dom?"* Marty bent forward and kissed Dom. He wrapped his arms around her as he hardened and began thrusting inside her.

"No, of course not. Only from the best. Only from the world's most fabulous, most delightful, most adorable, iniquitous, immoral whore."

"Now, I'm hearing the man I love, talking." Marty began rocking her vagina back and forth against Dom's penis. She felt her clitoris begin to swell. She knew an orgasm was in her not-too-distant future.

"Something tells me I have not yet heard the full story on Jen. Tell me, oh Goddess of all that is immoral and of all that I love; what more have you two been up to?"

Marty didn't answer Dom right away. She first unleashed a series of rapid Kegel squeezes on Dom's penis. She studied his face while he smiled and groaned in incomparable pleasure. He became putty in Marty's hands when she fucked him like that. His penis strained mightily, achieving his maximum hardness. His penis head touched her cervix. It was all natural enough. They had reached this intense state of intimacy many times before. Dom knew his ejaculation was near now.

As he placed his hands upon Marty's hips, he felt an outpouring of love and adoration, His fingers tightened against her hips. He confirmed that she was Goddess woman and he was merely a man. She held all the power of feminine sexuality. He was as helpless and vulnerable as a little child. His face expressed his upwelling of love and passion; his feelings of eternal nirvana.

Only Marty could make him feel this way. Only Marty could take control of his mind and make him experience love so intently. He became spellbound, captivated by her sensual powers. Whatever she would ask of him, he would do; whatever she would want from him, he would give her. Anything; everything; his very life, he knew he would give everything he had and all his love to this captivating, possessive, profligate, unapologetic, irresistible whore; his Marty.

Marty studied Dom's face intently while she resumed rocking her vagina back and forth against his erection. The honest innocence of an awed little boy's face stared back at her. His eyes looked dreamily into hers, as if to say that he would give her whatever she asked. Dom was ready. She knew he would say yes. It was time to tell him.

"Dom, Jen's been through a terrible ordeal with the divorce. She's poured out her soul to me. She needs us, Dom. She needs us to help her feel worthy as a woman. She needs us to help her find her confidence as an adult who is ready to strike out on her own. And she especially needs us for affirmation of her life and her importance in this world as a human being, with all her needs and feelings. And, Dom, she absolutely needs to feel secure in our love and appreciated as an adult, with all her adult needs."

"So, you are saying that we need to help her take wing; leave the nest, so to speak?"

"Oh, yes, Dom. We do. Her mother will never do what's needed for Jen. Her mother seeks to stifle her. We need to liberate her and actualize her as a woman. And she needs to feel affirmed and secure in our love. I've already done all I can do to help her on her path. She feels that connectivity and honest love with me. And now she needs to know she also has it with you."

"Of course, she has it with me. I'm her father. She knows I'll provide for her; give her whatever she wants. I just bought her that BMW convertible. She knows she'll inherit billions when I die. How can she not know that she has honest love with me?"

"Dom, oh dearest Dom, you are very good to Jen. You are an excellent father. Of course, you are. Most girls would kill to have a father like you. But Dom, you can't see yourself as a young woman sees you."

"I can't?"

"No, Dom. You can't. When Jen thinks about you, what do you think she sees?"

"I don't know. What? A cash flow machine? A man who worked his ass off every day of his life to provide a good life for her? What?"

"That's just it, Dom. Jen sees this powerful, strong man; a workaholic, indestructible machine that never stops plowing ahead through life. Dom, Jen does not see your heart!"

"What? What are you talking about? I'm always bringing her things. I went to lots of her little girl things when she was younger. I watched her perform in her ballets. I went to her soccer games and watched those. I suffered through her violin recitals. What didn't I do?"

"Yes, Dom. You did those things. But you were always a spectator. You were always there in the audience watching while little Jen put on her performance shows for you. And you clapped for her and hugged her afterwards and told her that you were proud of her."

"Yeah, I did that stuff. What's a father supposed to do? What was wrong with that?"

"Dom, tell me. How was that different than going to a rodeo or stock show and cheering for your horse while it did its tricks; or cheering for your prized bull when his handler paraded him past the judging stand?"

"Well, Jen is my daughter. That's the difference."

"You're missing it, Dom. That's what's wrong. Did you have talks with her every day? Did you ask her about how she felt about things? Did you ask her what she and her friends talked about? Did you go on walks with her and your family dog? Did you explain to her how things worked; how trees made leaves and why they did that; why earthworms came out on the ground at night; why crickets chirped in the fall; things like that?"

"No, not really. I never thought about getting into the minutia of her life like that, Marty. Jen was a smart kid. I could see that. I suppose I just figured she'd learn about most of those things in school. And as far as her friends and the things kids talk about, I figured that was her mother's area. I focused on making money. That touchy

feely stuff is just squishy bull shit, anyway. I don't like getting my head mixed up in it." Dom shrugged his shoulders, implying that he wanted to drop the subject.

"It's not squishy bull shit, Dom. It's the sharing of feelings that is so important to a young girl and to all women. It's what tells us that you are interested in our lives and that you care about the things that we see and think about; and about the things that make us happy and the things that frighten us or that we don't understand. You see, Dom, for women, life is a shared experience; and we love the sharing of the experiences with those we love. You men look at life as a battle that needs to be joined and won; and to hell with the collateral damage that you inflict on others."

"And you understand this stuff?"

"Better than you, Dom. This stuff is what I missed out on when my own dad died. He was the one who understood me. He asked me about the goings on in my life every single day when he was home. He explained things to me. He went on walks with me and my dog, Barron, every day he was home. I felt that bonding to him. Ever since he died, I have not had that."

"I'm sorry, Marty. You miss him still, don't you?"

"Yes, terribly. You have no idea. But at least I had it for a while. Jen has never had that closeness to you, Dom. She has a void that's even greater than mine. I feel for her. I'm doing everything I can to help her compensate for not having that closeness to you. I truly am. But I can't do it all. I need your help."

"What can I do at this late stage in Jen's life? She's not a little girl anymore."

"That's your misunderstanding talking again, Dom. In Jen's heart and soul, there's still a little girl inside of her, who is crying out desperately to be loved by her father."

"Well, I do love her, Marty. You know that. What am I supposed to do?"

CHAPTER NINE

You can't just jump into debauchery one night and expect to get the hang of it by morning. It takes years. (Jennifer Crusie, Strange Bedpersons)

Those among us who are unable to deceive themselves have invented vice and refined debauchery, which is another way of laughing at God and paying homage, immodest homage, to beauty. (Guy de Maupassant)

Despairing of love and of chastity, I at last bethought myself of debauchery, a substitute for love, which quiets the laughter, restores silence, and above all, confers immortality. (Albert Camus, The Fall)

If you are a man who has never made love with a porn star, nor tasted her wonderous pleasures, are you then also a man who has never ridden a thoroughbred race horse, nor driven a formula one race car? And have you never once sipped the finest spirits or wines; never tasted the choicest filets; never allowed your eyes to feast upon the finest art; never allowed your ears to appreciate the best symphonies, or jazz; never allowed yourself to embrace the immersive wonders of the oceans or gazed upon the exhilarating Rocky Mountains? Good heavens, man! Do you believe yourself unworthy of life's finest joys? Is it not time to experience wondrous pleasures? After all, you are a man! (Rosemary Lightfoot Ness-Bitner, Author)

INFERNOSS DECADO

"I'll help you with this, Dom. I'll tell you what you need to do. But first I need to tell you what Jen and I have done. Your little Jen is an extremely sensitive and brilliant woman. And she desperately needs to feel that you understand her needs and what she's decided to do with her life; and that you fully approve. But not that your approval is key to her knowing that you love her, Dom. She needs to feel it through the closeness she has with you; that closeness that she has missed all these years, okay?"

"Okay, I guess? I don't know where this is leading, Marty? So, tell me what you and Jen have done.'

'We've done some market analysis. We've determined that there's an untapped market for explicit erotic pornography, offered to high net worth and high-income individuals, corporate, foundation, sports, entertainment, and political leaders in a highly discreet, private, exclusive venue."

"Huh?"

"Dom, we've done our homework. Society has bifurcated into haves and have nots. Most people, regardless of wealth, income, or status, love pornography. Jen and I decided that our challenge was to provide an exclusive venue, for those who could afford to pay, where aficionados of premium explicit porn would be willing to congregate with others of like means and minds. By creating the right venue, we believe we can reach the necessary critical mass of cash flows to sustain a superior, premium experience for our target market audience."

"You're going to show movies to an exclusive audience? Why? They can watch porn at home."

"More than movies, Dom. We intend to immerse our audience in the porn experience; make it a lived and unforgettable experience; something they will rave about and want to repeat on a regular

basis; like some viewers will watch porn daily, we believe some in our exclusive target audience will become hopelessly addicted to the experience and will pay to repeat it often."

"So, where are you taking this idea? What have you done so far?"

"We bought a villa on the Mediterranean coast near Barcelona. We've gotten all the permits and all the local agreements necessary to offer gambling, prostitution, liquor, and recreational drugs. I've invested five million to buy the place and another thirty million to do renovations, including a heated swimming pool, an indoor theater with stage and lighting effects; and we are presently adding a hotel wing. I've made all the arrangements and agreements for booking and hotel management service. I've contracted with Celt to have prostitutes available during all our exclusive bookings. I've arranged with a casino in Nevada to provide gambling management and personnel. I've personally licensed retail gift shop space from Jen, for my gift shop that carries our premium bikini line and linge- rie lines as well as sex toys and props for BDSM.

"Jen, myself, and Roger, Ross, Alex, and Nelson have carefully reviewed the porn films of the top thousand ranked women. We decided which fifty girls aroused and stimulated the male libido best. From that list of fifty, we've arranged bookings in our private theater for live, on stage, with audience participation, porn performances for the first twelve months."

"So, this will be on a charter basis? This club will be a flagship?"

"That's the marketing emphasis. But we also have exclusive individual memberships where our members are given passwords on their mobile phones at the front door. The casino people manage that as part of their security services."

"I see. Sounds like you've thought of everything. Has the club got a name?"

"Jen named it. It's the 'Infernoss Decado,' Latin for 'Flames of Decadence.' She's also designed and posed for the enterprise logo.

Her artist created a beautiful painting of Jen's vagina, held open, displaying a white semen pool with a man's wedding ring floating on the semen. The words surrounding the picture say: 'Gloria Est Immorality,' or 'Immorality is Glorious.' The restaurants in the club and the lounge at the club's bar will all have napkins featuring the logo; as will the hotel's bathrobes, linens, towels, and washcloths. The club's glassware and the glasses from the bar also bear the logo. The idea is to promote immoral promiscuous behavior as accepted, normal and encouraged."

"My little Jen. Who'd have thought that she'd go all in on immorality; follow so closely in your footsteps like this, with the mother that she's had?"

Marty grinned sheepishly, shook her head slowly while kissing Dom and softly stroking his penis. *"I'm helping her rebound from her mother's oppression. I'm helping her claim her own life, Dom. It's what she wants. I'm her enabler. Dom. I plead guilty as sin. I corrupted your sweet innocent daughter. Are you going to whip me; cast me out of the kingdom; ban me from your chambers?"*

"Of course not, you adorable, incorrigible whore. Jen had no chance at a meaningful life the way her mother stifled her. You've saved her from her mother's drowning moralizing clap-trap and phobias. You've managed her transition to becoming a mature, aware, thinking, consciously competent woman of the world. I see how she's developed into a good decision maker. I see how she's gained the correct perspective on moral and immoral behaviors; and how she's gained the necessary self confidence in her own decisions to make good ones; and for the right reasons. Yes, I admit I was first taken aback when I learned she was making porn films.

"I thought doing porn would lead to her ruin. But thanks to your help, she's learned how to manage it, leverage that activity into opportunities; and find that something within herself, that confidence and assuredness, that security in liking who she is, in her

own skin. What helped me cross over from skepticism to pride in her decision to create porn was the realization that kids love to fuck.

"I said to myself: Dom, either your precious daughter is going to live by her mother's rules where she'll end up not knowing what she's doing; sneaking around with some stupid love-struck boy, and ruining her life and her self-esteem by getting herself pregnant; or, by paying attention to Marty and learning from Marty's experiences, she'll get a thorough understanding of the world of sex, men, and relationships. She'll learn how to manage herself, her beaus, and her affairs. She'll be in control of events, instead of reacting to them. And, no doubt, she'll learn that sex is wonderful and enjoyable. I've watched her films. Speaking as a man and not as her father, I must compliment you, Marty. She's got it. She knows how to romance the cameras and dangle her sex appeal. She drives those four boy friends of hers out of their minds crazy, doesn't she?"

"Oh Dom, I'm so glad you see the positives of what Jen and I have done. Thank you for your confidence in Jen and in me. And yes, she does drive those little boys wild! They cannot get enough of her." Marty undid Dom's pants, took out his penis and began sucking it. She felt like a kitten had awakened inside of her. She felt like purring. Dom's approval always warmed Marty in this way. She loved hearing his compliments. She adored his liberal mind set and openness to new developments. Dom quickly empathized with a woman's perspective and feelings like no other man could. And now, she wanted to show her appreciation. She wanted sex.

"Marty," Dom chuckled, *"I see where this is going. And I love how we are going to end up fucking our morning away. But before you slip my little friend inside you, my love, would you answer one question that perplexes me, please?"*

"Sure, Dom. What is it?" Marty rubbed the head of his penis against her outer lips. She was already hot, wet, and slippery. She stroked his penis slightly faster now; implying that her libido was

anxious to engage him in her pleasures; and that she didn't wish to be forestalled or denied.

"It's the Spain thing, Marty. Why did you two decide to site the Infernoss Decado in Spain? I mean, why not Las Vegas? Why not Paris? Why not on a yacht that could keep it offshore? I know you, Marty. I know you think of everything. But I cannot, for the life of me, think my way through your reasoning. Why did you choose Spain?"

Dom got his question out. Now he succumbed to Marty's desires. With a very slight uplift of his pelvis, his penis found its way past her outer lips and into the firm clasp of her inner lips. Her vagina was the most delightful place his penis had ever known. This morning's slide into conjugal bliss confirmed what his little friend had come to adore and appreciate. Dom clasped his huge arms around Marty's waist while he pushed his little friend deeper into her love channel: *"I love you, woman. I love you more than any man has ever loved any woman. You know that's the truth, don't you? Forgive me for loving you so much."*

"Yes, Dom. I know how much you love me. And I appreciate your love. And I love you more than any man I have ever loved. You know that, don't you?" Marty ran her fingers through Dom's hair and squeezed his face tightly against her breasts.

"Yes, I know; and I believe you. And I think I must not be the only man you have spoken those words to; but I don't care. I love you anyway. Now, tell me what is so wonderful about Spain?"

Dom began sucking Marty's nipple while his powerful hands clasped her ass and pulled her hips closely against his groin. His penis found its way deeper; thrilling to the touches of the thousands of her sensitized nerve endings, inside her vagina; delighted in its head touching the opening of her cervix; and intuitively understanding that coital intimacy and the explosions of their mutual orgasms was close at hand.

"Dom, my dearest, sweetest love. It was Jen's decision to site it in Spain. I have contracted with the club to perform live porn there two weeks every quarter for the next year. Live porn will be the signature drawing card of the club. You'll see. I've also worked to select and contract seventy-two other porn stars to come to the club and perform live porn. Jen's club will be the rave of the in-crowd. But it is Jen's club, Dom; not mine. It's important to her that she is the one who explains why she sited the club in Spain."

"So, when will she tell me?"

Dom frowned slightly. He didn't like being kept in the dark about things, especially as they pertained to his daughter. But his frown quickly disappeared and turned into a blissful smile. Marty had begun flowing; and the warn gush from her flow triggered his little friend to release. He was flowing a tremendous volume of semen into Marty's vagina. He again buried his face in her breasts while whispering:

"I love you so much more than I love God. You know that, don't you?"

"I know, Baby. I know. And I promise you this: I will always give you better sex than God does. Okay, Baby?"

Dom nodded his head without removing his face from between her breasts. He knew that Marty had control of his emotions, especially at times like this. He kissed her breasts while he waited patiently for her to reveal when he would learn the mysterious reason why the Infernoss Decado Club was on Spanish soil.

"We're going to Spain next week, Dom. I'm scheduled to perform live, on stage porn on the club's opening night. Jen thought that, during one of the two nights while I was performing; instead of watching me, you and she could have a quiet dinner together at the club's exclusive four table restaurant. You will have the entire restaurant to yourselves. She'd like to use the occasion of the club opening

to tell you the reason for Spain. And she wants to do that where she can be alone with you; in private."

Dom's lips found Marty's other nipple and began nibbling and sucking it. He now understood that, whatever Jen's reasoning was for Spain, it would be profound. Now he did what he was so skilled at doing. He summoned his talent for focusing and concentrating on the task at hand, like no other man on Earth could do. He knew he was, somehow, mysteriously, beholden to this illusive, incorrigible, and loving sex goddess. He loved her beyond all his abilities to describe or express to her how deeply he cared for her or how profoundly grateful he was to have her in his life. He knew he could best express his feelings to her now, in these precious moments, by lovingly coaxing her deliciously adorable nipple until he stimulated her release of a second orgasm.

"Oh, Dom, you dear, beautiful man. You are doing something wonderful! I'm coming again! You're taking my mind away to someplace it rarely goes; and I am loving it! Oh, I'm really flowing, Dom. Please keep doing what you're doing. I love you, Dom. Oh, it feels soooo good! I'm coming!"

"Yes; and I love you, Marty,"

Dom whispered as he paused briefly from his licking and sucking. He kissed her fully on her mouth while his fingers found her clitoris and rapidly stroked it to help her continue her orgasmic flow. He was delighted to hear her squealing in delight and begging him for more. In his thoughts he said to himself:

"There's nothing more wonderous in this entire world than a glorious porn star who truly loves you." And then, whispering aloud, between his kisses: *"And very soon, my dearest love, we'll be leaving for Spain!"*

Jen's entourage of Marty, Dom, Roger, Ross, Alex, and Nelson arrived at her Infernoss Decado Club two days before its grand opening. Dom and Jen checked with the individual management staffs for hotel, casino, gift shop, swim, and spa managements; programming management for erotic films and live pornographic shows; and with the concierge for guest and prostitution services. They assured themselves that everything was perfect and ready for the Club's grand opening. Dom was particularly impressed that the club's twenty closed circuit wide screen televisions would each continuously play different porn films from the world's top ranked porn stars. When Dom and Jen perused the reservation list, they recognized many high profile corporate and political people who had committed themselves to stays of one to two weeks.

"I never would have guessed that the demand for exclusive high end prostitution services was this widespread," commented Dom.

"Father, if our research is anywhere near accurate, we are only now beginning to scratch the surface of it. By all indications, our low-key brochure mailings and emails to political elites were highly successful. If all goes according to my marketing plan, word of mouth will ensure repeat bookings and an expanding market."

"And then, what will you do for an encore?"

"Oh Daddy," chuckled Jen, *"I'm already researching the logistics for siting Decado clubs in Germany and Italy, where the age of con-sent is fourteen; and in Japan where the age of consent is thirteen. I already have three offshore islands and a chartered yacht where our club members can receive private services. I'm having discussions with Celt to procure one hundred underaged girls for each of our future clubs. Each girl must prove she is promiscuous by showing us a film of her having sexual relations with at least two men or boys, as well as a release from liability signed by one of her parents. I'm also studying acquiring a full-sized yacht and modifying it to site a replica of the Infernoss Decado offshore, near Miami. The age of consent for our offshore girls is sixteen."*

"And Celt thinks he can get you a steady supply of girls?"

"Absolutely. He offers successful applicants a ten thousand dollar signing bonus for a six-month commitment; plus, free dining at the clubs and three hundred dollars per half hour of client contact time; plus, half our club charge for her intimacy time; plus, free medical care, and psychological counseling."

"Why shrink time?"

"Old boy friends. Some of them can't cope with their sweethearts doing prostitution. They lay guilt trips on the girls. The shrinks help the girls get over that. Also, some parents try to lay on religious guilt trips. Our shrinks help the girls keep their proper perspective."

"And you come out ahead on your money with all those costs?"

"The club charges a minimum of five hundred dollars per half hour of ordinary contact time. Our premium porn stars fetch three to five thousand dollars per half hour of intimacy time."

"Twat time?"

"That's what Celt calls it when a girl is engaged with a club member, through his appointment with the prostitution concierge, for one of our prostitutes to place his penis in her mouth or her vagina."

"That half hour rate for one of your premium porn stars; isn't that a bit pricy?"

"Not at all, Dad. These are the crème de la crème of the hottest, slipperiest, youngest vaginas available anywhere in the world; and the most fantastic, innocent looking girls on the planet. The best obtainable are only for the well-heeled; not for bargain shoppers."

"I see. And how is the girl is paid?"

"Half her rate; plus, her appointment visitor is also encouraged to tip her. Some girls get tipped anywhere from an extra thousand to more than double their rate. We don't take a cut of the girls' tips. We want our girls to be happy and loving their work. We also make money on our room rates; and on the casino and gift shop."

"And you've covered the legalities?"

"Yes, Daddy. Celt takes the risks there. He uses one of his Danish companies to produce forged birth certificates. He gets signed

consents from both parents that their daughter is sixteen and that they approve of her employment for prostitution at my clubs. We hire girls as young as thirteen; but their birth certificates show they are sixteen, seventeen, or eighteen."

"What if you get charged with trafficking a minor?"

"Got it covered, Dad. If a law enforcement person poses as someone else. We plead entrapment; our girl testifies that she was proposed marriage. We bribe prosecutors, juries, and judges; gum up the process. Then the case becomes a money shakedown. We plead out to a fine equal to a girl's income for a month. The authorities don't want to shut me down. I employ people and pay taxes. I comp free club memberships to judges and prosecutors; so, I always cut a plea deal."

"Good, Jen. Then what happens to the girl?"

"She gets suspended from working in the club until she's at the legal age of consent. I simply reassign her to one of the islands we own for private client servicing or to one of my chartered offshore yachts. She just works at a different location."

"So, my clever daughter has figured out how to make the illegal, legal?"

"That's right, Dad. Aren't you proud of me?"

"Very proud of you. You think like I do. And these girls don't get homesick? They don't develop morality issues?"

"No, Dad. Their parents are free to visit them. They can take vacation time off. We give them a month off for every two months of work. Most don't take much vacation time. They love the lifestyle, the glamor, the attention, the food, the clothes, the money, the contacts, and connections. They forget church and boyfriends. They get their emotional security by being with other girls and by being in the clubs. Basically, our girls love being whores. They all love to fuck. They are highly motivated. That's the main reason they join us in the first place."

"I see. And do you get any head cases? Does your psychological counseling handle those well?"

"Yes, we get some heartthrob cases. All our girls are stunningly beautiful. Many of them have boy friends with whom they already have intimate relations. Some have stars in the sky romantic notions of marriage, etc. Some of them need to talk their emotions out with a shrink to assure themselves that it's perfectly all right to do prostitution; and to have a loving boyfriend for their recreation times. Dad, you can't imagine how sexually active these young girls already are! I was shocked to learn the extent of underage promiscuity. It's rampant! It's common for many of these girls to have had sex with five to ten boys before they've even turned fourteen."

"Yeah, I've heard that kids nowadays love to fuck."

"Yes. I envy them. Mother kept me in a cage. I missed out. But about our shrinks, Dad: They are all disciples of Mrs. O'Dell. Their orientations towards sexual relations are extremely liberal. They counsel the girls that prostitution is perfectly normal and healthy. And they encourage them to consider the positives: that they may fall into romance with a man who is even more loving, more handsome, wealthier, and a better lover than their current boyfriend. So far, every girl we've signed to perform prostitution at the Decado has performed willingly and enthusiastically."

"Mrs. O'Dell?"

"Oh Daddy, I forgot. You've never heard of her. I hope you'll meet her someday. She's wonderful. Marty introduced me to her. I've used her myself for quite a few hours. She understands how to place feelings and emotions into context better than anyone else in the world. She's world famous and she has written many books on sexuality and pornography. I absolutely love her."

"I see," Dom searched Jen's face, hopeful that she might reveal what she and this Mrs. O'Dell had discussed in their sessions. But Jen revealed nothing by words. She only smiled confidently and nodded lovingly to her father.

Having satisfied themselves that the club was ready for the opening, Jen, Marty, and Dom treated themselves to the amenities of the Infernoss Decado. They swam in the hundred-meter infinity pool. They basked in the Mediterranean sun on Infernoss Decado's pristine white sand beach. Later, after they showered, they walked through a twenty-meter tunnel that had illusions of flames lapping at its walls, arriving at the Hologram of Sin. A voice then told them to walk through the hologram, which was an eight-foot-high replica of Jen's dark pink-light pink vagina, spilling out a continuous stream of bubbling white semen. Once on the other side of the hologram, the voice congratulated them for leaving all their inhibitions and morality behind them; and welcomed them to the deliciously wonderful world of immoral pleasures and endlessly sensational promiscuity. The voice assured them that they were all kings and queens here; and that all their activities would be kept in strictest confidence within the Club. Standing on the other side of the tunnel, Club guests were greeted by no fewer than ten of the world's most alluring porn stars, all dressed in evocative negligee; and all smiling suggestively. A minstrel sat nearby, strumming soft romantic chords on his Spanish guitar.

"This is, by far and away, the world's most fabulous whorehouse, dear daughter. Your porn stars are all mouthwatering beauties. You've outdone yourself. You're trying to top your own porn movies, aren't you?" Dom held his arm around his daughter and squeezed her closely to him. He beamed with pride at Jen's business acumen and her willingness to trample morality in order to make money. He reflected that she was a lot like him.

"We'll soon see, Daddy. Our grand opening is tomorrow night. Do you like the girls? They are all in the world's top one hundred; and they all have performed in at least ten porn films. They all have mastered exceptionally beautiful intimacy. They've all succeeded in

placing the world's most exquisite, amorous, artistic, erotic qualities of sex under their belts; or should I say inside their panties? You are welcome to any of them you wish, compliments of the Club." Jen responded to her father's squeeze by kissing him romantically on his neck.

"Thank you, Jen. But I don't think any woman could please me more than Marty already does."

"Well, perhaps tomorrow evening. After we have dinner, you may wish to reconsider. Marty will not be with us. She'll be performing live porn on our theater stage with Roger, Ross, Alex, and Nelson.' Jen squeezed against Dom a second time. And again, she kissed him on his neck.

CHAPTER TEN

The greatest problem in the world today is intolerance. Everyone is so intolerant of each other. (Princess Diana of Wales, former wife of King Charles)

I am no bird and no net ensnares me: I am a free human being with independent will. (Charlotte Bronte, English novelist)

What does incest feel like? For me it is mind blowing orgasms. I love fucking my dad and have been since a young age. He took my virginity and showed me an insane amount of pleasure and love. I absolutely love fucking my dad and I still do, to this day even though I'm married with my own family. Something about feeling your own father's big hard penis thrust inside you until you are in euphoria and hearing the pleasure your own father feels from being inside you is utterly euphoric. Being able to sustain long sex sessions and cum together at the same time with your dad is indescribable. Something about the naughty taboo secret nature of having an intense pleasurable closeness sexually with your father and being pleasured often is hard to describe unless you have lived it and enjoyed it. For me I never resisted or denied my dad as I wanted him inside me as much as he wanted to be inside me. (NataliaLoves, internet blogger)

It's the best feeling in the whole world. I love feeling my step-dad's cum inside me. Having sex with my bio dad is an even different feeling. It feels naughty as I bounce up and down on his penis, jiggling my tits in his face. (Rosanna, AKA nana: from her twitter feed)

It happens.... Sometimes. (Spoken by character Forest Gump in the movie: Forest Gump)

INCEST

Jen was pleased. She was having dinner with her father in the Toga Room, an exclusive, four table restaurant in her *Infernoss Decado Club*. The room provided the perfect intimate setting for guests that wished to not be overheard. It also had retracting booth backs which retracted into the walls and reclined. When the booth backs reclined, the booth seats lifted and fitted into the lower section of a queen-sized bed which appeared from beneath the restaurant and automatically slid into place. This night, there were no other guests. Jen had reserved the entire restaurant for herself. A servant named Rodrigo stood at attention, awaiting Jen's instructions. She was looking over the Decado's financial performance report from its first day of operation. After all prorated booking and promotional costs and adjustments for gaming bet losses, her Club netted her three hundred thousand dollars. She was on track to earn ninety million dollars from her first club in its first year. She smiled, appreciating her own success. She then turned to Rodrigo and instructed him to bring them a bottle of Chardonnet in an ice bucket, and two glasses. Rodrigo did as Jen requested. He delivered their wine and poured their glasses.

"You may leave us now, Rodrigo," Jen smiled to the sommelier, *"We will not be needing anything further this evening."*

Rodrigo bowed respectfully and left, locking the doors of the restaurant behind him. *"He's locked us in here?"* Dom looked at Jen, perplexed.

"We're safe, Dad. I have a key that will let us out when we are finished. I didn't want anyone to disturb us. I wanted absolute privacy tonight."

"Well, that's a relief. So, here we are, father and daughter."

"Yes, Dad. Here we are. I want you to see this." She shared the report with her father, Dom.

"That's excellent for your first business venture, Jen. Congratulations!" Dom, ever the bottom-line guy, beamed. He was pleased with the figures he saw.

"Well, I had lots of help from Marty. She had all the right contacts to help me set everything up. All I came up with, honestly, was the theme and some of the marketing ideas." Jen shrugged her shoulders while looking dreamily into her father's eyes and placed her hand on his knee.

"Your life has changed a lot since she came into it, hasn't it, Jen?"

"Oh Dad, you have no idea!" Jen then proceeded to tell Dom what her life was like as a little girl, living under her mother's thumb. She recanted all the restrictions that her mother made her live under; all the forced attendances at church before and after the divorce, as well as the after-church meetings with her mother's hate-prayer group, and her forced visits to a creepy, unkept shrink who told her she didn't need a father in her life. She told Dom of the many times she saw her mother flip him the bird behind his back; how she often saw her mother defy Dom's wishes by buying things they didn't need, like a new car and wardrobe every year; and an extensive remodeling of the house which left Jen disliking the house more, after the expensive remodel, than she disliked the house before the remodel. Dom and Jen laughed together. They had both considered that house Mom's show house; and they had both thought the remodel, which she had demanded, was ridiculous.

"I had no idea how hard she was on you, Jen." Dom sounded contrite, taking on blame for his daughter's frustrations.

"No, Dad, don't take this on. You were working to provide for us. I could see that. Mom weighed on you like an anchor. She was always holding you back. I could se that. She never appreciated you. She was spoiled by her parents and she expected you to continue spoiling her. It's just amazing that you pulled all that weight and

made yourself rise from being a man who had nothing into being the multi-billionaire you are today. How did you do it, Dad?"

"It wasn't that hard, Jen. Mostly, it's listening to people and being discerning about them; and about what they are telling you; and, when you have identified a person with ideas and talent, just working with them. Get yourself a piece of the action and help them manage it. Trust them; but don't trust them, either. Make sure that you and your partners and associates are always honest and loyal to each other. When a problem comes up, you want to always be the first to hear about it; and you always want to hear about it right away. It's okay for people to make bad decisions and fuck up. That's natural. That's business. Expect it. But, be open and honest about it. Demand that your close circle of friends is always open with you. I hope that helps."

"It does, Dad. Open and honest. Like you are with Marty, right?"

"Yes. She bares her soul to me and I bare mine to her."

"And now that you are into my club business for ten percent; like Marty, who also has ten percent; open and honest with you both, right?"

"Absolutely, Jen. And you have been. We're all good."

"Not as good as we should be, Dad. There's something I need to tell you."

"What is it, baby?"

"Well, first, I need to tell you about Mrs. O'Dell. Okay?"

"That's the shrink that you and Marty use?"

"Yes, Dad."

"Well, what about her?"

"I saw her because Marty thought she could help me with my problem."

"Did she?"

"I think so."

"Well, what is your problem?"

"It's guilt, Dad. It's how terrible I feel about how Mom treated you and how I just stood by and let her abuse you like she did."

"Don't blame yourself. You were just a child."

"Yes, but I had these feelings; and I couldn't do anything about them. Let me explain, Dad. When I was a girl between the ages of five, until maybe twelve, I loved to come to you and sit in your lap. Do you remember?"

"Yes. And you used to hug me tightly. I remember."

"And do you remember how you used to bounce me on your lap?"

"Sure. We even sang nursery rhymes while we did that."

"Yes, it was beautiful and sweet. But Dad, in my mind there was something more going on. I was pretending, with all my little girl's might to believe, that I was taking you away from Mom and saving you from her. Sometimes she watched us and I could see in her eyes that she knew what I was thinking and she hated me for thinking it. That's when it started. That's when Mom began to really get mean with you; even meaner than she had been before. And that's when she began to hate me."

"Jen, do you really believe that your mom hates you?"

"Yes. And I'm right about that. Mrs. O'Dell confirmed it to me. She told me that it's not unusual for a woman, like Mom, to feel threatened by another woman for control of her man. The threat of my sexuality as a young girl becoming a woman drove Mom sharply into control mode. She made me wear baggy clothes and go to that awful church and say those ugly hate prayers with her. Mrs. O'Dell says she extended that control to restricting my hours of freedom and keeping me from dating boys. She alienated you by becoming a total shrew. She sought to crush your spirit and make you succumb to her wishes and controls."

"Well, that explains some things."

"Yes, and when you couldn't deal with Mom anymore, you called Marty and became involved with her. When Mom figured *out that you were seeing a porn star, she went into this sort of con-vulsive reaction. Her controlling behaviors morphed into hatred of you. And Mom became terrified that I might also come under Marty's influence. So, Mom practically made me live in a social straight jacket. I couldn't even twitch without first getting her permission. My life became hell, Dad."*

"Bad? As in run away from home, bad?"

"Yes, that; but also, suicide, Dad. I thought about ways to kill myself. You have no idea how bad it was for me, Dad," Jen hugged Dom. Then she pulled herself away to arm's length and looked into his eyes. She was crying. Tears were spilling from her eyes and rolling down her cheeks.

"It's okay, Jen. You can tell me."

"Dad, I came so close to ending it all. I went to the top of this one skyscraper. I got up onto the roof of it and I stood looking fifty stories down at the tiny cars on the street below. I thought if I jumped, I'd be free of Mom and I'd join those little cars; just kind of roll away with them into another world. I even felt myself getting dizzy while looking down. Mrs. O'Dell says I had a case of vertigo and I was lucky that I started reeling backwards and that I landed on my tushy instead of reeling forwards and dying from the fall."

"Oh, Jen, my poor, sweet, baby, Jen. I had no idea."

"There were other things like that, Dad. I thought about using a gun to shoot myself. I thought about getting into a warm bathtub and slitting my wrists. I even started taking a bottle of aspirin; but I was only taking them one at a time and I started throwing up."

"Jesus, Jen."

"Yeah, I know. I didn't have the guts to go through with it. Then, for a while, I thought about killing Mom; even planning how I'd do it. I thought about poisoning her. But then I watched these TV shows where these crime lab forensic people always figure out how some-one dies and they always get the murderer; so, I gave up on the idea

of killing her. But I was going totally nuts inside. And, thankfully, that's about the time you bought your new house and moved Marty in with you."

"But you didn't care much for Marty, at first."

"No, I didn't. I saw her as just another woman who would keep me away from being with my dad. But, at least I had someplace where I could go and be away from Mom half the time. That was so wonderful! When I was with you and Marty, I felt like a free, liberated human being."

"Then, you and Marty became friends."

"Yes, close friends. Our friendship started out slowly. I don't think either of us trusted the other at first; but the friendship just kept growing as I began noticing the differences between Marty and Mom. Mom loves to control people. Marty never tries to control anyone. Mom lives and breathes everything the Church teaches. Marty doesn't even believe in God. Mom tries to keep me from growing, especially by denying me relationships with the opposite sex. Marty encourages me to have relationships with the opposite sex. Mom hates sex. Marty loves it. Mom thinks she's highly moral; but she's very destructive about it. Marty is shamelessly immoral; but she's open and friendly, and creative about it. If Mom were an animal, she'd be a clam. She'd live in a shell and never come out. Mom fears life. If Marty were an animal, she'd be some bird that loves fucking other birds; or she'd be one of some chimpanzee species that loves to have constant sex; and, she's so loving about it. Intimacy is so natural and beautiful for her. Marty loves life."

"And Marty led you to doing porn and then to meeting with this Mrs. O'Dell?"

"Yes; but, no, Dad. Marty didn't lead me into porn. I kept pushing her to open the doors to porn for me. Marty has no guilt for the way my morals have turned out. That's all on me, Dad. I wanted to become a porn star. I begged Marty to help me get started.

I desperately wanted to become an immoral woman. I wanted to release myself from Mon's controls, Dad. I wanted to fuck every man on the planet."

"Well, you've achieved our goal, dearest daughter. You now have several porn films to your credit. You have your own Private Member Service. And now you have the most exclusive live porn club in the entire world, don't you?"

"Then, you've arrived, haven't you? You've accomplished all you set out to accomplish, haven't you?"

"Almost, Dad. There's only one more thing. It's you, Dad."

"Me?" Dom's eyebrows lifted as he turned his head to ask the question.

"Dad, please help me with this. You're the only one who can help me here. I need to completely unburden myself." Jen got up from her chair and sat beside Dom. She put her arm around his big shoulders and hugged him while kissing his cheek.

"Jen, tell me. You don't need to beat around the bush with me. Tell me." Dom looked into Jen's eyes. He saw her as a woman now, no longer his little girl. And he loved her.

"Mrs. O'Dell explained to me that I needed to release myself from all my pent-up past frustrations. I need to feel absolved and forgiven for all those times when I went along with Mom's agenda and willed myself to hate you, when I never hated you. I always loved you. I need to know that you understand what I had to go through while my brain and my emotions were still forming. I need you to forgive me for all the damage that I caused myself. And I need you to understand that I couldn't help doing what I had to do, Dad.

"And now, I need you to accept me as a total woman. I need to understand why I've chosen to take the path of immorality; and I need you to accept me for becoming what I have become; and I need you to approve of my path in life; and I need you to love me for taking that path. I need your love, Dad. I mean, as Mrs. O'Dell *explained it to me: I need you to share your intimacy with me; and accept me into your intimate world. It's very important to me, Dad. It will release all the uncertainties and doubts I carry around inside myself and allow me to flutter freely as a total uninhibited, unashamed, proud, and beautiful woman. Can you understand that, Dad? Please tell me that you understand me."*

Dom reclined his head upon the back of their booth, and stared up, into the ceiling. *"Oh, my dearest, sweetest Jen. I do want to help you. I want you to be free of your demons. You know how much I love you. Believe me, I will do anything and everything to help you. And, maybe by helping you, I'll also be helping myself."*

Jen helped Dom remove his shoes and pants; then his boxer shorts. *"Dad, Mrs. O'Dell said that this experience will be transformative for me; and likely also for you. She said that we should just be in the moment and not try to overthink the consequences of what we are doing. She explained to me that, in many cultures, incest is viewed as a necessary validation of a young woman's transition to being a fully actualized woman, with equal powers as the men in her life. She said we should try to see it that way; and that, that is the healthy way to see it."* Jen paused her monologue while she lifted Dom's penis to her lips. It had not yet stiffened. She began kissing its head while gently stroking its shaft.

"In Spain, Portugal, the Netherlands, and several other European countries, incest is perfectly legal, Father. And here, in Spain, the age of consent is seventeen. So, you need not concern yourself about legal matters. Marty investigated everything and arranged the services of the right legal team. She's been immensely helpful."

"So, this is why we came to Spain, isn't it?" Dom lifted his head. His eyes met Jen's. He nodded his head in understanding and grinned.

"Yes, Father. I've become a legal resident of Spain. And, I fully consent to having relations with you." Jen began sucking her father's

penis. *"You're getting very hard, Daddy. You have a splendid penis, don't you know?"*

"Tell me, my sweet daughter. Tell me what you know about the male penis." Dom lifted Jen's chin so he could see his daughter's face while he spoke. He touched her cheek with his other hand.

"Well, Father, speaking as a budding young porn star who has already amassed a good deal of experience with male penises, I must confess that I have never before seen a penis as immense as yours; let alone held it in my hands or my mouth. I must confess, dear Father, that I am getting very hot and wet inside, just thinking about how pleasurable it will be to feel the head of your magnificent penis penetrating my outer lips for your first visit into my vagina. Please allow me to indulge myself." Dom's penis was now fully erect and anxious to enter Jen's vagina. Jen held the penis firmly in her hand. Then, as she had done many times with her partners in her porn films, she slipped out of her panties. And, while facing Dom and rubbing her free hand over his massive chest, she mounted her father's penis, settling her vagina over its head.

"Oh, Daddy! This is even more wonderful than Mrs. O'Dell said it would be! It's totally mind blowing; fantastic! I'm feeling so much more than the sex of it. I'm feeling one with you, Father. I'm feeling like I am finally completing the love that I have always felt for you. You are so huge inside me! Oh, I'm swelling up already! I'm going to come. I don't want to hold it back. I can't hold it, Daddy. I have to let myself go; so soon like this! Ohhhh, there it is! I'm releasing already. Oh, Daddy. I love you so much! I've waited for this moment since I was a little girl!" Jen bent her body forward and hugged her father tightly.

"Jen, Jen. It's all right. That was beautiful. I love you. I love what you just did. How do you feel?"

"Oh Daddy. I can't explain it. Everything inside me has come alive. I've wanted to do that with you since I was five years old. You

feel so good inside me! That was the best sex I've ever had! I loved it! I feel so good about who I am; about everything! We must do this often; over and over, please, Dad? There are so many ways I want to make love with you. I want to do all the positions that Marty taught me. Can we do that? Please? Did you like me, Dad? Was it as good for you as it was for me? Am I good for you, too?" Jen sat upright again. She began rocking her vagina back and forth over Dom's penis. Shortly after she began her rocking motion, he came inside her.

"Jen, Jen, my dear sweet Jen," whispered Dom while hugging Jen close to him and kissing her breasts, *"yes, it was beautiful. You were beautiful. I loved every second of it. Of course, we'll do it again. I had no idea how wonderful it could be. You are so slippery and warm! I loved being inside you. Is this the effect your Mrs. O'Dell told you about? Are you feeling the way she said you would feel?"*

"Yes, Dad. It's as she described it; only better. I feel like I'm your equal now. I feel so complete as a woman. I know now that I am your daughter, your dearest friend, your partner in business, and your lover. I now feel like I mean everything to you in every way. I feel so inseparable from you. This feeling warms me inside and gives me this sense of incredible power and self-confidence. Oh, Dad, I am so glad we made love. I love you, Dad."

"How does your Mrs. O'Dell think we fit in with society overall, now that we've opened this door, Jen?"

"Oh Dad, she's told me we'll need to be discrete about it until society comes around to accepting it. She will soon be publishing her research findings which will explain that women who have experienced consensual incest with their fathers are women who have more self-esteem and more confidence than women who have not benefitted from consensual incest. Her work will show that those who have had consensual incest are more assertive in their relationships with other women and with their husbands. They are

far less likely to be bullied. They don't allow anyone to shame them for expressing their sexuality, either. They are more complete and psychologically well-balanced women than women who have not enjoyed consensual incest with their fathers. She will be advocating a bold new approach to feminine sexuality. She argues that, as soon as a young girl reaches puberty and has her first period, her mother's duties must be to supply her with birth control pills and introduce her to the male penis."

"How, exactly, does she propose that mothers do that?" Dom looked confused.

"Direct intervention. And she insists that for maximum self-esteem and confidence building, it needs to be done with the girl's father."

"She.......?" Dom's eyebrows lifted and his jaw dropped.

"Yes," Jen nodded, *"She wants both parents involved. She wants the mother to introduce the girl to the father's naked body. Then, she advocates the mother's duty is to suck the father's penis until it is hard. Once it is hard, the mother is to position her daughter's vagina over the father's penis; rub the penis against the daughter's outer lips until the mother is satisfied that the daughter is lubricating sufficiently to entertain her father's penis shaft. And then, the mother needs to gently work with her daughter's hips while her daughter's vagina slowly slides over and engulfs her father's penis. In this process, the girl's hymen will be ruptured and she will bleed; but the mother's duty will be to assure her daughter that this is perfectly normal. Then, after the daughter has successfully fucked her father for the first time, the mother must clean the blood from her daughter's vagina. A day or two later, the family must repeat this process; this time to help the young girl understand that intercourse feels wonderful and that it's a perfectly normal, beautiful, human activity; and that she should feel free to have sex often and with many different male partners."*

"Mrs. O'Dell believes this is the way to go? And she thinks that young girls will grow up to be more assertive, self-confident, and sexually liberated, right?" Dom extended his jaw and nodded. *"This Mrs. O'Dell seems to have thought all this through, hasn't she?"*

"Yes, Daddy. And she backs up her position papers with lots of research. It's hard to go against her when all the other side has is historical religious taboos."

"She thinks she can change our entire culture, doesn't she?"

"Yes, Father. She believes the Pilgrims brought with them a ton of misconceptions about women and got a lot of their clap trap codified into laws. And she says that we have science and experience and data now. And we can afford to take this bold step. We can unleash the enormous pent-up power that women have by freeing them sexually and accepting them as true equals to men. Mrs. O'Dell will be advocating that all states reduce their age of sexual consent to fourteen; and that all states eliminate consensual incest from their criminal codes. She will be meeting with pro-incest advocates all over the country to help them draft pro-incest legislation for the various states. She says it is time to liberate women from the MRT's"

"And what is an MRT, Jen?"

"Oh, sorry, Dad. That's Mrs. O'Dell's shorthand for Misogynistic Religious Types. She includes in that grouping all male religious leaders and many males; but also, many females. She calls Mom a MRT Mom. These are people who, based upon their wrong-headed religious convictions, cause immense emotional harm to women; especially young girls and women in their most formative years when their attitudes and feelings about their sexuality is being set for life. Mrs. O'Dell has told me that Mother has caused me considerable harm in my relationship and sexual development by denying me closeness and intimacy with you when I was a young girl. She has encouraged me to do everything I possibly can to establish a

permanent, continuously intimate relationship with you, now that I've reached the age of consent in Spain."

"I see. And this explains why you've become a resident of Spain and incorporated Infernoss Decado here. Am I understanding this?"

"Yes Father. We must always be careful that our relationship doesn't cause you legal problems, even though I am the one who sought our incestuous relationship. The laws are blind, Dad. They presume all incest between a father and daughter is rape. Many jurisdictions make no allowances for consensual sex. They derive their laws from the MRT mindset and go after the fathers with a vengeance because incest represents a challenge to their religious based authority."

"So, I must come to Spain to see you and make love with you?"

"Only for this short vacation. I have a plan, Dad."

"Okay, surprise me! I'm sure you've thought of everything. And I imagine that Marty also has her hand in this?"

"Yes, Dad. I've thought of everything. I incorporated a company that has purchased an oceanfront mansion in Newport, Rhode Island. I'll be moving there after I leave Spain. It's a huge place with forty rooms. I'll be doing extensive renovations to it; so, you will have an entire wing of the place to yourself. You'll be set up with a complete, modern office, all your exhaustive corporate files, and your own living quarters with you stuffy leather sofas and chairs. I'll have separate quarters, but I'll be a frequent visitor to your quarters."

"But, what about Marty?"

"Well, Dad, let's talk about Marty. I've studied her schedules. She's only with you about twenty percent of her time. She's also visiting Bob, David, Carl, Marshawn, Josh, Ed, And Fred on a regular basis. And she takes time to service her Premium Members and to create her porn films. She's even going to be doing ten full length erotic films that you are producing, Dad. So, eighty percent of the time, you will essentially be batching it, without her. Look, Dad, I know you love her.

I know you are crazy about her; and about how much you love how promiscuous and immoral she is. I also know the two of you have a lot of business things that you work on together. But Dad, she's leaving you free and available eighty percent of your time! And I would love to have some of that time with you, Dad. Remember the film she did when she was kissing Marshawn and he was thrusting his fingers into her vagina while he was removing her panties? Remember how turned on she made you when she met his thrusts with her own? She was doing that to make Aaliyah, Marshawn's wife, jealous."

"Yes, I remember. Fantastic seduction scene."

"Well, Dad, I want to do that same scene many times with you. I can be even more irresistible than Marty. I'm wilder than she is. And I want to feel that I'm making Mom jealous. I want to punish her for the way she raised me and how she kept us apart all those years. I want to have sensational sex with you, Dad; like Marty does; only even better than Marty. I want to be your lover every bit as much as she does. What do you say? Can't we be lovers; and not just Father and Daughter?"

"So, while she's away, we'll play. Is that your thinking?"

"We've already talked about it, Dad. Marty is such a love! I love her. You love her. Everyone loves her. So, Dad, even while Marty is home with us in our Rhode Island mansion, we can have threesomes, if you like. Marty said she'd love it. I know I'd love it. Would you be okay with that?"

"Well, if both of you want that, who am I to say no to you?"

"Then, I can tell Marty your answer is, yes? She can move in with us?"

"Yes, Jen; absolutely yes."

"Oh, Daddy! You are such a love." Jen kissed her dad and stroked his penis until it stiffened. She then guided it inside her a second time. *"Oh, Father, I've never been so happy. I'm the happiest woman ever. I love you so much!"*

"So, mastermind daughter, when you and Marty don't have me screwing my brains out, what do we do in Newport, Rhode Island? Are we supposed to stare at the harbor and the ocean?"

"Yes, some of that, Daddy. It's beautiful there. But mostly, we are going to take this time out of our busy lives and you are going to teach me how you look at companies to invest in and acquire. You're going to show me what you look at in different industries; and what you look for in company 10k and 10q filings. You're going to train my mind to see situations as you see them; how you can smash companies together, merge or acquire them; which type of accounting will work best to satisfy your bankers; what cost cuts to make, etc."

"Wow, daughter! I don't even allow my closest investment contacts to understand everything I see. You are blood-thirsty little predator, aren't you? And what am I supposed to get in return for imparting all my knowledge to you, my dear?"

Jen ignored her father's predator question. But she assured him that he'd be well paid for his knowledge. *"You'll get the eternal gratitude of your loving daughter, Father; and you will have unlimited access to my fabulous, deliciously immoral, whoring, sex-crazed, hot, slippery-wet vagina. You should know, Daddy, that Intimacy Magazine is doing a feature piece on me. I've been voted one of the ten most sensational, up and coming young porn stars in the world, Daddy. You can be proud of me. And, in Newport, you will get to have me whenever you want me! I intend to fuck you to near exhaustion; and often, my dear loving Father. Your penis will know it's having the best time it has ever had! We will have the most wonderful time of our lives, Daddy. I promise you. And, Daddy, I love you. I love you very much."* With that promise, Jen delivered a strong Kegel squeeze to Dom's penis while kissing him on his mouth. His pleasured groan was her confirmation that everything Mrs. O'Dell had told her about consensual incest was true.

CHAPTER ELEVEN

'but she makes hungry where most she satisfies; for vilest things become themselves in her; that the holy priests bless her when she is riggish. (Shakespeare: Anthony and Cleopatra)

There is no hope for the satisfied man. (Earnesto Bonfilio, AKA Fred Bonfils: Founder of the Denver Post Newspaper)

SATISFACTION

Three years had passed since Jen made the move from Colorado to Rhode Island. Much had transpired in those years. She felt the pace of change was causing her to hurry her decisions, and she didn't like that. She had so many things on her mind that she wanted to examine and talk out with a trusted confidant. But who? She was having restless nights where she found herself standing in her kitchen and staring out at the ocean without having a particular thought in her mind; instead, her mind just seemed to race and flit from one concern to another, without resolution of anything. Jen knew enough about herself and decision making to realize that her night habit was leading her nowhere. She was also becoming more reliant on hot black coffee to stimulate her and help her slog her way through her days. After some thoughtful consideration, she decided to call on Mrs. O'Dell. Who else knew her history better than she? Who else understood a woman's pressures and cravings better than she?

Mrs. O'Dell was older now. Officially, she was retired; but she was still very alert, up to date, current, and engaged in matters that concerned women's issues. When Jen called her at her cabin in British Columbia, she was pleased to hear from her. Jen was one of her greatest success stories. The old psychologist was proud that Jen had shed her cocoon and 'fluttered into life,' as Mrs. O'Dell described Jen's transformation. When Jen told her that a man from her personal security detail would pick her and Bud, her talking cat, up at her cabin and bring them by helicopter and Jen's private jet to Newport, Mrs. O'Dell readily agreed. She looked forward to seeing Jen again. Jen had always trusted her guidance. Over the course of Jen's twenty sessions the two women had bonded and become personal friends. Over the intervening years, Jen had sent her greeting cards with little hand written notes, letting her know about her successes with her porn films and the mushrooming growth of her *Infernoss Decado* clubs. But in the last year, Jen had gone curiously silent.

Today the world-renowned shrink sat on a white wicker rocking chair on the open veranda of Jen's mansion. A teal-colored warming shawl covered her legs and a rust-colored vintage cloth hat with visor rested on her head. She was comfy warm and content, staring out at the beautiful harbor and the goings out of colorful sailboats, away to the open ocean.

'Of all my patients, I believe I loved Jen the most. I loved Marty, too; but Jen was always more demure and subtle than Marty. Marty burned with passion and her immense cravings for life. But Jen was the brightest; the most open to new ideas; and the one with the greatest career potential. That impish face and adorable pug nose of hers tells people that she is the Spirits' great gift to the world. I can see why her foray into porn was a huge success. Both Marty and Jen took to porn. I deserve some credit for that. They both saw erotica as a business. Marty saw it as a business in which she could perform

and excel. Jen saw it that way, too; but only as much as she needed to in order to understand the nuances of the productions. She took it one step further. Jen learned how to capitalize on the demand for porn and manage it into an empire. Like Marty, she's a natural femme. And, like Marty, she's highly promiscuous and free. Her face captivates. But then her highly toned long legs and tight tushy holds a man's interest. And her natural charm never lets him go. I wonder what's got her troubled?' Mrs. O'Dell smiled from her thoughts. She returned a robust wave to two young couples passing by the front of Jen's property in their sailboat. *'Ah, the young! Bless them. I'll bet they're going to have one hell of a romp once they get that boat out on the ocean!'* Mrs. O'Dell's mind never strayed very far from matters of human sexuality.

Jen was brewing tea; Mrs. O'Dell's favorite of chamomile and lemon. Set beside Mrs. O'Dell was a patio table and a tray of orange peel biscuits, another favorite. Jen had even thought of Bud. While she had no live mice to offer him, she did have a small tray of fish heads. He seemed satisfied with Jen's selection. He held one head between his forepaws and was busily chewing away on it, crunching into its skull. Jen had promised to join them shortly. Bud sat by his mistresses' side; snacking and occasionally purring.

"Lovely day; lovely view, isn't it?" Jen smiled a prideful smile as she approached the table with her tray of hot tea, a variety of honeys, and offerings of finger sandwiches and sweet cakes. Jen poured Mrs. O'Dell a hot tea and one for herself. Then she settled back into her own wicker rocker. She was wearing a pair of light blue summer pants and a simple white cotton blouse and a light blue woolen sweater.

"Lovely, indeed. And just enough breeze to keep flies away and bring the taste of ocean salts into my nostrils. This is a lovely place, Jen."

"*Thank you, Mrs. O'Dell. I'm so glad you could come. And I want you to know you are welcome to come and stay here, with me, whenever you wish and as often as you wish.*"

"*Why that is most generous, Jen. I don't know what to say.*"

"*Say yes; and please take me up on it. I'm serious. I love your company. And I appreciate my friends.*"

"*Yes, I will come visit again. But tell me, please, my dear. What's going on in your life. I've read all your notes. I know about the success of the Infernoss Decado clubs. There were four of them, weren't there?*"

"*Seven, when you include the yachts offshore.*"

"*And you sold them?*"

"*Had Dad's holding company acquire them as a separate subsidiary. Tax and liability wise that made the most sense.*"

"*I see. And did you ever get any blowback about using under-aged girls?*"

"*Not really. We had two sets of parents that wanted to make trouble. We simply showed them the appropriate laws, the consents they signed; and then we paid them to sign non-disclosures and simply go away.*"

"*Grifter types?*"

"*Definitely. It wasn't the girls' idea. They were loving it. They cried when they had to leave.*"

"*And how many young girls did you liberate into the sex trade?*"

"*All together, over all seven clubs, over the years I owned the business, Celt supplied me with over three thousand young girls.*"

"*And customers?*"

"*Oh, that's a bit fuzzy. Some only came to gamble and see the live shows. Men who used our concierge prostitution services numbered around thirty thousand. Men who repeated more than five times were some twenty thousand. Oddly, most of the repeats went back to their original girl.*"

"What does that tell you?"

"People crave sex; but more than sex, they crave love."

"I agree completely. But enough of that. Tell me, Jen, why did you bring me here? What's troubling you?"

"She's a woman. There's always something; that's what!" Bud stopped his chewing and looked up at the two women. It was his male dominance thing. He couldn't help himself.

"Now Bud, you just stop that; right now!" Mrs. O'Dell snapped her fingers. Bud grabbed a fresh fish head and moved a few feet further away. *"You promised you'd be a good kitty. So, I've brought you along on a nice trip. Now you need to keep your word, young man."* Bud turned his back on the women and engrossed himself with his new, fresh, fish head.

"I'm not sure what it is," Mrs. O'Dell, *"I think, possibly, it's burn out. But maybe it's something deeper than that. I thought if I talked out my feelings with you, you could help me see what it is."*

"Of course, my dear. We'll do that. We'll take as long as it takes. Bring me up to date, will you? Three years is a long time.""

"Yes. Well, I moved Father in with me. We had the most wonderful times together. You were right about consensual incest. Dad and I became inseparable. We spent endless hours together. There was the beautiful intimate sex; but so much more. Dad taught me all about how to look at companies; how different industries operated; what their risks and opportunities were; when to buy and sell the companies in the different industries; how to acquire them, friendly or hostile takeover; how to assess my odds of success. Honestly, after those years with Dad, I feel like I'm this huge gorilla, picking my way through the forest of companies; eating this one and that one and always moving along, looking for new companies to gobble up."

"And now he's gone, isn't he?"

"Yes. I sent you an obit. Your note was so kind. Thank you. Now that Dad is gone, I feel so empty. I thought the emptiness would go

away; but it won't leave me. Now I'm learning the meaning of lone-liness. And I hate it."

"And Marty? What's going on there?"

"That's just it, Mrs. O'Dell. No one seems to know; or if they do know, they aren't saying. She disappeared. The last she spoke with me, she said she was going to be in Colorado for a while. She wanted to spend some time with Bob and a few of her others; but mostly, she wanted to have some alone time to think about what she wanted to do with her life. And then, nothing. No calls; no text messages; nothing. I called her phone several times. Her voice mail was full, so I couldn't even leave her a message. I've written to her twice and have not heard back. It's been over four months now. I worry that something has happened to her. I got a call from a Plaintown detec-tive. I told him everything I told you. He said they were looking into her disappearance; but so far, nothing has turned up."

"Oh dear. I hope she's all right. She's such a bright light; such a stunning, vivacious woman."

"I hope so, too. I' m worried."

"Well, dear, there's nothing more to do until we hear something. Now, what about you?"

"Dad's death was so sudden. Heart attack. He was still a young man; only fifty. He's left such a huge hole in my life. I can't tell you how many hours I've sat here in these chairs, staring out at the ocean. Here I am, twenty-six, with Dad's billions; and I feel like my life has suddenly gotten stuck. I want to move on; but I don't know what I like doing. I don't know where to begin."

"Well, dear, can't you just keep doing what you are doing?"

"Well, I can; and I try. But my heart isn't into it like it was when Dad was here."

"What's changed?"

"Well, nothing; not really. It's just that Dad got such pleasure out of ripping into a company and slashing costs. I loved to se him being

happy while he did that. But, Mrs. O'Dell, honestly, that isn't me. I don't salivate at laying people off. That was Dad's thing."

"Well, looking back on your life, what made you feel good? What gave you the most satisfaction?"

Jen reflected for a while before she spoke. *"I guess, honestly, it was creating porn. I loved the idea that I was making those films. I loved knowing that people could see something that I created and get some pleasure from seeing it."*

Mrs. O'Dell sipped her tea and munched on an almond scone a bit before she responded. *"Jen, I want you to think for a minute. Was it the action on the porn set that you loved? I mean, was it the thrill of fucking before the cameras that gave you your satisfaction; or was it something else?"*

"Oh, gee, I don't know. I mean fucking is fucking, whether in front of a camera or in a dark bedroom. No, it wasn't the fucking. I think it was more my knowing that some men I've never met and would never meet would see my films and get pleasure from them; possibly jerk themselves off while watching me fuck."

"So, could you say that you got your pleasure from knowing that you were creating something beautiful for others, to, see?"

Jen sipped her tea. She didn't answer right away. She thought about what Mrs. O'Dell was trying to pull out of her. *"I guess you've touched on something,"* Jen nodded. *"I think what I loved most about doing porn was knowing that I was creating something. That's it, isn't it; knowing that I was in the process of creating something."*

"And that made you happy?"

"Yes. That's what got me enthused about going on set; taking down a man's pants; and sucking and fucking him. It was not the sex, per se. It was me knowing that I was doing something that would mean something to someone else, whom I didn't even know."

"Well, then, Jen. Maybe you have your answer. Maybe you need to go back to doing porn. Have you thought about that?"

"Yes, I've thought about it. But now I don't feel like doing it any-more. It's hard to explain; but I can't see myself going back to it. It's like there was this wonderful chapter in my life. I lived that chapter. And now I need to move on to a new chapter. Can you explain that?"

"Yes," smiled Mrs. O'Dell. placing her hand on Jen's arm. *"You need a new challenge. Porn would not seem creative to you. You've already done that. There wouldn't be anything new about it for you. It would bore you now."*

"Yes, I think that is true. But I also know that I still love sex."

"Oh, Jen; you will always love sex, until your body tells you that you simply can't do it anymore. Men who want sex with you will come along for another forty years. Have no fear about that. But we are after something else here; something deeper in your psyche, Jen. Tell me, if all your money was gone tomorrow and you had nothing; no place to live; but you needed to do something to make yourself feel like you had a purpose for your life; not to please anyone else, but to please yourself, to make Jen feel good about being Jen; what is it that you would do?"

Jen didn't answer. She stared into Mrs. O'Dell's eyes and sipped her tea. She knew her answer was important and she wanted to be sure it was the truth; nothing flippant; nothing ridiculous; just the bare, unvarnished truth. *"I'd want to draw a picture of that sailboat out there, the one with the ocean spray coming off its bow and with the billowed sail; and the men crewing her, leaning over her wind-ward gunnel; making her point high; making her go fast. I'd love to paint that picture. I'd love to put my feelings into it; the sea, the wind, that boat out there, flying over the water like she is; the wind into her sails and those men's' faces like that. Yeah, I wish I could paint that. But I can't paint. I can't even draw a straight line."*

"Wait a minute, Jen. Forget that you have never painted before. Why do you want to paint that boat?"

Jen chuckled. She looked into Mrs. O'Dell's eyes, searching for the answer to her mentor's question. *"This is important, isn't it?"*

"Oh, yes dear. This is important. This is how we get to know our own souls. So, tell me: why do you want to paint that boat?"

Jen thought long before she answered. *"I don't want to seem silly, Mrs. O'Dell. It's not my boat. But it is a beautiful boat. And the way those boys are sailing it is such a sight. It takes my breath and my imagination away. Just looking at it and them makes me feel like I am a part of them."*

"And if you could paint; and if you could capture what you see, what would that do for you, Jen?"

"I'd have it. I'd have it forever. I'd possess what I see and feel. I'd capture that moment and it would become mine; or, I could give it away to a friend or sell it and I would be giving these feeling that I have captured to them. And that would please me and make me feel good about myself. That would make me happy."

"Is this the only time you've wished you could paint something, Jen?"

"No, no; there have been lots of times when I have felt this way about lots of things and scenes. I've just never done anything about it because I can't paint. So, I've gone into town here and other places and acquired paintings that I liked; artwork that made me feel something. I just bought things that struck me as things I liked."

"But buying a painting wouldn't give you the same feeling about that painting as you'd feel about a painting that you created yourself, would it?"

"Oh no; not even close. I see what you mean. But Mrs. O'Dell, I can't paint!"

"You can't paint because you are thinking like a girl!" It was Bud again. He preferred hearing a can-do attitude; and he let Jen know it.

Mrs. O'Dell clapped her hands together. This shocked Bud. He looked up at the two women with a look of confusion and dismay. *"You need to leave us alone for a while, Bud. We must have an important girl's talk. You take a fresh fish head over there, to the other side of the veranda and entertain yourself. I'll call for you when we finish."* Bud did as he was told. Sullenly, he snatched a fresh fish head from the plate of fish heads and trotted off to the far end of the veranda. Mrs. O'Dell and Jen heard him crack into the fish's skull.

"That seems to have him settled, for now," smiled Mrs. O'Dell to Jen. *"Now, Jen, let's return to what's important. Suppose you were to paint that boat and after you finished painting it, you looked at your work and you saw that it was not exactly as your mind had seen the real boat out there on the ocean. How do you think you would feel?"*

"I don't know. I suppose I'd feel like I had more to learn and that I needed more practice why?"

"Well, yes; I suppose you would have those feelings. I'd expect that you would have those. Those are more feelings of realization of facts. But wouldn't you have some other, deeper feeling, Jen? Be honest with yourself."

"Oh, gee. You never cease to amaze me, Mrs. O'Dell. I think I know what it is that you are looking for in me. Yes! I see it now. I would feel proud of myself for having done the work and creating that painting! That's it, isn't it? No matter how badly it came out, I'd still feel proud and good about myself for having created it; for making the effort and creating something, wouldn't I?"

"Yes, dear. I believe you would. And isn't that the same feeling you had when you were making your first porn films?"

"Yes, Mrs. O'Dell. My best films came later; but that is exactly the feeling I had then."

"Okay then. So, there you have your answer, Jen."

"What is it, then. Tell me.'

'Jen, you'd be happy; you'd have a purpose; you'd feel self-fulfilled if you painted."

"But I............."

"Yes, I know," interrupted Mrs. O'Dell. *"You don't know how to paint, right?"*

"Obviously not. No. I know nothing about it."

"But here you are in this beautiful setting with so many things you could paint. And nearby, all around you are forty or fifty colleges. Surely you could find some art courses if you looked. Surely you could pick up technique about lighting and colors and depth and motion. A place like this must be brimming with artistic types, don't you think?

"Come on, Jen. New skills to learn; new friends to make; a whole new appreciation for the world around you! What's not to like? Do you think the world's great artists simply picked up a palate and brush, sat down at a canvas and whipped out a masterpiece? Hell no, Jen. It took them time to learn. It took practice. But it was their journey, Jen. It was fulfillment in the doing of it. It made them feel good about doing what they did when they turned their imagination into a painting."

CHAPTER TWELVE

But he is a very fine cat. A very fine cat, indeed. (Samuel Johnson: Boswell's life: On the death of Mr. Levett)

I've never known a bad cat. They are all good kitties. (Rosemary Ness Bitner, author)

BIFSTER

In the weeks that followed, Jen changed her life. She hired top flight corporate executives to manage her holding company and its forty-three subsidiaries. She remained on the board as the majority stockholder; but she appointed a man she and her father had trusted for years to the chairmanship. For the first time in years, Jen was a passive investor. She then enrolled in an art studies course at a local college. She learned about many different types of paper, colors, mediums, depth, and lighting schemes. She attended lectures by visiting artists and made frequent visits to area art galleries. And Jen began painting.

She arranged her mansion to be artist friendly. She enlarged the first floor's drawing and smoking rooms into a single room with full floor to ceiling windows that captured natural daylight for those times she wished to paint indoors. She glassed in the western corner of her veranda and installed a space heater so she could comfortably paint there during cold, blustery days. Much like a nesting bird, she was in these transition days. Frequently she flitted off to a local art supply store to obtain or order what she fancied would help her canvas show the exact effect she sought to convey. This business left her no time to realize that she was lonely. That feeling of isolation didn't occur to her until one rainy day during the last week of winter.

She had not seen him arrive. She was intent on capturing her vision of a sailboat's stern, sweeping the sea aside as it tacked into the wind. She heard him first. *"Meow!"* he screamed, startling her. She looked at her glass door. And, there he stood. He wasn't exactly a proud cat. Defiant was a better descriptive word for him. He was an oversized tabby cat. He looked up at Jen to survey her. In doing this, he revealed his front teeth. They seemed to be in perfect condition. His fur was also in good condition, except for a patch on his foreleg where something had torn the fur away. Obviously, he was feeding well somewhere on something. But his face told a different tale. His was a face that knew combat. One eye was missing and partially grown over with fur. His good eye was rheumy with a crusted mess of dried tears plastered fast to his face, from his watery eye down to his mouth. His right foreleg had a reddish patch of scab in place of his missing fur. Obviously, he had been fighting.

"Oh, you dear fellow. You're quite the mess, aren't you? What have you been up to? Been fighting? You're a feral cat, aren't you? No collar? Of course not! A big tough guy like you wouldn't be caught dead wearing a collar, would you? No mistress will ever sissify you, will she? No, I didn't think so. You like being out and about and free, don't you? Wouldn't give that up for your life or your other eye, would you? No. Of course you wouldn't. I think I shall call you Bifster One, for bruiser with one eye. That suits you, doesn't it, tough guy?"

And so began Jen's great love affair with this fierce male of a different species. Their friendship was birthed out of the cat's insistence that Jen feed him and Jen's heartfelt compassion for this male who needed her attention. Bifster defined the parameters of their relationship, initially. Whenever Jen approached him with a bowl of the finest cat food, he puffed up to twice his size. His tail stiffened and swelled, also to twice it's normal girth. And he scowled and hissed menacingly, as if were Jen to make the slightest move towards him, he would surely become a furious frenzied maniacal shredding machine.

This cautionary stand off continued into the middle of Spring. By then, Bifster was showing up for his feedings twice daily. He had his prickly ways; but Jen had hers. And she took a liking to him. Every time he appeared, she spoke cheerfully and softly to him, constantly reassuring him that she was a non-threatening friend who appreciated his company.

But on this spring day their relationship would change. Jen had decided, for Bifster's own good, he needed to be neutered and tested for diseases. Today Bifster would be seeing a veterinarian. By now, the cat had relaxed his guard slightly. He was letting Jen get closer to him and he had stopped his hissy-fit routine when she placed his bowl before him. And that slight relaxing proved to be Bifster's downfall. Behind her back Jen held a beach towel. While Bifster chowed down, face buried in his food bowl, Jen pounced. She cast the towel over him and very quickly gathered him up and whisked him into a large sized cat carrier. Once in the carrier, Bifster howled.

"There, there. This is for your own good, you know," Jen spoke softly, trying to assure her friend that she meant to cause him no harm. *"There are younger Tomcats coming along, you know. And every day they are getting stronger. And you are already in your prime. One of these days an upstart boy is going to take you on. You don't want to lose your one good eye, do you? You don't want big chunks of your pretty fur ripped away, do you? And you want to be a happy kitty, don't you? Of course, you do. When you heal*

up from your neutering, Jen is going to let you come inside. You'll have a nice warm bed by my fireplace. You'll have a food bowl that's always got food in it. You'll have a water tap running a continuous drip so you'll always have fresh water. No more drinking from dirty mud puddles! You'll like that, won't you? And you'll be able to come sleep in bed with Jen when you get used to having me around. Won't that be fun for you? Sure, it will! And when you get accustomed to the cat carrier, Jen is going to take you on trips with her. We'll motor over to Cape Cod, to this lovely beach near P (Province) town. It's so beautiful and secluded. I bought a small, rustic cabin there. You'll love the place. You can prowl around on the dunes; walk on your paws over the soft, white sand; and you can chase lots of mice and birds, too! Jen will take you there often. You'll come and sit by me, while I paint; or you can be near me while I make love with one of the yummy young boys whom I've met in my art classes. We'll have fun, together, you and me. We will, Bifster. You'll see. You are going to be a very happy, pampered kitty.'

The local vet gave Bifster a clean bill of health. No feline leukemia. No distemper. Now neutered, he became an ideal companion for Jen. The accomplished corporate raider focused her energies on a merger that, by all appearances, was impossible to consummate. Joining Mr. Bifster, from Kitty Kingdom, to Jen's World, with its moments of silent study and periods of frenzied movement; capturing a scene or a lighting effect, would be challenging. Jen knew that going in. But she decided Bifster and his friendship would be well worth her efforts. After all, he was a unique sort of cat with his attitude complex and one good eye. And he had come to her on that cold February morning. Jen convinced herself that Bifster wasn't just some grifter cat scrounging for food. No, he was much more than that. He was a feisty, brave soul; a modern-day knight of the feline species. And the real reason he sought her out was he wanted to be her friend. Bifster had planted the seed of friendship. Now that the ordeal of his neutering had passed, their friendship could sprout and grow.

"You didn't want to stay a feral cat, did you, Bifster?" Bifster looked up at Jen when she talked to him now. Sometimes her even purred at the sound of her voice. Today, he seemed to understand that she was confiding in him and seeking his agreement and forgiveness for the mutilation of his testicles. It was one of those times when an animal knows that, somehow, its fortunes are tied to a human's willingness to take it in and care for it. Poor things, especially stray cats, have no real say in the matter. They can only hope, if they know how to hope, that the human who adopts them is a good human. Bifster was lucky. Jen was a kind heart. And she was very good to him.

"You didn't want to spend your life fighting other cats and hiding from foxes, did you?" Jen was very expressive. Her animated gestures were intended to draw Bifster into her monologues; make him feel like he was part of the conversation; and that the decisions she had made for his welfare were his decisions.

"Goodness no!" she shook her head emphatically, and opened her hands to him. *"You wanted Jen to love you and pamper you, didn't you? And you wanted to live a good long life, didn't you? Well, of course, you did. And Jen will make sure that you do. Okay, big guy?"* After a brief silence when human and feline exchanged stares, Bifster meowed. Jen took that to mean that Bifster agreed with her agenda. She picked him up and hugged him. And he let her.

Her next challenge was working with Bifster to get him accustomed to her cat carrier. It was difficult and stressful, at first. Bifster would see the carrier; then run and hide. But Jen was persistent. She would hunt him down; bag him in a towel; then plop him into the carrier. And then, she would reward him with a kitty treat and a pinch of catnip in a bag, for going through the exercise.

This became a daily game. Eventually, Bifster stopped running and hiding when he saw the carrier. He realized, after some thirty attempts at escaping, that he was fated to lose. One day, he simply surrendered. When Jen brought out his carrier, he just stood still and looked up at Jen. He then allowed her to pick him up and settle him into his carrier. He knew by then that his trips to this odd cat purgatory never lasted long. As soon as he finished his treat and Jen had given him his catnip, she lifted him out of the carrier and he discovered himself a free cat once again. Bifster allowed his cat logic to convince him that his mistress, Jen, was a kind and merciful jailer. Finally, by the end of Spring, he trusted her.

By late summer Jen and Bifster had made six trips to her Cape Cod cabin. She had managed to replicate her Newport art studio in her cabin. She loved both her worlds. She loved the atmosphere of both places. There was the culture and colors of Newport with is art galleries and coffee shops and her college nearby. It was all so stimulating. And there was the raw wildness of the Cape; and the feel of salt grasses on her bare feet; and the freshness of ocean breezes lifting her hair away from her face; and the taste of ocean spray in the air. All this raw nature, here with her; filling her with life and the sheer awe of all of it! And the near constant sometimes harried and sometimes laughing callings and squawks of the seagulls. And the surf! The lovely ever present, reassuring pounding of the surf breaking against the shore. And then its ominous withdrawing sound, as its waters retreated from the beach; as if leaving behind its retreat its admonition to never forget for one moment the ocean's immense powers; and how it could, suddenly and without warning, snatch a mortal woman away and carry her to its mysterious, haunting, Neptune deeps.

And then they came, predictably, inevitably; the unstoppable rising swells and breakers, roaring back in their fearsome assault upon the beach once again; to pulverize the white sands again, as they have done since the beginning of time, into ever finer, more granular grains of powdery white sand. Jen loved being here; being a part of it all; feeling the insignificant smallness and the blessedness of being able to immerse herself in the wonderment of it; and being able to drink in the immensity of it all. Often, she would sit on a blanket on the seaward side of the dunes while sketching or painting the ocean. And Bifster would stop his mousing or birding or running down hapless spiders and insects and come sit beside her. It seemed to Jen in those endearing moments that Bifster understood the importance of this special place and that it refreshed both their souls to be here. He often sat next to her now and even let her place her arm over him. Human and feline faced the vast ocean, feeling the air; tasting it; savoring it; appreciating each other's warmth and the pounding roars of the ever-changing sea. Together, Jen and Bifster understood eternity.

CHAPTER THIRTEEN

I long to talk with some old lover's ghost who died before the god of love was born. (John Donne: Love's deity)

When you make love with a man and it feels so right, consider you may have been lovers in your previous lives. (Rosemary Ness Bitner, author)

THOR

It was inevitable. Thor Ragnar, a young art student, took an interest in Jen. Their relationship began innocently enough. Thor asked Jen how she created the color contrasts in her seascapes, and she showed him. He invited her to coffee to thank her and she accepted.

"I couldn't help but notice you, Jen. You seem so diligent and focused. You take your art seriously, don't you?"

"Yes, I do."

"Are you planning to exhibit somewhere, sometime soon?"

"Oh no, I doubt if I'll ever do that."

"You don't need the money then, do you?"

Jen's caution flag went up when Thor broached the subject of money. She knew that living in her mansion labeled her as a woman of considerable means. She was open to relationships with members of the opposite sex, as long as the relationship was centered about her and her male friends' interests; not about her money. Despite the caution flag, Thor held Jen's interest. She gauged he was six feet, three inches tall. His thick red hair and broad shoulders were accented by his face. He had a manly face; a fierce face with penetrating deep blue eyes, a light, slightly ruddy complexion in the Viking tradition of Nordic seafarers; and a mouth and jaw that held a Jen's imagination:

"I wonder if he's a good kisser? I wonder how well he knows how to use that mouth of his? I wonder how I'll feel when he attaches it to my vagina? You know you want to fuck him. You've got to assume he has a fabulous penis. I wonder how much he knows about me? Is he just some happy go lucky puppy with big feet and big ideas; or is he a man who appreciates a woman for who she is? I think I'll just answer questions and not ask any. I'll find out more that way. I've noticed a few girls in class flirting with him. I'm sure he's had his share of girls already. I wonder if he's mastered cunnilingus; or if he even knows what it is? I like the way his eyes hold mine while he sips his coffee. He's not in a hurry. That's a good sign. He nibbles his coffee cake; never takes big bites. That's a good sign, too.

"Maybe he's sensuous? Maybe he's very good with that mouth? Maybe those huge hand of his understand how to touch and pinch and caress and finger a woman? Maybe Thor even has a brain to go with that face and body? Maybe he'll develop into a good friend?

"And there are the speed bump things. There's the age thing. I'm four or five years older than him. There's the background thing. I've done incest; put corporate deals together; steered boardroom decisions; worked with Dad to build my conglomerate empire; and I've done porn. Yeah, if anything, I'll bet he's figured out that I've done the porn thing. Has he, possibly, seen my films? Is that what got his nerve up to ask me for coffee? Possibly he wants to find out what it's like to be with a woman who loves to fuck? Maybe he wants to compare me to the girls he's already had? Maybe he wants to find out if he can perform well enough to give a porn star three orgasms?

Maybe he's only interested in creating beautiful art? Maybe he thinks I'm the key to bettering his technique?

"Well, I suppose I'll be like Mr. Bifster: guarded, circumspect, attentive, and open to possibilities. What the hell? Maybe the two of us can become better artists. That is what I want, isn't it? And, it couldn't hurt me to have a younger lover. It might be fun. I'd feel like a teen again; like when I started doing porn. That was exciting; mouthwatering. It would be thrilling to suck a young man's penis again. Yes. Yummy. Yes, I think I'd like that. I'm sure he'll be able to keep it up. And I imagine his ejaculations will feel hot and fabulous. Yeah, I'm sure I'd love feeling his cum shots gushing over my clit. It's been months since I've done it. I've even had the urge to make some calls to producers and do some porn again; but I've decided against it. I've outgrown it. I used to fall in love that way: thinking Roger, Ross, Alex, and Nelson. But they are only in my memories now. I've moved on. They've moved on. I couldn't fall in love with a porn partner again. It would seem too forced; trying too hard for something that is more than just the sex. But why not play along with this puppy? Why not see if he tries to bed me? Yeah, why not?'

Coffees, lunches, sitting on benches together between classes followed for Jen and Thor. He revealed bits and pieces of himself between their discussions about art. Jen was more guarded. She didn't invite him to her mansion or to pick her up or drop her off there; nor did she give him any hint that she had a yacht and billions in assets. She never wore any jewels that might give her disguise away. She kept herself plain vanilla Jen; simple clothes, minimal make up; and always art centric, focused on mediums, technique, expression through contrasts, etc. But Thor was no dummy. He noticed things. He caught glimpses of Jen's long, firmed legs and her tight buttocks. And her manners. There was refinement there. She was brought up to be respectful and demure. And her grace-fulness, the way she carried herself; the confidence with which she spoke, and the conciseness of her word choices. Curiosity got the best of Thor. He searched her last name in the local library's newspaper records.

"Jen, I have a confession to make to you," They were in Jen's car, having just returned to the College after lunch at a cozy bistro. Thor's head dropped slightly and his eyebrows lifted. He was ashamed of the snooping he had done. But he had feelings for her. He understood that her money placed them worlds apart. He surmised that her stint as a porn star had likely jaundiced her. She'd already made love with some of the world's handsomest, most experienced lovers. What appeal could he possibly have to a woman as worldly as her? Yet, there were those times when they connected over something in their art. And there were those times when Jen laughed at something he said. Then, too, were the ways she smiled at him; the ways her eyes flashed interest and friendship; and, yes, even that hint of love. He was certain of it, especially the ways her lips lifted or dropped when the message her eyes carried was telling him that there were real feelings there, behind those alluring eyes. Yes. It was often there, in her lips.

Her feelings betrayed her. He was sure of it. He detected her true feelings for him. He intuited that Jen loved him. *"I got interested in you. You intrigued me; and I realized I had feeling for you. So, I found out about you. I investigated newspaper records. I had to know. You've been so…. well…. circumspect. I thought you might be hiding something; possibly even a criminal record. The unknowing of whom you were, while I had these feelings of wanting to be near you; with you, just kept gnawing at me. So, I looked. I learned about your money and your mansion. I learned about your father and how powerful he was. And I know about your friendship with Marty Mallory, and about your own films. Jen."*

He blurted out, *"I don't care about any of those things. Honestly, I'm not interested in you for your money or for your porn experiences. Honestly, I'm not. And if you don't believe me, then you don't. I can't help how you feel about me or what I've done. I just want you to know that it's you that I'm interested in; just you, Jen. I just love being with you. I'm being completely honest."*

Jen leaned back against her car door and stared at Thor. No man had ever confessed that he had investigated her. She nodded to Thor: *"So, now you think you know all about me, don't you? My porn films?"*

"Yes." Thor nodded.

"My father, and how he raided companies and laid people off?"

"Yes." Thor nodded again. This time his head came back up more slowly.

"And you know about my wealth, too, don't you?"

"Yes," Thor shrugged his shoulders sheepishly.

"And my highly publicized friendship with Marty Mallory, Queen of Porn. You know about that too, don't you?" Jen's eyebrows lifted in amazement at Thor's diligence. She noted that he again shrugged his shoulders; but this time his face wore a sheepish smile. She decided to assess whether his interest was that of a perverted stalker, a gold digger, or a young man who had become smitten by her. *"So, tell me, Thor, are you repulsed; enamored perhaps? I need to know why you kept digging? I mean, once you learned I did porn, didn't that tell you all you needed to know? Why did you continue digging?"*

"I was trying to piece your life together, to understand why you did porn, Jen. It didn't make sense to me. Here you were, a girl who had everything. You had the world at your feet; and yet you did porn. I mean, most girls who start out doing porn have very little money and they use porn as a way to make a start in life. You didn't need to do that. It made no sense to me. So, I tried to put the puzzle of your life into context so it would make sense to me."

A light rain had begun to fall. The isolated drops on the windshield were getting heavier and coming more frequently than just a few minutes earlier. The sky to the south was filling with a white line of advancing clouds, and looming behind them the sky was turning more ominous darkening gray. A precocious thought crossed Jen's mind. *"So, you wanted to make sense of my life, did you?"*

"Well, yes. I find you most intriguing."

"I'm glad I intrigue, Thor. I'm going to help you figure me out. Get out of my car."

"What? It's starting to rain?" Thor reacted with shock to Jen's command. He thought he stood on firmer ground. Now, he was being ejected from her car and, he believed, from her life as well.

"Get out, Thor. Right now. It's really going to rain soon. You'd better run for it." Jen pulled her lips tight in a matter-of-fact grimace. It was her way of letting Thor know that she disapproved of his sleuthing.

But she was not finished with him. She decided to teach him that there is a much better way for a man to learn about a woman. She followed Thor in her car as he half-walked, half shuffle-marched in quick step towards the college. He was getting wet. Perfect! That was exactly the effect she wanted. After five blocks of watching his distressed shuttle walk, she decided he'd had enough. She pulled her car slightly ahead of him and leaned on the car's horn. She giggled when he jumped; but she didn't let him see that. She lowered her window and shouted to him:

"Thor, get in the car. You're getting soaking wet!"

"What do you want from me?" He scowled back, indignantly.

"Understanding would be a good start. A little respect, maybe." She shouted in turn.

"But I don't understand you! I don't even know where to begin!"

"That's obvious. Get in the car. You'll catch cold standing there in the rain. You can try to understand me later." Jen canted her

head, implying this was Thor's moment to choose. He could make amends with her; learn about her, her way; or he could just keep walking; and that would be the last he'd see her. Her look also implied that she didn't intend to give him much time to choose. As Thor dropped his scowl and ran toward the car, Jen had a silent thought: *"Thanks for your lessons, Daddy. You always were the greatest negotiator!"*

Once Thor was in the car, Jen asked: *"So, what did you learn about me?"* Her head was lifted high and her eyes were upturned.

"I don't know," Thor shook his head. His dismay was obvious.

"Want to learn more?" Now Jen tilted her head toward his and smiled mischievously.

"What? You're going to jerk me around? I've heard that women are unpredictable; but I never expected to………"

"Be put out like an unwelcome cat?" Jen finished Thor's sentence for him.

"Yeah. Did you have to do that?"

"Yeah. I did."

"I don't understand."

"I know you don't. You will."

"Huh?"

"Get your art kit and your sheets and canvases. Meet me in front of the college in two hours. It's one now. I'll pick you up at three."

"Where are we going?"

"You'll see."

'*When are we coming back?*'

"Sometime. Maybe next week."

"But I have classes. There's the brush seminar series over the next three days. I really need to get to those for my work. I can't miss them."

"This is a more important lesson than your classes. You can pick up that technique stuff later. If you need it, we'll hire that professor

to tutor you. We're in front of your dorm now. Get your art things and a bag of your personal things. I'll be here for you in two hours."

"That's it? You're not even telling me where we're going?" Now Thor pleaded.

"*Two hours. Right here!*" Jen shook her head and gave a playful smile, as if to assure her young beau that his lessons about understanding a woman would not be medieval torture.

CHAPTER FOURTEEN

Thy kingdom come. Thy will be done. (from the Lord's Prayer)

I was a child and she was a child; but we loved with a love that was more than love; I and my Annabell Lee. (Edgar Allen Poe; Annabell Lee)

KITTY KINGDOM

Thor met Jen in front of the college. He carefully laid his portfolio case and backpack in the trunk of Jen's car, then slid into the front passenger seat.

"What's that?" Seeing an oversized animal carrier on the back seat, Thor looked alarmed and confused.

"He's not a that. Thor, say hello to Bifster One. Bifster, say hello to Thor," commanded Jen.

"Hello, Bifster One," Thor mustered a tentative greeting to the creature in the animal carrier. *"What is he, Jen?"* Thor looked questioningly at the driver of the car. His voice and face indicated he was somewhat miffed. He had presumed that the trip was for him and Jen to get acquainted, hopefully on a romantic basis. He had not imagined that Jen would bring along a companion cat.

"He's, my friend. He's a perfect gentleman. And he happens to be a cat."

"And he travels with you?"

"When I travel by car; yes, he does."

"I didn't know you liked cats."

"*I don't. I feel ambivalent towards most cats. I can take them or leave them; but I happen to like this cat.*"

"*He's special then?*"

"*Very special.*"

"*What makes him special?*"

"*He came to me, seeking a relationship with me. He was a feral cat. I fed him when he was hungry and we became friends. He doesn't ask much of me, except he likes being with me. He's still got a lot of feral in him.*"

"*He won't go nuts and attack me?*"

"*Not if you don't suddenly attack me. He's protective towards me. I don't think he'd set well with that. I've had him neutered and checked. He has no diseases. And he lets me pet him now. And he even purrs sometimes. He is still protective of his belly when I try to rub him there. We're working on that.*"

"*How did you decide he wanted a relationship with you?*"

"*He had other choices. He had very good fur when he introduced himself. But he preferred that I feed him. Then, after the second time I fed him, he rubbed up against my leg.*"

"*And that was significant?*"

"*Very. It certainly was. It was his way of telling me that I was welcome in his Kitty Kingdom.*"

"*Kitty Kingdom?*"

"*Yes, the world of Bifster One. It helps you to understand his world better if you train your mind to think like a cat thinks.*"

"*They think?*"

"*Yes, they do. Better than most men. And they think great thoughts, too. Don't you, Bifster?*" Bifster stayed silent. "*He's just being quiet until he gets to know you, Thor. When you hear his meow, you'll know that he accepts your presence.*"

"*So, I'm the subject of some kind of approval test? Whether Bifster decides to like me?*"

"No, nothing like that. I'm not some fickle nut hatch, Thor. I just like him and there's no reason why he can't be included where we're going. He likes having fun, too."

"I see. Well, now that we are on our way, would you please tell me where we're going?"

"To my cabin on Cape Cod." Jen offered a sketchy description of her cabin, and its location and surroundings. She was scant on details; preferring her tendency to understate, then deliver a positive surprise.

"Sounds like a terrific place," approved Thor. The three travelers drove on silently for another fifteen minutes; Thor and Jen both turned over their private thoughts.

"Thor, it's my turn to ask some questions. Do you mind?" Jen glanced away from the road and smiled innocently into his eyes. She had the subject of her interest exactly where she wanted him. He needed to be truthful and convincing. She was wary of any man who stalked her or investigated her history or financial wealth.

"No, not at all. Shoot." He was relaxed and comfortable. He had taken his shoes off, put his seat back and reclined.

"What went through your mind when you first asked me if you could carry my books?"

"Jen, you're a very beautiful woman. And you intrigued me."

"You had not researched me before you asked to carry my books?"

"No, I didn't. Besides, how could I? I didn't even know your name until later. The instructors are strict about not calling on us by name. Honest, Jen, I didn't know who you were. I had no clue. Besides, when I introduced myself, you told me your name was Bridgett Abadie. There's no such person anywhere within two hundred miles."

"Okay; so, what prompted you to ask me whether you could carry my books?"

"I wanted to meet you."

"Why me? There are twenty other girls in the class. And a lot of them are very pretty. How did I get so lucky?"

"Well, I started to notice how you carried yourself; kind of proudly and unhurried. And I noticed that you didn't seem to talk with the other women. You had no interest in them. And you showed no interest in any of the men, either. You seemed to be a real loner. That's true, isn't it?"

"I tend to mind my own knitting, yes. So, you thought I was lonely?"

"No, that wasn't it. You always seemed to understate yourself. You wear simple shirts and slacks, mostly. You don't overdo makeup. And you are the only woman in the class that never wears jewelry. That kind of intrigued me about you. I thought you might be trying to disguise yourself. But two things gave you away."

"Pray tell me, great sleuth." Jen cracked a smile. Thor was amusing her. She was pleased to hear about the machinations the young man's mind went through while on the discovery trail.

"Well, most days you wore brand name tennis shoes while other women wore flats. That told me you took good care of your feet."

"Lots of women wear tennis shoes."

"Yes; but then there was a day when you wore flats and a white silk blouse. Do you remember that?"

"Oh, yes, I do remember," Jen recalled that she had come to class after a charity's board meeting. *"So?"*

"Well, your flats were made of soft leather. There was something about them and the way your feet seemed to melt into them that excited me."

"You have a foot fetish?"

"Yes, for your feet, I think I do. But it wasn't the shoes that made me want to give chase. It was your blouse."

"A white silk one?"

"Yes, you wore no bra. And the way the light touched your blouse when you turned your body to sit down, allowed me to see your breasts through the silk. That brief caption of your breasts and your nipples played with my mind for weeks. I thought about your breasts so much, I had trouble sleeping. I tossed and turned nights imagining how it would feel to cup your breasts in my hands and kiss your nipples. I dreamed of softly biting and sucking them. I couldn't get you and your breasts out of my mind. I didn't want you or it out of my mind, understand. I was obsessed with thinking about how I could approach you. That's when I got up the courage to ask you if I could carry your books."

"Oh my! Fish on!" Jen let out a spontaneous laugh.

"Fish on?" Thor looked perplexed.

"That's girl talk, for when a woman knows a man is interested in her, Thor. I remember when you first asked me. You were so obviously interested, I almost let out a giggle. But I didn't want to chase you away; so, I acted surprised and very pleased for your offer. You caught my smile when I accepted, didn't you?"

"Yes. So, why didn't you tell me who you really were?" Thor's face was curious with a touch of miffed.

"Well, Thor, a woman can't be too cautious these days. What did you expect me to say: Gee thanks, handsome guy I just met. Let me drive you to my place. Can I take your pants off and have a quick fuck?" Jen chuckled. Taunting him was fun.

"That's not very nice, Jen." Thor's face was crestfallen. He never took her for being a vulgar woman.

"Come on, Thor," her voice chided, *"Get real. You know I've done porn. Don't tell me you expect me to be an ingenui from a bible study group."*

"No, I know you're no virgin, Jen. I'm not stupid. It's just that, to me, you're very special. I wish you understood that."

"Well, that's what I'm curious about. How is it that I came to be so special to you? How did you even find out who I am? How did you come to know my history? How did you find my porn films? How's a woman supposed to know she's not just being hustled?"

"You already know. I told you. Remember when I first asked you to carry your books, I didn't even know your name. You do remember that, don't you?" Thor's voice was raised; dominating.

She liked his assertiveness; his willingness to take command. *"Yes. Sorry. I forgot. You really were attracted to me, weren't you? It was the way I carried myself, my demeanor and how I dressed myself like a plain Jane."* Jen relaxed a bit, now assuring herself she was hearing the truth. This younger man was smitten by her. *"And my flats and that silk blouse that gave you that peek at my boobs. That was the sum of all of it, wasn't it? That was what made you hit the bait, wasn't it?"* Her eyes searched his to understand his truth as he nodded. The truth was there. He was smitten then. And smitten now. And his little hurt from her vulgarity and distrust showed through, too.

"Yes Jen, that sent me out of my mind crazy for you, honest."

"So, after you learned there was no woman named Bridgett, how did you learn who I was?"

"I followed you."

"How? I drive and you walk."

"I saw the direction you took when you left school. I cut class and waited along your route with my bike; and followed at a distance until I saw where you lived."

"You saw me drive into my mansion's garage?"

"Yes. Then I wrote down the address. I found out that it was held in your father's trust for you. I found out who he was; his connection to Marty Mallory; their business ventures; your parents' divorce. I was curious about Marty and why a man who'd been married fifteen years would toss his marriage for her. So, I watched five of her

films. And, not only did I see why a man would leave his family for her; I also discovered you. There you were, in a trailer film tagged along with Marty's film. You were doing four guys at a waterfall. I was struck by how sexy you are, Jen. My testosterone was blowing gaskets in my mind. The ways you sucked and fucked those four boys took my breath away. You must have been fifteen or sixteen when you made that film, right?"

"Yes, sixteen. Almost seventeen."

"Well, I fell in love with you then, watching that film and knowing who you are. I'm being honest. You're the most beautiful, sexiest woman I've ever seen."

"Sexier than Marty?"

"Yes, honestly. Your smile captivates me. You remind me of a cute fox. I just want to take you in my arms and hug you. I've felt that way since I saw you in the silk blouse. No offense to your friend, Marty, Jen; but you intrigue a man. You're mysterious. A man wonders what it's like to hold your body close and kiss your mouth. And a man looks at you and thinks you deserve to be loved. Not to take anything away from Marty; I've never met her, in person. But in her films, a man knows what to expect, and, as wondrous as she is, that knowing detracts from the enchantment of it. With you, it's like falling into a wonderland with no end. In all truth, Jen, I adore you."

"But you've never even kissed me."

"I don't care. The feeling is real. It's an obsession thing. And when that one boy performed oral sex on you in that film, I ......, well, I don't know how to say this, Jen; but I laid awake nights and prayed that I could do that with you, too; someday. I called the number to your private service, on the porn site that carried your film. But the voice mail said your voice mail was full. I figured you discontinued it. You did some prostitution, connected to Marty somehow, and then you just dropped out of site, right? No more porn; no more prostitution, right?"

"Yes. I just dropped out of porn and prostitution altogether."

"Why? I mean, you are the most adorable, fuckable babe ever. I'm sure the demand was there."

"Thank you. That's enough with the compliments, okay? Yes, the demand was there. I just outgrew it all. It stopped being exciting."

"So, why did you do it in the first place?"

"Thor, that's touchy. I never needed the money. I just loved the freedom that porn gave me; that boost to my self-esteem; that attitude adjustment that convinced me I didn't need anybody's approval for the decisions I made for my life. I loved doing porn for the while that I did it. But the feeling didn't last. My decision to do porn had to do with rebellion issues I had with my mother. Marty helped me; put me with good people; gave me confidence. She was so precious and so understanding. She became my best friend." Jen's voice trailed off. She sounded maudlin when she spoke of Marty.

"I thought diamonds were a girl's best friend? Come to think of it, you never wear any jewelry, do you, Jen? Do you even have any diamonds?"

"Yes, I have tons of diamonds; but I seldom wear an of them. I don't want to show off; and I certainly don't want to make myself a target for bad people. Wearing bling is passe, anyway. And diamonds are not a girl's best friend."

"No? What is then?"

"The pill, Thor. The birth control pill is a girl's best friend, because it lets her have what she really needs, without worrying about becoming a slave to an infant child and getting trapped in a marriage to some guy who wants a child so he can have someone to play with.'

'What she really needs? You mean......?"

"A penis, Thor. A penis is right up there near the top of necessities for a woman; right alongside of a car, a dwelling place, and food, and energy for her car, cooking, and warmth. You see, Thor, once a

woman has the necessities, she wants satisfaction and vindication of who she is. A penis gives her those things and the confidence that she deserves having them. The penis completes her as a valid human."

"Not her money?"

"Nope; not even close; only the male penis. Once a woman has sufficient money, the male penis becomes her biggest priority."

"And is that why you are taking me with you to your cabin on Cape Cod?"

"Yes, Thor. I'm going to fuck you. I'm going to fuck you so wonderfully and beautifully that you'll remember this week for the rest of your life."

"Oh wow, Jen. And can I do cunnilingus with you, too?"

"Yes, you'd better!" Jen smiled her most affirmative smile. "And let's see how many positions we can do it in, agreed?"

"Agreed. I've never had a conversation like this before; not with any other woman. You're so direct, Jen. Talking about sex doesn't bother you, does it?"

"No, why should it? Father always told me to be direct; rarely circumspect, unless you are unsure of the other party. That's why I was circumspect with you at first, Thor. I needed to be sure of whom you are. A woman can't be too careful."

"You learned a lot from your dad, didn't you?"

"Yes. My years with him before his heart attack were the best years of my life. He and Marty were both so good to me: business associates; best friends; confidants; and intimate lovers. We were inseparable; an unbreakable trio. They helped me put the Infernoss Decado Club together. We had seven locations, including the cruise ships, before we folded it into Dad's holding company. Now, they are both gone."

"Jen, you were intimate with your dad? Incest?"

"Yes; for three beautiful years. We loved each other on a level few people will ever know or understand. It was wonderful. It completed me as a woman."

"You miss him, don't you?"

"Terribly. I've been in mourning these past several months."

"Heart attack, right?"

"Yes."

"Was that a shock to you? He was only in his early sixties. He had a lot of life left to live."

"Yes, he did; but I didn't see it that way. I'm twenty-six. I'm still young and beautiful. I have the best years of my life right in front of me. And no, his heart attack was not a shock to me."

"I don't understand?"

"Thor, it's like this. Marty explained spirit souls to me. She told me she has the spirit soul of a temple priestess who performed prostitution rituals twenty thousand years ago. This man had a wife who tried to separate her husband from the tribe. Marty had the woman murdered while she fornicated with her husband, right in front of her."

"Devilish femme; control freak, right?"

"Something like that. Well, the husband became a lover to the priestess prostitute; and he gave his daughter to be raised by the prostitute. So, the daughter learned all sorts of pornographic seduction methods. She became an exemplary temple whore. The priestess educated her about the beauty of incest."

"It's beautiful?"

"Yes, absolutely it is, when it's understood in a loving way; in a way that helps a young girl appreciate the power of her sexuality and the freedoms that her sexuality gives her."

"Okay, so, this daughter was doing her father?"

"Yes."

"And this relates to you, somehow?"

"Wait for it, Thor. Be patient. I'll explain everything."

"Okay."

"*Well, this father decided, because he was doing his daughter and had given her to the priestess, that he could short change the temple. He tried to cut back on his required tithe. The priestess didn't take kindly to that. She decided to punish the father.*"

"*Okay, I'm following.*"

"*Well, to bind the girls' loyalty to the temple, and really to herself, the priestess decided that the girl should punish her father by murdering him. The father was brought before the priestess on charges. He pleaded and begged, but his daughter showed him no mercy. She decapitated him.*"

"*Wow, wicked women.*"

"*No Thor, not wicked women. Women who asserted their rights and took what was rightfully theirs.*"

"*So, what has this got to do with you, Jen?*"

"*Marty swear that my spirit soul is the same spirit soul of that decapitated father's daughter. The father was the lover of both the priestess and his daughter, just like my father is the lover of Marty and me.*"

"*Okay, I'm seeing something here. Go back to your father's heart attack.*"

"*All right. Well, from my perspective, I was in much the same situation as the girl in Marty's story. You see, Daddy was getting along in years. His penis wasn't nearly as strong as the penises of my porn partners. And Daddy had all those billions that he couldn't possibly ever use, except to buy more companies and make more money. And Daddy had already taught me much of what he knew about acquiring companies. You know, all the calculations that go into valuing companies; all the tricks to use in proxy war take over fights. So, you see, I was much like that temple prostitute girl. Her father and mine had a commonality. Neither father was of much further use to his daughter. Are you getting this, Thor?*"

"Sort of. So, you were actually happy that your father had a heart attack and died?"

"More than just happy, Thor. I made sure he had it. And I made sure he couldn't recover from it."

"Jen! Why are you telling me this?"

"Because I need you to appreciate that I am totally immoral. I want no secrets between us. And I can easily deny everything I'm telling you. I'm also unapologetic and fearless. Do you still think you love me?"

"Oh, Jen. Yes, I love you. So, tell me how your father died."

"I fucked him to death."

"What? How?"

CHAPTER FIFTEEN

Murder most foul, as in the best it is; but this most foul, strange, and unnatural. (Shakespeare: Hamlet)

    Murder is born in love, and love attains its greatest intensity in murder. (Octave Mirbeau: The Torture Garden)

MURDERESS JEN

"We had sex, like always; but I ground up two of his erection for longer pills and spiked his cocktail with them. He stayed rock hard through three of my orgasms. I was really happy for him. He was loving the intensity of our sex; living my orgasms with me. It was beautiful sex. Then, he started complaining of chest pains. He asked me to run quickly, and get him an aspirin. I told him I would, but I just needed him to hold on a little longer and help me get off one more time. Daddy really loved me. He kept at it. He tried very, very hard. Then, when his heart attack started, his entire body shuddered and convulsed. He gasped and moaned. I quickly changed positions. I told him I was certain his chest pains would pass if I just sat on his face for a moment. I positioned my vagina over his mouth and I sat down hard on his face. I made sure his nose was smothered by my buttocks' cheeks. I pressed my ass down hard on his face, making sure he could not breathe. I used my buttocks muscles to hold his head upright each time he tried to roll his head to one side or the other to get air to breathe. I kept pressing my ass down very hard

into his face while his legs thrashed wildly. I held his arms down with my hands on his wrists. I knew he was in agony; but I suffocated him as quickly as possible."

"Didn't you feel sorry for him; or any remorse for what you were doing to him?"

"No, not really. The thought that went through my mind at that time was that here was my corporate raider father. Here was this man who had ruined countless lives and companies. Here was this man who had taught me to be ruthless in my dealings with others. Here was Daddy, getting the immoral ending that he rightly deserved. I told myself that to be as ruthless as Daddy; to show him that I had learned the lessons that he had taught me, I needed to murder him. And I think his mind smiled while I murdered him, because he was pleased that I had become so much like him."

"And you never paused to reconsider what you were doing? You weren't worried about getting caught?"

"No. I only thought of myself as a predator. I was killing my victim. It was all just part of nature. I knew Daddy and I were alone. I knew I had ample time to be unhurried and methodical. Once I had Daddy in his favorite cunnilingual position, I knew murdering him would be easy. My thoughts shifted to thinking that this was now all just a process. So, I kept my ass-tight grip clamped down onto Daddy's face until his legs stopped moving and I was certain that he'd stopped breathing for several minutes. While he was in his final struggles, I thought about this young man named Thor, whom I noticed in my art class. I thought about inviting him over to my mansion after Daddy's remains were interred. I remember wondering what it might be like to make love with you, Thor; to fuck you in all sorts of ways. Then I looked at Daddy's legs and arms. I was convinced he was dead. I felt very proud of myself in those moments. I had taken something for myself, as Daddy had taught me to do. After a few minutes of reflecting that I was now in charge of all of

Daddy's companies and all of his wealth; and that I needed to be a responsible custodian of things, I lifter my tush off his face. I got a wet rag and towel from the kitchen and thoroughly cleaned Daddy's face. I dried him off. Noone could tell what had really happened. Then, I sat there, beside him, holding his hand. I checked his pulse to be doubly sure that he was dead. That wasn't really necessary; but I had nothing better to do. I waited for a full hour before I called for a paramedic. Daddy was beyond resuscitation when they arrived. They pronounced him dead of a massive heart attack."

"The paramedic asked me how it happened. All I said was: 'I don't know.' Daddy had taught me that when you're being pressed for an answer or explanation that you don't want to give, the best thing to say is: 'I don't know.' Daddy called that answer his 'Drop dead' answer. It causes your antagonist's mind to switch gears from trying to get the answer out of you to making up his own answer that fits things together in his own mind. That fit then fixes your interrogator's belief. That belief sets in his mind, like cement curing. Once that mental cement hardens, it's very hard for him to change his mind."

"You're amazing."

"I'm glad you think so. Daddy said the same thing. He often told me I was amazing after we had sex. That always made me feel proud of myself and my sexuality. Marty said that incest helps a young girl develop pride in her sexuality; and she was right. Poor Daddy. His heart just suddenly exploded from all that exertion. I like to think that I our last fuck was the greatest fuck that Daddy ever had; even better than any fucking he had with Mommy or Marty.

"Anyway, I know Daddy didn't suffer very long. The medical examiner wrote that the wall between his ventricles had a major rupture. Blood just flooded from the side that pumps blood out of the heart into the side that sucks blood back into the heart. The heart just suddenly stopped working. Daddy's death was sudden. So, just

like the father of the ancient temple whore received a quick and merciful death, Daddy also had a quick and merciful death.

"Maybe Marty's right," Jen pouted and sighed. "Poor me. Maybe I do have the same soul of that temple prostitute who was also a Daddy's girl? Maybe I'm ruthless and sinful and fuck crazy, just like she was? Heck, according to Marty, her soul lives inside me. Maybe I am She. And, you see, now I have all of Daddy's money. Isn't that wonderful? And, now I know everything he knew. And I also have you, Thor. Like Daddy, you are also very smart. And I felt your penis with my hand, in the car on our ride up here. I could tell it's huge. I can't wait to hold it in my hands and put it in my mouth and inside my vagina. I know I'm going to love your penis much; much more than I ever loved Daddy's. I can tell you have a fabulous penis, Thor. You're going to love having it in my mouth and my vagina. It's one of the main reasons why our love will be so special. I'm going to love fucking you. I'm totally getting into the mood to fuck you, can't you tell? You do want to fuck me, don't you? You'll love fucking me often, won't you?"

"You are an amazing, incorrigible, heartless whore, my love. Yes. We will fuck like there's no tomorrow."

"I am incorrigible, aren't I? I'm a woman who takes what she wants. Don't you want that trait in your partner? Do you like that about me? Does knowing I made money by sucking penises and lying on my back and fucking in porn films excite you? When I was lying on my back with my legs spread wide while I was caressing my partner's face and saying: 'Yes, yes, Ohhhh, yeses. Fuck me, Yesssss, fuck me,' Did you find yourself wishing you were him?"

"Yes."

"Did you find yourself wishing that it was you shooting your cum into my pussy instead of him?"

"Oh yes, Jen. Very much. I went to bed many a night wishing you were there in bed with me, fucking me. Many a night I prayed I could hold you in my arms and tell you how much I love you."

"Honest?"

"Yes, honest."

"But I'm such a naughty girl. I'm not the kind of girl a boy takes home to meet his mommy. You need to appreciate me for what I am. Do you think you can do that?"

"Yes. I know I can."

"You could love me, even though I have no morals; even though I am a total whore? Are you sure; or does it intrigue you that I can be heartless and ruthless? Daddy said those were good traits to have in business. Knowing how sinful and wicked I am; knowing I'm perfectly willing and capable of being intimate with multiple lovers, do you think you could truly love me? I don't believe in boundaries. I have the heart and soul of a whore, you know."

"Yes, you really are a very naughty woman, Jen. And yes, I know I can love you. I already do love you. I appreciate how determined you are to get what you want. I love you for that. I find myself loving you more with each passing day. I'm fascinated by your immorality. I've never encountered a woman like you before. I've studied your porn films. They tantalize me. I get crazed obsessed with thoughts of fucking you. I'm certain I'm going to love everything about you and your fabulous pussy."

"Do you think I'm beautiful?"

"Yes, You're gorgeous, stunning, dazzling."

"More beautiful than Marty?"

"Yes, much more beautiful. But when will we see Marty? Tell me. Where is she? What has happened to her?"

"No one seems to know. She seems to have disappeared. I hired a private detective; but he turned up nothing. Authorities have interviewed her mother, Susan, her business associates, David, and Bob. They talked with all her know past lovers and porn associates, including Celt, the man I used to procure underaged girls for my clubs. They checked her phone records; her travels; her porn partners. But no one has a clue. Everyone seems to have air tight alibis

for the day she was last seen. She just disappeared. I fear for her. It's not like her to not call me for this long. I'm afraid she's met with foul play and I'll never see her again."

"And you and she were lovers, too, weren't you?"

"Yes, the closest and the best. She was the most sensual person I think I'll ever know. I loved her. We had beautiful lesbian love. I miss that very much. So many men and many women loved her. She was so giving of herself; so free with her love; so passionate about her love-making. Being without Marty in my life is tragic."

"I'm sorry, Jen." Thor's voice conveyed his heartfelt feelings. After seeing Jen's porn films, he appreciated how much intimacy meant to her. He felt a stirring in his penis. He intuitively knew that Jen hoped he would help her fill some unspecified void in her life. The trip took on a new importance to him now. He felt needed and inspired to please; not disappoint.

They arrived at the cabin as the sun was setting. Jen let Bifster out of his carrier. His sense of freedom renewed; the cat disappeared in the direction of the dunes.

"Should I go after him and catch him and bring him back," Thor became alarmed as he watched Bifster fade into the shadows.

"No. You'd never catch him anyway, if he doesn't want to be caught. He just wants to explore for a while. He'll be back when he's ready to be fed."

"What's he looking for?"

"Anything that moves. He sees better in the dark than we do. If there's a mouse or a moving insect or small bird that's still fluttering before it nests, he'll find it. He'll come yodeling and running to us with a prize in his mouth."

"What should we do with it?"

"Nothing. He'll just present his prize to show us that he's a good cat. That's all. If he brings something, just let him have it. Don't try to take it away from him. He'll play with it for a while until he tires of it; then he'll lose interest and drop it; then he'll go do something else."

"Does he kill many birds?"

"A few. Usually, one or two every day I'm here."

"Don't you think he should be trained to not do that? Don't you feel sorry for those little birds?"

"No and no, Thor. You can't untrain his natural instincts. He wouldn't understand. He'd just get neurotic and then I'd have a bad relationship with him."

"But those poor little birds!"

"Don't feel sorry for them, Thor. If they are stupid enough to be caught by a cat, then that's their bad luck. That's all. It's nature. Be proud of him if he brings you a bird, Thor. He'll be showing you that he's a good cat. Pet him, if he'll let you. Reward him with a kitty treat."

'For killing an innocent bird?'

"Yes. Some creatures are meant to be victims, Thor. Don't feel sorry for them. Let's get the car unpacked and go inside. I'll make us hot soup and sandwiches. We'll eat light tonight. And I'll leave the door slightly ajar so Bifster can come in when he pleases."

"No worries about crime, Jen?"

"No. We're isolated. No one comes by here. Besides, I have security around this place. Intruders get shocked and a security fence comes out of the ground; bright lights and sirens go off. My private security comes. They're armed. Don't worry. We're safe here."

Inside the cabin, after their soup and sandwiches, Thor seemed ready to relax.

"Where's the TV? I'm not seeing it."

"That's because I don't have a TV."

"Oh. What do you do for entertainment?"

"I entertain myself. There's lots of good books here. We can read and sit and think about the messages the authors are trying to relate to us. And there's a large room where we can set up our easels, if we decide to paint or sketch. Relax while I freshen up."

"Okay. So, what would you like to do, Jen?"

"Tonight? Oh, I thought I'd break up my routine a little. I thought you and I should take this time we have and get acquainted with each other."

"Like how? Board games?"

"We could do some of those, if you like." Jen's voice faded as she went into the bedroom. When she reappeared five minutes later, she wore only a sheer silk chiffon, see-through white mini-length nightgown. Her nipples were clearly visible, as was the fleshy mound and love channel of her vagina. *"We could also play a game I especially love playing, if you like?"* Jen tilted her head and smiled her most coquettish naughty smile. She walked over to the recliner where Thor had settled his tall frame; and twirled around in a full circle, giving Thor a complete reveal of her lithesome body. Her Marty's Blend ™ of gardenia and lilac oil, with its hint of sandalwood left Thor breathless with desire. He instinctively reached out to her and placed his big hands on her hips. Jen had made up her mind about this moment before they even left Newport. She settled onto Thor's lap and ran her fingers from one hand through his hair. She leaned her head to his, kissing his mouth with her soft, inviting lips. Her other hand found his penis through his pants and began gently stroking it. *"Could I interest you in intimacy, Thor?"*

"Oh, Jen, yes! A thousand times, yes!" Thor buried his face in her stomach and squeezed her body close to him.

"Are you sure I'm the woman you want, Thor? You've seen my porn films. You've seen other men fucking me and you've seen other men's semen flowing from my love channel. I've told you that I did prostitution though my Private Member's Service that linked to my porn films. So, you know what a naughty girl I've been. You know I've done girl-girl sex with Marty, the world's most notorious whore. I've told you about my Infernoss Decado Clubs and how I've legally exploited thousands of underage girls. You also know I've done incest

with my father, for years. And, Thor, lest you forget, I'm four years older than you. That might not seem like a big difference to you, now; but if our paths are joined and we continue seeing each other, I promise you, it will become an issue for us. So, before you pillage me with your glorious penis, Thor; before You experience the most wonderful sex you've ever known in your life; ask yourself whether I'm the kind of woman your family can accept in your life. Seriously, Thor, many people can't stomach a woman with my morals being anywhere near their son or brother. How do you feel about that?"

Thor returned Jen's kisses and placed his hand on her breast. His finger and thumb found her nipple. It instantly hardened to his touch. *"Finally,"* he sighed, *"I'm with the woman I love. I'm with the woman I've gone crazy dreaming about. My family is me, Jen; okay? You'll always be young and beautiful to me, Jen. I promise you; I swear on my soul. I love you, and I will always love you."*

"Well, my sweet, handsome Norse God, let us not overthink all the permutations of what if's tonight. Let's retire to the bedroom, shall we? Let's make love." Jen stood; then taking Thor by the hand, led him into her bedroom. It was a well-appointed room, complete with a California King bed. And they made love.

And for the next three days Jen and Thor made love obsessively, in the cabin and on the dunes overlooking the beach. The fourth day of their love fest found them lying together, Jen's head resting in the hollow of Thor's shoulder when their dreamy thoughts were interrupted by Bifster's yodeling. They sat up to see what had the cat so excited.

CHAPTER SIXTEEN

Alas, regardless of their doom, the little victims play. No sense have they of ills to come, nor ills beyond today. (Thomas Grey: Ode on a distant prospect of Eton College)

I hated doing it; but in my books, I murdered butterflies. (Rosemary Ness Bitner, author)

MURDER PLAY

"Jen, look!" Thor voiced his alarm. *"He's got a Monarch butterfly in his mouth! It's flapping its wings frantically! Should I hit him and make him let it go?"* Thor shot a consternated look to Jen, expecting her to grant him approval to swat her cat. But no approval was forthcoming. The butterfly was stuck on Bifster's face; obviously doomed to be tortured by cat play, until its life drained away. While Thor's sympathies were clearly with the victim butterfly, Jen's were anything but.

"Don't you dare lay a hand on him, Thor," she barked in alarm. Then, more calmly, *"Just let him be. He's a cat, remember? He needs to have fun with that butterfly. It's his kitty plaything."* Then, turning her attention and softer voice to Bifster:

"Oh, well, well, Mr. Bifster. Just look at what you've brought to me to see! It that a present for me? It is? Well, thank you very, very much. You went to all that effort to follow that butterfly, and track it down. And then you waited until you could pounce on it and bring it to me, didn't you? You are such a wonderful, precious, kitty. Yes, you

are. Jen is so proud of you. Thank you for showing me your present. You are such a darling, wonderful man. Jen loves you very much." Jen reached out her hand and Bifster came under it, allowing her to pet him. He dropped the injured, hapless butterfly by her side and purred. *"That's a good kitty. You are such a good, wonderful kitty. Yes, I am very proud of you. You are the best kitty in the entire world! Yes, you are!"*

Thor's sensibilities, observing this macabre ritual between cat and mistress, were nonplussed. His sympathies clearly lied with the wounded butterfly. *"Should I pick it up and take it somewhere where he won't get to it, so it might have a chance to survive?"* He looked furtively at Jen. His anxious voice was pleading for a life.

"No, Thor. Let it be. He'll pick it up in a minute. Watch. As soon as it flutters again, he'll pick it up and take it away where he can play with it. He'll bat at it until it stops fluttering. Then, he'll yodel while he rips its wings off. He'll probably eat the body afterwards."

"And you just let him do that? He's torturing that poor butterfly! Are you enjoying watching him victimize that thing?" Thor's alarm was palpable.

"Yes, I am enjoying it. I let him do that, Thor. He's having fun. Don't begrudge him his pleasures, Thor. He's a cat! That's what cats do! And yes, I am happy to see him having his way with that butterfly. It's giving him pleasure to bat it around and pounce on it. Can't you see how superior he feels when he puts his paws on it and tears its wings off with his teeth? See how proud he is?" Jen's voice flared her defiance. *"And I am very, very proud of him. And you should be, too! Look at him! He's only got one eye. Obviously, he is handicapped. But, despite his lack of depth perception, he bravely went out into the world today to do what kitties do. He hunted. He probably worked very hard to hunt down that butterfly. And he caught it! And then he brought it to us to let us see what he could still do, despite his handicap. He's got a wonderful heart, Thor. He's a very good kitty.*

My goodness, can't you see how important it is to him that we love him and accept him?" Jen searched Thor's face for understanding.

Then she turned to Bifster. He had just chewed the body of the butterfly in half and eaten half of it. He moved close to Jen and looked up at her for approval. She assured Bifster that he was her pride and joy:

"You are such a wonderful kitty, Bifster," she assured him in her soft, pleasing voice tones. *"And you were so good to show Jen how you took care of that pesky butterfly,"* she nodded to her cat's face in approval; then she reached out her hand to pet him and draw him close beside her. Bifster purred, signaling his delight to be included in Jen's world. He rolled over and allowed Jen to rub his belly. *"Oh, you are such a brave, wonderful kitty; and such a wonderful hunter. Jen loves you so much."* She picked up her cat and gave him a loving hug.

Jen turned to Thor and gazed into his eyes. *"Surely, Thor, you can see the world from his perspective if you'll just allow yourself to accept that nature has its ways about things. Moralizing over a stupid butterfly is not going to change the way Bifster sees his place in the world; now, is it?"* Her eyes questioned his to see if he could accept the butterfly's fate; see whether he could transfer his sympathies from the victim butterfly to the victimizer cat. She smiled a warm peace offering smile to him; a welcoming smile; a smile that invited him to abandon his tendency to moralize; and, instead, embrace her immoral world view. She leaned in towards his face, offering him her irresistible innocence; by her body language, imploring him to capitulate his morality and surrender his soul to her immoral, pagan faith-based, new world order.

Thor's consternation relaxed. *"So, that's Bifster's trophy, isn't it? I should just mentally write off the butterfly as a lost soul; already dead while its wings were still fluttering?"*

"Yes, Thor. That's a good way to look at it. That's his trophy but-terfly. It's his. He's earned it. We should rejoice over his capture of it; and we should be happy for him while he is torturing it and killing it." Jen nodded her assertion.

"So, in our minds, by your way of thinking, we should set aside our feelings for the victim?" Thor searched Jen's face, trying to learn her heart.

"Yes," she nodded without the slightest hint of uncertainty. *"Victims are losers."*

"And we should rejoice in Bifster's glee while he tortures and dis-members butterflies and birds and mice? And we should praise him for his hunting skills after he devours their bodies," Thor grimaced.

"Yes, Thor, absolutely." Jen smiled, while placing her hand on his penis. *"You didn't know I could enjoy sadism, did you? You didn't know I could enjoy seeing someone being tortured and destroyed, did you?"* She rolled her body towards his, pressed herself against him, and kissed him passionately on his mouth.

"I had no idea, you gorgeous whore. Even your own father. You felt no remorse while you killed him, did you?"

"No, none. The predator in me saw that he was vulnerable to me. I knew that killing him would benefit me greatly; and I knew I could get away with it. So, I killed him. Simple as that. It's just nature, Thor."

"This is a side of you I never would have expected." Thor felt sen-sations he had never had before. Was Jen thoroughly evil; perhaps fiendishly evil, or just selectively evil; calculating, he wondered? And, what was it about her evilness that suddenly infatuated him? What was it that made his penis harder than it had ever been before? Was it her casual reveal about her attitude towards murder? Why did he now crave her so intensely? Why did he feel this overwhelming urge to enter her and hold her? And why did he suddenly want to love her like he had never loved any woman

before; and, yes, adore her; adore her wickedness; her predilection to casually enjoy the suffering of another creature? How could she be so matter of fact; so nonchalant about her murder of her own father?

Jen slid lower onto Thor's naked body. Her mouth found his penis; and, taking her leisurely time, she placed her mouth over the head of it and began kissing and licking it, intermittently, making her fellatio a natural component of their conversation.

Thor asked himself: *'Why do I now, suddenly, feel this powerful compulsion to shoot my semen into her and bind my life to hers more than I had ever felt any other force in my life? How has she vexed me this way? Was it the way she confronted me over the murder of the butterfly; that strength of her immoral convictions? Her narcissism? Her willingness to place her own needs above her father's very life? Was it the way she asserted to me that a cat's cruel deed was somehow natural, normal; and good, desirable, even praiseworthy? Did watching the dismembering of a beautiful innocent make Jen's loins become hot and wet? How did she get this way? And why do I love her so much more deeply because of it?'*

Thor searched his own soul, reaching down to the foundation of everything he was ever taught to believe. He admired Jen's strength and conviction; but he could not articulate the answers to his own questions. He could not explain why his love for Jen had suddenly intensified like it had; but he knew the intensity had strengthened. Perhaps his soul contained a secret? Perhaps it secretly revered evil and evil doers? Perhaps he was drawn to the pleasures that evil offered; the blood lust intrigue of seeing another being suffer? Was he, possibly, a secret sadist? Thor could not articulate his new phenomena of feelings. But he felt them; felt them pulling him forward and deeper into Jen's world. His soul was peeling away from its safety place; its mother star. It was flying, slowly at first; but now faster and faster, irretrievable, into Jen's soul; becoming one soul united with her immoral, uninhibited, natural ordered world's pagan soul. His love burned inside him now. It was a hot, furious, hungry flame. He was obsessed with her now. He had to have her; often; always; forever. He remembered how Bifster seemed smitten by his catnip treats when Jen dolled them out to him. He now asked himself whether he was any different from the cat. And he knew in his heart of hearts that he was no different. He had become obsessed with her. He had to have her; hold her; kiss her; enter her and love her; and never let go of her.

But he had to understand the why and the how of it. What made Jen the way she was? How did she get this way? Where had her hardness towards the butterfly victim come from? That coldness of heart; her deafness to the plight of the mortally wounded; her seeming embrace and love of something horrifyingly macabre and immoral; her indifference to another creature's pain; where did all that come from? He had to know how Jen's mind worked.

Did she have a moral compass; and if so, in which direction did it point? If he was going to love her, commit to her, love her for all his life, he had to know. But even if he discovered the truth, even if it was revealed to be a terrible truth, he knew before he searched for his answer that it wouldn't matter. He knew his obsessions would overrule whatever cautions he would uncover. His thoughts were spinning: *'What if Jen is a career criminal; perhaps a murderess? Would knowing those things about her turn me away from her? If she sometimes lived on life's dark side, would that quell my lust for her? I know it won't. I know I'll love her, even if she is a murderess.'* But he wanted to know what it was that he would be subjugating, regardless. And why? Perhaps, he told himself, so he could become as immoral and addicted to evil as she was; so, he could become like her in every way; so, he could love her more.

"Jen, I'm curious. Do you feel the same way about the children in Africa who are starving to death as you feel about that butterfly? I

mean, do you just mentally write them off as unfortunate souls who have no hope of even living; and not feel empathy for them; not try to help them in some way?"

"Oh Thor, you really are one of those bleeding hearts, aren't you? You're one of those who answer those television pleas for money for their lost causes, aren't you? What do you think would happen if I gave them billions of dollars?"

"You'd save lives."

"Wrong, Thor. I'd be making it possible for them to breed faster and create even more poverty; making the poverty problem, the poor homeless victim problem, even worse. Dad told me that some things are best left alone; and I believe he was right."

"I see. And those thousands of underaged girls that you employ in the Infernoss Decado Clubs; do you ever have regrets about leading them down the road to perdition?"

"Thor, darling, where are your doubts coming from? You obviously don't understand me. First, I'm in tune with today's morality. Porn and whoring exemplify the new, Modern Morality Standard. Traditional faith based Western morals are circling the drain. People no longer blindly accept dogma. They no longer give religious hypocrisy a wink and a nod. The mumbo jumbo homily spewers have used up all their get out of jail free cards. People now question their moral authority. Who is good? Who is evil? Who gives some priest the authority to say if you do this or don't do that, you'll go to hell or to heaven? That only works if you let your mind suspend disbelief. That also depends on your perspective and your time horizon, doesn't it?

"And where is heaven, exactly? Ever met anyone who's been there? No? I didn't think so. Is it in our solar system, somewhere? How about somewhere in our galaxy, or in another galaxy? Six thousand years ago people didn't think much about the possibilities of Space. They just listened to the theories of the religious spewers and accepted. That's not good enough now. Now people want real *answers; not faith-based mumbo jumbo. People see what pleasures my girls can give them. Those pleasures are here and now, and people want them. People don't need to live their whole lives like Goody Two Shoes, hoping their souls will go to some idyllic place. They can have heaven now, in my clubs, with my girls.*

"Second, I'm providing a valuable service and fulfilling a human need. People need a break from their daily grind. They used to depend on religion for that relief. But the organized religions started in the Middle East, thousands of years ago. They spread to Europe and the Americas. But religion isn't modern America. Religion takes time. It's ritualistic and it's slow. The world is faster paced now. People don't have time to devote a Sunday to Church. They want instant relief from their everyday reality. So, they turn on a porn film on their computer or their phone. They see a new star. And, lo and behold, she's one of my girls! That spreads the word. It's cross marketing. It brings her fans into my clubs. My clubs are displacing the Church. I'm taking religion's cash flow. It's just business, Thor.

"Third, everything about our Clubs is legal. Every girl and every girl's parent signed consents. Those consents stipulate that their daughters will be engaged in prostitution and pornography; and the girl and her parent agree to it. In every jurisdiction where the Clubs are located prostitution and pornography are completely legitimate businesses. I have no legal exposure or guilt feelings about what I'm doing, Thor. And I care about my girls. Those girls are examined and tested, often, by a nurse. They all lost their hymens before they joined the clubs; they are all health checked and blood tested weekly. Thor, my sweet love, have you any idea how a girl feels after her puberty?"

"No."

"Well, let me assure you. Many of them are eager to discover what it feels like to fuck; and a lot of them do fuck. Many begin having sex from the time they are eleven, twelve, or thirteen. When

they turn fourteen, in some jurisdictions, they can have sex legally; and, they can legally become prostitutes."

"So, you have a valid business model?"

"Yes, legal, and valid. Father taught me to look for business opportunities; know my markets and my market's rules. He taught me to think like the customer thinks; see what demands the customer has that are not being met; and meet those demands. That's what I did when I created the Clubs, Thor. There are literally millions of men who would love to have sex with an underaged girl; who would love for their penises to experience a young girl's hot, wet slipperiness; who would love to hold her in their arms and become her lover; many, many millions of men, Thor.

"So, I put demand for underaged sex together with underaged girls' cravings to have sex, and created a marketplace for premium underaged sex with gorgeous girls and very well-heeled men who can afford to have sex with them. And I don't just throw my precious girls to the wolves, Thor. They are highly trained courtesans. They are trained in every technique of flirting."

"Like, what?"

"Oh, Thor, sweetheart, I can't tell you those things. How do you think you got here?"

"I wanted you?"

"I knew that, silly."

"So, you enticed me here?"

"Yep; and you never even suspected, did you?"

"No. I thought I was the one who instigated everything."

"Silly boy. Did you play football? Hang around in the locker room? Hear talk about girls? Girls who did it? That sort of thing?"

"Yeah, sure. Why?"

"Why? Well, I bet at that stage in your life you thought we girls were bundles of hormones walking around with cunts between our

legs; just hunting for a man to take care of us; and willing to let him stick his dick in us to guarantee our security. Have I got that right?"

"Yeah, pretty much. You got that right. Is there more to know about you girls?"

"No, not really. You've got a lot of that right. But that's where our Club girls are different. They don't approach seduction from the 'me' perspective. We train them to think about seduction from the male's perspective."

"I don't get it."

"I know you don't. Here's the difference. We train the Decado girls to not think of their own sexual needs. We train them to prioritize the male's sexual needs; train them to understand what makes the male mind tick."

"And what, darling, makes my male mind tick?"

"Your penis."

"What?"

"We know the male mind is governed by the male penis. So, we make sure our girls have a thorough understanding of the male penis. We bring in experienced prostitutes and male porn stars to acquaint our girls with the male penis."

"You're serious?"

CHAPTER SEVENTEEN

Tobacco and alcohol kill thousands of people every year. To my knowledge, no one has ever died from a blow job. (Florynce Kennedy, author)

Oral sex connects like nothing else. (Rosemary Ness Bitner, author)

ORAL SEX

"Yes, very. We stress that a deep understanding of the male penis is essential to a deep understanding of the male mind. We start by explaining the anatomy of the penis, its blood flow before and during sex, it's relationship to its companions, the male's prostate gland and testicles. We then have our instructors demonstrate with live sexual intercourse how the penis behaves at the various stages of foreplay stimulation and copulation, including before and during ejaculation, and after. Using our male porn stars, we train them with hands on experience how to recognize the signals that the penis is giving them.

"We have group sessions where a girl practices her fellatio on a male porn star while the other girls sit around her and watch. We hold critiques of her progress all through her performance. She discusses her feelings at several intervals of her performance. And, this is very important. So does the male performer. He explains how her fellatio is making him feel; his emotions. And, this opens the girls' eyes. They hear him express how he first loves the sensations.

He describes them in vivid detail. And, as the fellatio progresses, he explains how he feels himself becoming emotionally bonded to the girl. He explains how he's now thinking about her. Thinking about whether she's liking what she's doing. Asking himself whether he'll see her again, Asking himself whether his penis pleases her more than the other penises she has sucked. And then, a miracle happens. Before and during his ejaculation, he fells this overwhelming sensation, He feels an intense empathy for the girl. He feels he wants the very best for her life in every sense of meaning. And, he tells the group, that he now feels a strong emotive love for the girl. He loves her! And that is exactly what happens in these sessions. The male porn star tells the group that the girl's fellatio has caused him to fall in love with his partner."

"Is that true? Do these male porn stars actually feel love for the girl who is performing fellatio on them?"

"Yes Thor. It is absolutely true. It's true of all males, except the most sociopathic ones. The penis is the key to the male limbic mind. And fellatio arouses the passions in that limbic mind. It's a phenomenon like an aphrodisiac; but much stronger than an aphrodisiac. The male becomes powerless to feel anything other than love for the girl."

"And you want your girls to understand this?"

"Oh, yes! Most definitely. These fellatio sessions are very important. They help the girl appreciate the power of her sexuality. We inculcate in all our girls the belief that those men who receive their fellatio will become their devoted lovers; and that they will be loved by these men, likely forever. The sessions are a tremendous boost to a girl's confidence. They dispel all her inhibitions about performing fellatio. After her lessons, she understands the enormous powers she has. She becomes a freshly minted nymph with a clearly understood purpose; making her customers fall hopelessly into love with her; forsaking all other loves. She feels no embarrassment or hesitation

about initiating flirtatious seduction and performing fellatio. She looks forward to performing it. She loves performing it. She sees it as her certain method of achieving a dominant relationship with her male customer. After her lesson sessions, she becomes a confident, highly desirable sex goddess; eager to be on the Club floor striking up flirtations with customers; anxious to induce them to have intimacy with her; and especially anxious to perform fellatio with them."

"And these lessons foster a deep understanding of the male mind. That's really what you're teaching your girls, isn't it?"

"Yes Thor. The lessons help them recognize and understand where the male's mind is with respect to our girl's seduction techniques; and during and after actual intercourse with her male porn star instructor. The girls practice their seductions and copulations with real, live male porn stars in these group sessions, so they can learn firsthand how to interpret what the male penis is telling them; and how they can relate those penis signals to the things they should be thinking and saying during their intimate encounters. Each girl openly expresses her honest feelings during her lesson experience; and the other girls observe and provide their own thoughts and feelings to the girl who is performing. The girls sort of compete with each other and learn from each other. It's a very healthy way of dispelling inhibition. They learn to love the male penis and performing fellatio with it. And it builds comradery among the girls.

"We continually stress the importance of the male penis and its subtle signals as it relates to the male's limbic mind. This assures our girls that they will be experts at saying the right things and initiating the right phases of seduction technique at the exactly right time. They learn to interpret their own vaginal cravings and moisture readiness in relation to the signals they are receiving from the male penis.

"We train our girls how to be patient and relaxed about their conquests; how to have a shameless and casual, loving, enjoyable attitude towards sexual intercourse. And we instill in them the belief

that their promiscuity will facilitate many rewarding long-term relationships. This gives them confidence that their erotic intimacy events will sexually satisfy them as well as their customers.

"Before they seduce their first customer, my Club managements train them on how to seduce a customer; fondle a man's balls, lick and stroke his penis; suck his penis; run their hot wet lips up and down the shaft of his penis; tickle his penis with their fingertips; tickle it with their fingernails; massage twist the penis with one hand and two hands; manage the penis's ejaculations; and we teach them how to make the penis feel sensational coitus inside their vaginas, in six basic positions. They are also trained in the rigors of meticulous sanitation; groomed in the arts of makeup, dress, seductive facial and body gestures.

"But most of all, we teach our young prostitutes their attitude. They are taught to believe that they are divinely chosen to feed the hunger cravings within men's souls. Their training emphasizes that, even more important than their seduction moves and sexual positions, their thoughts about and communications with their partners must focus on the spiritual. Our program is closely modeled on religious teachings. It's a catechism of prostitution thought. When our girls have completed their learning, they believe they are answering a higher calling than merely offering up their bodies for sex. They believe that they have become the sacred vessels through which their partners offer up their life 's experiences, hopes, frustrations and tensions to the Great Spirit of All Living Things; and that they, as Decado girls, are performing a divinely, joyful, celebration of life and life's creation, which enables their partners to discover personal freedom and their own true souls.

"Essentially, through the splendor of their fornications and their creative love making, our girls help their partners rise above and brush aside traditional moral and religious teachings; help them discover the sacred solemnity of human connectedness and immoral

love. Our girls help men discover their true, liberated souls; free them from unbearable burdens; unshackle them from stigma and shame; guide them into more humanized lives, lived in the world of the Modern Morality Standard. Here," said Jen while retrieving her phone from her purse, *"this will help you understand our indoctrination program from the girl's perspective. This is a video our instructors made of Bridgitte, one of our most sought after fourteen-year-old trainees. She uses the name 'Lolita' as her Club name, after the heroine of Nabokov's novel by the same name. Pay close attention to her face while she describes her first two months at one of our exclusive offshore clubs."* Thor watched the short film on Jen's phone. The club manager was interviewing Lolita:

"Tell us, did you experience sex before you joined Infernos Decado, Lolita? Could you tell us about that? And could you tell us how you came to join Decado?"

"Well, yes. I had already been having sex for about a year before I joined. You see, my dad left me and my mom. Mom met this man whose wife had died; and he had a son named Jaques. After Mom and me moved in with Jaques and his dad, Jaques and I started doing it."

"How old was Jaques?"

"He was fifteen and I was thirteen."

"And did your mother know you were having sex with Jaques?"

"Mom never mentioned it to me; but I'm certain she knew about it; and I'm certain she was okay with it."

"How so?"

"Because one morning I woke up and there was this package of birth control pills on my night stand. And every month there was a fresh, new package of the pills there. And one morning at breakfast, Mom winked at me and said: 'Remember to take your morning pill.' I think Mom was letting me know that it was cute that I and Jaques were having sex and that she approved of it. It fit. Jaques' dad and

Mom giggled about Jaques and me a lot and remarked how cute we looked together; and how we were probably made for each other; and that we'd probably get married someday."

"How did you feel about that?"

"About what?"

"About marrying Jaques someday."

"Oh, I didn't want to give that much thought. I thought Mom was just having one of her whimsical moments when she said that. Getting married to Jaques was not even on my mind; not in the slightest."

"But you liked fucking him?"

"Yes. He was my first. We did it every single day. We always found a way to be alone together."

"Did you, or should I say do you, love Jaques?"

"Well, yes, I think I love him. But I don't know how to answer that. You see, I loved fucking him. It was the highlight of my day, every day. But I can't say that I love him or who he is or that I want to be married to him. I just loved fucking him."

"You said loved, past tense."

"Well, yes. Jaques was before I joined Decado. Now it's different. There are so many men and all of them are better lovers than Jaques was. He's still a boy and I think I'm the only girl he's had experience with."

"I see. So, How did you come to join Decado?"

"Oh, that was my girlfriend, Josephine. She knew I liked doing Jaques. We talked about everything. She told me about Decado and how exclusive it is. She wanted to teach school and work with little kids, so Decado wasn't for her. But she thought I might like it. And she told me about this man named Celt who could fix things with the paperwork so I could join Decado. She gave me Celt's number. I called him. He talked to Mom and got the consents and the other papers I needed. The I joined."

"*And you don't miss Jaques?*"

"*No. I can still see him when I visit Mom. I can still fuck him. None of that has changed. But no. I don't miss him.*"

"*So, we were just watching your training session on the round day bed. You were doing a threesome, weren't you?*"

"*Yes. This is my second training week to prepare me for making porn films with multiple partners. My first training week was all solo partners. Right now, I'm learning to have relaxed and carefree expressions while I'm doing two men at the same time.*"

"*What were you practicing, just now?*"

"*Concentration and modulation, my instructor calls it. As you saw, I was on the bed. I was straddling my first partner. He was lying down facing my face. I was rubbing his penis against my pussy lips while my right hand was stroking his penis. My second partner was standing beside me. I was performing fellatio with his penis and using my left hand to stroke his penis while I sucked it.*"

"*I see. And was that a difficult maneuver for you?*"

"*At first, it was. But that's why we practice. At first, it was hard to get my coordination down. If I concentrated too hard on my fellatio, I would tend to stop moving my pussy lips against his penis and my right hand would tend to stroke my first partner's penis erratically. I was pretty uncoordinated.*"

"*But you've overcome that?*"

"*Yes. Practice helped a lot. I first learned to rapidly shift my concentration from my right hand to my left hand, so my stroking became pretty seamless. Then, I learned to kind of automatically do a simulated faux twerk on my first partner's penis while keeping my head strokes and my lip and tongue stimulations going on my second partner's penis. It's all a learned mind and muscle coordination; kind of like playing a piano. By repetition the muscles and the mind kind of get into synchronicity. After doing that for three sessions a day, for five days, the motions become pretty automatic.*

And then, when I make my first threesome porn film, the scene will look extremely breathtaking and erotically beautiful."

"You mean, like you're a completely uninhibited and shameless nymph; and you love pleasuring two penises at once?"

"Yes. And that's true. I really do love it. I love doing it with two partners at once like that."

"Now, before we began talking, you were on the round day bed with two different partners. What were you practicing just now?"

"Positioning. Relaxing and positioning. My pussy was getting very creamy. I knew I was very slippery wet. This hot sensation was flashing from my pussy down my legs. A kind of shield passed over my mind. It blocked out all my other thoughts. My mind could only think of fucking my first partner; all my other thoughts went blank; even my fellatio thoughts. I desperately wanted to fuck my first partner. Then, at this same time, my first partner said he wanted to be inside me. I was so thrilled to hear him say that. I immediately inserted his penis in my pussy. I was so ready to fuck. I couldn't wait to begin. I stopped doing fellatio on my second partner and collapsed my body onto my first partner. I kissed his mouth and rubbed my hands through his hair while I bumped and twerked my pussy on his penis. It felt so wonderful. I can't put into words how much I loved fucking him. I kept fucking him until he came inside me. I orgasmed twice while we fucked. So, part of my training is to learn to smile and look at the cameras and have a happy, delighted facial expression while I orgasm. I did that perfectly during that practice session. I felt like I was a divine goddess or an angel from heaven who was here on earth fucking my partner. Before my practice sessions, I've always felt this way while I fucked my partners; but now, because there were cameras recording the scene, I needed to put into words how I felt. It was about expressing myself. It was remembering to put into words how I felt. I remembered to say nice things in a soft voice to entice him to enter me with his penis:

'Yes, I want you to do it. I need this. I really need you to do this. I love how it feels in my hands. It's so big and hard. Here, I want to rub it on my pussy lips. Ohhhh, that feels sooo good. Yes, that's it. It's sooo big. That's okay, don't be afraid. I can take it. It's all right. Yes, that's it. Push it in. Yes. Yesssss, deeper. Good. That feels soooo good. That's it. Now push into me. Yes, all the way inside me. Ohhhh, yes.'

"And then, while I orgasmed all over his penis. I remembered to say lots of things like:

'Oh, oh, I'm going to come. Yes, yessss, I'm coming. Mmmmmm, Mmmmm. That feels soooo wonderful. Mmmmmm. I love fucking you. Keep fucking me. Yessss. Fuck me harder. Faster. Yes. That's it! Harder and faster. Yes. Yes. More. More! OHHHHH. YEEESSSSS! I'm coming again. OH my God! Yes! Fuck me. I love this. That was soooo wonderful! I could fuck you all day and all night and never stop. UMMMM. Push your penis hard up inside me. I want to feel all of you. UMMM. I love how you're fucking me. This is soooo beautiful. Can you tell how much I love what you are doing? Ohhhh! You're coming now! I feel you. You're shooting! I feel your hot cum all over my clit. Ohhhh, that's so wonderful. You made me come again. I'm loving this. We're so good together, baby. MMMMM. Do you like how I'm moving my pussy all over your penis? Do you? Oh, I love how you feel inside me. I can feel you everywhere inside me. Do you have any idea how close to you I feel right now? Can you feel me? Can you feel how much I love this? Push. Push. Push harder. Harder!!! Yessss! I love when your cum is shooting inside me. You're doing it again! I'm coming again; my third time. Third time! Ha Ha HA! OHHH. Oui! Oui! I love your penis inside me. Can you feel how I'm creaming all over your penis? It's so wonderful; so beautiful. Oh. You are draining me. I love this so much. You're soooo goood! We have to do this again. Many times. Okay, baby? Yes, okay. Just call me. Call me whenever you want to fuck me. I want you to call me. Don't make me wait. Please some see me again, soon. I love

fucking you. I totally love how you fuck me. I feel so wonderful. You know I love you, don't you?'

"*And, while I'm having my orgasms, I need to remember to express my joy with my facial smiles. After a while that also comes naturally. I no longer wince or show any serious concentration sort of look on my face while I'm fucking. My face shows I'm totally casual and naturally relaxed while fucking my partners; and that I'm thoroughly enjoying it; actually, loving it; more like I'm totally consumed by the glorious wonderment of it all. Those are the kinds of looks my instructor wants me to have; and I'm mastering them. Now that I'm mastering my facial expressions, they are coming more naturally. They're kind of automatic. My instructor told me the more often I fuck, the more automatic my expressions will become. I'll soon be working with my expressions while I'm performing fellatio and intercourse with multiple partners. I'm ready to get started. My instructor tells me that beautiful porn is transformed into exquisite, divinely gorgeous, mouthwatering porn by the facial expressions a girl makes while she's having sex. Those expressions are what make viewers relate to a girl. They sear an indelible memory of her porn scene into her male viewers' minds. That memory impression can never be erased. It stays with the male forever; and it builds and builds his desires for her until he obsesses over her. That's when her smiles and her happy eye expressions are make them fall in love with her. They buy her films. They call her. They can't get enough of her. She becomes a god-like persona to them. And they worship her and everything she does.*"

"*Well, Lolita, it sounds like you are progressing well. Your enthusiasm literally beams from your face. Tell us, how do you like your time on the Club floor with real customers?*"

"*Oh, wonderful. I Love being on the Club floor. I've been out there, mingling with the Club members for three months. I've met many heads of companies, politicians, judges, even royal aristocrats.*

I've made wonderful friendships with many of these men. I've had sex with over thirty different members already; some of them two or three or four times; and many of them have booked me to spend private time with them. I am surprised that so many of male members want to perform cunnilingus with my pussy. They pay really top money to do that. They seem to love my pussy because they've seen me fuck so many male porn partners. One of the other girls explained that cunnilingus is a male dominance thing that men do. I don't understand it; but I love it that men love to do it. I feel completely connected to a man while he's doing that with me. I love him for doing it. I just feel like I'm in heaven. And I love all the money the men pay me to let them do that. I've already earned over one hundred thousand dollars! Just by spreading my legs and letting my male customers lick my pussy! It's a wonderful way to make money! I love it! I'm learning so many things about men! They amaze me!"

"Why do you think they like cunnilingus so much?"

"I'm not sure. I asked one of the older girls about it. She explained it to me the way Marty explained it to her."

"Marty?"

"Yes, the woman who was the world's most notorious porn star for about five years. That Marty. Well, Marty explained that it's a Pagan religious thing. She believed it was a natural worship kind of thing that's a kind of hold over from temple worship times of twenty thousand years ago. Marty told her that men believe, in their souls, that the way to eternity and the reincarnation of their souls is through the female cunt. The cunt is the way to eternal life. The cunt is the pathway to eternal enlightenment and eternal life. And no man can experience this enlightenment unless he submits to the female cunt and sups its juices and connects his mind and soul to the female's mind and soul by causing her clitoris to be pleasured until it orgasms. It's a pleasing of the eternal God that lives within the female cunt. And it is this cunnilingual communion with the female

cunt which gives the male his salvation. It's his way of submitting to the cunt's eternal powers; and adoring and revering the cunt's powers. It's a kind of heaven for the man as well as the woman. Marty said it's the best fruit from the forbidden Tree of Knowledge in the Garden of Eden. She said when you partake of that fruit, which means you are tasting the fruits of the female vagina, you acquire the same knowledge that the Hebrew God has. And you actually become like God and Goddess when you engage in cunnilingus. So, now, whenever I'm engaged in the cunnilingus act, I imagine I am offering myself to perform, with my partner, a very special, time honored, sacred religious ritual."

"And you make good money by allowing men to perform oral sex on you?"

"Yes. I look at it as a sacred Pagan communion service that helps these men refresh their souls. The money they pay me to perform cunnilingus is their religious offering to the Eternal Spirit. My cunt is their divine pathway to reach the Spirit. It's like communion for them. Many need it weekly. That's what's so wonderful about the Club and why I love the Club so much. It's where many men come to worship my cunt as their most sacred religious experience."

"I see. And you've also been able to get your customers to gamble?"

"Oh yes! The Club has already made over four hundred thousand off my customers. And the Club pays me ten percent of those losses."

"And the winnings?"

"Well, I get a portion of those, too. My male customers have given me jewels and furs. One even gave me his time share in Aspen. This winter we're going to spend a week there, skiing, eating gourmet restaurant food, going to shows, and fucking long and slow beside the fireplace."

"Lovely. And what do you do with your times away from the club and the members?"

"Well, those aren't too many days. Whenever I'm away, I try to promote myself. I love going to car races and posing for photos in my Premium Bikini next to the race cars and on the hoods of the cars. I wear a thong or nothing at all for those poses. I love to flash my pussy for the cameras. Men can't resist that. When they see my pussy, their curiosity about me just skyrockets. They want to know who I am; how to meet me; what they need to do, and what they need to pay to spend time with me and fuck me. I get lots of lunch and dinner dates from going to car races. I bring my publicist with me for those events. He shoots the new photos. He also brings along lots of my autographed porn photos. I hand those out to men I want to spend time with. And I write the phone number for my Private Service on the photos. I get lots of calls and new Private Service members that way.

"Then, I hit the dance clubs after the races. I love to bump to the beat of the music and take my top and bra off and just let my titties bounce free while I drink in the sounds of the saxophones and the horns and the strings and the piano playing. My body is very sensitive to the different instruments. My body feels this incredible freedom. I love kissing my dance partners right there, on the dance floor, in front of everybody. I'm uninhibited and shameless that way. I love it when they feel me and finger me, right there, out in the open, in front of everyone. I encourage that. I love being fondled. I never resist them or say no when they do that. I just hug them and kiss them with my long sole kisses. Sometimes, when I'm in the mood, I'll take a swig of alcohol into my mouth and I'll kneel down on the dance floor and suck a guy's penis; get his penis really alcohol cool hard; make him crazy out of his mind to take me someplace and fuck me. I tend to draw a crowd when I get all activated like that.

And I like that. I want that image. I want to be known as a notorious 'fast woman,' like Marty was. I like attracting attention and getting my name around.

"But usually, when I'm not at the Club, I'm with one of my Premium Members. Being a Club girl means my body is a kind of male time share. And I'm totally fine with that. My Private members are all very sweet. There's one older man who takes me to the opera with him. He has a private balcony box. We just sit there and enjoy the show. Sometimes he holds my hand for a few minutes, but that's all he likes to do. We've never had sex. Another man, he's in his early forties, takes me to this secluded beach in the Bahamas. We lie on a beach blanket near the water's edge. He likes to hug me and kiss me for the longest times. Then, we have sex before we swim in the ocean. Then, he brings me back to the Club. Another guy, he's a football player, takes me to sporting events. We mostly go to basketball and hockey games. Then, we go to his hotel room and do it. I usually spend the night with him. After we have sex, I fall asleep while he sits in bed studying his football playbook. Then, in the morning, he brings me back to the Club."

"And, it doesn't trouble you to have sexual relations with many different men?"

"No. Why should it trouble me? It doesn't trouble me at all. I went to the guest lecture that Marty gave. She explained the effect of butterfly DNA. She explained the eternal spirit and the nympho effect. She explained the majesty and glory of intimacy. She explained how misogynists use religion to control women and deny us our rights and freedoms. She emphasized it's normal for women to crave sex. It's normal to want different men; just like a lot of men want different women. And by the new Modern Morality Standard, there's nothing wrong with having sex with many different men. So, no; it doesn't trouble me. Not at all. There's nothing troubling about it. It's mentally healthy and liberating and wholesome. Besides, I

love doing it. And I want to do more of it; lots and lots more of it. I love the discovery part of it. I love having different men. Every man fascinates me; getting to know a new man; getting to know how I feel about having sex with him; how he feels about sex with me; how we can work together to make our sex more meaningful and more beautiful. It's all wonderful. It's exciting. I totally love it. If I could have ten new partners every day; if I could fit all of them into my schedule, I would absolutely do that; absolutely, I would fuck all ten of them, every single day. I love sex and the experiences with my partners that much. I just do.

"Like Marty said: 'There comes a point in your life where you just need to acknowledge who you are and what you want out of life. And then you need to just take it.' So, no, I'm not the slightest bit troubled."

CHAPTER EIGHTEEN

Marriage rhymes with horse and carriage. And both are becoming obsolete. (Rosemary Ness Bitner, author)
Marriage is nothing but a civil contract. (John Selden: Libels)

MARRY?

"Very good, Lolita. Now, after three months with the club, would you consider leaving the Club and going off with your boyfriend Jaques or some other man and getting married?"

"No way! Not a chance."

"Aren't you interested in marriage? Not even with a handsome man with means to take care if you?"

"No. There are plenty of those and I'm not interested. Look." Lolita reached into her carry bag and retrieved a letter. *"This man is one of my private customers. He sent me this. A lot of men say things like this; but he put it all in writing. Go ahead, read it."*

The instructor held the letter and read it aloud:

'My Darling,
I write this to convey the seriousness of my proposal. As I said, I cannot live without you. I lie awake nights, beside my sleeping wife. I am nearly mad, thinking only of you; your perfect breasts; your delightful peach with its glistening moist lips; your smiles and laughs. I wish to kiss you and hold you in my arms, every night, for the rest of my life. I

have no need for family or faith. My only belief is in you, Lolita; you, only you, and in the many lovely ways you sin. I adore you and everything about you.

You live in my heart and soul and in every breath that I take. The sounds of your voice expressing your joys while making love echo and resound endlessly, hauntingly in my mind, while I am awake and while I dream of you:

'Oui! I love your beautiful penis! It's so big and hard! I love how you're fucking me. Yes! Yes! Oui! Oh, my love. That's it. Fuck me harder. That feels so wonderful. Yes. Come inside me. I want you to. I love it when you come. Yes, darling, come. Come. Come. Yes. That's it. You're soooo wonderful.'

Lolita, you are my life. I must have you. I go to my factory. I watch the belts moving the goods of the company I built. But it means nothing now. When I'm in bed with my wife; with every breath she draws, my spirit takes another step towards death. I'm on my private conveyor belt to my soul's abyss. Only you can stop it. You can reverse it and renew the young man who lives within me. My soul leaps, grasping for its freedom. When I awake, white cum cream covers my hand. And I feel guilty; not for withholding my seed from my wife; not for defiling God's wishes. No, my guilt is that I did not give my spilled seed to you. Only you deserve it. You are my God now.

I obsess. These feelings I have, these passions, must never end. I must have you, Lolita. I must kiss you and love you and kiss your gloriously delicious peach. I am your smitten, devoted supplicant.

Morality, I command you: Leave me! I no longer need you or want anything to do with you. I only want Lolita. I need only her. Her. Her! Her and her glorious sinning. My heart bursts with passion quests for her; only her.

Lolita, pray hear me. I need you; only you; my destiny's obsession; delectably tantalizing tart; dazzling coquette. Your love arrows have pierced my heart; barbed me; hooked me fast to you. Those moments when your eyes meet mine beguile me. Do your laughing eyes speak of your love? I wish and pray that is true. I can only hope that they shine with your love for me. Your eyes know you've captured me. They know you hold my heart, my very life in your delicate lovely hands. They know I love you for love's sake, like others must love art for art's sake. Yes, I must love you, because you are you. Lolita. You are love. Your love means everything to me.

As I proposed: If you agree to marry, I will divorce my wife. I'll leave her and the children. We will move to the South of France and buy a chateau near St. Tropez, on the beach. I will gladly surrender fifty million dollars, half of my wealth, to my wife to gain my freedom from her. I will give you, my love, thirty million of my remaining fifty million, to prove my proposal is serious.

And I will love you with every breath I take until the day I die.

Please say yes, my glorious love. Please agree to marry me and come away with me.

Your truest love,

Louis'

"I hear this sort of thing from several men. And I have no interest. I'm not going to confine my life to the whims and pleasures of one man. No way!"

"That letter is a serious proposal."

"Yes; but it is beneath my consideration. If I am his true love, why give his wife fifty million and me thirty million? He makes no

sense. If my love means everything to him, why not give me his entire hundred million?"

"You think you should have everything? All his wealth?"

"Of course I do. I am a whore. My cunt is a priceless asset. It's uniquely mine. He wants it. He must be willing to pay everything he has for it; for me, since I mean everything to him. He can fight with his wife later, after he has given me everything."

"And if he did give you his hundred million, would you then marry him?"

"No, of course not. The whole idea of being married to a man and being under his thumb is ridiculous."

"So, you'll not consider marriage to any man, regardless of his sex appeal, status and wealth?" Her instructor sought to confirm Lolita's commitment to the Club.

"Ha! No! Not until I'm twenty-nine or thirty. I wouldn't leave the club because, in addition to the money and the lifestyle, I love the Club's philosophy that shared intimacy is a beautiful and wonderful thing. It brings people together; frees them from inhibition; connects them in love. They become open and connected. I love that way of thinking. It's so different from religion. It's so free! And, I'm learning so much about men! I know I'll meet many more men just by staying with the Club. There are many men who will pay me millions to spend a week with them. Why should I limit myself when I can make so much more by being available to many men? And having multiple lovers is much more satisfying. No, I won't leave the Club. I'll only consider leaving when I can't attract customers anymore."

"Not even if a prince made you a sensational offer?"

"Nope. I know myself. I need to have sex with more than one man. Many men. One man could never keep up with me. I'd go crazy sitting in some castle staring at tapestries and getting dressed up to go to parties where I'd need to smile and wave to people. That's too stupid for words. I'm being honest. It's my nympho butterfly

DNA thing. Unless he'd be willing to let me continue doing porn and seeing my private clients; no way!"

"So, you like the Club lifestyle?"

"No. I love it," gushed Lolita. "*I Like, totally, totally, LOVE it! I love it all, very, very much! The customers, my porn partners, the many opportunities I get to perform live porn at our different clubs, and make porn films; and the money, and my sexy clothes; and my trips to exotic places with my Premium members. Absolutely, I love it! I totally love all of it! I'm constantly meeting new penises and fucking new customers. It's like living in a never ending, exciting, new wonderland. And I learn about so many things from my customers when they talk about themselves and their lives. I learn about all sorts of different things that I never would have thought about before.*

"Heee, heee," giggled Lolita, "I can't believe all the fun I'm having; all the men I'm meeting. I heard before that Decado girls had great lifestyles; but I had no idea how fabulous it would be. It's like I'm learning new things and learning new things about men, their lives, and their sex preferences, nonstop. Like this one man. He comes to see me every week, just to perform cunnilingus. I asked him if he wanted to have sex with me, and he said: 'No,' he just wanted to taste my juicy peach. He said it was his way of honoring the wonderful things he saw my pussy doing in my films. I never expected to hear a man say that; but there it was. He actually said that. I think it's a male dominance thing, like when animals put their scents on things to mark their territory. So, he comes every week to give me oral sex. He's quite pleasing in the ways he does me. I enjoy it. So, like I said, every man is different. And then there are my sex lessons with my porn partners. My partners are simply out of this world wonderful. They are really into making a girl feel wonderful while she's having sex. I totally love being a Decado girl. It's the perfect life for me. It's kind of like getting an advanced degree in sociology, I think."

"And do you ever have concerns about your customers' wives or girlfriends? Do you ever feel concerned about being labeled a whore?"

"No and no. As far as wives and girlfriends: When I'm with a man, I make up my mind, he's going to be mine. When I take my bra off and he starts kissing my nipples, I know he's leaving his other woman behind, for me. When his hand slides into my panties and touches my pussy, I know he wants me; not her. And when I'm rubbing his penis against my pussy's lips and I hear him saying he wants to be inside me; and then I guide his penis inside me and I start fucking him, I know the other woman has no chance of ever winning him back; she'll never get him away from me.

"From the moment he first penetrates me, I make up my mind that he'll become addicted to having sex with me. I make up my mind that our sex will be the most wonderful sex he's ever had. I know I'll be fucking away all his thoughts and feelings for the other woman. I, my touches, my tastes, my smells, my body, and my mouth and pussy will drive all thoughts of the other woman away; push her out of his mind, forever. I'll be the only woman he wants, ever, from his first penetration and afterwards, forever. I'll make him obsess over me; over my laughs and smiles; over my fellatio and over his cunnilingus with my orgasming, sex craving pussy. And I know I'm going to love every minute of our intimacy while I'm doing that. I know I'll make him come inside me. I'll be patient and resolute about our love making until I feel him shooting inside me. When he does that, I'll kiss him and I'll suckle every last drop of semen from his penis; very lovingly, for a long, memorable while, afterwards. After he experiences my lovemaking and my passion, he'll be mine for as long as I want him.

"And as far as being called a whore, I'm totally fine with that. I'm actually very pleased to wear the whore label. It enhances my reputation and desirability. Men have a curiosity factor, you know. A lot of men want to know how it feels to make love with a notorious

whore. Many prefer a whore to a girl who wants to be monogamous. We whores are more enticing and more stimulating than reserved, religious girls. That's how men really are. They might like having meek women whom they can dominate. But when it comes to intimacy, men prefer promiscuous women. We're more fun. Sex with us is more satisfying and enjoyable. We're not inhibited about having sex. We don't have mental hang-ups over it. We just love to fuck. We're more challenging for most men because they know whores have had many men and we'll compare male performances. So, the sex act is a kind of a male challenge thing. And real men like rising to the challenge of pleasing a whore. That's the honest truth. And that makes for great sex."

"I see. Very good. Well, what are your immediate goals, Lolita?"

"Next week I'm going to have a Monarch Butterfly tattooed on my upper thighs, right up against my vaginal lips; exactly the same way Marty had hers done. I wish to make an immediate, unmistakable impression upon the men I'm seducing. I want them to instantly recognize me as a carefree flutterer, like Marty was; that I will not be tamed or caged; and that making love with me is about discovering eternal personal freedom."

"You really are committed to sexual freedom and messaging that, aren't you?"

"Yes. Totally."

"And your longer-term goals?"

"The Club, as you know, has me scheduled to create four more porn films and to also perform live porn at two of our offshore clubs. I'm just looking forward to those experiences and gaining a reputation for creating exceptionally gorgeous pornography. You know, the kind that men salivate over and cannot forget. And my long-term goal is to have a huge following of devoted fans who will buy my films and want me for private intimacy sessions and who will fall in love with me."

"I'm sure you'll be a huge success, Lolita. Thank you."

"You're welcome. Good bye."

Jen turned off her video and put her phone back in her purse; then she turned to Thor:

"You can see, Thor, our girls are not common street sluts. They are specially chosen, beautiful, eager, willful, highly trained, well cared for, pampered prostitutes. We encourage their promiscuity and train them how to be sincere and loving. We teach them proper nutrition, oral hygiene, and dental care; and how to take excellent care of their bodies. My girls and my clubs thrive on repeat customers. We want a man to come to the Club and stay for a week or longer at a stretch. We want him to experience and savor the joys of living the Modern Morality Standard. We want him to relax, have fantastic sex, enjoy the massage services, which naturally include prostitution, become regular patrons of our live, on-stage porn performances with the world's top porn stars; and, of course, enjoy the company of our prostitutes at our gaming tables. We coach the girls on how to encourage their male customers to wager boldly."

"And you have no trouble finding beautiful young girls?"

"Oh, no trouble at all. You wouldn't imagine how many girls approach Celt, our liaison for procuring our girls, to work in our clubs. For every girl we accept, train and sponsor, we reject fifteen. And the ones we reject are attractive girls, Thor. They are just not the crème de le crème of drop-dead gorgeous, promiscuous femininity. And why do you think so many thousands of girls seek to work in my clubs, Thor?"

Jen proceeded to answer her own question: *"It's the money, Thor. A Decado girl makes two to ten times what a woman makes as a professional career woman."*

"By fucking?"

"Yes, of course by fucking; but also, by all the nuanced things we teach them. We hold classes for them that cover everything from the

most sensuous ways to lick a penis and how to tease it with her outer vaginal lips to the techniques of binding a man's affections to her, possibly forever; and everything in between that initial encounter and the enduring relationship. We examine the history of whoring, from the early pagan goddesses and prostitution worship to the phenomenal successes of famous seductresses like Sarah and Cleopatra. We infuse attitude into their psyches that they are special women; placed, as the ancient Roman and Greek prostitutes were, at the pinnacle of society for their beauty and their abilities to seduce and charm men. We invite top porn stars to visit as guest lecturers. They explain their seduction techniques and erotica specialties and show our girls with hands on demonstrations with live partners how best to make a man obsess over them; and how to make a penis desire to be inside them. Because of our training and attention to detail, our girls make fabulous tips. Your eyes would pop at their take home pay.

"Thor, we do everything we can to promote our girls. We pay for them to create their first three porn films with the industry's best directors. The directors help them lose all inhibition and greatly bolster their confidence. When the films are finished, they are highly polished, professional works of intimate artistry. The girls see their work and their self-esteem skyrockets. Many film producers then pay the girls to create more films. Their reputation and following builds. They become like shooting stars. They know they are adored. They know they are irresistible goddesses and worth premium monies for their services. Their films show explicit close ups of their faces and their vaginas while seducing and copulation and while receiving ejaculations. And on the films, we run a trailer that tells the viewers that the girl can be reached through the Club's call center; and we mention that she is available for personal contact under certain jurisdiction and member suitability qualifications and introductory fees."

CHAPTER NINETEEN

Why is it immoral to be paid for an act that is done for free? (Gloria Allred, attorney)

Sex is one of the most beautiful, wholesome, natural things that money can buy. (Steve Martin, comedian)

Prostitutes rent their bodies. Married women sell them. (Rosemary Ness Bitner, author)

PROSTITUTION

"You operate a prostitution empire, don't you, Jen?"

"Yes, but Club membership is only offered to men and women who meet our high standards. We screen and background check membership applicants carefully. We don't allow thugs, cretins, psychos, or perverts anywhere near our girls, Thor. We have safeguards. We protect our girls; give them a safe, protected, working environment. We treasure our girls. We invest heavily in every one of them and we love them. They are like my extended family. We build trust between them and the clubs. They know they are appreciated, always protected, and never abused. They are the assets that make the clubs work. We also promote their goodwill by helping them jump start their careers. We give them exposure through our porn film partnering program and we avail them of the opportunity to perform live porn, on the big stage at the clubs. It a girl wants to broaden her appeal by doing dozens or hundreds of porn films, we try, whenever

possible, to pair her on stage with top ranked porn stars. We offer many girl-girl, threesome, and orgy opportunities for them to show-case their techniques and their expressions before live audiences."

"And that helps them?"

"Oh yes! Sure; of course, it does. Often enough, audience members will see something about our novice porn star that attracts them. We've had girls get offers from audience members to create films. Lots of our club members are willing to risk some capital producing porn films that feature a new girl. We encourage audience members to sponsor our girls. Some of them go on to highly successful porn careers; and that reflects well on the clubs. The world is always hungry for new porn talent, Thor. We promote our girls every way we can. We even fly them to different club locations so they can gain valuable, varied experiences with at least a hundred different penises."

"Penises?"

"Yes, Thor, penises. We encourage our girls to take full advantage of the Decado's wide geographical footprint. We help them become highly versatile prostitutes by having broad experiences with many different men. We believe a variety of male customers gives the girls a sense of self-esteem and greater confidence in their self-worth. It's the same concept as helping a beautiful flower receive its necessary pollination. We train the Club girls to think of every male penis as her human pollinator and true customer; not the man himself. We encourage our girls to please those male penises; make those penises go crazy for them; make those penises want to keep coming back to them for more.

"And we encourage the girls to ask their customers whether they believed the services they received were worth the money paid; or perhaps even more. That results in higher tip income for our girls. Some customers tip lavishly, even giving twice the costs of the services they receive. Many of our girls make thousands every night. If

a girl attracts a multi-millionaire repeat customer, she often gets eye popping gifts. Some girls have gotten cars, jewels, furs; some have even gotten condominiums. We're happy for them. We let them keep all their tips. We celebrate their successes. We pamper them and give them paid vacations. We want happy girls."

"Aren't you concerned about flying underaged girls around for prostitution, Jen? I mean there are human trafficking laws."

"Oh, goodness, no, Thor," Jen laughed. "Don't you know me by now? Don't you know I'm very detail oriented? The Club has two private jets and two helicopters. We always fly the girls on our private planes. There's no passenger manifest, no record that any authorities can see. And we tip our airport Fixed Base Operators very well to maintain our Club's privacy. We also own three private islands in friendly jurisdictions. If a well-heeled man wants small group or individual privacy; and if the girls he selects are willing, we accommodate that. Our islands are equipped with the very finest gourmet kitchens and chefs, the finest wines, spirits, and recreational drugs; and our facilities and staffs are outstanding."

"You are the quintessential international madam, aren't you, Jen? You think of everything, don't you?"

"Yes, absolutely; everything for the penis, Thor. I am driven to please the male penis. Our club's motto is: The penis is our king. And, if a particular market segment, like our pleasure porn islands, will bear my prices for the services requested, my clubs will meet the demand."

"Your focus really is pleasing the penis. Nothing is too much for you to do, is it?"

"No, to be the best, Thor, one must commit to excellence, whatever that takes."

"I believe you. But after all this investment in your clubs and your girls, aren't you concerned that the girls you sponsor and cultivate will just up and leave you, Jen?"

"No, that doesn't concern me in the slightest. I happen to have ownership interests in ten different companies that are in the business of producing premium porn films. And those businesses are booming, Thor. The public can't get enough porn or enough new porn stars. Much more important is the feedback effect that a girl turned porn star has on our club's businesses. Very few of our sponsored porn stars leave our clubs."

"Why is that, Jen?"

"The money, Thor. They make more by staying with the clubs."

"I don't understand."

"Let me help you here. Let's say a customer has seen one of our girls performing in a porn film. He then comes to the club and sees her there. When he recognizes her, what does he see?"

"Her, I guess. What else?"

"Oh Thor, he does not just see her standing there in her Premium Bikini under a silk chiffon nighty. No! Through her shimmering gauze chiffon, he catches a glimpse of her outer lips beneath her vaginal hood, suggestively peeking out from her mons pubis. A sudden surge of eroticism floods his frontal lobes; his jaw opens and saliva courses into his lower mouth and washes the underside of his tongue. He cannot simply pass by her sensational, mouth-watering gem. It's impossible for him to ignore the treasure that's before him. She is sex personified. Between her legs, he knows his nirvana awaits. It begs for his attentions. His limbic mind takes over. His penal gland floods his thoughts with recalled images. It's her! It's the beautiful, uninhibited girl who captivated his imagination with her porn! His mind pushes away all logical, rational thought. Images of her from her porn film pulsate and resound through his memory mind. He recognizes her face. Indeed, it is she! She is the one; our glamorous nubile porn star; the same girl who performed such memorable explicit erotica in the film! Yes, he is certain it is her. She's the girl who laughed and giggled mirthfully while mocking morality

and religion. She's the defiant one; that one who pleasured herself with that dildo which was shaped like a crucifix; the morally absent vixen who enthusiastically licked and sucked the stem of the cross between the times she plunged it into her vagina. When she smiled to the cameras, her face spoke without saying: 'I control Jesus. See how I let him come out of me for air? You can see I have no need for God. You don't either. Join me. Accept my vagina as your God.' That porn film scene already clued our friend's limbic mind that our girl is decidedly immoral; committed wholly to the pleasures of sinfulness; not beholden in the slightest to religious admonitions or moral restraints. She is completely committed to her whoring and her pornography; dedicated to it, from her creamy white skin through her bones to her soul.

"Then, our customer member remembers when her porn partner appeared in the film. He sees that she notices her partner-stud. In her film, she smiles innocently while wrapping her arms around her porn partner and kissing him. She then squeals with delight and bounces up onto her tiptoes as her partner clasps her behind with both his hands, squeezes her buns hard while pulling her hips closely against his penis.

"Our customer sees this gorgeous underaged fifteen-year-old child-woman, on screen, giving tongue to her porn partner's mouth while his hand finds and massages her vag; and while her hand locates his penis and begins stroking it. Our club customer notices that she has no inhibitions about the seduction she's performing; no moral qualms whatsoever; no trace of guilt or even any self-consciousness over her naughtiness. Her rush to iniquity personifies pure, natural, honest, licensed, expected, accepted, immoral innocence. Apparently, our club member concludes that our porn girl has suffocated and drowned every vestige of virtuousness she ever had; obviously asphyxiated and eradicated all traces of any past moral teachings. And she appears to have done this purging of her

chastity willfully, shamelessly; with no reservations whatsoever. He concludes that any residual hints of morality in our uninhibited, carefree whore have been overpowered, destroyed, and subsumed by her obviously insatiable lust for penises and wealth. We at Infernoss Decado have trained her well! We are proud of our work. Our customer has assured himself that he observed her genuine comportment. Clearly, she is committed to profligate whoring. Obviously, she loves what she is and what she is doing. Most importantly, he, too, loves what she is; adores what she does; and feels within himself a budding love for her.

"He looks up at one of the club's televisions. Our secret club monitoring cameras have noticed his interest in our porn star nymphchild prostitute. Conveniently, the closed-circuit screen presents one of her porn films, showing her beginning a seduction. That our club member is suddenly immersed in images of her titillating debaucheries is no coincidence. Our member stares at her eroticism on screen; then he turns to her. She stands beside him, lifts her face towards his, implying that she wishes to prove she is every bit as promiscuous in the real flesh as she is on screen; and by moving her mouth close to his, that she also would like to be kissed. She asks him if he likes her; if he likes what she did in her film; if he'd like her to do those things with him. He tells her yes and embraces her. She welcomes his touches and places her hand upon his penis; implying that sexual wonders lie ahead. He chooses to risk a first kiss. She responds to that kiss with her warm lips, open mouth and flicking touches of her tongue. She knows that her kiss will set off a flame in his loins. She presses her body against his, confirming without words that she is eager and anxious to have sex with him.

"Suddenly, his mind reels with desire. He remembers from her film how she smiled and writhed to her partners' touches; how she oohed and aahed with pleasure from their fondling of her breasts and their kisses on her nipples. He recalls her asking them if they

thought she had nice tits; and did they like feeling them. And he remembers her telling them how much she loved it when they felt and massaged them; and how their touching and pinching her nipples excited her libido, making her hot and slippery wet; making her want to be their special bad girl. He remembers how she lifted her head back and taunted them, asking them if they had any idea what a shameless, penis-hungry, cum slut she was while she smiled and stroked their penises; and he remembers how she cooed like a happy bird when she held their two penises and first licked them; and when she told them how much she loved feeling how hard they were and how she could hardly wait to have their penises inside her; and how she laughed so naturally and uninhibited as she bantered with her porn partners and how she giggled with joy at the playful revelry of it all.

"Now brought to the forefront of our member's mind's focus are her laughs and giggles and her taunts, while asking her two porn partners if they had any idea how an innocent, pretty girl like her could have become so naughty; and why she loved being naughty more than anything in the world? Our member next feels his breath being stolen away. His most revered memories of our aspiring porn star now reappear upon his mind's theater screen. He remembers seeing her naked, straddling one of her partner's penises; sliding her pelvis back and forth while rubbing the opened lips of her vagina over his penis. He remembers her words: her asking her partner if he had any idea how hot and slippery wet his penis was making her vagina feel; whether he had any idea how good his big hard penis felt against her vagina's eager lips; whether he had any idea how much she was going to love sliding his big, hard, penis inside her vagina and sliding her penis-thirsty vagina up and down on it. And he remembered her then taking her partner's penis in her hand and guiding its head to her vagina's welcoming outer lips. He remembers how her outer lips gleamed with their slippery, anxious moisture as she

began settling her vagina over the shaft of her partner's penis. And he remembers how she oohed and aahed with her moans of pleasure and how her face seemed radiant and divinely blessed as she raised and lowered her vagina over her partner's penis, while rocking her pelvis back and forth over it; performing this motion slowly at first; but then faster as her libido demanded greater stimulation.

"Our member also recalled his cherished memories of our whore's gleeful smiles while her porn partner performed oral sex on her. Our member vividly recalled the spectacle of our young porn star holding her legs widely, shamelessly welcoming open while her porn part-ner held her vagina open while bringing his face flush against it. He was entranced seeing her triumphant, glorious smiles and hearing her encouraging words of: 'Yes, that's it. You're getting it. You know what I like. Oh, that feels so wonderful. Yes, your tongue is touching my clit perfectly. Do more of that. Oh, I love this so much! Don't stop. Oh, yes; I'm coming! Oh, I love this. This is so wonderful; so beautiful!'

"Our member remembers how her porn partner placed his face against her vagina; how he lowered his face to get the maximum angle of reach and penetration of her vagina with his extended tongue; and how his tongue pleasured her, patiently and persistently, until her pelvis lifted and her hands grasped her partner's head and held his face flush and hard against her opened lips while she released her explosive orgasm. And he recalled the serenity that then appeared upon her face and remained in her contented smile as she slowly moved her head back and forth, savoring her pleasures from oral sex.

"Our member then heard her confirm all he surmised. He clung to her words when she sighed and told her porn partner how much she loved being an immoral whore; and how she wanted to be a whore and fuck penises for the rest of her life, because she loved the experience of sexual pleasures so much. Our member then heard

her ask her porn partners whether they cared that she was a cum slut and a professional porn star; and whether it turned them on to know that she would most definitely be performing an orgy tomorrow; joyfully sucking and fucking four other men; and whether, knowing that, were they excited? And whether knowing that excited their penises so much that they wanted to fuck her again, right now? In the film, the men replied that they totally approved of her lifestyle and that they adored her for being a cum slut. And they again, taking turns, both fucked her a second time.

"Our member remembers still more from that film. He recalled how, after both men had fucked her a second time and had come inside her a second time, she then thrust her vagina into one of their faces, telling him how she loved feeling his tongue on her clit; and declaring how that made her come and made her feel totally fuck-crazed. And her partner performed oral sex upon her a second time; after which she sucked both her partners' penises until they became hard again. She then, using her hands, helped her partners put their penises inside her. And then she fucked them doggy, and missionary styles, and while sitting front and backwards facing, upon their penises. And, often while in her throes of fucking, she clasped her hands against the bed and grasped the bed sheets from the sheer unbridled ecstasies of her orgasm experiences.

"Our member appreciates that our budding porn star loved what she did with her porn partners. Now, standing next to him, her body pressed against his, and having tasted the warmth of her welcoming kiss and tongue touch inside his mouth, he no longer thinks of her as a mere woman. She is, in his mind, transformed. She is now a divinely unholy nymph goddess, placed here beside him, in her living flesh, to bless him with pleasures which he, before, could only dream about. With his arm now wrapped around her waist, he still visualizes her stomach heaving in the throes of penises' explicit thrusting in rhythm with her mons, and the way she held her partners' heads

and touched their shoulders, to release the inexpressibly delightful thrills from her oral orgasms. He still sees her fornicating with a penis inside her vagina; while holding her partner tenderly in her arms, caressing him and kissing him; whispering sweet encouragements to him; and expressing her delight while holding his penis tightly inside her, until it finished filling her vag with its ejaculation. Our budding vixen porn star understands the effect that her porn film is having on our member's mind. She knows his limbic zone has become flooded with burning desires for her sexual favors. She plays with our customer's imagination by stroking his penis while they stand together, getting acquainted, getting familiar, getting ready for intimacy. She knows her craft. We have coached and trained her so very well.

"And, our customer can never purge from his mind how spellbound he was when, at the end of her porn film, she smiled and bantered with her porn partners and told them how wonderful and hard their dicks' were; nor can he forget how she belly laughed with carnal joy when she asked her partners if they were ready to give their cum to her; and how she squealed and chortled as her partners released their semen onto the welcoming tongue of her open mouth; nor can he forget how she praised them, telling them that their semen tasted delicious and yummy, confirming that she was already an expert connoisseur of cum; nor can he forget that, while kissing and stroking their penises a final goodbye, she urged her porn partners to call her, come see her, and fuck her again. He is awestruck that our Decado girl does not have one moral fiber anywhere in her entire body.

"Our member will never forget how our newly minted minx smiled through her partners' ejaculations; how she burbled their semen; how uninhibited and shameless and proud of her ribald performance she was; how she blew kisses and winked at the camera; and at him, her viewer, after she swallowed her partners' semen; and

how gleefully immoral she was in her final scene when she held her vagina open and chortled with pleasured pride while she displayed her partners' semen flowing out of her. Our member looks up at the screen in time to witness a penis rubbing against her vagina's outer lips, begging admittance to the nirvana between her inner lips. She opens her legs more widely for this newest friend of her welcoming vag; her hand guides the penis's shaft home. She smiles like the Cheshire Cat. She is confident of her femininity, sure, of herself; thrilled to have a hard, fresh penis inside her again; pleased to be fucking again.

"Just then, another film of our budding porn star appears on another screen. She is naked and performing a massage on yet another porn partner. She first bathes him in a shower; then slathers him in oils and rubs him sensuously, all over his body. He hears her say to her porn partner: 'Did you have hectic day at the office? Are your wife and kids giving you a hard time? Did you know that married men turn me on? You are married, aren't you?' When her porn partner says yes, she continues her enticements: 'You probably didn't know this about me; but I love being a very bad girl. Yes, I do. I especially love helping married men relax their tensions. I especially love helping married men who are twenty years older than me. Why? Because I know that men who are thirty-five and older have had some experience. I know that your penis has seen and done a few things. And I love having an experienced penis inside me.

"I'm first going to give you a full body massage. I'm going to totally relax you and take away all your tensions. Part of my massage is the special care that I'll give to your penis. I'm going to give your penis the most wonderful fucking your penis has ever had. I promise, your penis will be happier tonight than it was on your wedding night. Yes, I'm certain of that. I'm going to want an honest evaluation from you, okay? I want to know whether you agree that this sweet, innocent-looking bad girl has fucked you more wonderfully

than you've ever been fucked before, okay? And why do I want to fuck you so wonderfully? Why do I want to make your penis so happy? I'll tell you why; because after I fuck you, I don't want you to go back to your wife. No, I don't, not ever. I want you to stay with me and fuck me all the time, several times a day; every day. Yes, I'm serious. That's how much I love your penis. I love how big and hard it is; and I want it inside me, shooting your cum into me; only me. Okay, baby?'

"Our member is spellbound by the insatiable penis thirsting passions of our young porn star. He holds our nymph goddess's body tightly against him. He's losing all rational thought now. He hopes to possess her all for himself. He now kisses her mouth while he looks up and sees her now sucking her new massage partner's penis; then he watches her sliding his penis into her vagina. Our member is immersed in erotic sensations. His limbic zone has taken control of his abilities to reason. He is smitten; obsessed, much like a wild stallion now, intent upon fornicating with our delectable fifteen-year-old nubile nymph; willing to do anything within his abilities to please her and marry her affections to him. Before he even feels the sensation of his penis inside her mouth or her vagina, he is already hopelessly in love with her.

"Yes, there you have it, Thor. That is what the customer really sees when he sees our cute, nubile, innocent looking fifteen-year-old porn star. He savors her soft, seductive kisses. He hugs her close to him, feels over her nightgown, slides his hand into her bikini bottom until he brings it to rest on her vagina. She offers no resistance to his hand; rather she flexes her buttocks and rubs her mons pubis softly over his hand. She confirms, like a purring kitten seeking closeness, that she is receptive. He senses her warm wetness, his nirvana. He's almost home. He imagines how tasty, slippery hot and wet her vagina's inner lips will be. By now, he desperately wants to place his tongue and penis inside her. It's love at first sight, Thor. We create that sensation through our club's porn program affiliates."

"And they make more money by staying with the club than just doing private service work?"

"Yes, absolutely. We coach our girls well, Thor. Let's say our man approaches her and tells her that he's seen her film; and that he loves what she does in a bedroom. Our girl will then tell him that he can have all that, and so much more, if he can win her one hundred thousand dollars at the craps table. She tells him that craps are her favorite game. It helps her get incredibly slippery wet and turns her into an erotic maniac who wants to fuck the entire night away. She mentions that she loves to sixty-nine. And she assures him that he'll love tasting her while she sucks his cum from him. And she promises him that that will just be the beginning of their fantastic night. She assures him that she will fuck him five different ways before the night is over; and that he will cum inside her every time. Our girls are taught how to entice and tease.

"After he loses two hundred thousand, our newly minted porn star informs him that she has a sudden emergency. One of her porn partners has had a family emergency. She needs a stand in for her first on stage live porn orgy tomorrow. Would he please stay and be one of her partners? He agrees; but that isn't the end of it. After her performance, she bats her eyes at him; tells him he was the most fabulous sex partner she's ever had; but she has another problem. The Club's resident porn film coach is demanding that she star in an additional ten porn films before she turns fifteen and a half. Her coach insists that she produce more content to keep her marquee showplace status at the club. Could her new member friend be a good sport and stay with her at the club for another few days while she performs in three new films? She reminds him of how much he loves sex with her. She coos and purrs and strokes his penis and kisses him; telling him that his other commitments and wife can surely wait; telling him to make up some excuse to spend more time with her. After all, she implores him; surely, he can appreciate that nothing is more important than her porn career and the wonderful

intimacy that they share. Surely, he wants to be one of her closest and most reliable friends. He agrees.

"That's her first bat, when she disrupts his agenda and bends it toward her agenda. I'm so proud of this girl, Thor. She's one of my favorite porn kittens. She has such a promising future with the clubs. She's just turned fifteen and she's already mastered many of the nuances a girl needs to create exceptional porn. She understands how to carry her body when she walks into a room; how to run her fingers through her hair and widen her eyes, implying that she's contemplating doing something important and wonderful; how to arch her back to emphasize her ass, and slowly twist and move her hips to show that she has a gorgeous ass; how to look over her shoulder and smile a naughty smile, a smile that not only opens her mouth, but also displays her tongue suggestively touching the back of her upper teeth, revealing the delicate underside of her tongue. She's also mastered the art of undress, Thor. She plays with her bikini straps and teases the camera by slowly revealing her breasts and nipples. I've watched her raise her arms over her head and stretch her body, full length, as if she's a lioness; then slowly move her ass and twist it back and forth while she performs slow twerks for the cameras. She's really got the moves that entice the viewer. Her body, her pretty face, and her naughty smiles telegraph that she is eager to fuck. She prolongs this slow twerk and twisting of her ass while smiling naughtily, driving the viewer nearly mad with lust for her.

"Just before she greets her porn partner, she gives the viewers a hint of the treats they are about to see. She spreads her legs slightly, revealing her thong string that barely covers her vag; and she then uses both her hands to lift her buttocks and move them slightly from side to side. I kid you not, Thor, she entices the viewer to near madness for her before she even begins the seduction of her porn partner. Then, her final enticement, before she performs with her partner is to face the camera and smile widely and naughtily, displaying again

her open mouth and tongue's delicate underside. She winks. She's letting the viewers know that they are in for the most unforgettable porn spectacle they've ever seen.

"In all her porn films, when she first approaches her partner, she immediately presses her body to his and kisses him full on his mouth. Her hand caresses his head while she lifts one of her breast nipples to his mouth. As her partner begins sucking her nipple and fondling her breasts, she arches her back and smiles joyfully, telling him that she loves how he's making her feel; while her other hand searches for, discovers, and begins stroking his penis. Before she even undoes her bikini bottom; before she reveals her vagina to the camera, she kneels before her partner, undoes her partner's pants, and holds his penis before her lips. She smiles enthusiastically at the penis, exclaims how large and beautiful it is, and chortles mirthfully how happy she is to be fortunate enough to suck it.

"As she begins her fellatio, she uses her hands well. One hand fondles her partner's testicle sac while the other strokes in gentle, twisting strokes. And she doesn't just suck the penis. She takes frequent pauses to look into her partner's eyes and tell him how much she loves his penis and how much she loves what she's doing. She works so well with the camera men, Thor. She instinctively knows when to slow her head strokes for a close-up shot. She knows when to stop stroking altogether and pause, look up while smiling enthusiastically and while batting the penis against her lips; and then displaying her tongue as it licks the penis, slowly, from its underside to its tip. Only after she has sucked for a full five minutes does she stand erect and remove her bikini bottom. She is sensational, Thor, she never hurries. Whether we marry or not, I want you to meet her and fuck her. She's one of those unforgettable sensual women you just need to experience for yourself.

"She next sits her partner upon a sofa or bed and faces him; then she stands over him and straddles him, very slowly and deliberately,

very sexily, as if she knows she's about to deliver the greatest sensation her partner has ever known. Then, she takes his hard, erect penis in one hand, positions it against her outer vaginal lips, and lowers her vagina onto the penis. She fucks deliberately, with enthusiasm and great happiness in her face, and with demonstratively slow, sensual twerking of he hips. She laughs enthusiastically as her partner increases the rapidity of his strokes. And when she senses that he is possibly about to come, she lifts off him; holds his penis in her hand momentarily to settle it; and then, again, performs fellatio. This time, her fellatio emphasizes her tongue licking the penis from the stem to the tip of its head, much more than sucking.

"She next mounts his penis a second time. Only this time she faces her partner's feet while she inserts the penis into her vagina. Once inserted, she props herself up with her arms and front-twerks her vagina against the erect penis. The cameras move in for their explicit close-up of her spectacular vagina while it thrusts and gyrates upon the penis. She throws her head back and laughs boldly, proclaiming that her partner's penis is giving her the best fucking she can remember; declaring that she loves how his penis feels against her clit while they copulate in this position; and that she's just about to have an orgasm. After another minute of front twerking in this position, she shouts out that she is coming; that he's stimulating her clit so perfectly, so wonderfully; that she's loving this so much; that she's releasing now; and that her ecstasy is beyond wonderful; and that she's loving this; and that he has a fabulous, adorable, penis. The cameras come in for another close-up as she dramatically slows her front twerking and grinds her vagina down hard to fully engulf the penis. The penis is captured by her forceful, circular pelvic motion; thus, continuing its clitoral stimulation and prolonging her orgasm fluid flow. She rapidly hand rubs the hood of her vagina while she does this slow, further stimulating her clitoris; all the while continuing her forceful, rotating grind

upon the penis; all the while shouting out how much she loves the way her partner is fucking her.

"Just when she perceives that her partner is about to come, she dismounts from the penis, holds it in her hand briefly, and again performs fellatio on it. You can see she does not want the penis to ejaculate just yet. She's not finished with it. She has more fucking and more positions in mind. She makes it obvious to the viewer how much she enjoys fucking; it's apparent that she wants to experience the full range of pleasure feelings she can enjoy, in the many different positions she can assume, while fucking her partner's penis.

"After this latest session of fellatio, she kneels on the sofa or bed. She displays her vagina to the cameras from her doggie position. She takes her moistened fingers and rubs lubricant over her vagina's outer and inner lips; and beckons her partner to come to her and insert his penis into her vagina. He does as she asks. She smiles widely and tells him that she loves feeling his penis in her this way; commenting on how hard and huge it feels; how she loves feeling it all the way into her, bumping up against her cervix this way. And then she twerk-fucks while her partner thrusts against her buttocks. She displays her consideration for her partner's penis while she performs doggie style. Her twerks are gradual and combined with a rhythmic, rolling twisting of her tush. She never does a sharp exaggerated twerk, which can injure a penis. She loves soft eroticism; the kind that fires a man's imagination. She's already got the moves of a top porn star. She shouts out how much she loves feeling her partner's thrusts; how wonderful it feels to have her partner's penis pleasing her this way. She frequently turns her face to fully face the cameras; smiling, nodding her head, voicing the words: oh yes, fuck me, fuck me more; yes, I could fuck like this forever!'

"Again, when she senses that her partner is near ejaculation, she uncouples from his penis and performs fellatio, keeping him hard. She then assumes the missionary position. She holds her vagina

widely open to reveal her pink inner lips and love channel to the cameras. She then inserts his penis into her vagina; all the while smiling enthusiastically to the cameras and laughing, bantering with her partner; asking him if he likes fucking her in this position; lifting her torso, propping herself up with her hands and kissing him with her soft lips fully on his mouth, obviously teasing his mouth by inserting her tongue in his mouth; and asking him if he'd like to come soon; and asking him if he'd like to come inside her. The camera then moves in for another close-up of her vagina, now fucking in the missionary position. She and her partner begin their rhythmic thrusts, slowly at first. Our darling vixen nymph uses this opportunity to smile and banter-babble to her partner; drawing her audience into her as a person; helping them relate to her; helping them fall into love with her.

"She asks him whether he thinks she is sexy enough to become a top porn star. He, naturally says she is more than sexy enough. He declares that she is the sexiest, most sensuous woman in the world. She then asks whether he thinks a man who passes her by on the street would think she is an innocent school girl or whether he might suspect that she is a very naughty girl who loves to fuck and perform in porn films. While her partner thrusts into her, he pauses briefly. He looks sincerely into her eyes and tells her that she can easily be both a carefree, innocent school child and a glamorous, gorgeous, delicious, lovable, breathtakingly wonderful, delightful porn star. He assures her that when the world sees her films, every man in the entire world will fall in love with her and they all will want to fuck her. She giggles when she hears that. She puts her hand on his chest, rubs his chest, and teases him. She asks him if he's just saying that so she'll ask him to make more porn films with her. He assures her that he's being truthful.

"Then she asks him if her vagina fucks as good as the other vaginas he's fucked. He affirms that hers is the tightest, wettest, hottest,

most slippery vagina he's ever fucked. She gets him to reveal that he has fucked eight other porn stars and to confess that her vagina gave him the ultimate in sexual pleasure. Then she gets very personal. She asks him if he's married. He reveals that he is. She asks him if he thinks she's a better sex partner than his wife. He tells her that, absolutely, she is; that there is no comparison; that his wife doesn't even hold a candle to her sexuality. She then asks him how he thinks his wife will feel if she sees this film and sees him coming inside her. He tells her that he doesn't care what his wife might think; that regardless, he would love to come inside her and make more porn films with her. She then asks him if he'd leave his wife for her. And he declares that definitely; he would leave his wife for her.

"He then asks her whether she'd want him in her life. She tells him that she'd like to think about it; that he needs to understand that a girl in her position has many men who would love to fuck her; and that her porn career is just getting started; that she plans on having a serious porn star career for another ten to thirty years, because she loves fucking so much; and that she expects she'll get many offers of marriage; and that she can't be expected to just rush into marriage. Then she says she'd first like to know how her vagina feels while he's ejaculating his cum into her. She laughs pleasantly, asking him if he could please, when he comes inside her, keep holding the head of his penis against her clitoris and not withdraw from her vagina until after all his spurts are finished, because those hot pulsing shots of semen flowing over her clitoris often makes her orgasm; and she'd love to orgasm again; this time simultaneously, with him. And she tells him that she'd love to make more porn films with him; especially since he believes that she's a better fuck than his wife. She tells him that it upsets her to know that some married men feel deprived of sex; and she wishes that, instead of feeling deprived and frustrated, that they'd join the Infernoss' Decado Club so she could meet them and fuck them.

"There, Thor, can you see why I love her so much? She knows how to entice men to become members. She knows how to seduce them and keep them coming back for more; and she knows how to bat them."

"Bat them?"

"Oh, that's prostitute slang. It means how to knock a man off balance when he's trying to get away from you; make him feel that he needs to stay with you; support you; help you. It's a technique to keep and strengthen the relationship bond while draining the man's pockets of his money. It's analogous to what Bifster One did to that butterfly. He played with it until he drained all the life out of it. Our sweet little porn star plays with her customer until she drains all his money out of him.'

"Your little kitten star did that to that member, didn't she?"

"Definitely. She most certainly did. We trained her well. After the first time he tried to get away and she got him to stay and perform in a four-partner orgy with her, he tried to escape a second time. But by then she was ready for him. She batted him again. She told him that she needed him to come with her to a photo shoot because she greatly valued his opinion. She got him to come and sit for three days. The first day, she dressed in scantily clad outfits and gradually peeled them off; ultimately revealing her vagina; holding it open and positioned in dozens of different positions. She had him go through each of hundreds of photos of her and tell her which ones turned him on; excited him; gave him the strongest erection.

"On her second and third days, she posed with male porn partners while he watched her. Our photographers took hundreds of photos of her in a dozen different outfits, first dressed, then in various stages of undress until she was naked. All the while she was kissing her partners; holding their penises; licking and sucking their penises; placing their penises inside her vagina in a myriad of different positions; doing cream shots with their penises while they

ejaculated onto her boobs, her vagina, her ass, her lips, and face, in every position imaginable. They had a series of finale shots where she performed orgy scenes, including one with her head hung over the side of a bed, receiving semen into her open mouth after sucking a penis, while partners ejaculated on her boobs, her stomach, and her vagina; and while one man held her vag open to display a voluminous white cum pool as other men ejaculated into her open vag."

"And her bat victim didn't object to this? Didn't he think he had a relationship with her?"

"No, he didn't object, Thor. He couldn't. That's the strange thing about men and porn. When they see a porn star receiving ejaculations while making porn, they love her even more that before, no matter how many porn films she makes. They adore her for being a cum slut, Thor. That's why I invested in porn production companies and why I encourage my Decado girls to do porn. Men crave more and more porn content. Did you know that for every minute a man watches a regular movie, he will spend ten minutes watching porn?"

"I don't think the studies bear that out, Jen."

"Those are survey studies, Thor. People lie in surveys. We did our own surveys based on Club members' habits, what they watch in their rooms, even when their wives are with them. They watch ten minutes of porn for every minute of regular movies. The demand for porn is consistently underestimated. It is enormous; and it is growing. The demand for fresh content from beautiful new, young porn stars is skyrocketing, Thor. And I am racing to meet that demand."

"So, how did your nymph porn kitty bat her man and separate him from his money?"

"Simply and smoothly. When she wasn't performing her porn scenes, she took him to visit the gaming tables with her. She persuaded him that his luck could change and she wanted to see him become a big winner, so she could fuck him for an entire week. He tries. He doubles down his two hundred thousand; loses; doubles

down again; and again; and again, until our casino closes off his credit. He pleads with our young porn star to stay with him, explaining that he loves her and that his wife is filing for divorce. But she informs him that the club has told her that his credit is no longer any good and she can no longer see him; besides, other, more well-heeled gentlemen are demanding her time and attentions; so, she'll just have to contact him later, when she sees he has cleared up his financial problems. He will never see her again. She will no longer return his calls. Their brief affair was never love; and it's over.

"You'd be amazed, Thor, at how many men take our fifteen-year-old porn star to the tables and lose two hundred thousand to the house to win her that hundred thousand. You'd be surprised how many men have put up property and stocks and gold and silver to reach their hundred-thousand-dollar goal to earn their night with our porn star whore. Would it surprise you to learn that many of our porn star girls become multi-millionaires before they reach the age of nineteen?"

"Really?"

"Yes, it's true. Now do you understand why Celt turns away three girls for every girl we accept?"

"I can appreciate your business model now, Jen. Tell me, has any man gotten so involved with one of your girls that the girl got him to lose everything he owned at one of your casinos?"

"Yes, Thor. That happens all the time. We've had at least five hundred men become members; fall hard for one of our girls; then lose everything they had at one of the casinos, all in the hopes of winning more of her favors, more of her time. The demand for hot, young vaginas is insatiable."

"Oh, wow! I had no idea. Were any of them married men with families?" Thor's eyes widened, revealing his sympathies for families that lost everything.

"Yes, all of them. Every one of them was a married man," Jen smiled widely and nodded in pleased affirmation. She kissed Thor and rubbed her hand over his penis. *"Why, my love, does that bother you?"*

"Well, honestly, Jen, it does a little. I mean, how do you feel about putting a mother and her children into the poor house?" Thor looked disconcerted and unnerved. His eyes searched Jen's eyes for some trace of human compassion.

"Oh Thor, you are a bleeding heart, aren't you? Listen, I didn't incur those gambling losses, the club member incurred them."

"But, Jen, your girls. They are so sexy and irresistible. And you coach them to persuade the male members to gamble and double down when they lose, right?"

"Yes, we coach the girls to do that. In all our casinos prostitution with teen aged girls is legal; gaming is also legal. It's even legal for our girls to give a man head right there at the gaming table, in front of other gamblers. And we encourage that, Thor. And our girls do that. They are uninhibited and shameless. We encourage our girls to do whatever it takes to get club members to bet. Men have lost anywhere from a few hundred thousand to seventy million dollars; going broke, doubling down, just to get their penises into one of our girls, one more time."

"And you're proud of that? You're proud of what you coach these girls to do?"

"You bet I am. I reward the girls when we collect our gambling debts. We give the girl ten percent of whatever we collect."

"You aren't religious, are you, Jen?"

"No, Mother was. She tried to force it on me; but Marty rescued me; showed me a different way to see the world."

"And your Clubs' girls? You brainwash them into becoming Pagan whores, don't you?"

"Not exactly, Thor. I unbrainwash them. I free them from the mental angst that religion imposes on people. Our girls are liberated from religion. We helped set them free of all that claptrap. We acquaint them with the proverbial Tree of Knowledge. We teach them that tree's forbidden fruit is tasty, nutritious, and rewarding; that there is nothing wrong with partaking of it; that it is a rewarding lifestyle. We teach them to feel free about partaking from that tree and enjoying the pleasures that it teaches them. We teach them that there is an alternative to letting the male misogynists take control of their lives and bodies and turning them into baby factories. We teach them that they are, before anything else, precious humans and entitled to life's pleasures."

"And the wives of the men they seduce? You don't feel sorrow for those men's wives and their children?"

"No, Thor, I honestly don't. These women know what they married. Many of them used sex to bag their husbands in the first place; so, they shouldn't feel shocked when a sexy young porn star takes their man away. Sex is a nature thing, Thor. It's that simple."

"And the children?"

"Come on, Thor. Some kids just get a bad break in life. It's not my fault that their parents split up. I'm not running an orphanage. Look at it this way, Thor. I once saw a stupid song bird fly down from the sky and land next to a playful little girl kitten. The kitten was curious, playful, and full of life. She sees the little bird and thinks it wants to play; so, she bats it with her paw. The bird falls from the bush and flutters; but the bird is cripped now. It can no longer fly away. The kitten has captured the bird. The bird is in the kitten's world now.

"It can't get away; but it isn't dead, either. It continues to flutter on the ground. It tries to get away from the kitten. It walks and hops, injured; and tries to distance itself from the kitten. It would like to escape and avoid further injury; but every time it tries to get away,

it flutters its wings and excites the kitten more. The kitten thinks the birdie wants to continue playing; so, this hoping and fluttering excites our kitten more. She senses that the birdie is her helpless victim. She decides to have fun with it; and this batting by our kitten continues.

"Eventually, the kitten's mom cat notices that the bird was on the ground and she decides to end the silly game between the birdie and her kitten. She pounces on the helpless birdie. She pins the bird's head down with one paw while she tears its wings off with her teeth. The birdie is still alive while the mom cat pulls its breast's feathers off and bites off a chunk of the birdie's breast flesh and eats it. The mom cat then encourages her kitten to come to the mortally wounded birdie and do the same. The kitten also bites off a chuck of breast flesh from the still living bird and eats her share of the bird. The two felines then leisurely take turns biting and tearing the flesh from the bird's breast. They eventually get to the bird's heart and they eat that, too; and the bird dies.'

"You watched this and didn't try to stop it?"

"Yes, Thor, I watched it. Why stop it? It's the natural way of things. It's a mother and her baby bonding by killing and eating a bird. Afterwards, the mother licked the blood and feathers off her kitten's face. It was so sweet and endearing. Watching them bond like that made me feel all warm and wonderful inside; at peace with the ways of nature."

"So, why are you telling me this, Jen?"

"It's an analogy, Thor. The hapless bird was a lot like a club member who gets too involved with one of my young porn stars. His emotions draw him to her. My nubile nymph is curious, irresistible, and innocent. She wants to prove, to herself, that she can be successful. Our aspiring porn star cripples the club member by flooding him with her playful sexual favors. She 'bats' him: persuading him to gamble, to win more of her time and favors. We call her behavior

batting the member, meaning she hits him with suggestions to risk more of his money so he can buy more time with her; fuck her more. Eventually, after the member has incurred losses, our sex kitten bats him again. She tells him his luck might change; and that sex with her is worth the risk. She encourages him to double down on his loses with a single bet. He bets and loses. He tells her he needs to get back to his wife. But our kitten doesn't let him flutter and run away. She bats him again. She tells him that she needs him here, with her. She needs him to support her between her porn filming and picture shoots; fucking her to keep her confidence high; reassuring her that she's still desirable to him after doing all that porn. She tells him that, surely if his wife is worthy of him and if she is understanding, as a wife should be, that's she'll accept his explanations when he sees her a week from now. Our man wants out of his dilemma. He wants our porn star and his wife. He's desperate, like an injured, grounded bird. The only way to have both women is to get his money back. So, he doubles down again, and again, until he loses everything he has."

"Then, you become Mom cat. Am I getting this, Jen?"

"Yes, you are getting it. When we know the member can no longer raise sufficient additional collateral to cover his losses. I step in. I take his notes and file for judgements. My lawyers work with law firms all over the world. Once I have court ordered judgements, I perfect them. I seize the member's properties, his stock and bond assets, his business, and his bank accounts. I levy liens; obtain orders for garnishment, place charging orders on all his accounts. In a manner of speaking, like the mom cat in the analogy, I tear his wings off; I rip out all his assets and his heart. Essentially, as in the analogy, I eat him alive. And, in many cases, I foreclose on the man's home and serve eviction notices which throw the wife and kids out on the street. I am iniquitous and merciless. I am a business woman. My clubs are not charities.

"But I am also generous. I give ten percent of the debts I collect to my wonderful kitten-nymph porn star, who batted the member

repeatedly, until the Club casino took everything he had. Like the mother cat licked the blood off her kitten's face; by giving my sex kitten a percentage of the debts I collect, I reassure her that what she did was good and wonderful. I praise her and honor her by financing more of her porn films. And that encourages my kitten to repeat her behavior with other men. That bonus money I give her is in addition to her prostitution rates and her tips. That's just good business, Thor. It encourages the girl to persuade other love-struck members to gamble; removes any inhibitions she may have about using her sexuality to entice them to gamble. I reward her for batting them to double down. Giving her a piece of breast meat helps her appreciate that whoring and performing as a porn star is a fantastic, wonderful business if she stays focused and trusts my management."

Jen smiled smugly and matter of factly to Thor, as if to ask him whether she disgusted him. Thor returned her look. His face showed comprehension and appreciation for the lack of empathy that Jen had for those who fell into debt to her. Jen turned her head slightly, lifting her smile, as if silently asking Thor whether he could love a woman with her villainous, immoral ethics; whether he could accept her as his life partner as well as one of the world's consummate, heartless whores.

Thor answered her silent smile with a question:

"And the same way you explained that I should love and appreciate Bifster for what he is and the way he is with butterflies, birds, mice and the like, you are asking me whether I can love and appreciate you for the incorrigible whore that you are and the things you do to succeed in business; aren't you, Jen?"

"Thor, do you believe it's possible to succeed in business and be ethical? Do you really believe that? If the government orders you to do something and pushes you to do it when it's against your moral or religious beliefs, would you do it; or would you not do it, knowing that you'd get sued and regulated out of business for being ethical and true to your beliefs?"

"I guess if I wanted to avoid the risk of going out of business, I would do it."

"So, if I have concluded that being immoral and unethical is the optimal configuration for a business model, how am I so different from a business that gets pushed into doing something immoral or against the business owner's religion?"

"I guess there is no difference, except that you embrace immorality willingly rather than reluctantly."

Jen knelt and lifted her head from her intermittent fellatio dalliances with Thor's penis. She straddled him and took his upright penis in her hand; and guided it to her vagina, touching its head against her outer lips. She knew that Thor's penis would recognize how hot and slippery wet she was. But before she lowered her vaginal lips onto the head of Thor's penis; and before she began her rhythmic strokes, up and down over it with her insatiable vag, she replied:

"I think that begs the essential question for us, doesn't it, Thor? Can you love me the way I am, an immoral, unethical business woman, without trying to change me? Can you accept the things I do to people who owe me money and to people who are my adversaries, without becoming squeamish about it? When people tell you that your wife is a bitch and a cunt, can you look them in the eye and tell them that you already know that about me and you love me despite those traits; even tell them that you love me because of those traits? Can you love the cat more than you feel sorry for the bird, Thor?"

Jen's face and eyes now implored Thor to understand her; to love her as she was; beseeching him to throw his life in with hers; to embrace her piratical, marauding, rampaging, vicious, unethical, immoral approach to life and business; to embrace her and love her as a whore, a madam, and a wife; and to become one in spirit with her.

'Yes, Jen. The answer is yes. I can love you with unconditional love; and I do; and I always will. I wish to partner with you and sire your children; and I will love you until the day I die.'

Upon hearing Thor's answer, Jen lowered her vagina over his penis until she engulfed his entire shaft.

CHAPTER TWENTY

She looked at me as she did love; and made sweet moan. And sure, in language strange she said: I love thee true. (John Keats: La Belle Dame Sans Merc)

Take my hand, take my whole life too; for I can't help falling in love with you. (Elvis Presley, the King)

Love is wonderful. Fill your life with it. (Rosemary Ness Bitner, author)

LOVE

"Then, I shall also love you, Thor; until the day I die. You will be my love; my man; my trophy. We shall become like a pair of mating Monarch butterflies. I have fluttered above the Mexican jungle canopy, waiting for you to find me, Thor. Now that you have, I shall mate with you. We will produce human offspring; and also, from our butterfly souls we will create fertilized eggs. I will seed those eggs upon the victim milkweed leaves. Those eggs will become our caterpillars, our business ventures. They will devour the innocents and they will thrive and become butterflies like us. And our sinful, immoral ways will continue forever."

"I'm glad you revealed your thinking and your ways to me, Jen. Now, help me understand another thing: What is it that you look for in a girl besides a beautiful face and body?"

Jen rocked her vagina over Thor's penis, smiling down at him; pleased with his declaration, savoring it before she answered his latest question:

"Well, it's not that complicated, Thor. We want girls that have not been brainwashed by religion, who love to fuck, and who want to make a lot of money. It's a dog-eat-dog world. We want girls who have a predatory predilection; who have no sympathy for a man who goes broke at the game tables; who has no sympathy for the wives and kids that get thrown onto the streets. We probe for telltale signs of religious or moral attachments. We want girls whom we can mold into thoroughly immoral, uninhibited, shameless whores; girls who have no misgivings or second thoughts about becoming porn stars; girls who aspire to becoming wealthy."

"You are against religion, aren't you, Jen?"

"No, I'm not, Thor; really, I'm not. I understand that people need to believe in something; and for many people that is a belief in God via some venue path to their God, in some form or another. I get that. I accept that. Good for them. They are getting what they need. Religion gives them that. But I view religion and morality as a marketplace where different faiths compete for market share. Much religious belief has been debunked by evolution theory. Many people made global warming their religion; now, lately their new God has become climate change. Okay, there are people who believe in that stuff. There is no sure proof that their beliefs are well founded, just like there's no proof that there was ever a God who created day and night and animals and humans the way the bible says they were created. In fact, the opposite is true."

"Really?"

"Yes, really. You see, Thor, the DNA strand that created the human gnome first expressed itself nine billion years ago. About six or seven billion years ago, somewhere in the universe, human female DNA experienced an unusual mutation. Several

primate-like females' double helix strands were pried apart in one place, and one of their two strands were severed. A serpentine, bent and twisted DNA molecule was spliced into their severed strands; then, these modified strands were reconnected. These modified strands were then rejoined to their companion strand in the DNA helix. These females were purposely DNA modified in order to make them more promiscuous than non-modified females. In effect, this new human woman was created to be more promiscuous, breed more readily and more often; and to evolve more rapidly than other primates.

"Evolutionary change as a result of this DNA modification began very slowly, because it took billions of years of breeding for the population pool of DNA modified humans to grow sufficiently large; so that the promiscuous progeny not only sustained the population level; but increased its size. By five billion years ago, before the Earth was even formed, the human promiscuous population was already increasing. Approximately five to ten million years ago these modified humans were introduced to planet Earth. There was, initially, interbreeding between these modified alien humans and other primates. The various species that this interbreeding created propagated and flourished for some millions of years; but they were doomed. They died out because the modified alien human species, the purebred alien descendants, possessed greater intelligence and were more aggressive. They were also more promiscuous. Eventually, these modified alien humans subjugated, dominated, or otherwise eradicated all other species of animals on Earth.

"So, you see, Thor, promiscuous women were present on Earth and driving civilization's progress millions of years before any religious concept of a deity appeared; millions of years before the Sumerians, Hebrews, Hindis; well before Islam, Christianity, Buddhism, Judaism, Hinduism, or Sikhism."

"Jen, where are you getting this? And what are you telling me?"

"My trusted source of all things relating to human evolution, morality, and spirituality is Mrs. O'Dell, my shrink. She keeps up with all the latest theories and developments in humanity's morality and progress. She assures me that her information is based upon scientific facts; not fairy tales propagated by misogynistic shepherds and goat herders. What I'm telling you, Thor, is that modern women are the product of billions of years of human evolution that began somewhere in the universe and was introduced to Earth many millions of years ago. The religious versions of human development are just wrong. The religious types naturally defend their illogical beliefs. They seek to censor and condemn those who use science to disprove religious dogma. This is why Mrs. O'Dell lives hidden in a cabin in the wilds of British Columbia."

"And you believe her, don't you, Jen?"

"Yes. Absolutely."

"What are the implications, Jen? What do you see?"

"It's obvious, Thor. People are becoming more accepting of promiscuity, prostitution, and pornography. A voracious whore, such as myself, is the natural result of humanity's evolutionary progress. Everything about my immorality is natural and healthy and normal. Embrace me and my ways; and love me. You will see, as time goes by, people becoming more skeptical about their beliefs. There are lots of skeptics about religion; lots of skeptics about climate change; lots of skeptics about government. I see that as a market opportunity. I think that's why so many people have turned to porn; many are even making porn the centerpiece of their lives; for many, pornography has become their religion. I think, more and more, people are waking up to the one thing that has been constant throughout human history."

"And what's that?"

"Simply that the human female vagina is integral to human creation. Historically, first there was prostitution worship. The religions

and the stuff governments want us to worship, like climate change, came afterwards. But the afterwards things aren't working. Society is fragmenting, distrusting, disbelieving religious thought and government mandated thought. So, what are people doing? They are returning to prostitution worship in the form of porn, Thor. They are deciding, once again, to return to their awe of creation forces. They are returning to their natural worship of the female vagina. It is natural, Thor. The vagina is beautiful, awe inspiring, powerful, and mysterious. It can make men lose their minds with lust for it. It makes some humans bind their souls and spirits to the soul and spirit of the porn star. The female vagina can launch armies and navies. It can give pleasures of the carnal type that religions and governments' claptrap mandates cannot give. The female vagina is humanity's one true god, Thor. It's the bedrock of faith in the continuation of the species. People are returning to it. They are changing their beliefs. They are accepting of prostitutes and porn stars as beautiful and good women; women to be adored and worshipped. I am at the forefront of that wave of change, Thor. I offer people the very best prostitution clubs and the most beautiful, most desirable porn stars in the entire world."

"Wow, Jen. Your thinking amazes me. What else do you look for in a potential Decado girl?"

"We want girls who are willing, without any hesitation or reservations, to transform their lives and become porn stars. They must want the notoriety and adulation as well as having a hunger for money and the finer things in life. They must love knowing that men are enthralled watching them performing explicit erotica. They must be uninhibited and shameless; but they must also demonstrate joy and exuberance while performing with a porn partner before the cameras. They must convey to the viewer that they are thrilled to be performing explicit sex scenes for all the world to see. You'll experience what I'm talking about when you meet our newest, most *promising stars. I especially want to introduce you to a girl whom I affectionately call 'My Kitten.' Her real name is Lolita Bunny Joyful."*

"The girl I saw in the film on your phone?"

"Yes. She is Kitten; I am Mom Cat. She personifies our new golden age of porn, Thor. She's the perfect porn star. A complete nymph. She has no morality; no inhibitions. She does not equivocate. Porn is her life's obsession. She even had a legal name change to help her porn career.

"You'll meet her. We'll spend some time with LBJ. I want you to taste her vagina and fuck her, Thor. You'll appreciate what I'm saying. Once men have been fucked by LBJ, men swear they've died and gone to heaven. She's typical of the girls we seek; girls who want to make serious money; who consider prostitution a noble calling, a profession; who appreciate that their vaginas are incredible assets which our clubs value enhance. We want girls who want to belong; girls who appreciate that my clubs advance their goals."

"And you're not worried about pairing me with this underaged sex siren?"

"No, I want to watch the two of you. I want to see how you feel while you come inside her, and into her mouth. I want to see how much cum you give her. I want to feel turned on. Then, when we make love, I want to ask you how you felt while you came inside her. I want you to tell me how good it was and how wonderful it felt to fuck her; because that's going to make you want me more, Thor. I want to know that you love her vagina as much as I do. That's how I'll know your mind associates our love making with the most fantastic sex available anywhere in the world. I want you to feel this way while you fuck me because I want us to fuck often. I want us to fuck so much that you won't have time for anything else."

"I had no idea you were a minx, Jen."

"I am, dearest; one of the most sex crazed nymphomaniacs on the planet."

"And this Lolita; how did you decide to accept her into the club?"

"She was fourteen when we interviewed her. She started having sex with Jaques when she was twelve. She then had sex many more times with four different boys. Her friend, Josephine, gave her Celt's card; and things progressed from there. She was a natural sex pot; absolutely loved fucking; loved fucking more than anything else. We only needed to ask her some qualifier questions. When we interview any potential girl for our porn star program, we ask pointedly uncomfortable questions to see their faces when they answer."

"Such as?"

"Okay.

'You are given a choice. You can fuck a sixty-year-old fat man and make a million dollars, or you can fuck an Adonis twenty-five-year-old man and make three thousand dollars. Which man would you fuck? Your father discovers that your mother signed your consent forms without his knowledge. He threatens to never see you again if you do not quit the club. Do you quit the club?'

"We use variations of those kinds of questions to probe for a moral core and to test the girl's greed factor. If we think she has an inflexible or equivocating moral heart that won't adapt to a porn star's immoral lifestyle, we reject her. There are too many girls who are more than willing to become immoral, shameless porn stars. We're not running a convent."

"And Lolita checked all the boxes?"

"Oh yes! She has no qualms about doing older men; no qualms about lying, cheating, or stealing. She'd commit murder if it paid her well, and if she couldn't get caught. No morals; none. Her soul is committed to pleasing male penises. When we explained our porn star program, her eyes lit up. She begged to be included at her young age. We watched her do a porn demo with one of our male partners. She convinced us. She adores the penis. She's intrigued by everything she can do with it. We knew she was a natural for the cameras."

"And you want me to fuck her?"

"Absolutely I do. Why not? Are you afraid of her; her age?"

"No. I'm just making sure that's what you want for me; for us."

"I do, Thor. It is exactly what I want. Don't be provincial. I want the best for you. I want you to have that experience so I can transfer that eroticism to our love making. I want you to have her as often as you want her. I know what I'm doing. Trust me. It's a phenomenon that takes place in the mind. It's hard to imagine it now, but our love making will become that much better."

"All right then. Jen, I'll do your Miss Lolita Bunny Joyful."

"Good. I'm pleased."

"So, tell me, I'm sure some men go ga-ga over your girls. Surely, you encounter men who are troublesome. How do you deal with them?"

"I hire out that problem. I've engaged a private security service. They can be rough. If a man persists in being a nuisance, I will not put up with him. The service detail takes him swimming."

"Swimming?"

"Yes, Thor, I told you I'm very detail oriented. All our clubs are located near oceans or large lakes, or they operate on yachts at sea. We take our troubles out of sight of land and let them swim."

"What if they are good swimmers?"

"Thor, no one swims well with their legs weighted with twenty pounds of concrete blocks and wrapped tightly in chains."

"You murder people, Jen?"

"Well, don't go there, Thor. Remember, I hire security people. How they handle things is their business. I don't know the details of that. I only know that troublesome men are kept away from my clubs and my girls."

Thor held Jen in his arms and kissed her.

"I've fallen hopelessly into love with you, Jen. Please tell me if I'm ever making you unhappy."

Jen's vagina stroked Thor's penis more rapidly; and she held him close to her.

"You'll never make me unhappy, Thor. Think positive thoughts. Think fun thoughts. If you want variety, spend time with one of the girls. I'm fine with that. I'm a free spirit, Thor. I want you to be happy."

"I'm happy, Jen; very happy." He held her close and kissed her. *"And what happens to your girls when they become adults?"*

"Some stay with the clubs. We love our long-term girls. We keep them on as long as they bring in the revenue. Some fall in love and marry one of their customers. That happens. People need intimate, compatible love and many find that in our clubs. Others go into the business world. Having Infernoss Decado Club hostess on a girl's resume is a real door opener, Thor. You'd be surprised how many companies use sex to sell their products and services. Many Decado girls get placed near the top in corporations.

"Executives like having women on the payroll who have no qualms about having sex with them while they are working late hours or while they are out of town on business. They also love being able to offer the favors of beautiful women to their customers. Sex helps make business transactions happen. That's the silent side of corporate life that companies don't like to talk about. But it's very real. Immoral liaisons have become integral to modern day corporate life. Some of our former girls have gone on to become top executives. Many girls who went the corporate way have reported back to us, thanking us for helping them launch their corporate careers."

"I had no idea!"

"Oh, Thor, you are such a baby. Tell you what: Assuming I do decide to marry you, how would you like having our two-week honeymoon at one of my clubs? How would you like sampling two different, fuck-crazed beautiful teen aged girls every day for fourteen

days? How would you like to sample the very finest, hottest, juiciest female vaginas available anywhere in the world?"

"Jen! What about us? I mean if we married, would you want that for me? When would I see you?"

"Oh, you'll see me plenty, Thor. Three times a day, at least! I haven't forgotten my porn experiences. Surely by now, you know how much I love to fuck!"

Jen laughed. She lifted her vag off Thor's penis and lowered her head to it; and began giving him head.

"We'll have a fabulous time! We'd do lots of threesomes with the girls. They could sit my face while they licked me and sucked you. I could sit your face or kneel and put my vag in your face while you fucked them. They could sit my face while you fucked me. And they could sit your face while I had oral sex with you. Can you imagine how much combination fun we'll have?"

"Yes; so, you are not contemplating a monogamous marriage, are you?"

"Goodness no, Thor! That's a lot of Victorian claptrap. Marty and Mrs. O'Dell straightened out my thinking about that. Put religious sermonizing and the self-righteous homilies out of your mind, Thor. Those are just methods that narcissists use to gain power and control over people. Preachers, sham hucksters, and do-good organizations beat those drums for their paychecks. There never was a Garden of Eden. There never was original sin. That's all a prop for the homilies that give impressionable people their fears and guilt trips and make them surrender control of their lives. We, that is our marriage, will have no part of that stuff."

"So, you are not worried about me straying?"

"Oh Thor, don't underestimate me. I'm already investing in two different companies that are creating the most advanced feminine lubricants in the world. My scientists are creating unique blends of low viscosity oils that infuse molecular graphite into the molecular

chains of their products."

"Why would you do that?"

"To create a lubricant that makes an eighty-year-old vagina even more slippery, hot, wet, and fuckable than a fourteen-year old's vagina. That's why!"

"You want that for eighty-year-olds?"

"You're still not getting me, are you, Thor? I'm always thinking ahead. I want that for me! I want to stay a hot, juicy vagina for you. I want to fuck you, Thor. I want to fuck you lots! And I'm always trying to see opportunity. Many eighty-year-old women would love to fuck, if only their vaginas could still excite a penis. That's a huge market! There are tens of millions of sexy older women, Thor; and some day, I will be joining them. And I know myself. I'll want to continue fucking you until the day I die; so, your sweet, innocent looking Jen wants to be sure that she can still excite you, no matter how old we are. I intend to stay beautiful and sexually active, Thor. I'll have surgery maintenance done when I need it. I'll keep my pretty face. I'll keep my pretty boobs. I'll still have my die-for, tight, penis loving tushy. And, when nighttime comes, I'll still want to feel your wonderful penis inside me; understand?"

"Yes, Jen. I'm beginning to understand you. And I'm loving you more with each passing day."

"Then let's stop talking. Let's make love."

And they did.

CHAPTER TWENTY-ONE

The excellence of every art is its intensity, capable of making all disagreeables evaporate from their being in close relationship with beauty and truth. (John Keats: Letters to G and T Keats)

The two most important days of your life are the day you are born and the day you find out why. (Mark Twain, author)

KNOWING JEN

Thor was drawn to Jen now, closer than he ever dreamed was possible before they came to Cape Cod. He felt it happening. His soul was trying hard to know her soul, to appreciate the beauty of it; treasure the freedom its immorality enjoyed, and share in it so that he could somehow love her more. He had come to appreciate that she was a high energy, driven, success-oriented woman; and he loved her immoral character, more and more, with each passing day. They had made love several times a day for their first three days. It was an intensely physical coming together. Thor felt it. He was certain that Jen felt it, too. During the many times they made love, in the throes of their intensity, he recalled the enthusiasm and tenderness with which she performed the explicit erotic scenes in her porn films. He now knew that Jen wasn't acting. The real Jen was there, performing in her on-screen love scenes; loving the eroticism of it; consumed with pleasing the penises of her partners; making their pricks and the pricks of millions of other male viewers rock hard and erect; driving them insanely wild with their desires for her.

During these last three days Jen had been every bit the minx that had left him spellbound from watching her films. Only, now real and in the flesh, Jen was a million times more alluring. Her touchings, the feel of her body against his, her kisses, her scents and her smiles were vivid now; imprinted into his mind, forever. Yes, he told himself, he was certain. This was a forever thing kind of love. He knew he was born to love this woman. For their first three days they had ravaged each other, Then, on the fourth day, they had run a mile down the beach and back. They laughed and hugged and sat side by side in the surf, hugging and kissing. The waves washed up and over their feet, and then retreated to the sea.

That fourth night Thor had gone to bed early. Jen said she wanted to lie awake and read awhile. When Thor awoke, hours had elapsed. Jen was sound asleep, and her bedside light was still on. He turned her light off and pulled her duvet up closer to her chin, covering her. That's when he noticed her journal. It was Jen's personal, leather-bound treasure that chronicled her thoughts and feelings, day by day. He couldn't help himself. What better way to know and understand her? He turned back to her entries from the day she first saw him. He read selected passages, and his thoughts followed:

'Very handsome one joined the class today, two weeks after we started. Tall, Nordic, love his chiseled face and bod. Name is Thor (T). Felt it. Wonder if I'll ever get to fuck him? Remember, girl, you are off the pill.'

'She noticed me! She wanted me from the get go. Why didn't she ever reveal herself? Why so coy?'

'T asked to carry my books. Fish on! Mrs. O was right. I baited, and waited. He's an awkward pup. He wants me. Who is he? Why me?'

'She's unsure about me. That explains the questions she gave me.'

'He let me grill him. Answers okay. Still seems weird that he picked me to hit on. There are other pretty girls. Flashy dressers. Obvious attention seekers. But me? Mrs. O. knows men.'

'She's still skeptical. Mrs. O must be the Mrs. O'Dell she talked about. Does she have mental problems?'

'At the cabin. Made love with T. He's hungry for me. It's an obsessive love; need based. Why? B came in with bottle tail. He saw something. What riled him? No hissing, no cat fiffs; no dog barking. A person? A deer?'

'Yeah, I was hungry for her all right. Wanted her more than I ever wanted anything or anyone.'

'Made love on and off all day. Better and better. Knows a woman's body. Loves oral sex; huge plus! Very good technique, reminds me so much of Marty. T has a woman's intensity about the clit. Not like Roger; not an enjoyment thing with T. It's still mostly need based. Obsession. Yes, obsession. Not like Dad; not a sharing of joy, camaraderie based; not honoring me, treasuring me, like Dad; but needing me. Why does T need me?'

'She knows me by how we make love; compares me with Roger. Who's Roger? Her dad? Yeah, she said she did incest. Obviously, she loved incest with her dad. No, her dad's name was Dominick. Roger must have been a porn partner. She wants to dig into my psyche. Should I tell her? Maybe I should. Maybe if I'm honest I can chase her doubts away. She might freak out, though. Take the risk? Watch her mood.'

'Fantastic love making again today. Curious. T does the under tongue exactly like Marty; taps my clit exactly like Marty; vibrates it like Marty did. Could it be? Coincidence? He's that good at pleasuring a woman? He's drawn to it more than straight sex; loves licking my vag in every position. Bif freaked out T today over a stupid butterfly. T overly sensitive about a victim insect. Weird.

Wonder what he thinks now about the underaged girls I use? What is he? Saint? Preacher type? How to corrupt him? We could do so much! Dear God, help me. I love to fuck him so much!'

'She suspects! It's right below the surface. Should I tell her; just trust her?'

'Ran the beach with T today. Great. Loved sitting in the surf, watching the ocean swells breaking; having him next to me. Thinking about eternity; like I always do when I look at the sea. Couldn't wait to get back to the cabin and fuck again. What's happening to me? It's love. I'm sure of my feelings; but not sure of him. I want him. Creation partners? I'm sixteen again!'

'She feels it too. Time to tell her? Maybe better to tell her than letting her find out? She will find out, you know. You've had so many flashbacks. There must be truth in them. Tell her? She may think you're crazy! Tell her you remember clearly; how vivid it all is:

'You were Moses and she was Baaleezebelle. Zeporah and her two sons were her victims. You realized that she had arranged their murders. They were about to be thrown to the crocodiles and you did nothing to stop it from happening. You wanted it to happen. Baaleezebelle motioned to you to come to her; consort with her while your family was being devoured. And you di go to her. And you kissed her forehead in twenty places with loving kisses. And you kissed her lapis tinted, taupe painted eyelids. And you kissed her mouth, ignoring Zeporah's screams ordering you to stop.

'And you became smitten by Baaleezebelle when she took your penis into her hands and began kissing it. You smiled at her and kissed her mouth a second time when she spoke so softly to you:

"Ummmm. You have such a wonderful penis. It's so huge! And so hard! I'm going to love fucking your penis more than any other. But first I need to help it understand how much I love it. I need to bond with it and become one with it. I need to kiss its head and lick it all along its entire shaft. And I need to hold its testicles in my

mouth to let them know how much I appreciate the semen they will make for me. And I need to do this acquainting for a long time, until I'm certain that your penis truly loves me and wants to be inside me. I want this to be wonderful, Moses. I want your penis to love me forever."

'And that's when you knew the true heart of Baaleezebelle! That's when you saw her soul for the first time. You suddenly saw her, not as Egypt's most notorious, incorrigible whore; but as an artist who performed spectacular intimate artistry. Yes! You could see clearly then! Her pornography was beautiful artistry! It caused the human mind to embrace its limbic needs and soar to fresh heights of emotive feelings; to feel this unrivaled outpouring of love and passion lust; and to embrace that outpouring because it is the natural order of humanity and it sets the soul free! And in that instant, you fell into love with Baaleezebelle! You knew, in that moment, that nothing else and no one else mattered to you or your own soul than Baaleezebelle and her love.

'And now, here you are again. It's seven thousand years later and now your soul is in Thor and the soul of Baaleezebelle is in Jen. And you love her! You must have her, only her, for your lifetime! You must reveal this truth to her. Give her your total honesty. Honesty. But to an immoral goddess? A madam of brothels? You must confess that you adore the morals of a whore? That you want your soul joined to hers for your lifetimes? Yes, you do. So, do it! You must! Love is based on truth and trust. Now you know her for what she is. This is an eternal thing. Your souls have found each other again! You know you love her. You love what she is; everything about her; what she means to you. So, do it!'

It was the morning of the day before they planned to go back to Newport. Jen made poached eggs, bacon, and marmalade toast. She sat across from Thor at her small breakfast table wearing her silk chiffon nightgown, opened; her breasts revealed; nipples pro-truding. They did that sometimes without even being touched. That's how sexually charged she was. Jen was the first to bring up relationship questions:

"I sneaked a look at your sketches. All me. Why all me, Thor? My face at different angles; front, sides, my face close-ups. And those drawings of my boobs? How many ways did you need to draw my left tit, Thor? My nipple? I couldn't imagine how you got so obsessed over my boobs and my nipple? Are you okay? I mean, if this is obsession, can you handle it? Care to tell me what draws you to me like this? Where is it coming from? Was it something with another woman; your mother, maybe? What?"

Jen smiled, trying to make her inquiry seem as innocent and light hearted as possible.

"Wow, okay. You've guessed it, all right. It's obsession, Jen. I can't get enough of you. And I can handle it. Don't you think I'm handling it?"

"You are, Thor. It's just that you're younger than me by almost five years. You're going to meet so many other girls; kiss so many other soft lips; hug them, hold them; fuck them; pleasure them. And you deserve that, Thor. They'll all love you. You are a fabulous lover. I think you already know that. Hundreds of women would die to have you pleasure them in the same ways you pleasure me."

"But I don't want to pleasure hundreds of women. I only want to pleasure you. When I see the wind lifting your hair from your face while you sit there on our blanket staring out at the sea, I know I am with the love of my life; everything I've ever wanted in a woman. It's all in you, Jen. No one else; just you. I'm seeing the enormity of life and the eternity of time and the sea. And I'm feeling those same winds, Jen. They are our winds. They are caressing our faces; telling us they understand our love; whispering to us that we share a common, eternal bond. They know we love each other and they

know that love is all that matters. I feel our souls have traveled time together and they have rediscovered each other and they know our love is all that matters. They know, Jen. They know everything. I want you, Jen. I want a life with you. I want to marry you and create a family with you. Will you marry me, Jen?"

"Thor, please. We are going so fast with this; and we don't need to go fast. Just because Bifster rubbed against your leg yesterday and we talked about marriage in hypothetical terms, doesn't mean that I also totally accept you. I get it that you are ready for me; but I'm not sure I'm ready, Thor. Jen's kingdom sets a higher bar than kitty kingdom does. It takes more than a week of great fucking to be accepted. Thor, you hardly know me. And I'm not even sure I know who you are. I do love you. I already told you that. I know I love you; but love is blind. I'm sure you've heard that. Some things just leave me feeling like there's so much more that I need to know."

A long pause followed while Jen tilted her head as if the things she needed to know were hiding under Thor's chin: *"about you and about myself."*

She bit down on the edge of her marmalade toast and stared into Thor's eyes, as if to tell him that if there was something he was not telling her, this would be a good time to come clean. Surely, he was smart enough to know that with her money and connections she could have him researched and vetted, knowing everything he did from the time he was born to the present. She munched her toast. She was enjoying this. She reached his foot with her toe and rubbed it. And she was liking her marmalade toast.

"Okay, Jen. I think you're wanting to hear total honesty."

"Well, I think you and your fabulous penis have had the time of your happy lives this week, Thor. I think I'm entitled to hear honesty; and only honesty, don't you?"

"Sure. Yes. Time for games to end. Let's start with my poor boy routine, okay? Jen, I'm not in your money class. But I'm not poor. I'm

the sole beneficiary of a family trust worth over fifty million dollars. Dad had a tool and die company that he sold out to a conglomerate, much like your dad's. So, I'm free to do whatever I want. But it's you I want, honest."

"Okay, great start, Thor. Now about how we met. That was no accidental happenstance, was it? You staged that gig about carrying my books, didn't you?"

"Yes, I confess. But it was only because I was dying to meet you."

"Go on. Where did you first see me?"

"Honestly, I told you. I happened to see one of your porn films. But I believe my soul met your soul seven thousand years ago; and now our souls have rediscovered each other and they insist that we join together for our lifetimes."

"I'm not buying what you are selling, Thor, darling. If it's me you want, you need to divulge the whole truth. Corny hokum half-truths won't cut it. I want to hear all of it."

"You might throw things at me. You might kick me right out of your life, Jen."

"That's my decision, isn't it? If you believe we have something, you'd better tell me. Don't underestimate me. That would be a fatal mistake. I've also felt this soul thing you are talking about. I know there's something there, driving this. But I do not suffer fools, Thor. If you are playing me, I'll figure you out. And then you will be out of my life. And there won't be any coming back. So, do you want to try again?"

"Yes. It was Marty, Jen. I got addicted to her films. I joined her Premium Members. I paid $5000 an hour for three separate hours with her. I watched all her films. And then I noticed the two films that you tagged with hers. Then I searched porn sites and found your other ten films. I watched every film you made several times, Jen. I became addicted to you; honestly addicted."

"Now we're getting somewhere. That's good, Thor. Honesty is a great place to start. So, you're a whoremonger, aren't you? I mean

you do love whores. You obsess over whores, don't you? You pre-fer the company of whores to regular women, don't you? You love watching whores doing all the sexy and perverse things they do, don't you?"

"Yes; that is, no. I mean I was once a whoremonger. I studied the films of about ten porn stars until I found Marty and joined her service."

"Why did you join her service, Thor?"

"I just had to have sex with the woman who fucked and sucked so many penises. I mean, I watched what she did. She fascinated me. She's beautiful and so uninhibited and casual. Her porn made my mouth water. I felt this overpowering lust. I had to have her. It was like I needed to fuck her myself; just to honor her for being the spectacular, glorious whore that she was. So, I did."

"But you stopped seeing her after three times; three hours?"

"Correct."

"Why?"

"You, Jen. I saw your films. That's when I lost all interest in Marty. I mean, you did this one scene where two men came inside you. You were streaming cum; and then you positioned your vagina over this third man's face and set yourself down on him. And he was licking you while swallowing the cum from those other men. But you didn't care about his struggles; only that he was pleasing you. You had this countenance about you. You had this faraway look of pleasured bliss on your face. It was like you understood that you were, by far, the most sensational, glorious whore in the entire world. And your face showed that you knew it was that third man's great fortune that you allowed him to pleasure you. It was the way you took command of his body and his mind that captivated me. I became smitten and beholden to you. Watching that scene, you became my goddess. I had to have you."

"More than Marty?"

"Yes. Much more than Marty."

"And Marty taught you the techniques you use for cunnilingus; I mean the ways you use your tongue and fingers, didn't she?" Jen smiled. The truth was all coming out now.

"Yes," Thor lowered his head in submission. *"All of it. Everything I know. She worked with me on it until I pleased her."*

"She taught you well, Thor. You please me beyond measure. And then, was it Marty who gave my name to you?"

"Yes. I told her that I wanted to meet you personally and possibly join your premium service also. She gave me your name and the name of your production company. I hired a private detective to find out everything. He told me who you really were and where you lived; the college you were attending, everything. So, I rented a house in Newport and enrolled in the college and signed up for the same art course that you were taking."

"You did all that just to meet me?"

"Yes."

"Why didn't you simply join my premium service?"

"You had already discontinued it and dropped out of the adult film industry."

"Oh, yes, that's right. I had quit porn. I was working with Dad putting deals together and building the Infernoss Decado clubs."

"Yes, I knew that, too. But I had no idea you were in an incestuous relationship with your father."

"Well, I was for about four years. I loved fucking him. How do you feel about that?"

"Oh, Jen, I love you more than I can put into words. I believe you are my eternal love. And I love that you did that with your dad; that you could be so immoral like that. I love that you use underaged girls in the Decado clubs. I love your immorality; all of it. And I understand it; how beautiful and liberating it is; how badly humanity needs it. But aren't you taking legal risks doing that?"

"All legal, Thor. I told you. Totally legal. And with third party protection. They all worked for Celt."

"I heard of him. You liked him?"

"Liked him? I loved him. I loved him enough to fuck him many times, Thor. We got past the incestuous thing our first time and never looked back. We loved each other in every way, Thor. I hope that doesn't crush your moral compass."

"Oh, you are my everlasting darling whore. It doesn't crush my compass. I'm happy for you that you had that love. I totally love you; all of you; all of your immorality. Have I answered your questions?"

"Almost. What are your goals other than fucking me for the rest of your life?"

"Well, I want to build boats. I want to start with a small yard and build some of my own designs; then race them; see how they do. And I want children with you, Jen. We could create life together; help them grow; teach them so much."

"Children? Do you mean that?"

"Yes, I mean that more than anything."

"I won't do diapers, Thor."

"You won't. We'll have a nursemaid and a nanny, and a potty tender. Our kids will have good help. And you, my love, will fuck and suck to your heart's content."

"Just you, Thor?"

"No, I expect that you will have others, whenever you wish. I never want to change you. I had this dream. You and I had this boat building business. We were very successful. We had graduated to building yachts that sold for two hundred to three hundred million dollars each. And you were a huge reason for our success. We made this film of you with your first porn partners. What were their names?"

"Roger, Ross, Alex, and Nelson."

"Right, now I remember. Well, in my dream film you posed on one of our yachts for about a hundred porn photos with one or more of those four studs. You were wrapped in the sails, smiling blissfully, getting your vagina licked; standing at the helm, looking like a divine

goddess in your Premium Bikini, with Roger's arms wrapped around you and his fingers pinching your nipples; you again; licking and sucking all four of their penises in the master stateroom bed; and then fucking all four of them; playfully sucking Roger's penis while stroking it; causing semen to bubble up from it; then you again, smiling like a kitten taunting a mouse, while you lapped Roger's semen up; and you continued repeating this licking and stroking and kissing his penis's head and lapping up his semen. It was indescribably erotic! And you again, always you; lying on the forecastle deck with your glorious vagina held open, revealing your delicious pink inner lips and your love channel; and with creamy white semen gushing out of you. And you, of course, standing upright in the galley with your leg extended and propped upon a cabinet while Ross kneeled beneath you, licking your vagina. And more of endless images of you; this one of you, standing naked on deck, the wind gently lifting your hair while you held onto a mast stay with one hand and stroked Alex's penis with your other hand...."

"*Okay, okay, Thor; I think I'm getting it. You want me to be your whole package; wife, mother to our kids, business partner, company whore in charge of marketing; and porn star, performing live porn at trade shows for our serious buyers. Am I understanding you?*"

"*Yes, Jen. All of it. All of you; all in. What do you think?*"

"*Let me see,*" Jen smiled her naughtiest vixen smile.

"*Do I also get to fuck our buyers when we make successful sales; if I like the buyer?*"

"*Yes, absolutely. I'd expect you to. I want you to have the happiest libido any woman ever had. Honest. That's true love, Jen.*" Thor nodded approvingly.

"*For our larger boats, say the ones we sell for fifty million and up. How about it?*"

"*And do I get to design our company logos? I'm thinking it would be cool to show my open vagina with one wedding ring floating on a pool of cum. I'd call that our Adventure Line! That might make us a 'must see' at the boat shows, don't you think?"*

"Oh, absolutely; definitely. You have a perfectly shaped, glorious, love to put my face and tongue into it, vagina, Jen. Men will stop for a look!"

"And another, larger, five times life sized logo of my open vagina and four wedding rings arranged like a four-leaf clover, floating on a pool of creamy white semen; implying that your business partner is a profligate whore who loves doing orgies. I'll call that our Lucky Line yachts! And the implied promise is that the buyer also gets lucky with me. What do you think?"

"I love it, Jen. I love the way your mind works. Are you on board with me on this business concept? And are you sure you want to? I mean you already have so much money!"

"Choo, choo! Whooo, Whooo! Yes, absolutely I want to. A girl can never have too much money or too much sex. You should know that about women, Thor. Whooo, whooo! The doors are closing. The train is leaving the station; and I'm on board! Lots of money and lots of fucking! When do we start? But Thor, ask yourself: are you sure you want to share your wife with other men? I can be a very naughty, immoral slut. And once I'm hot for a man's penis, it's impossible to get me away from it. I tend to take what I want. Do you understand what I'm telling you? I might leave you, maybe for a while; possibly even for good, someday. Are you sure you want to be married to a profligate, greedy, incorrigible whore?"

"Yes, totally sure. I'll take my chances; anything to have the woman of my dreams, even if I eventually must lose you. But why did you say greedy, Jen?"

"Well," Jen lowered her head and blushed.

CHAPTER TWENTY-TWO

There is no danger to a man who knows what life and death is; there's not any law that exceeds his knowledge; neither is it lawful that he should stoop to any other law. He goes before them and commands them all; that to himself is law rational. (George Chapman: Byron's Conspiracy)

'When a man loves a woman,' if she's bad, he can't see it. She can do no wrong…. (Lyric lines from the song by Michael Bolton)

MURDER RATIONALIZED

"There is this nasty rumor going around that I fucked my poor, dear Daddy three times the night before he had his heart attack. And some people say I was intentionally exhausting him; straining his heart; fucking him so hard and so often like that; making sure he was overtaxing his aging heart and getting all those severe chest pains; and that I was never giving poor, poor Daddy any rest; so, I'd be certain that he'd have his massive coronary; and that I deliberately did all that fucking with my poor, dear Daddy, just so I could get all his power and money ten years sooner; so, I could be free to go find myself a younger, stronger penis. Can you believe that people would think that way about sweet, little ole, innocent looking, me?"

"I don't care what people think, Jen. A lot of people have dirty minds. It doesn't matter what caused his death. He's dead. And I'm here, now. You are as pure as the driven snow. I know you are. I love you. I love your kisses, your nipples and boobs, your tight ass, your

fuck-crazed vagina; and I especially love your mind. I just want to love you and film you and watch you lick and suck penises and fuck our qualified customers with all the passion you put into having sex. I adore what you do. I love your character; your calculating immorality; everything about you. I want to be a part of you. You know I do."

"And you don't care that I'm immoral, cruel, opportunistic, domineering and ......"

"Sensuous beyond words that could ever describe you."

"And that is what you want in a woman?"

"Not any woman, my love. You. Mother of our children. This woman." Thor stood up from the breakfast table. He went to her side, took her toast from her hand, and kissed her. Jen responded:

"Thor, let's stay here a few more days. And let's stop talking. I want to fuck."

Jen laid on the pillows, relaxed and smiling. They were lying on the cabin's California King bed. It was after coitus. Thor was kissing her face and tracing her lips with his finger. She loved his love making.

"I'd like to get used to this, Thor. I've fallen in love. I didn't think I ever would, but I have. Tell me something, would you? You seem to love it when I sit your face. You even go there without my asking or even hinting that I want that. Why is that?"

"It's hard to put it into words. I just feel so connected to you when we do that; especially when you gush. I feel like I am one with you on a spiritual level; inseparable, like we're fulfilling some divine purpose. And I love the tastes of you; can't get enough, I guess."

"Is it the porn thing? I mean, while you're doing that are you believing you're doing it with me, as Jen, the porn star who sat on that man's face in that film you obsessed over?"

"No; not anymore, honest. It was that at first; but now it's simply you; you and me, connecting like we do. My love for you really

exploded when I saw you in a later film. A porn partner was about to make love with you. You had already sucked his penis. He was all hard and hot to enter you. But you stopped him. You held his hand and noted that he wore a wedding ring. You looked at him and kissed him while you took his ring off and placed it inside your vagina. You already had a semen pool from the two men you did before him; and you held open and placed his gold ring on the white pool. Then you looked up at him again, as if to ask him if he really wanted to give up his marriage for you. He nodded yes. And then, only after hearing his yes, you fucked him. That scene was so beautiful, so immoral and so incorrigibly naughty; and it made me go crazy over you, Jen. I knew you were domineering and you took whatever you wanted; and I loved that about you."

"You do love me; even that possessive selfish side of me, don't you?"

"Yes; very much; deeply. I care about you. I often ask myself how a woman, who has such a wonderful mind with so much going for her, makes the decision to do porn?"

"Okay; my turn. I'll tell you why. It was my individual choice. Marty and I talked about it. I also talked with Mrs. O' Dell, my shrink, about why I did porn. I think the answer is a combination of things, Thor. I really do love sex. I love licking a man's penis and sucking it until it ejaculates; and I love fucking; absolutely love having a penis inside my vagina and feeling it pulsing its ejaculation into me. That was a big part of it. But a woman can get sex from many men without going to the troubles of creating porn films. Mrs. O'Dell said my sex drive is natural. It's partly because of my female DNA's mutation. That's a natural thing that's taking place in many women as evolution advances. With every succeeding generation, we women naturally crave more and more sex."

"So, what was Marty's take on it? Why did she do it?"

"For those same reasons I just told you. She and I had some deep discussions about it. We concluded that doing porn helped us with more than our sex drive thing. We also needed to find some venue to emancipate ourselves from our mothers' controls over us."

"A rebellion thing?"

"Something like that. Marty had a friend named Maria. Her mother was a hopeless drunk who had a love-hate relationship with her; nearly drove Maria to suicide. Maria ran away to Montana and became a camp cook. She did prostitution tricks on the side for extra money. She eventually married a fun guy; an oilman who hit several big discoveries. Maria is now riding high; lots of money; kids, she loves kids; having her perfect fun life.

"Then, there's Marty. Her mother abandoned her; dumped her off at a boarding school when she was five. Marty seethed with resentment; hated her mother. She got promiscuous to find the love that her mom wouldn't give her; naturally gravitated to porn for the money, and loved it. But Marty became destructive. She dove into the Modern Morality cult. Mrs. O'Dell encouraged her promiscuity and urged her to leverage her porn into world wide fame. Her notoriety comes from wrecking high-profile marriages. She got great tabloid press for doing that. So, Marty got the adulation she craved through porn; but love for her was all over the place. She got some pieces of love from many different men. She had Bob, her steady guy; Carl, her dream penis guy; Marshawn, her defiance of world norms guy; Josh, her dream lover; and lots of others that she met through her promiscuous adventures. But there was also this guy named David. She always mentioned him in guarded terms. I think she loved him; and feared him. I often wonder whether he had something to do with her disappearance. Their relationship seemed very dark and secretive."

"And what about you, Jen? Why did you do porn?"

"The sex and the mother thing again. My situation was not like Maria's or Marty's. I had a religious nut hatch for a mother. She

wanted to keep me in a straight jacket; totally control every aspect of my life. And no dating! If Mom had had her way, I'd have become a nun, living in a convent. I couldn't stand living with her anymore. Then Marty met Dad. Thank goodness! Mom was furious when Marty took Dad from her; but Marty didn't back down. She wanted Dad and she simply took him. That helped me see how powerful sex can be. That's when I began seeing the female vagina as an asset. Then Marty took me under her wing and helped me free myself from Mom's control, through porn. She set everything up for me; made all the right calls and introductions. I loved porn at first. I did twelve films, total."

"So, why did you stop doing porn? I mean, honestly, Jen, you are so beautiful and you have such a phenomenal body, I think you could become the world's number one porn star if you continued making films; put your soul into it. You've got that sweet girl- next-door face and you have a to-die-for body; and you know how to make love to the camera. You are so seductive!"

"Well, that's a nice thought and compliment, but porn isn't me anymore."

"Why not?"

"Well, you know I don't need the money. Porn is a great way for girls to make an income; but that isn't me. It never was me. It was my rebellion path to get free of my control freak mother; that's all it ever was. And I got bored with porn. I'm not like Marty. I don't crave the stage and the spotlights. I got to where it seemed like doing one film was much like doing previous films; just substituting different locations, men and combinations of men, and different positions. But there's only so much you can do. Fucking is still just fucking. After doing thirty different guys, I felt porn became boring. I loved the sex, don't get me wrong. Porn opened my eyes to how wonderful sex can be. And it removed all my inhibitions about having intimate relationships. I lost all fears of intimacy through doing porn. Porn even gave me the courage to begin my incestuous relationship with

Dad. I really connected with him. We had a wonderful love, Thor. And I miss him. We were partners in business; friends; and lovers. Dad mentored me. I was his junior partner. Our sex life was fabulous. It was all so wonderful. It's tragic that he died. Sometimes I blame myself for that. I often wonder whether I fucked Dad to death. But I can't dwell on it. It just happened. We stopped doing it while it happened. Well, we had to stop. A man can't perform while having a heart attack."

"So, what are your goals now, Jen, after porn?"

"I talked with Mrs. O'Dell about this very subject. She asked me so many questions. And then she came to it. We concluded that I love to create things. I loved creating companies with Dad. I love creating art because I can put my feelings into my paintings. I can come here to the dunes and watch the ocean; see the swells breaking and smell the salt air; feel the spray on my skin; observe the different lighting effects on the sky and the sea throughout the day. And I can sit with Bifster looking at it all; and the people who walk past; the ships and sailboats that go by. I feel like I'm part of eternity while I do that. And then I paint what I see, putting my feelings into it. I don't care whether my art ever sells. I just love creating it. I love messing with my papers and canvases; my mediums of oils, acrylics, water colors, inks, and paints; and my palette knives and brushes. I even screw around making homemade brushes with scraps of broom weed and tree branches. It doesn't matter what I do, according to Mrs. O'Dell. When I'm involved in the process of creating something, my mind goes into it. My tensions and worries evaporate. I'm very happy and content."

"Jen, with all your money, why don't you just invest in stocks or mutual funds and forget all the hassles of managing all your businesses?"

"I like the hands-on of business life, Thor. I like to know and control what I own. That's why I use the cash flows from my businesses to buy land with mineral rights, oil and gas leases, and mining claims.

Dad explained to me that, by the time a company with a neat new product makes it to the market with its initial private offering, it has already had three to five rounds of private financing and all the real money has already been made. The public comes in late, chasing the crumbs and depending upon market momentum and the Fed's game to lift market values higher."

"Fed's game?"

"Yes. The way Dad explained it was that the Fed keeps expanding the money supply to a debt bases economy. And the market operators use that credit expansion to artificially prop up market values by using margin credit to finance derivatives. There are quadrillions of derivatives, Thor; and their values depend upon counterparty solvency. Dad said the markets are like a grand casino and the public is doomed to lose big time when the markets deflate to real valuations. Dad said I was better off operating my own casinos, which I do. Every one of my clubs has a casino operation. I have complete control. I love being in control."

"Jen, you amaze me. I want to marry you. I mean it. I love you."

"Thor! You can't mean that. I'm not the kind of woman that a man should marry. You know I have no morals. You know what that means, don't you?"

"You must have some morals."

"No, I don't. None. None whatsoever. I'm the opposite of morals. Think, Thor; do you really want to marry a woman who loves to get slutty? Do you want to see your wife giving hummers to other men?"

"Hummers? I don't understand?"

"Thor, darling. You're such a baby. It's when I take a man's balls completely into my mouth and tickle them with my rapidly vibrating tongue, while I hum a tune that makes my throat and lips vibrate; and while I'm stroking his shaft with my fingers. I did it in a few of my films. Marty, my Mother Superior, taught me how to do it. We practiced on some penises together until I got good at it."

"How do you know?"

"Know what?"

"Know that you are good at it."

"Oh Thor; can't you figure it out?"

"No, Jen," Thor kissed her mouth. He was intrigued. *"Tell me. How can you tell?"*

"By his cum shot."

"What?"

"By how quickly he ejaculates and by the volume of cum he shoots. When I get a quick ejaculation and a huge volume of cum, I consider that a successful hummer."

"And you like doing this; giving hummers?"

"When I'm in the mood with a guy I like, I love giving him a hummer. See? I'm a total slut, Thor. I'm a no morals, cum dumpster, fuck bunny. That's who you'd be marrying. And when I dig some guy and want to give him a hummer and fuck him senseless, you won't be stopping me; understand?"

"Okay. If you're happy doing that; it's fine."

"Fine?"

"I mean wonderful; joyous. I'll be happy for you. I'll love you even more. I adore your sluttyness."

"Really? Thor. You really do love me for my sluttiness. Okay, I believe you. But I'm a woman who murdered her own father. I'm capable of anything. You can't seriously want a life with me."

"But I do, Jen. I love you. And I love the whore in you. I love the total you; the entire package. A life with you is exactly what I want."

"Are you sure, Thor? What do you and I have, besides sex? Why would you take our relationship and complicate it with marriage?"

"It doesn't have to be complicated. We'll let the lawyers work up a prenuptial agreement. If we decide to split up, you keep your money and I keep mine. I'm a fifty-million-dollar trust baby. I want you; not your money. No common accounts. Things will be just like they are now."

"Then why bother doing it?" Jen's face was puzzled.

CHAPTER TWENTY-THREE

First it was ordained for the procreation of children. (From the sol-emnization of matrimony in the Book of Common Prayer)

There was an old woman who lived in a shoe. She had so many children she didn't know what to do. (Gammer Gurtland's Garland, nursery rhymes)

CHILDREN

"Children, Jen. I want to have children with you. We'll create some beautiful babies. We'll create wonderful people out of those babies and we'll have fun doing it. Bifster will have playmates! They can crawl around after him. You and I could teach them so much!" Thor's face glowed with excitement at the prospect of creating life with her.

"You want children with me, Thor? Seriously? You really do want that?" Jen leaned back from him and took a deep breath. Her heart began pounding. She felt a deepness in her breast; an indescribable longing. She looked into his eyes: *'Is he serious?'*

Something triggered her flashback. His soul telescoped into hers. She saw all the things she knew were there when she saw him for the first time in her art class. She had intuited that she'd seen him before; but she couldn't remember where or when. But now everything became clear. What had happened before happened again. Her vision recalled everything. There he was!

They were together again, back in ancient Egypt. She was Baaleezebelle and he was Moses! They had made love and consummated their agreement to marry. Then, after the fertility rites ended, Pharoah Akhenaten married them under the authority vested in him by his one god, Atim. The feast followed. Moses led the prized Apis bull up the sacrificial ramp to the alabaster altar. Taking the bull by its horns, his muscles and abs glistened in the sunlight. He twisted the bull's head until it collapsed on the altar. How strong Moses was! Six priests fell upon the bull, quickly slitting its throat and disemboweling it. Their obsidian blades quickly separated its hide from its flesh; then expertly carved the meat from its bones. One priest crawled into the carcass and separated the tenderloin strips from the animal's spine. Slaves brought vessels of water from the Nile to wash the altar clean of blood, guts, excrement, and bile.

After the butchery, the choicest cuts of meat were passed to Pharoah's royal family and his harem whores. The priests then took their share. Lesser cuts, entrails, and scraps were given to the assembled multitude. Then, more animals: pigs, sheep, and fowl were sacrificed. Moses supervised the distribution of meats; baskets of dried, salted fish; grains of barley, sorghum, wheat, chickpeas, and fava beans.

Jen had seen it all. She recognized Thor as Moses in their previous lives. She knew how strong he was. She saw how he took charge of matters. He was a proven leader of multitudes! He would succeed in everything he set out to do. As Moses, he had proven he could change humanity's religious orientation from many gods to one. As Thor, she would discover, he would be wildly successful in building the world's most prized boats. His boats would become iconic standards. They would win races. They would carry people safely across the world's oceans. And Thor would have the same passion he had as Moses while he created his boating empire.

Moses had not wanted children. Joshua was her way of getting the child she wanted then. But today's Thor was different from yesterday's Moses in one compelling aspect. Thor wanted children! And, she intuited, he would be a wonderful father to them!

Suddenly she knew she needed what Thor was offering her; needed it more than anything else in the world! Needed it more than all her money; more than her clubs; more than all the lovers she knew she could have. Children! Family! Yes, what Thor offered her was something more than all her thieving, whoring, scheming, and murdering could ever bring to her. Happiness! Family! Family! Family! Thor had not spoken the word 'Family;' yet it resonated and reverberated through her mind. Yes! She wanted Family! And she's known it all along, somehow, somewhere deeply inside her, she knew now. She knew it all along. It might not be perfect, like her mother's family was not perfect; but then, whose family is ever perfect? But that didn't matter. What mattered was that it, perfect or imperfect, would be hers. Her family! A family she would create, with Thor!

She trembled slightly. This was everything. Life was all about this; begetting of more life! Nothing mattered more than this. And this beautiful man, this man who deeply loved her, this man who was pouring out his guts to her, wanted to create a family with her! Her! Jen, the madam; the porn star whore! Wow! Her head was spinning. Her whole purpose for living suddenly became clear! Thor had awakened her deep maternal instinct. He had dug deeply down into her, below all the stuff that really wasn't important; below her pornography and her clubs and her murders. And there, below it all, he finally found her; the real her. Suddenly her entire perspective about life telescoped into a new kind of focus.

Thor's purpose for seeking marriage to her was noble. Yes! Unquestionably noble! He wants a family with her! Here was a highly eligible man proposing to her; not for her money; and not

even for the torrid sex they would surely have; but for the best reason of all possible reasons; a shared life and a shared legacy. With
her! Not with some other woman! With her! She now looked upon
a man whom she suddenly held in the highest possible esteem;
where before she only saw a man with whom she could have liaisons. This man wanted to be the father of her children!

"Thor, you aren't just saying that, are you? Jen's voice trembled
with cautious uncertainty. Tears of happiness welled up in her
eyes. *"Kids are a huge responsibility. You must know that kids are
a really big deal, Thor. They grow and they grow on you, too. They
become part of you. And they are work, Thor. I mean there's mid-
night feedings, the diapers, the chaos of children getting their cuts
and bumps and boo boos; their sibling temper tantrums; and taking
them to their activities and their lessons; and getting their meals
ready; and on and on. Do you really want all that? I mean do you
really want to take on a challenge like that?"*

*"With you, Jen. Yes, I do. That's exactly what I want. That's
everything I want. You, the ways you think, our kids, and all the
kissing and the fucking and exploring everything about your glorious pussy for the rest of my life that comes along with it. I want all of
that; more than anything I ever wanted before. Marriage with you
would mean everything to me. We'd have a family!*

*"And don't forget. We can afford it. We can hire a nanny and a
night nurse and a clean up crew. We can do as much of the messy
stuff or as little of that as we want. We'll create life, Jen. And we'll
show our children the world. Our kids will be with us. They'll be part
of us. We have so much to give them. We'll teach them all sorts of
things. We'll help them grow. It will be beautiful! And we'll have fun!
We'll make a fun life together with our kids. We can put our love and
feelings into them."*

*"But what about you, Thor? What do you want to do with your
life? You'll need to do more than obsess over my cunt and play with*

our babies." Her puzzled face with tears streaming down her face returned to Thor's eyes; but this time it wore a hopeful smile.

"Boats, Jen."

Thor's answer was spontaneous and direct. His eyes lit up when he thought of boats. His man face was that of an overgrown boy's face who had never stopped being a boy.

"They are in my Viking blood. I want to design and build boats. I want to create sailboats that people love to have and love to sail. And I want to build boats that go the fastest and win the most races. I want the challenge of it. I've done sketches of my ideas. I've read a lot about sailing. I've studied fluid dynamics, aerodynamics, and materials and methods of shaping things. I want to put it all together into building the world's most desired boats. My boats will be of the highest quality in the world. Premium boats. The world's fastest boats. Quality boats. The best boats money can buy. I'll start small, in Newport. I'll get a half-acre of ground near the water and put a building on it so I can work year-round, whatever the weather. I'll be creating, Jen. I'm like you that way. I love to create."

Jen saw the fire in Thor's eyes when he was speaking of family and creating boats. She saw the same desire to build something that she had so often seen in her father.

"You are so much like Daddy, Thor. People say that girls marry their daddies. Tell me something: if we married, could I join you in the boat building business? I bring a lot to the table, Thor. I know how to organize and schedule things. I have experience in building businesses. I built the Decado clubs. I've helped Dad put many deals together. I understand regulations and regulators. You'll need skill sets that I already have. I also have a deep pocket. I'll put up five billion dollars into building boats with you for a half interest. Our salaries will be capped at one percent of sales; the business will carry our expenses and our automobiles, agreed?"

"Yes, Jen, agreed. I'll love having you building our business together with me. We'll create together. We'll love it. A thousand yesses!"

"Thor, before you agree to partnering with me, you need to understand that I also love to create. I'm an independent woman and I have a vision for the future that I intend to fulfill."

"Sure, Jen. What's your vision?"

"I want to make prostitution and pornography commonplace family values. I want to push religion off center stage and at least make religion share that stage with prostitution and pornography. I want to change peoples' perspectives about sexual relations. I want the world to see the sex profession as something beautiful and humanistic. I want women who work in the sex trade to feel free and open about it; to not have any stigma attached to what they do; and I want them to feel proud to serve in a necessary and vibrant industry."

"So, how will you bring this about?"

"By making pornography mainstream, Thor. As I see it, people will pay to watch sporting events. I want people to visualize porn stars the same way they visualize their favorite football, basketball, and baseball players, and their favorite golfers and Olympic athletes. I want to create a venue for porn stars to excel. I visualize a world-wide contest, conducted every year or half year, or quarter. There will be open entry for any woman who wishes to pay her entry fee to participate. Each woman will get a half hour to perform whatever sex acts she wishes. I'll supply thousands of willing, penis qualified, disease-free males to accommodate whatever the women wish to do on stage. I'll have layered competition, including semi-finalists and finalists. There will be judges, participants, sponsors, magnificent trophies of gold, silver, and bronze; honorable mention awards for participating; huge monetary prizes. I'm thinking mind

boggling trophies. I'm thinking we'll do something more stunning than Michelangelo's David. The boys have their statue of David. We'll have our statue of Bathsheba. It will be huge! A massive bronze statue of a glorious naked woman holding out her arm with a butterfly on her finger."

"I like your thinking."

CHAPTER TWENTY-FOUR

His soul shall taste the sadness of her might, and be among her cloudy trophies hung. (John Keats: Ode on Melancholy)

But for the general award of love, the little sweet doth kill much bitterness. (John Keats: Isabella)

Oscars, Golden Globes, Emmys. But trophies for best porn stars? Absolutely! (Rosemary Ness Bitner, author)

TROPHIES

"Yes! And we'll have real trophies. They'll be one hundred ounces each and made of real gold for the first-place winners; real silver and real bronze for the second and third place winners. We'll call the trophies Martys, in honor of our dear friend and pioneer in the wonderful world of pornography. We'll have categories by age groups; say, ten age groupings. We'll have categories by venue, like erotic romance, threesomes, orgies, cunnilingus, fellatio, masturbation; contortionist; best improvisations to different musical themes, like jazz, hip hop, rock, country, classical, patriotic, macabre, big band swing, acapella, etc."

"Ten age groupings, seven or more venues, maybe ten or so musical scores, Jen, you're talking about two hundred million, plus, in trophy costs alone!"

"Yeah, so what? I've got billions. Anyway, it's not about money. It's about doing what's right. We need to encourage more women to feel open and free about their sexuality. We need to help them peel

away their inhibitions. They need to have the incentive to leave their religious and the institutional constraints that they live under; throw off their oppressors, and declare their desires to have unlimited, uninhibited freedom. It's what Marty would have wanted, Thor!"

"Yes, she would have loved something like this."

"I'm excited! It will be more popular than golf tournaments. There will be age divisions of competition from fourteen- and fifteen-year-olds to women over the age of sixty. And......"

"Wait, Jen. There are laws about underaged girls doing prostitution."

"I understand. And I've already studied those laws. We can have our fourteen- and fifteen-year-old aspiring porn stars paired with boys who are sixteen and fifteen and fourteen. And those competitions can be held in Jurisdictions that have Romeo and Juliet laws, where the age of consent is fourteen as long as the boy is sixteen or younger. Underaged girls will be allowed to compete for free. I'll have my lawyers check out every detail further to be sure everything I do is legal. But as I was saying, I'll have media at these competitions. I'll have an adjoining convention hall where the porn stars can rent booths and the public can pay admission fees, so they can freely mingle with their favorite porn stars; take their business cards, sign up for their publicity releases, join their premium services, arrange for dates, and escort services with them."

"And you think this will be widely accepted?"

"Absolutely! Can't you see what's happening? The entire world is in the process of changing its morality. People are yearning to throw off their religious and institutional yokes. They are ready to rebuild society from the ground up. And prostitution and pornography will be essential cornerstones to the world's new morality codes. Can't you feel it, Thor? The entire world is going through a catharsis. People are throwing off their old gods and adopting new gods. Porn stars are the world's new gods. Marty is God for millions of people.

Heck, many people even consider me to be their God, even though I don't actively perform anymore. When I did perform, I knew I felt something, Thor. It came through in the fan mail and the tabloid interviews and the paparazzi chases. These people were desperately seeking me as, not just some woman to fuck; but as a woman to worship and adore and cherish. It was maddening.

"You're a man. You should understand male psychology. Many men adore these porn stars. They fantasize that their favorite stars are happy; that they are joyfully fucking someone, somewhere; that their every wish and whim is being indulged; and that they are pampered and properly pleasured at all times. They have vicarious love affairs with these women. And many women have vicarious dreams about these women, also. Of course, our porn tournaments will be widely accepted. It may start as a novelty, but it will grow over time and become huge; even more popular than the football Super Bowl.

"And, unlike annual sports tournaments, our tournaments will be held every three months! We'll advertise and promote the events. We'll encourage women to participate; help them lose their inhibitions; help them gain their self-awareness and confidence. Thor, at least seventy five percent of men and forty percent of women watch porn. We're going to help these people become unashamed to admit that they love porn. We're going to help them declare that they love porn. We will prevail, Thor! Sex attracts! Sex fascinates! And sex sells! Yes, our project will be a huge success. I'm highly confident. We will change the world!"

"And do you think you'll attract a sponsorship following?"

"I'm certain of it. Of course, we will. Business is about sales, not morality. I'm looking at my second sponsorship pledge."

"Me?"

"Yes. The Infernoss Decado Clubs will be the host sponsor and event organizer. Many of my club girls will participate. The clubs will pay their entrance fees. It's great publicity for the girls and the

clubs. It's just good business, Thor. Our boat business will be the second sponsor and keynote, signature sponsor. At the porn venues we'll have your boats on display. Porn stars will be seen holding and kissing their male partners on your forecastles and sterns. Inside your cabins, in your master staterooms, a porn star will be performing with two male partners. She'll be lying comfortably on the bed, maiden position, and fornicating; while simultaneously performing fellatio on her second partner. The boat, with its porn stars performing their erotic stimulations, will be shown on the huge stadium screens for thirty and sixty second segments during the grand pornography final competitions.

"And the world's top porn star will be given a boat as part of her prize package for being the most glorious intimate artist in the world! Think of the publicity for Thor's boats! You will have orders for hundreds of boats, Thor. I know you will. Sex sells, Thor. Trust Jen on this."

"Will this idea make money, Jen?"

"Yes, Thor. Lots! Daddy taught me to think big. Marty taught me to think inclusively. This worldwide porn competition will make us billions, annually. We'll give away cars and travel packages to the porn star winners. The world will go ga-ga over this new acceptance of porn. Businesses will see the galactic, sea change shift in morality from religious domination to hedonistic domination; and businesses will want in on the action. Hundreds of businesses will clamor to be accepted as paying sponsors. They all know that sex sells. Everyone will want in.

"Just watch, Thor. As the tournaments grow in popularity, our sponsorship fees will increase. We'll have lots of fun with this. Remember, many top executives and top marketing people will love having the opportunity to mingle freely and openly with the world's most glorious porn stars. What's better than having a sex filled week coupled with a tax-deductible sponsorship fee? Trust me, Thor. We'll have hundreds

of top corporations pounding at our door. And many of them will need a corporate yacht! You are going to be so glad you married me."

"Okay. I love the idea. I'll do it. I'll sponsor and I'll contribute one boat, ten boats, whatever you want, Jen. I'm in. I'll do whatever you ask, Jen. Count me in."

"Good, Thor. Well, then, it's almost settled. There's only one more thing I need to know before I'll agree to marry you, Thor."

"What? You know I love you, woman. You know I'm crazy about you. What? Just tell me."

"Let's go out to the dunes and see."

And Jen and Thor and Bifster went out of the cabin to the dunes. At a secluded spot where they could look over the ocean and survey the beach for two miles in both directions, Jen pitched her blanket on the ground. She asked Thor to strip naked. She did the same. It was mid-morning. The air was fresh and balmy warm with only a hint of a breeze. Jen directed Thor to sit. Then, she excited him to erection and straddled him, facing him. She placed her nipple against his lips.

"This is something else I must know before I marry you, Thor. I must know whether you arouse my feelings sufficiently, while we make love in this position, for me to experience orgasm."

Jen had her quirks and demands. This was, perhaps, her most intensely private one. But with Marty's coaching, she had come to orgasm this way with Roger and with Dom, her father. In all her experiences of making love while doing porn, this position with a penis pressing firmly against her clitoris while receiving mouth stimulation through her nipple, uniquely sent Jen's emotions into erotic nirvana. She loved making love this way.

And Thor did what a good and dutiful lover should do with his woman love. Jen felt the beginnings of an explosive orgasm. She rejoiced by shouting:

"*Yes, Thor! Yes, yes. Oh, yes, my love. Lift your hips up just a little. Yes! That's it, Thor. You've got it. You're pressing against my clit perfectly. Now slide up and down over it. Yes! Oh my God, yes! That feels so good. I needed this. Oh, I love you so much, Thor.*"

Jen's thoughts about her life and future telescoped into her love making:

'*So many men have been vulnerable to me. All the letters I received when I did porn; all the offers of romance and marriage. But I never allowed any of those, even the ones I had made love with, to capture their dream girl. And now I am about to allow Thor to capture his dream. Yes, girl, everything feels right. It does. He is the one. I first believed that Thor pursued me because he needed a mother substitute. Maybe our romance dance started out that way; but now his dream of creating family and beautiful, fast sailboats no longer sound like the ravings of a child dreamer. It's a big dream, a real man's dream; a dream that wants me as a full partner.*

'*And he is wholly unlike those perverts who wrote me asking whether they could pay me to lick my vagina or massage oils and creams onto my breasts and vagina; or those who sought a personal demonstration showing them how I controlled male ejaculation pulses with finger squeezes, strokes, and tongue licks; or that one creep who asked me pointedly whether the first spurt of cum I lapped from Roger's penis tasted as good or better than or less good than his second, third, fourth or fifth serving of white, creamy cum, which I licked up and burbled and savored and swallowed?*

'*Oh, I was tempted to take that man's bait; tempted to tell him that the final offering of cum yum is decidedly tastier than the first. Getting kinky with that fan sounded like it might be fun. But I didn't respond to him, lest I be drawn into an endless spiral of perversions with him, culminating in me giving him personal demonstrations. I sometimes had pangs of regrets that I avoided that one.*

'*So, what does that say about me? Oh, I guess I know. I love to experiment with my sexuality in all sorts of ways. Whatever; he may have been interesting to know. He was a voyeur with intellectual curiosity; a rarity. But I didn't take up with him. I've moved on. I can't know the inner workings of every man's mind; understand all those sexual vectors. Yet I never categorically reject my thoughts of entertaining their perversions. If that man ever comes to one of our boat shows or our porn tournaments, and if I like him, I think I will love fucking him, even though I'll be married to Thor; even though I'll probably have children. Funny, isn't it, how the libido often governs choices? And what does that say about me?*

'Then there is Thor. Thor is unlike those low lives who only want sex from me; not that I'd never give in to any of them. But Thor offers me relationship; more than mere mindless perversions of sex. He wants me, Jen; every dimension of me; even friendship. He is a serious man who craves an authentic, intimate life with me. He's not a boy anymore. His dreams are the foundation planks of a man's life, lived with purpose. And I shall be the keel that steadies his wonderful world. I can be the steady hand in our family, even if I do allow myself some picadilloes. I can't help myself from going off track sometimes. No man, not even Thor, will ever take the whore out of me.

'But that's what's so wonderful about Thor. He loves the whore in me and he wants me to be even more of a whore than I already am. Girl, you have hit the jackpot! I have changed Thor; and he has changed me! We will both be happier and better souls for it.

'I love hearing him tell me how wonderful I am; how his love for me intensifies when I sit his face and orgasm. Then, I know I am woman; and overflowing with love. I know this is so right and wonderful. I can see the two of us together with our family; me being a thousand times better and happier me than the former me in my aloneness. Clouds, stars, the ocean swells are all more vivid and meaningful now. I will be an essential part of all of it! And Thor promises me that he will never try to limit me in any way. Yes, finally, I have captured the world to which I belong!

'There is so much to do! No time to waste. We must fuck; even more often now! And with our important purpose; the purpose of creating. How wonderful! So much more than mere pleasing; so pleasurable; making love with our creation purpose! All those things that constantly swirled through my mind before: my sketches and paintings, my companies, and my board meetings; the operations of every entity and the myriad personalities of every board member; and my endlessly conflicting schedules all fade into irrelevant background noise now.

'I must focus on fucking now; my main purpose as a woman. Yes, I must be vigilant for my opportunities to be fucking during my morning waking moments, and in my afternoons and evenings. And I must vacuum up every drop of Thor's precious semen into my fallopian tubes and ovaries, hoping that one of his tiny warriors succeeds in impregnating me. Yes, I must fuck Thor whenever he comes home and before he goes out; and wherever we travel, we must fuck there also. There is not a moment to lose! We must fuck! We must create! Oh, how much I want to do this! Oh, I am so happy! I am going forward with life now. I am creating. I have grown so much! I am a complete woman!

'And I will do so many delightful things with Thor's marvelous penis! I will torture it with my wicked sexiness and make it do unimaginable lust filled things with me. I will tease it mercilessly, until it begs me for refuge from my tongue and my mouth; until it cries out for the sanctity of my welcoming vagina. I will become Thor's goddess and the naughtiest whore who has ever pleasured him. I will show him things and positions he never imagined a woman could do. He will crawl to me on his hands and knees as my devoted sex slave, begging me to sit my insatiable vagina where his tongue can savor me. Yes, he will be my sex slave; and I will be his. I, Goddess Jen, will go to where Thor rests his head; and I will kneel *over him and rest my vagina over his lips and feed his addiction to me; and make it even stronger. Oh! I do so much, love this man!'*

Jen's thoughts returned to their lovemaking. She intended to coach up Thor's techniques; teach him the delicious, explicit nuances that she'd learned from her years with Marty; help him achieve ever higher pinnacles of female pleasuring through his newly learned, uninhibited eroticism:

CHAPTER TWENTY-FIVE

Orgasms are mother nature's Ambien---without side effects. (Rashida Jones)

Some day every woman will have orgasms, like every family will have a colored TV. (Erica Jong: How To Save Your Own Life)

PROCREATING

"Now, bite softly on my nipple, Thor. Yes! Yes! That's it! You are doing it perfectly. You're sending glorious chills down my spine, Thor. I feel them reaching all the way down into my vagina now. That's it. Nibble; bite my bud softly; suck it; tongue tickle my whole areola. Oh, yes! You are a fabulous lover, Thor. Now use your fingers. Reach them into my vagina and rub them rapidly against the tip of my clit. YES!" Jen screamed squeals of joy. *'Yes, Thor, that's perfect. You are stimulating me so wonderfully! I love how you are working your fingers and your penis. So heavenly! Oh, let me lean down and kiss you. I love you so much. You have such a wonderful penis.*

"Wait! It's happening, Thor. Oh my God! Oh my God! I'm coming. Oh, goodness! I'm squirting! I've never done that before. What a wonderful release! What a beautiful orgasm you just gave me. Oh, I do love making love with you. We are going to fuck so often, Thor! We will make fantastic love. I know we will. You'll see. I've never had feelings like this before. We must do this often, my love.

"We will marry. I shall throw my birth control pills away; and we will create babies. We will create a family and build a business

together. I want everything, Thor. I want everything with you, more than I've ever wanted anything. I will be a wonderful wife to you. I will be your total woman. You are making that possible. You are opening a whole new world to me. And I love you for it. Promise me you will fuck me often with your fabulous penis; promise me you will drive me crazy with your fingers, this same way we are doing it now; just like today. Promise me!"

"I promise you, Jen. Always. Just tell me when. I'll be there for you."

"And in the many new ways and techniques I will show you. Promise me!"

"Yes. I promise. I love you, Jen. I'm so happy that this position does it all for you!"

"Well, Thor; almost all, but not all."

"There's more?"

"Of course, my love, there's always more. All you need to have more is your imagination."

"Tell me your more, Jen."

"Sure, gladly. More is the same position we just did, but with add-ons."

"Add-ons?"

"Yes, while you are doing me like you were just doing me, we'll have four additional partners for me; say, Roger, Ross, Alex, and Nelson. While I sit on your lap with your penis in my vagina and your mouth on my nipple, Nelson massages my neck and shoulders; kisses my neck and temples. I'll suck Roger's penis while fondling Ross and Alex. After you come, our partners will take turns ejaculating inside me. Anticipation of what I'll be doing will make you incredibly rock hard, Thor. Afterwards, vivid images of your cum slut wife will dance through your mind while we make love. My porn films made you crazy for me. I want that prurient, limbic lust sensation imprinted vividly in your mind, from real, sex in the flesh, *experiences, while you ravage me, Thor. I want to be the sex goddess in your mind; every time we make love."*

"And you'd like to do this partnering from time to time?"

"Absolutely! It's better sex! It gives me my nirvana feeling; that sensation that I am a pleasured goddess, pleasured; adored in an Elysium field. I love being a liberated modern woman. I love living by the morality of Mrs. O'Dell's Modern Morality Standard. I want that freedom from morality. I need to be your completely free, uninhibited wife-whore. You see, Thor, everyone must have a goal in life. A businessman, like my father, Dominick, seeks to build an empire. A politician seeks to become President or Prime Minister. A General seeks to win battles and defeat his enemies. But I seek to pursue that which is natural to me, peeled away from all religious institutions; separated from all the political virtue signaling; devoid of empathy for the plights of others' lives.

"And then you have me, reduced to my simplest, completely honest form. I love pleasure. I love the feelings I get when I am being pleasured. I love sex. I love sexual intercourse with men and women; and I love feeling completely free to enjoy the pleasurable feelings that having many different partners gives me. That is why I started the Infernoss Decado clubs. I could never be a hypocrite who professes to believe in this or that; who states allegiance to some rigid ideology; all the while living a different secret life or chafing in frustration at the life I profess to embrace. No; honesty is best.

"And what do humans exist for, if it is not to pleasure themselves? Do they exist for virtue? Is it virtuous to attend church so that I can be seen by others as believing what they believe, when in my honest sense of logic and truth, I cannot believe in the Church's teachings? So, why conflict myself? Why live in untruth's fantasy? What is virtue, anyway? I cannot define it or understand what it is. Can anyone? I don't think anyone can define it."

"Jen, did your father ever try to dissuade you from doing porn, or creating the Infernoss Decado clubs? Did he ever try to influence you to live a more traditional lifestyle?"

"While he was married to Mother, Dad was very traditional. We did church on Sundays. I was doing all the traditional activities that a young, righteous girl was expected to do. But after Dad met Marty, after he divorced Mom, he changed. He became a whole new man."

"And you liked him better as this new man?"

"Liked him? Thor, I loved him! With Marty's help he unchained me from my miseries and freed me."

"And you became his lover, right?"

"Yes."

"And, tell me honestly, did you make love with him so much that he had his heart attack?"

"You mean, did I fuck dear Daddy to death?"

"Well, did you?"

"I don't know, Thor. Don't try to lay guilt on me. Dad was very active; not just with me, but also with some of the Infernoss Decado girls. The weekend before he died, he had Cindy at the mansion. She was fourteen, from my club in Spain."

"He was doing underaged girls?"

"Yes, sure. Why not? Celt procured them and got all the legal consents and the paperwork. If there was ever a problem, Dad would have plausible deniability and from there we could just put out some bribes and it would all go away. That never even came up, Thor. You see, these girls all love to fuck and they love the lifestyle; and they and their parents love the money."

"Okay. So, you think this Cindy taxed his heart the weekend before the heart attack?"

"Oh, she definitely taxed his heart. Cindy did Dad at least six times that weekend before he died."

"*So, it wasn't anything you did?*"

"*Honestly, Thor, what Dad and I did was normal for us. We were lovers. I freely admit that. I loved Dad. We made love the night before he died. It was beautiful. He was like a baby in my arms. He needed my love and I gave my love freely.*"

"*So, this was pretty regular?*"

"*Thor! You know me! You know how much I love sex. Dad and I often did it three times a day. Where is this going?*"

"*I just want to understand how incest became so normal, that's all.*"

"*Well, okay. Dad was a very handsome and powerful man. He had a tremendous libido. He took copious quantities of Ginseng. Lycopene, vitamin E, B vitamins, especially B12, Creatin, Spirulina, Saw Palmetto, and all kinds of male fuel. And when he wanted to have a really long extended love making session, he also took the blue pill. Dad loved to fuck. He just did. He could fuck for hours. And he did. And that night before he died, we did it for a very long time; and he came inside me, twice.*

"*Marty showed him how beautiful sex could be. Marty convinced him to break with his past and go with her. Marty got him to love the explicit erotica of porn and to appreciate how much a woman loves sex. And then, Marty introduced me to my own sexual freedom and porn. Incest was a big theme with Marty. She believed in it. She believed it released a young girl from inhibition. She believed it was beautiful. She got Dad and me into it. And, she was kind of gifted and prescient that way. I think she understood that, once she got us started with it, that we would love it. And we did. Dad became one of the most wonderful lovers I've ever had, Thor. No amount of judging or criticism of what we did will ever take away from me the fact that I loved Dad very much; not just as a Father, but also as a lover.*"

"*He was romantic?*"

"Oh my God, yes. Yes, Thor, he was. I can't begin to recount all the times he would lie next to me in my bed and begin teasing my nipples and kissing my neck; or the many times he would come up behind me and place his arms around me and nuzzle my neck and fondle my breasts. He excelled at foreplay. He loved performing cunnilingus. He knew how to please me, as a woman; never hurry me; always ensuring that I had complete pleasure. And he brought me little gifts, not that I needed anything. I already had everything. I've always had everything. But he'd get me little baubles just to let me know he was thinking of me and that he loved me as a lover. We totally forgot that we were Father and Daughter, Thor. We were lovers; lovers in love; totally, happily in love."

"I see. Well, do you miss him?"

"Truthfully, I miss him as my Father. I miss his wisdom about markets and companies and mergers and acquisitions; and how to tear companies apart and unlock their values and put them together with other companies. I miss his genius. But I do not miss him as a lover. I now see our love was a celebration of our mutual freedom from Mother and her religious clap trap; freedom from all the social pressures and hypocrisy that seemed to swirl around Mother. And I can now compartmentalize all my childhood years with Mother, because of Dad and our incestuous love, and Marty's help with that. And I now look at my life in a forward looking way with you, Thor. You are my new love; and I do love you. I love you dearly. Honestly Thor, it is a deep and abiding love; the kind of love that's true. And I look forward to many years of uninhibited love making and pleasures in a new life that I intend to build around our love."

"And you want pleasure seeking to be a central part of that, Don't you? I mean you want us to involve many partners, like Roger, Ross, Alex, and Nelson; and you want the Infernoss Decado girls in our mix, too. Am I understanding the kind of life you want, Jen?"

"Yes, I think so. Honestly, Thor, I believe there is no greater call-ing in one's life than the attainment of pleasure. We live to find ever greater pleasure in our lives, in all its forms. Thus, I freely admit that I am a nympho hedonist; and I am proud of my admission because it is the truth. Having many experiences and many partners opens up the world for me, Thor. I must feel free to take pleasures as I please and manage my pleasure takings as I wish to satisfy myself; but careful to not allow my pleasure quest to control me into a state of insensibility.

"But, yes, Thor, I am, in my heart of hearts, a profligate nympho whore. I am a sexaholic, given to pleasuring in joyous debaucheries. And I need you to love me for being the way I am. I need to have it all, Thor; all that life offers. I love the euphoria of that. I'll love it even more if you'll kiss my mouth and nipples; and massage my clitoris, while I'm doing our four partners; while my vagina is receiv-ing their ejaculations and while their semen is spurting into me and flowing out of me? Will you help me know the greatest pleasures I can possibly know? Will you stimulate me; heighten my sensations of pleasures? Will you love me even more, by giving me your enthusias-tic stimulations, while I'm joyfully fornicating like that?"

"Of course, I will. I will love to assist you in experiencing height-ened pleasures. You know I will."

"But Thor, my love, I need to know that your eyes are wide open when I tell you that I am an incorrigible hedonist. Can you live with and love a woman who is a determined sybarite, a connoisseur of BDSM and sadism without regard for the consequences to others, so long as my own pleasures are heightened? When my first partner ejaculates his hot semen into my vagina, he is spent; but do you realize that my sexual appetites are then just becoming stimulated and that I might be able to continue fornicating with another five partners and still not feel satisfied? Do you understand that when

I tell you I wish to make love with a group of partners, that I'm talking about having my vagina ravaged as if five freight trains had repeatedly slammed into it? Do you understand that I intend to fuck those men until my cervix aches and my vagina becomes sore from repeated ravaging? Do you understand that I intend to fuck until I am sweated and exhausted; and that I will only stop fucking because I physically can no longer participate? Do you understand that my nymphomaniac urges become so strong, that I never want to stop; that I become angry that my physical body can no longer continue fucking? I mean, Thor, do you have any idea how insatiable my urges are?

CHAPTER TWENTY-SIX

He speaks the kindest words, and looks such things. Vows with so much passion, swears with so much grace.... (Nathaniel Lee: The Rival Queen)

VOWS

"Can you appreciate that my urge is like a Monarch female's urge to mate; that it is so strong that she will fly thousands of miles, cross oceans, and brave dangers to her life because she must fuck her mate? And can you appreciate that, unlike the female Monarch, who only mates once and dies, my urges are such that I feel I must fuck practically constantly, and non-stop, at every opportunity I can seize? I mean, Thor, after I have fucked like that; after I have collapsed from exhaustion, could you still love me?"

"Yes, Jen. I do understand your condition. I've talked with Marty about it. She also had the affliction; and I know that it is a real addiction. She explained it to me. She said a nympho is a seed with an outer shell that needs to make love; but that seed also has an inner kernel which desperately needs to be loved and accepted as a whole and beautiful person. Marty found that love in Bob, her constant lover. And I offer myself to you, Jen, as your constant lover and true love, for I love you as you are; all of you. And I also know that you are a good-hearted soul and that you are capable of being in love unlike any other love I could possibly ever know. And I love you for that and for who you are.

"When you have fucked yourself to near death, you may count on me. I will carry you to your bed and cover you with a blanket and hold you close to me, because I will understand that is what you needed to do; and I am perfectly fine with it. I am fine with your nympho condition. I understand it. I accept it. And I'll love you, knowing full well what it compels you to do. I will hold you close to me and kiss you tenderly until you fall asleep. I swear it."

"And, should I stir with some life still remaining in me, would you also fondle me and kiss me and kiss my nipples and would you be gracious enough to make love with me, until I fall into a deep sleep?"

"Yes, my love. Of course, I would. You know I would. You know I cannot resist you. You know your peccadillos only make me lust after you more. My limbic mind controls my every thought. I become smitten and wild with desire for you. I long to place my tongue against your clitoris; to pleasure you in every imaginable way. An intensity of amore overwhelms me. I must hold you and kiss you and cherish you. I can visualize your partners' penises inside your vagina. I see them thrusting into you; ejaculating their huge gobs of creamy white semen over your clitoris and deeply inside you and through your cervical opening; and I am smitten by what I visualize."

"You honestly can imagine what is happening inside my vagina? You can visualize the penises thrusting and ejaculating inside me?"

"Yes. I do. I can see it all. It's as real as if I were inside you, kissing your clitoris and helping you come to orgasm."

"Which of my films is your favorite?"

"The one where you fuck the black man with the monster sized penis. It fascinated me. I saw how much you loved it. I tried to imagine how you felt with such a huge penis inside you. I saw the joy in your face. You weren't faking happiness for the screen. You really loved fucking that huge penis, didn't you?"

"I did. Fucking that man's huge penis made me feel like a total woman. I felt totally uninhibited; free from all the racial claptrap; just feeling the rapture; pussy elated, living her own nirvana; just savoring the fantastic thrusting and probing; spurring it on; Kegel squeezing down on it; teasing it; squirming on it; my orgasms popping, then flowing; sending me into convulsive pleasure seizures; trying hopelessly to hold onto my senses, but losing my mind and composure; unable to control my pleasure moans and my screams of 'Yessss' and 'Fuck'; and never, ever wanting to stop our glorious fucking; hoping we could go all night like this; hoping my partner could keep his erection hard as steel; hoping that splendid penis would never wilt inside me; wanting to fuck and fuck and fuck, until the end of eternity; sweating until my make-up ran and my hair went straight; thinking: the hell with the cameras, the hell with how I looked like an exhausted, fuck crazed barnyard pig. I didn't care. I was fucking my brains out and loving every mind-blowing moment of it."

"I could see that. I adored you for what you were doing and for the pleasure you were feeling. That film made me fall in love with you, and your fabulous vagina. It was like your vagina had taken on a life of its own, independent of your life. I thought I was seeing your vagina taking control of you; demanding never ending copulation; like it was royalty and it demanded that its needs be satisfied. It fascinated me. I 've watched that film at least ten times."

"Ten times? Really?"

"Yes, at least ten times."

"And my cunt fascinated you?"

"Yes. I was mesmerized."

"How? Tell me. What did you see?"

"Everything. All of it."

"No. What exactly? What went through your mind?"

"Oh, Gee. The whole sequence. The way your pussy lips gleamed from your moisture. The way your lips seemed to become gates that opened when the penis rubbed against them, asking permission to enter you. It was reverential; a kind of divine moment. I was spellbound. Then, when your pussy writhed and wriggled on that penis and thrusted while it thrusted, I felt like it was making a statement; that it was taking on a life of its own and controlling you and your partner. And later, when the penis came with its semen flow inside it, and spread some of its semen onto its outer lips as it pulled out of you, I felt this holiness toward it; like it had just performed the divine act of procreation. It looked so beautiful to me then; the way it seemed to pulse with pride and triumph over all those doctrines that say it shouldn't do anything for its own pleasure. I felt respect for it because it had stood its ground and taken its full measure of pleasure for pleasure's sake. And then I thought it had taken a kind of control over me. By doing what it just did, it had declared to me that it had no need for God in the religious sense of God, the way the religions try to describe God, because it is God; and it must not have any other gods before it; nor should I allow any other god to challenge its supremacy, because it, your glorious pussy, was the only god I would ever need.

"And now, after hearing you tell me how you murdered your father and how that tribal princess of twenty thousand years ago murdered her father, I realize that your pussy is my true god; that it is a jealous and powerful god that cannot tolerate having any other gods before it. And now, I also believe that the DNA of that tribal princess is somehow also your same DNA; and that her pussy has become your pussy. I think, like her pussy must have been placed upon a royal purple cushion where it freely fornicated and was worshipped by the tribal members, your pussy must likewise be esteemed as a royal god. It must be worshiped by your fans who adore your pornography. It's as if I was receiving a command from the Great

Spirit of All Living things to love your pussy as my God, with all my heart and mind and soul and strength. So, you see, Jen. I know I am fated to love your pussy as well as loving you."

"Knowing that my cunt is a murderess? You could love her?"

"Yes, absolutely. I desire to kiss her with the greatest passions she has ever known; and love and worship her with all sincerity, for the wondrous deed she performed. And what a beautiful way to be murdered! He had to know more joy than pain. He had to feel rapture while he lay there, dying. Bless your sacred pussy. I adore her and all she's ever done! She set you free from your father. She brought you to me through her starring roles in your films. She is my best friend. I want to be her lover and her best friend. I want to have oral sex with her. I want her to love the touches of my tongue. I want her to dance with joy on my tongue. I'm anxious to surrender my soul to her and join my soul to yours, Jen."

"Why Thor, darling, that's beautiful. She feels your desires. I can tell. She wants you to have her often, in every way. Thor, I do believe my films have transformed you into a porn addicted whoremonger. Can you accept that about yourself? You'll need to be very manly and accepting to be my partner. I'm telling you this, just so you'll know. I am a total whore, Thor. Can you go through life addicted to my whoring; obsessed with seeing me experience pleasures?"

"Completely, totally okay with it. More than okay. I am honored and blessed by some spirit that, through you, revealed the beauty of explicit erotica. It released passions within me that thrill me and give me joys I never knew existed. I want to become your pussy's true love as well as yours. I desire to worship her, often. I feel no shame in what I have become; only liberation and happiness. I love you for that, Jen."

"Oh Thor, I wish everyone had the same outlook and acceptance that you have. Unfortunately, religion has made so many women believe that they are only supposed to have sex to have children. So,

they become miserable by denying themselves sex. Then they become doubly miserable during childbirth and the smelly diapers that follow. I wonder about the males who organized and perpetuated these religions. I don't understand why they want half of humanity to live in misery. Do you?"

"It must be their control thing, Jen. I don't know their minds."

"Well, we'll be nihilists. We aren't going to be religious. It doesn't matter to me why they think the way they do. But what about your mind, Thor? Did your mind meet my mind? Could you feel what I was feeling while I fucked my partners; while I orgasmed? Was it beautiful? Could you see inside my mind? Was my mind beautiful? Was my joy contagious?"

"Yes. A thousand times yes! Your mind was experiencing most beautiful thing ever in the world, Jen. You knew euphoria! I witnessed your mind reveling in the pleasures I know I witnessed. My heart throbbed with desires for you that I never knew before. I can only express it this way: I must love you. I must be your lover. I must honor your quest for pleasure and help you obtain it in every way I can. So, yes, Jen. I and my mind would treasure your favors more than ever before. When you are experiencing orgasm and I am visualizing your pleasures with you, I know a oneness comes to us. It binds us. It's special and precious. Your joy is contagious. I see why your porn films did so well. Men's hearts long to hold you and love you. Your passions are infectious. I cherish your joyous moments, Jen; your shouts and moans and laughs and smiles. So beautiful, confident, deserving, carefree and unashamed. Glorious. I have no words to express it. I only pray that we will have those same, delicious, erotic moments, often."

"I love you, Thor. Know that no matter how many partners I have, you shall be my only true love; my trophy partner for my life. Let's not talk for a while. Let's celebrate our understanding. Let's make love now. I need you to take me in your arms and kiss me and

stimulate me in all the ways you do; and then you must make love with me. I need our lovemaking very much."

Jen then collapsed her body down onto Thor's. Her lips met Thor's and kissed him passionately. She satisfied herself that his warm lips loved her kisses. She wrapped her arms securely around him. Her vagina Kegel-squeezed his penis. She clung to the treasured source of her nubile bliss, now feeling its wild throbbing pulsations inside her vagina, eager to surrender its semen into her. And, thinking as she clasped her body tightly to his:

'Yes, we have concordance of our souls, at last. He is honest with me. He loves me. And he accepts and supports my sinfulness and all my iniquitous ways. He is much younger than me. He is a splendid lover. And his penis is so huge; so hard. And he uses it so beautifully! It feels so wonderful inside me! I love fucking him. I think I shall never get enough of his splendid penis. I remember Marty's description of Carl's penis and the wonderful sex they had; how she constantly thought about it; how she became addicted to it. She loved sex with Carl so much! I suspect that she eliminated his wife, so she could have him and his wonderful penis all to herself. I have with Thor what Marty felt with Carl. I'll never have enough of Thor's lovemaking. I could make love with him several times a day; every day. And I will! We will have a grand future!'

CHAPTER TWENTY-SEVEN

Shall my sense pierce love, the last relay and outpost of eternity?
(Dante Gabriel Rossetti: The Dark Glass)

Eternity was in that moment. (William Congreve: The Old
Bachelor)

ETERNITY

Bifster, meanwhile, sat stoically beside his two friends. He faced the ocean; seriously studying it. His good eye was focused far away, intently observing the haunting eternity of the sea. His fur-tufted ears were erect, forward bent; carefully monitoring the wave crests spilling over their swells' tops; acutely hearing the predictably familiar overtopping spilling sounds, reassuring himself that the surf breaks were keeping their proper rhythms; obediently surrendering their great strength, letting the shore break it into nothing; then signaling by defeated ebb sounds their retreat to the watery deeps. And politely leaving behind, for his amusement, an occasional shell or helpless, struggling sea beasty; offerings he expected the sea to give him.

Was he, perhaps, confirming that those fearsome monstrous sea sounds had not freed themselves from their waters; and were not now racing towards him and his friends? Was he reassuring himself that unseen brooding monsters had not escaped from the terrifying, unfathomable sea? Did he wonder with each swell break:

411

'Are the sea's mysterious monsters contained? Are they not charging towards us from across the expanse of white sand dunes? Do the dunes give us safety? Can they separate the ocean's mysterious wonders from the three of us?'

Jen turned her head to stare at Bifster. She pulled her lips away from Thor's lips to wonder aloud:

"Thor, do you believe it is possible to fathom the workings of Bifster's mind? Yes, he is a cat. And his mind is configured differently from a human mind. But he is also a loving creature who has feelings and need of friendship. And he is our dear friend."

Thor wrapped his arms around Jen and, whispering, pulled her lips back to his:

"I think he understands what's important. I believe he knows we accept him and each other; and I believe he loves us."

Thor released his semen into Jen. And Jen orgasmed beautifully while they
kissed.

More to come.

We are fluttering onward—come with me, Minna Morinette, as I take you on a scintillating story telling journey!

THE SECRET BUTTERFLY (tm) SERIES is an eighteen-part book series with a prequel and a sequel; a risqué saga filled with erotic romances, hidden sacred jewels, diabolical temptations, and determined grit.

PREVIEWS FROM
LOVE AND LOVERS

Was this the modern-day way of an Apache woman? Did she stake men out in the hot sun to let the sun bleach them? Wait, she was Lakota, not Apache. Well, then what? What was her favorite way of torturing a man? Just tie him to a tree and stand naked before him? Drive him insane? What? What, damn it? What is her 'we must wait' message all about? . . . . Chapter One.

David silently swore revenge upon Bob for all the wrongs that had ever occurred to all Jews throughout history. In David's demented mind, 'Never Forget!' also meant 'Never Forgive!' and 'Get Even! and 'Make the bastards pay!' He silently promised himself that this Gentile would become his personal project. . . . . Chapter Two.

David's wife was screaming hysterically from inside the house:

"I told you! You keep that filthy, louse-infested animal out of our house! You keep her out of your bedroom! You stop sleeping with her! If I ever see her in the house again, I swear I will kill her! I mean it. Don't ever bring her into the house again!" .... Chapter Three.

"Tell me, when you look into Bob's eyes, do his eyes tell you that he loves you?"

"Yes, Father."

"Do you feel the same about him?"

"Yes, Father. I cannot deny my feelings. I love him. I love him with my whole heart."

"Now, Sparrow, this is important. Tell me, when you look into David's eyes, what do you see?"

"I see an evil presence. David chills my blood when he looks at me. He makes the air cold around me when he is near me. He is like a kind of death that has not yet died."

"Then you must allow for more time."

"Why do I need more time?" . . . . *Chapter Four.*

"Well, lookie here. I think we just found ourselves a lady," said the first biker to his sidekick.

"Whatcha doing here, babe? You slumming? You lookin for action?" the second asked.

Marty welcomed the hit. "I'm passing time, fellas. Passing time and looking for someone." . . . . *Chapter Five.*

"Thank you, my love. I love you, Bob. Know that I love only you. I promise I'll love you forever. I'll even love you forever; after I die."

"You're not going to die, baby. Let's not talk that way. It's not good."

"I will someday; maybe even soon. I don't know. I get a strange feeling about death sometimes and it scares me." . . . . *Chapter Five.*

"Marty." Barbara broke the silence. She saw Marty was off in thought somewhere.

"Yes, Barb?" Marty's voice was clipped. She wanted this awkward scene to end.

"Don't you dare hurt him." . . . . *Chapter Six.*

"No! There's no need for that. We're finished here." David slammed his palms down hard on his desk. "I want your resignation on my desk in the next ten minutes. Get your things and get your slutty ass out of here. Immediately! That's all!" . . . . *Chapter Seven.*

"I wax it."
    "Why do you do that?" . . . . *Chapter Eight.*

We've learned that Marty's promiscuity is more than a passion lust quest. It's her personal war against the institution of marriage. It's finely tuned and calculated to capture males who are susceptible to her seduction messages. And, it's not new! Her spirit soul has been successfully waging this war for over seven thousand years!

Jen and her love affair with Thor resulted in marriage, children, and a successful boat building business. Her discussions revealed why Maria, Marty, and herself all turned to prostitution to emancipate themselves from their mothers' influences. Marty's view is that every woman should consider her vagina to be a very valuable asset, which she should consider monetizing. Jen had both a wonderful mind and a vagina that Thor obsessed over. Smart girl! She got everything she wanted, and on her terms!

Bifster One found his place in the world. He was at peace with his lot in life. He knew that Jen and Thor loved him. He appreciated their love and continued bringing them his trophies.

Our saga will next return to dear, sweet Marty. What became of her? Did Marty continue her quest to create a more immoral world? Could Bob, the one man who truly loved her, change her cycle of destructive behaviors? We listen as Marty visualizes herself the successor to her mother's clientele, seductress queen of the firm, and David's close confidant; all while advancing her erotic film career and private business ventures. David listens, intently, to Marty's aspirations. She is, undoubtedly, his ideal persona. He admires Marty's sociopathy. He adores her devil-may-care immorality. Those qualities make his decision difficult. Will he share his power with her, or does he have a different idea about the firm's future?

Our next segment is tumultuous and revealing, dear readers. Sociopathy reveals itself. Well, have courage. I'll guide you through it. I promise. Let's travel into the hidden world where two serial killers struggle to find mutual trust. I'm Minna Morinette, your audio book narrator. Come flutter with me as I narrate LOVE AND LOVERS, our eleventh book of THE SECRET BUTTERFLY (tm) SERIES.